NOBODY PUTS ROMCOMS IN THE CORNER

KATHRYN FREEMAN

One More Chapter
a division of HarperCollins*Publishers*
1 London Bridge Street
London SE1 9GF
www.harpercollins.co.uk
HarperCollins*Publishers*
Macken House, 39/40 Mayor Street Upper,
Dublin 1, Ireland, D01 C9W8

This paperback edition 2023
First published in Great Britain in ebook format
by HarperCollins*Publishers* 2023

1

A catalogue record of this book is available from the British Library

ISBN: 978-0-00-856033-1

Printed and bound in the UK using 100% Renewable Electricity
by CPI Group (UK) Ltd

To Andrew, Harry and Ben

The three most important men in my life. I love you to bits, even though you all moan when I suggest watching a romcom.

Prologue

Sunday morning and Sally was singing in the shower when she heard her phone ring in the next-door bedroom.

Leave it. This is you time.

But what if it's important? How can you relax not knowing?

With a silent curse she turned off the water and wrapped herself in a big pink towel. Trailing wet footprints across the wooden floor, she padded over to her bedside table to retrieve her phone. The number wasn't one she recognised.

'Hello?'

'Hi.' A deep male voice. 'Harry Wilson here. I think Trixie mentioned me to you?'

'Oh, yes.' Trixie was a friend of friend, or more precisely a friend of Kitty's, who was one of her best friends. 'You know her boyfriend, Mike?'

'He's my business partner, yeah. I hear you have a room for rent?'

'I do.' When Trixie had mentioned she knew someone who might be interested in the room, Sally had been unsure. Yes, she needed the money, but did she need it badly enough to share her space with a guy she didn't know? But only one other person had been interested, and, unlike Harry, that man hadn't come with the promise that he was highly unlikely to come into her room in the middle of the night and murder her.

'Any chance I can come and see it this morning?' He paused. 'Like in half an hour?'

Sally glanced down at herself and winced. She knew from Trixie that Harry had been sleeping on Mike's sofa for the last few days, so she could see why everyone was keen for him to find somewhere to live. And as she was pretty desperate to get the room rented, thirty minutes would have to be long enough to get dressed and tidy up the two-bed flat.

When she opened the door to him exactly half an hour later though, she wasn't ready for him, in any sense. Her hair was still wet and the kitchen still bore the debris from breakfast, but they were nothing compared to her reaction to the sight of him.

'Hi.'

She had to crane her neck up at an awkward angle to look at him – and she wasn't short by any means. 'Trixie didn't warn me you were so … tall.' Or so … wow-snatch-the-breath-from-her-good-looking, she added silently. Not pretty good looks, but gruff, rugged, sexy-enough-to-make-her-toes-curl good looks, though the light-grey eyes, framed with dark lashes *were* ridiculously pretty.

He arched a brow in that cool way some people could pull off. 'Is my height going to be a problem?'

'Not unless you can't fit in the bed.'

The bed had been her sister's and wasn't intended for six-foot-four hulking builders.

She led him down her hallway to the room at the end, opposite the bathroom. Unlike her en suite, the bathroom had a shower over the bath. Not ideal for the man behind her.

Neither was the decor of the bedroom, she realised belatedly as she pushed open the door.

Behind her, she heard a sharp intake of breath, and a quietly muttered, '*Jesus.*'

'It used to be my sister's room.'

'Big fan of pink, I take it.'

Amy had been, Sally thought sadly. Or maybe she'd never liked it, just put up with it because Sally loved the colour. 'You can change it, if you want.'

He nodded and glanced around. 'And the bed?' He looked towards the fancy wrought iron bed, currently sporting a floral duvet. 'Can I bring my own?'

She tried to imagine him lying there, and had to work hard to suppress a giggle. 'You don't like the flowers?'

A pair of amused grey eyes found hers. 'Compared to where I'm sleeping at the moment, this is a huge step up.' But then his shoulders seemed to drop a little. 'But yeah, I'd rather sleep in something bigger. And less likely to give me hay fever.'

Funny or sarcastic? She wasn't quite sure how to take that. 'I guess I can put that one in storage. Trixie said this is just for a few months?'

'Hopefully.' He glanced sideways at her. 'No offence.'

'Short term works for me. My sister might want it back and, besides, I'm not sure how I'll get on living with someone else.'

He huffed out a breath. 'I'm tidy, if that's what you mean. Plus I work long hours so I'll not be in your way too much.'

'Do you want to see the rest of the place?'

She walked back up the hallway and into the kitchen. It was a pretty good size, which was one of the reasons she'd bought the flat. That and the fact the kitchen had double doors out into a lovely big lounge, with two windows that could definitely be described as having a sea view, even if it was from several roads back from the front. Most people who saw it said something complimentary, but Harry's eyes weren't looking towards the view at all.

'Is the sofa going to be a problem?' she asked, mimicking his comment from earlier, trying to arch her brow in the same way he'd done.

He frowned. 'Are you winking at me?'

'No. God, no.' Heat scalded her cheeks.

'A single no would have done,' he countered dryly.

Turning so he couldn't see her embarrassment, she waved at the velvet fuchsia-pink corner sofa. 'My sister isn't the only fan of pink. The sofa stays, so if that *is* going to be a problem…'

'It isn't.' He smirked. 'Pretty sure I'm man enough to sit on a pink sofa.'

'But not sleep in a pink bedroom?'

His big body shuddered. 'Something wrong about the thought of waking up to pink walls.'

When she'd decided to rent out the room, she'd been hoping to share with a like-minded soul. This guy clearly wasn't it. Still, her spidey senses weren't on danger alert, Trixie's boyfriend had vouched for him and, judging from the only other person she'd shown round, she could do a lot worse. At least Harry looked clean. 'I presume Trixie told you the rent?'

'Sounds reasonable, considering.'

'Considering?'

He gave her a crooked smile. 'Considering all the pink.'

His sense of humour was going to take some getting used to. 'What do you think, then? Colour of the walls aside, do you want to give it a go? We can agree on a week's notice for either party, just in case the pink gets too much for you.'

'You mean in case I piss you off.'

'Or in case you piss me off,' she agreed.

He gave her a small smile. 'Sounds fair. I can paint over the pink walls today, move in tomorrow if that works?'

'I'll need to find a home for the rejected bed,' she pointed out, feeling a little panicked. He'd be living in her space *tomorrow*.

'No sweat. I'll take it to my house and swap it for mine.'

That made her pause. 'If you have your own place—'

'Long story.'

Silence stretched between them. 'Okay.' She pushed a wayward curl back behind her ear. 'Just reassure me your wanting to move in here has nothing to do with dead bodies you've buried in your garden. Or beneath your floorboards.'

He let out a low chuckle. 'No dead bodies I'm aware of.'

'But then you would say that.'

'Any axe-wielding maniac worth their salt would say that,' he agreed, eyes glinting. Before she could panic further, he held out his hand. 'Thanks. I'll be back in a bit with the paint. And the axe.'

He was gone before her stunned brain could come up with a reply, leaving her wondering what on earth she'd let herself in for.

Chapter One

Harry shoved the box of winter clothes into the rear of his truck and stared back at the house. His bloody house. The one he'd spent the last four years carefully and painstakingly restoring.

Now the hard work was pretty much done and it was time to enjoy the fruit of his graft. Except he couldn't, because his ex had refused to move out.

And this farce had gone on for so long he was now into a new frigging season, hence the box in the back.

The woman herself stood on the doorstop, hand on hip, looking as if she owned the place.

'Don't look at me like that.' Isabelle flicked the poker-straight hair that fell in a glossy dark curtain over her shoulders. 'It's your choice not to live here.'

'Are you going to leave?'

She gave him the stubborn chin and pouty lips. 'No.'

'Then it's not really a *choice*, is it?'

'Of course it is.' She sighed dramatically, something he'd been getting pretty used to since their epic row two months ago. The one that had led to him dossing on his mate Mike's sofa for a week before finding a room for rent in a woman's flat. *That* was a whole other story, but he couldn't dwell on it because Isabelle hadn't finished talking. 'You're the one who's decided to be stupid and leave.'

'You think it's sensible to continue in a relationship with someone who's clearly been having an affair behind my back?'

'For God's sake, how many times do I have to tell you? I didn't sleep with Charles.'

Harry let out a long, slow breath. Knackered from a day of knocking down an old conservatory and laying foundations for a swanky orangery, he didn't have the stomach for yet another round of pointless arguments. 'Whether you actually *slept* together isn't really the issue, is it? You certainly weren't working when I interrupted your after-hours *meeting*.'

He'd been feeling guilty that the drama of his parents' separation had sapped all his energy over the last few months, so when Isabelle had told him she was going to have to work late, he'd decided to surprise her. Telling his parents to find another referee to their spat, he'd booked a table at Isabelle's favourite restaurant and driven to her office.

See, he *could* be romantic.

But life wasn't like the romance films that Sally, the woman he was renting his room from, seemed so obsessed with. Sure, he'd not actually seen Isabelle and her boss in action, and maybe, just maybe, they'd not had sex in his office. Whatever they'd been doing though, she'd looked guilty as hell when she'd come out to find him sitting at her desk, waiting for her. And though he'd never worked in an office, he figured meetings with the boss didn't usually lead to messed-up hair, smeared lipstick and undone buttons.

'I made a mistake.'

He laughed incredulously. 'A mistake is forgetting my birthday. Reversing into my truck. Not shoving your tongue down your boss's throat.'

Her face fell and she bit into her bottom lip. 'Okay, call it a moment of madness I never intend repeating. Please come home.'

He hated that, just for a second, he considered it. Made him feel an even bigger fool than he did already. 'I'll come back to *my house* when you leave.' He reminded himself of the guilty look on her face, of the fact that it probably hadn't been the first time she'd left that office in a dishevelled state, and hardened his heart. 'I've tried to be patient but it's been two months, Isabelle. Plenty of time for you to find somewhere else.'

And plenty of time for him to get really frigging fed up with paying a mortgage on his house *and* rent on a room.

'I don't want somewhere else.' Her bottom lip wobbled. 'I want to stay here, with you.'

'Yeah, well you should have thought of that before you went tangling tongues with your boss.' The thought of what she'd been up to behind his back, how she'd lied to him... It made it easier to ignore those tear-filled puppy eyes. 'Start looking for another place to live or I'll get the lawyers on you.'

Her eyes widened. 'You wouldn't do that.'

He wished he could. Wished he wasn't too much of a soft touch when it came to women. But damn it, he'd had enough of living in a room in someone else's flat – especially when that person talked too much and was ever so slightly bonkers. *And cute and blonde.* 'Don't try me. You won't like the answer.' He looked straight into his ex's doe-brown eyes. 'Get out of my house, Isabelle. This is starting to really piss me off.'

Turning his back on her, he climbed into his truck, but just before he could jam the gear into drive, his phone rang. With a sigh heavy enough to fill the cabin, he pressed Answer.

'Hi, Mum.'

'Your father refuses to leave the living room. He says he's got as much right to be in there as I have, but that wasn't what we agreed. He gets the office and the snug, I get use of the living room. How am I supposed to hold my book club meetings if he's parked himself on the sofa? I need you to tell him.'

What a Friday night this was turning out to be. 'Where did he used to go when you had your meetings?'

'He was at work. Now he's home all day and getting in my way.'

It was the crux of why his parents were separating after thirty-five years together. He wasn't sure they'd ever been happy, but apparently now they couldn't stand to be in the same room as each other.

Much like him with Isabelle. Except they'd managed only twelve months.

And people wondered why he was such a cynic when it came to love.

'Harry?'

He exhaled a breath full of exhaustion and deep-seated frustration. 'I'll have a word with Dad when I get home.'

'Thank you.'

He hesitated, then decided what the hell. The day couldn't get much shittier. 'Are you sure this is what you want? That you guys can't just talk things through?'

Silence. When she answered, he could hear the

disappointment in her voice. 'I expected more understanding from you. Of course getting a divorce at my age isn't what I want, but it's what I need to stay sane. Have I asked you why you're not talking to Isabelle instead of going off to live in some bedsit?'

She made it sound like Sally's was a dive, when actually it was a cool space. A large two-bed, top-floor apartment in one of the squares a few roads back from Brighton seafront. The building was old, but the flat was modern, light and airy. His only criticism was the colour scheme. Pink was not a colour any sane person wanted to be surrounded by. 'Our circumstances are totally different. Isabelle cheated on me. Dad's never done that to you.'

'I've never given your father reason to cheat. Besides, there are other ways to hurt a person.'

Reason to cheat? The injustice of the statement rankled, but it didn't screw with his thirty-year-old head, not like it would have done when he'd been a boy. He'd stopped wishing he had a mum who took his side a long time ago. 'Okay. I'll call you tomorrow when I've spoken to him.'

The ridiculousness of the situation wasn't lost on him. Umpteen calls between him and his parents to try to solve an issue when all they needed to do was walk down the hallway and talk to each other face to face.

As he ended the call, a message popped up on his screen.

Sally: Bad day [grumpy emoji]. Going to watch *Dirty Dancing* [grinning widely emoji]. Want us to wait for you? [5 smiling emojis]

Despite his mood a smile tugged at his mouth. He'd never met anyone who used so many damn emojis.

He'd also never felt less like watching one of her crappy romances. At least … he assumed that was what it was.

Sally set the bowl of popcorn onto the coffee table next to the jug of margarita.

Yes, it had been that sort of Friday.

Not many people wanted to walk along the beach in the pouring September rain. Those who had found their way into The Love Bean Cafe, the coffee shop she owned in the arches on Brighton seafront, had left soggy footprints and very few smiles. Rain was cold and, yes, wet, Sally got that, but it was also vital to the planet's existence. To be celebrated as much as a dose of sun. Though apparently not many people thought like she did. Something she was kind of used to.

Add into the mix the coffee machine playing up, so those customers who'd been brave – or desperate – enough to slog through the rain had been left without their caffeine fix. And the worry of finding the balance on her bank account was less than the mortgage payment due. Oh, and the fact that her sister was being elusive again, which history suggested meant trouble.

It was no wonder she needed a giant, heart-shaped distraction.

'Who's got the remote?' A little of her usual joy returned as she contemplated the next two hours. Bad days could be turned into good nights just by watching a romcom. How incredible was that? And if she watched it with her two best mates, and added popcorn and cocktails, the bad day could actually be wiped out of her memory.

Vince waved his hand in the air. 'I have it, sweetie.'

Kitty snorted. 'Might have guessed. We all know how much Vince likes to be in control.'

Vince raised one of his beautifully shaped dark brows. His

was an elegant face, framed by soft dark hair and enhanced by sharp cheekbones. 'And your issue is?'

'No issue.' Kitty reached forward and grabbed the popcorn. 'As long as Steve enjoys it.'

'Err, I don't think Steve's opinion matters anymore,' Sally interrupted, plonking herself in between them on the giant pink corner sofa and starting to pour out the drinks. Thank God she wasn't opening up the cafe tomorrow.

'Sally's right. As of two days ago, all three of us are now sad singles … or footloose and fancy-free, depending on your point of view.' Vince smiled ruefully and grabbed a glass.

Kitty shot him a sympathetic look. 'You and Steve really split up?'

'What can I say, it wasn't working.' Vince took a deep swig of his cocktail. 'Other than finding each other spectacularly attractive, it turns out we had nothing in common. I mean, I couldn't even convert him to romcoms.'

Sally mock shuddered. 'Definitely time to ditch.'

As well as being one of her best friends, Vince managed the cafe with her. Kitty was an artist, but they saw her frequently as she worked from a studio in the arches a few spaces up from the cafe.

The three of them had been tight since secondary school, gravitating together as the odd kids do, the ones that don't fit. Vince had been openly gay at an age when most were still working out who they were. Kitty had always had an artist's temperament; she had strong feelings about most things and wasn't afraid to voice them. Just as she wasn't afraid to shave her hair – sometimes the sides, sometimes all over – or wear Doc Martens with her shorts. As for Sally… Okay, so she lived in her head more than most people, and yes, that meant sometimes she was in a fantasy world and not the real one, but if it made her happy, what was the issue?

Picking up her own glass, Sally raised it high. 'Here's to us all finding our prince. And, until then, we've got Patrick Swayze to cheer us up.'

'You are aware you don't have to look too far for a prince, aren't you?' Vince remarked, regarding her contemplatively. 'You only have to come to The Cat and Fiddle when we're playing. Adam won't quit banging on about you. *How's Sally doing? Is she coming to watch us tonight?* The man is smitten.'

Vince was a member of a band – The Brighton Boys – and Adam was their new recruit. As a bass guitarist he ticked the cool box, and with his high cheekbones and broad smile he also ticked the attractive box. Sadly, she'd not felt the fuzzies so far, though there was enough cinematic proof – *What If, One Day, Just Friends* – to suggest that love didn't always come with a big bang. Sometimes it crept up on you. 'Maybe I'll come and watch you next week.'

Vince threw popcorn into the air and caught it expertly in his mouth. 'Atta girl.'

'Enough matchmaking.' Kitty grabbed a cushion and hugged it to her before nodding at the TV. 'Let the joy begin.'

'Hang on a minute. I messaged Harry to see if he wanted to join us.' Sally reached for her phone on the coffee table. 'Let me see if he's replied.'

Kitty's eyes widened in horror. 'You asked Grumpy Pants to crash our film night?'

'He's not that grumpy,' Sally felt duty-bound to point out. Harry Wilson just had a very dry sense of humour. 'And he's hardly crashing if I invited him.'

'Forget the grumpy part, if we're going to discuss the nature of the man's pants, I'm in.' Vince waggled his eyebrows.

'Can we please not discuss my lodger's underwear?' Sally pleaded. 'I won't be able to look him in the eye tomorrow morning.'

Vince grinned. 'That's not where you should be looking.'

Nope, she wasn't going there. There would be nothing worse than being caught ogling her lodger. Her very attractive lodger. Scanning her messages, she read Harry's reply out loud.

This Dirty Dancing, porn flick or romcom?

'And that's one reason I've no interest in looking at his pants or any other part of his anatomy.' Quickly she typed out:

Only one of best romcoms of all time.

A second later he replied.

Oxymoron. Ta but count me out.

'The man is a sarcastic arse,' Kitty declared as Sally read out Harry's message. 'I don't know why you agreed to let him rent your spare room.'

'Because your friend vouched for him. Because I need the money. Because he's a builder so I get my leaking tap fixed for free. And because the only other person who enquired looked like he hadn't washed for a week and wouldn't stop talking.' Sally shuddered as she remembered that interview. 'At least Harry is clean and reasonably quiet.' When he wasn't being sarcastic.

'And nice to look at,' Vince supplied, frowning when both she and Kitty glared back at him. 'What? You two might be blind to his muscular physique, but I'm certainly not.'

'He's too brawny.' Kitty pulled a face. 'Men like that are Neanderthals.'

'Stereotyping much?' Vince tutted. 'I know you like the pretty guys – don't we all – but the big, macho, rugged types also hold a certain appeal. Back me up here, Sally.'

She wanted so much to agree with Kitty, but she *did* find Harry impressive to look at. And though he was a man of few words, most of them dryly sarcastic, he was proving surprisingly easy to live with. Clean, tidy, courteous. Yet if she admitted that, they'd both start watching her like a hawk. 'It takes more than a good body to be attractive.' To make sure there was no further discussion on her lodger's attributes, she pressed Play.

They'd got to the part where Johnny and Baby were practising the lift in the lake (swoon) when Sally heard the front door open. It annoyed her that instead of losing herself in the film she found herself listening for the familiar sounds of Harry's arrival: the clatter of his keys as he threw them into the bowl on the sideboard, the thud of his heavy-duty boots as he dropped them on the floor. The pad of his feet as he made his way to the kitchen – it was presumably hard for a hulking six-foot-four guy to walk quietly, even in socks. The squeak of the cupboard door as he pulled out a glass, the clink of the fridge as he opened it to find the orange juice. The splash as he poured it out... Okay, she couldn't hear *all* that, but she knew his routine by now.

And even though she was facing the TV, she felt his presence as he stood in the opening between the kitchen and the living room.

'The guy not got the girl yet?'

Kitty frowned at him. 'Shh. We're trying to concentrate.'

'Sorry. Didn't realise the plot was that complicated.' The clunk of his glass as he dumped it back on the counter.

'That's because you've got the emotional sensitivity of a … a worm.'

Sally couldn't help it. She burst out laughing. 'Worm? That's the best you've got, Kit?'

'Yeah, well, the two margaritas have dulled my usually razor-sharp wit.'

'You do realise while you're discussing my worm-like qualities, you could be missing crucial plot twists?'

Harry was no longer behind them. Her skin pricked as she felt his presence to her left. Her nose twitched as she smelled the outdoors on him.

'And you do realise you're ruining this film with your interruptions?' Kitty shot back, reaching for the remote and pressing Pause.

'Sorry. Just fetching my laptop, then I'll … wriggle out of here.' He stepped in front of them to grab his computer from the shelf below the coffee table before pausing and staring at the TV. 'What in God's name are they doing?'

Kitty let out a deep sigh. 'Practising *the* lift.'

'Right.' He paused, ran a hand over his short dark hair. 'Yeah, sorry, I still have no clue. What is *the* lift?'

Kitty let out an exasperated breath. 'Only one of the most iconic film moments. Ever.'

'Iconic, huh?' He shifted the laptop further under his arm. 'Guess it's not hit worm-land yet.'

Sally bit into her cheek to stop from smiling. Okay, occasionally her lodger could be kind of funny.

'Careful, or I might stomp on you,' Kitty muttered as she watched Harry saunter out.

He either didn't hear, or chose to ignore her.

'You were pretty mean to him.' Sally studied Kitty. 'Are you okay?'

'Of course.' Kitty huffed. 'Sorry. I guess he reminds me too much of those cretins at school.'

And this was the side others didn't see. Kitty might be loud-mouthed and act like she didn't give a shit what people thought, but that hid a vulnerable core. At school she'd been bullied for being different, so now, when she felt threatened, she got her attack in first.

'He's innocent until proven guilty, sweetie.' Vince reached for the jug and set about refilling all their glasses. 'Though he hardly looks *innocent*, if you get my drift.'

'I guess I should go and apologise.'

Sally took the remote out of Kitty's hand and pressed Play. 'Later. Let's watch Patrick Swayze get his girl first.'

'Duh. Spoiler alert.' But Kitty smiled.

After all, it was the seventeenth time they'd watched the film.

Chapter Two

Having checked his emails, had a long, painful conversation with his dad, and had an even more painful session trawling through websites claiming to provide help on quick, lawyer-free divorces, Harry closed the laptop. His stomach let out a loud rumble.

In all the excitement of dealing with his parents and his ex this evening, he'd forgotten to eat.

When he opened the door to the kitchen he was surprised to see Sally watching the TV alone in the adjoining living room.

'Your friends gone home already?'

She turned briefly. 'Yep. They're lightweights. Plus they're opening up the cafe tomorrow so I guess that gives them a good excuse.' She waved a glass in the air. 'I made too much margarita, so grab a glass and come and join me. Save me from the mother of all hangovers tomorrow.'

He wasn't a fan of cocktails – he was a beer man – but he could definitely go with the idea of alcohol to dampen the pain of the evening.

First, food.

Disappointment settled in his stomach when he opened the fridge. Sandwich it was then.

After slapping some butter between two slices of bread, he added a few chunks of cheese hacked from a huge slab of extra mature cheddar and shoved it on a plate.

For a fleeting moment he wondered what Isabelle would have made of it – she'd used to love cooking for him – then angrily shoved the thought away. The exotic stir fries, hearty roasts and elegantly filled lunch boxes had stopped a while back. Probably the moment she'd started to realise she'd got what she wanted from him.

He could imagine her to-do list. *Find a sucker prepared to let me live with him for free.* Mission accomplished. Next item, *gain promotion.*

Maybe he was being cynical again. Or maybe her boss would realise he was only a means to an end once Isabelle was made brand manager.

'Dinner or a late-night snack?' Sally asked, turning the sound down on the TV as he walked into the room.

He stared down at the plate. 'Dinner. Want me to make you one? Mop up the alcohol?'

She showed him the bowl of popcorn sitting next to her. 'Thanks, but this stuff is surprisingly filling. And low calorie, apparently.'

She smiled over at him as he took a seat on the other side of the sofa. There was something about the ease of it, the warmth, the way it lit up her eyes and sent dimples peeping out from either side of her mouth… It made him want to smile back. 'Yeah, probably. The margaritas not so much though.'

'True, but the lime, all that vitamin C, that's got to count for something, right?' She dug into the bowl of popcorn, threw a few kernels into her mouth and then washed them down with a large swig of cocktail. 'So, Kitty was going to talk to you before she left but you were on the phone. She wanted to say sorry about the worm thing. She's not usually so catty.' Sally started to laugh. 'Oh God, Kitty catty, she'd hate that. Anyway, you caught her on a bad day.'

'Or I rub her up the wrong way.' Through Mike dating Kitty's friend Trixie, he'd seen Kitty out a few times and had always found her on the cool side. A marked contrast to both Trixie and Sally.

'Maybe. Cats do hate that.' She winked, reached for the glass he'd brought in and filled it to the brim with the margarita.

'Whoa.'

'You're saving me from the hangover, remember?'

'Okay.' He guessed he could do his civic duty so he took a swig, decided it wasn't half bad, and took another. Then wolfed down a few bites of sandwich just in case it was more potent than it tasted. 'This is your thing after a shite day, huh?'

'The cocktails or the film?'

'Both, I guess.'

Those dimples appeared again and he wasn't immune to them, oh no, not by a long way. 'There's nothing like a good romcom to make you forget a miserable day.' He must have made a face because she narrowed her eyes. 'I get the feeling you're not a fan of romcoms.'

'Not my thing, no.'

A small frown appeared between her eyes. 'Love isn't your thing?'

He thought of the evening he'd had and a low laugh

escaped him. 'Funny thing, love. It's like the pot of gold at the end of that whimsical rainbow. People want to believe it exists, but evidence shows it's just a myth.'

She gave her head a vigorous shake, sending those curls bouncing. 'Tens of millions, no wait, hundreds of millions of people would disagree with you.'

'Today, maybe. But tomorrow? I bet a good number of them would find themselves agreeing with me. And the next day, a good number more.' As he was in danger of depressing himself, never mind her, he changed the subject. 'Didn't you finish the film?'

'Oh yes.' She looked back at the screen, which was now showing a curly-haired woman carrying what looked to be a giant watermelon. 'I'm just watching the best bits again while I finish my drink.'

Okay, that was like a loose ball inside the penalty box. He had to shoot. 'Best bits?'

She shot him a dark look. 'Of course. The whole film is amazing, but some parts are even better than others.'

'Like *the* lift.'

'Exactly,' she agreed, ignoring or missing his sarcasm. 'Let me show you.' She picked up the remote and began to fast forward.

He couldn't quite believe he was drinking margarita on a pink velvet sofa while being shown the *best bits* of a romcom. Mike and Jack would have a frigging field day. Mike wasn't just a friend, he was also co-owner of Wilson White Construction – and yes, maybe some of his reasoning behind bringing Mike on board had been to avoid owning a company whose initials were WC. Jack was a sparky who'd started contracting with them, but he'd gelled so well he was now on the payroll.

'Here.' Face glued to the screen, Sally shifted her feet onto the sofa and hugged her knees. 'Watch this.'

Earlier he'd seen the guy and girl in the lake. Now she was leaping off a stage and running down the aisle towards the same guy and … yes, okay, she jumped up, he caught her and raised her above his head.

Sally sighed. 'Isn't it incredible?'

'That's what all the fuss is about?' To say he was underwhelmed was putting it mildly. 'It's good he didn't drop her, sure, but iconic? The shower scene from *Psycho*, yeah, that was unforgettable. *Star Wars*, when Darth Vader tells Luke he's his father, was a real shocker. The scene in *Spider-Man* when Mike dives through New York buildings trying out his new suit? Visually stunning. The chest buster scene in *Alien* is a bit old now, but I reckon you could call that truly iconic. Your lift?' He nodded to where she'd paused the film. 'That's just a guy catching a girl.'

'Just?' She stared at him like he'd just spoken a totally different language to her. 'The shared trust in that moment, the way they communicate without words. It's a symbol of love, of belief in each other. It's beautiful.'

'Hate to burst your bubble, but any reasonably strong guy and reasonably active girl could do that. We could do that.' He grinned. 'Not saying it would be beautiful, mind.'

Her eyes skimmed over him and he felt his muscles twitch in response. Not for the first time since he'd started living with her, he became aware of her as a woman. Worse, he found himself wondering if she liked what she saw. Horrified at his line of thinking, he pushed the thought way, way down into his subconscious.

'You're strong enough, I guess.' Clearly her survey had been clinical, which was fine. More than fine, it was a bloody relief. 'But the reason the lift is such an iconic moment isn't about strength or agility. It's about what it symbolises. Baby's newly found confidence. The complete trust she has in Johnny.'

'Baby?' He snorted. 'Come on, guys lift babies over their head all the time. It's called being a dad.'

She threw a piece of popcorn at him. 'It's her nickname. And if you'd bothered to watch the film you'd realise it's apt because the film sees her grow up over the summer, become her own woman. Confident, sexy, thanks to Johnny. All of which is shown in that final lift.'

He thought she was making far too much of some mediocre film scene, but each to their own. 'Okay, so if you jump and I can catch you, will you admit the lift itself isn't actually anything to write home about? I mean you can read into it whatever you want, but it's just a guy holding a girl above his head.'

'Ryan Gosling repeated it with Emma Stone in *Crazy Stupid Love*.' Sally sighed again. 'That was also an incredibly romantic moment.'

'You're saying that because you fancy Gosling.'

'I'm saying that because it was sweet. And sexy.' She giggled. 'And because I fancy Gosling.'

He didn't know what pushed him, but suddenly he was on his feet. 'Right, let's do this. If Gosling can do it, so can I.'

Laughter spluttered out of her. 'Err, no thanks. I'm not playing Baby to your Johnny or Hannah to your Jacob.'

He raised his eyebrows. 'What about Sally to my Harry?'

Her big blue eyes blinked over at him. 'So you have watched some romcoms.'

'Never watched it all the way through, but the guys have

shown me the restaurant scene on YouTube.' He glanced across the room. 'Where are we doing this, then?'

'Where are we faking an orgasm?'

He smirked. 'Not to be a dick, but if we're doing *that* together, you wouldn't be faking it.'

In the split second it took for his words to register with them both, the atmosphere in the room changed. Suddenly he'd gone from having a laugh with his landlady, to staring at the curve of her breasts beneath her T-shirt and the midnight blue of her eyes. To wondering if those natural-pink lips would feel as soft as they looked.

By the way her breath hitched and her cheeks flushed, he reckoned he wasn't the only one thinking, however briefly, about the possibility of sex.

Sally swallowed, trying to add some moisture to a mouth that had gone very dry. This was ridiculous. The man dressed in a faded T-shirt and worn jeans standing in her lounge was the same one she'd been living with for nearly two months.

So why, instead of noticing his blue T-shirt, did she see the heavy muscles outlined beneath it? Why were his eyes no longer grey, but a glittering, smoky grey that pinned her to the spot?

'Where are we doing this *lift*?' he clarified, his voice sounding deeper, more rumbly. 'Not the orgasm.'

The word sent more heat to her face. And between her thighs. It had to be the alcohol causing this weird feeling. Why else did he seem soooo much more attractive than he had this morning?

There was only one way to squash the tension. 'I need a soft landing.' She stood, her legs feeling embarrassingly wobbly. 'I'm bound to end up flat on my face.'

He looked insulted. 'You think I won't catch you?'

'Pretty certain you won't, yes.' And it had nothing to do with his impressive upper body strength. *Don't think about it.* 'In case you haven't noticed, I'm not some eight-stone waif.'

'In case you haven't noticed, I'm not some lightweight who can't handle a real woman.'

Was there a compliment buried in there somewhere? Flustered, she started pulling the cushions off the sofa and into a line on the floor. 'Call it insurance, just in case you're not as strong as you look.' And yep, somewhere in *there* was a compliment, too. 'I mean claim. As strong as you claim.'

Amused grey eyes stared back at her. 'Which is it?'

She was getting herself into a right tangle. That's what happened when she drank too much. 'Are we doing this or not?'

'We're doing it.' He strode over to her and settled his hands on her hips.

'Wait.' Her pulse began to race. 'When you say *it*, what do you mean?' The alcohol was still interfering because she felt his touch everywhere. Not just the warm press of his hands but an answering tingle across her skin.

He cleared his throat. 'Lifting you?'

'But if we're doing the lift scene properly, I need to run up to you.'

'Sure, but first we should do it without the run. So I know where to put my hands.'

His face was impassive, but his eyes sparkled with mischief.

Before she had a chance to worry about what he was doing

26

with those hands, she was hoisted up in the air. 'Holy crap.' Slowly he raised his arms and she felt his feet shift as he tried to get his balance.

'You're … taller than I thought,' he panted.

'You wanted to say heavier.'

'Nope.' He moved again, arms swaying. 'It's the length that's hard to handle.'

Despite the fact she was perched precariously in the air, she started to laugh. 'Isn't that my line?'

'Funny.'

Hands still holding firm on either side of her waist, he slowly lowered her. As her breasts brushed against his chest she felt a sizzle shoot down her spine.

Shit, shit, shit, this was not good.

'Okay.' His Adam's apple bobbed up and down. 'I've got it.'

She heaved in a breath, fighting to regain her calm. 'It didn't feel like you had it.'

His gaze snared hers. 'Trust me, I know exactly where to put my hands for maximum … benefit.'

Her heart bounced, rattling against her ribs, and what had started out as a bit of a laugh suddenly felt a little dangerous. Yet as he stood there, hands on hips, all sure of himself, she knew it was too late to back out. 'We need to video it.'

'We do?'

'Yes. Because then you'll see where you went wrong. And I can use it to sue you if I break my arm.'

For a second his eyes bugged out. Then he started to laugh. 'Fair enough, but I'm going to catch you so it's not an issue.'

As she set up the phone, angling it to get the right shot, she was aware of him watching her, a faint smile on his face.

'Okay, that should do it.' Her heart gave a little anxious flip as she pressed Record and walked to the end of the room. Harry stood in between the cushions, arms by his side, the cocky smirk on his face reminding her of Ryan Gosling when he'd re-enacted this same scene in *Crazy Stupid Love*. For an excruciating moment she even wondered what Harry would look like without his shirt on.

Stop it. Harry wasn't out to seduce her, in fact he wanted to prove the opposite. That the lift wasn't about chemistry, about love and trust. It was just a strong guy lifting a woman above his head.

With those thoughts churning through her mind, she charged at him.

'Whoa.' His hands went to grasp her hips but it was too late. The momentum she'd created knocked him backwards onto the cushions, and she ended sprawled on top of him. 'Ooof.'

For a second she was paralysed with shock. For the next second she was aware how big and solid he felt beneath her. For the third second his eyes found hers and she felt a flutter in her lower belly.

Then he blinked and started to laugh, his whole body shaking beneath her.

'Give a guy a bit of warning.'

Acutely embarrassed, she struggled off him. 'You knew I was going to run up.'

'Yeah. But not like a charging rhino.' With a surprising alacrity for a guy his size, he jumped to his feet. 'Let's go again, but less rhino, more … cat.'

Less rhino. The bastard. 'You do realise if Ryan Gosling or Patrick Swayze had said that, the lift moment would have lost all its symbolic beauty?'

'Symbolic beauty, my arse. At the most, it's a bit of gymnastics. Come on, I'll brace myself this time.'

'Gee, thanks,' she muttered. 'Way to make a girl feel good.'

There was silence as she walked to the end of the room, but when she looked over at him, he gave her a small smile. 'You feeling good isn't the issue.'

And now she was embarrassed in a whole different way. Unsure how to handle his remark, she fell back on humour. 'Are you sufficiently braced for impact?'

'Do your worst, pussycat.'

Taking a deep breath, she jogged – not charged, note, *jogged* – towards him. At the last minute he bent his knees, hands settling on her waist again. This time she felt the power in his arms as he lifted her above his head. And wow, that was kind of impressive.

But then he moved and took a step back, clearly trying to find his balance.

'You're going to drop me,' she said, panicked. 'I can feel it.'

'I'm not.'

Though she could hear the strain in his voice, beneath it was an unwavering conviction that helped her pulse to settle. 'Good to hear.'

'Aren't you supposed to stretch out your arms and legs? You know, like a plank?'

'Like a plank?' Oh God, this was ridiculous. Placing her hands on his shoulders to steady herself, she started to giggle. 'First I'm a rhino. Now you want me to be a plank?'

'Planks are easier to hold above my head. They don't squirm.'

Another giggle burst out of her. 'Now I'm a worm?'

He grunted. 'Takes one to know one.'

His feet were now planted firm, so she risked raising her legs up. 'Does this work?' No way could she put out her arms. Her hands were attached to his shoulders like glue.

'You're the lift expert. You tell me.' She felt his feet shift once more, though his arms were rock steady. 'Have we cracked it? Proved anyone can do it?'

'I'll admit to anything if you get me down in one piece.'

He let out a huff of laughter and began to lower his arms. Panic bubbled at the thought of sliding down his body again, but this was no romcom moment. This was Harry.

He hunkered down and fell backwards, causing her to squeal as she dive-bombed into the cushions.

'You okay?'

'I don't know. I'm suffocating under a pile of cushions.' She heard a snort of laughter. Then a hand was thrust under her nose. Clasping it, she allowed him to pull her up. 'Thanks.'

She bumped lightly into him and automatically her gaze flew to his. When their eyes connected she felt a hum, a crackle of something that sent a shiver through her.

It's the lift. She'd associated it with an intensely romantic moment for so long, it was no wonder acting it had left her feeling unbalanced.

Harry swallowed and took a step back, shoving a hand over his cropped hair. 'Did we debunk your iconic lift then?'

'Never.' She went to stop the recording, steadier now there was distance between them. 'I will concede we proved you can carry me above your head.'

'Without breaking your arm.'

'Good point.' Eyes down, she played the video back. 'We also proved people do crazy things after drinking cocktails.' She started it from the beginning and showed it to him. 'This has to be the least romantic lift copycat scene of all time. You started off calling me a rhino.'

He looked a little wounded. 'In my defence, I thought we were just doing the lift. Didn't realise you'd be charging at me full pelt.'

'So what are you saying? That you can be romantic if you're not taken off guard?'

His eyes avoided hers. 'You'd have to ask my ex.'

Ah, so there *was* an ex. 'The fact she's your ex suggests the answer is probably no.'

The lines around his mouth hardened. 'You're assuming the fault lay with me, huh?'

Guilt wriggled through her as she realised she'd done exactly that. But why did a thirty-year-old man find himself suddenly homeless if it wasn't that he'd been kicked out? 'Sorry. It's none of my business.' There was an uncomfortable silence while she searched around for something to break it. 'I might upload this video onto TikTok. Do you mind?'

He shrugged and picked up his plate and glass from the coffee table. 'Knock yourself out.'

'It would be good to give it a tag line. Like, I don't know … what not to do after a pitcher of margarita?'

His expression returned to the one that seemed to be his default. That of quietly amused. 'Taking the rom out of romcom?'

She considered it. 'Not bad but maybe a bit obscure.'

'How to catch a charging rhino?'

She rolled her eyes. 'Thanks, I think I've got it from here.'

Settling back on the sofa she tweaked the video and settled on the caption:

Epic romcom re-enactment failure: When you drink too many margaritas and try Dirty Dancing *with your flatmate.*

It was only after she'd uploaded it that she realised Harry had gone back to his room, but not before he'd tied up the cushions, cleared away the empty glasses and put the dishwasher on.

Whatever reason he'd split up with his ex, it wasn't because he was untidy.

Chapter Three

Harry woke far earlier than he wanted to on a Saturday morning, thanks to his rumbling stomach. First task today, re-stock his shelves in the fridge so tonight he could eat something more substantial than a cheese sandwich.

As he stretched, he thought of other Saturday mornings, of waking up in his bedroom with a warm female body next to him. Sex. So much lazy morning sex that it was late afternoon before they'd make it out of bed.

His body twitched, wanting in on the action it wasn't going to get because, guess what, his hadn't been the only body Isabelle had been having sex with.

With a sigh he levered himself out of bed, his mood – and parts of his anatomy – now deflated. Shrugging a pair of sweats on over his boxers, he headed out of his room to find food. He was nearly out of the door when he clocked his naked chest and snagged a T-shirt out of his drawer.

Two months and he still hadn't got used to the fact he wasn't in his own home, able to do whatever the hell he wanted.

When he wandered into the kitchen he found Sally dressed an oversized bubble gum pink bathrobe. He kind of admired the fact she wasn't afraid to be seen in it. Or that she hadn't bothered to look in the mirror yet because surely if she had, she'd have done something with the riot of blonde curls that sat on top of her head.

Again his thoughts turned to Isabelle: silk dressing gown, poker-straight hair at all times. It was like living with her polar opposite.

'Morning.'

She glanced up and gave him a surprisingly shy smile. Made him wonder if she was still thinking about last night, and the fact he'd had his hands around her waist. Her body sliding down his...

Yep, now he was thinking about it too. Bad idea.

To distract himself, and to fill the empty hole in his stomach, he dragged out the box of Crunchy Nut cornflakes.

From the corner of his eye he saw her opening her mail. She started humming to himself and he winced. He could take music in the morning, but that sound she was making? It made his eardrums hurt. Suddenly the noise stopped.

'Everything okay?'

'Just for once I'd like to open a letter and find it's from a mystery admirer. A love letter, you know?'

He couldn't see why anyone would write a letter when they could phone or message. 'Can't say I do.'

She let out a huffing sound. 'Well anyway, this isn't that. It's a statement from the bank.'

'That's a letter I can relate to.' Maybe one day he'd have more money coming in than going out. As he watched her rip the letter up and shove it into the recycling bin, his eyes automatically dipped to her feet, and the fluffy pink slippers.

Then back up the length of her long legs, which the dressing gown failed to hide.

Jesus, she looked like a flamingo. Only with way sexier legs.

'Your lips are twitching.'

'Are they?' He tried to keep his face straight as he poured milk onto his cornflakes, but the thought kept zipping round his head.

'You rarely smile so this has to be funny. Come on, what are you thinking?'

Wondering what you'd look like standing on one leg. 'What do you mean I don't smile?' Yeah, better. Push her on the back foot. Though if she was only standing on one leg…

'I mean, you smirk a lot, but you don't give out many genuine smiles… You're doing it again.' She frowned. 'Have I got sleep goo in my eyes? Bed hair?'

He took a step towards her and studied her face, surprised to find his pulse gave a little jump as his eyes found hers. Damn it, when it had happened last night he'd put it down to the alcohol. Had her eyes always been that big? That shade of blue? Had her skin always looked so smooth?

Alarmed, he shifted back. 'No goo.' He winced as he looked at her hair. 'Bed hair is an affirmative.'

'Guessed it might be.' She patted it down, which did absolutely nothing, then picked up her phone. A second later she let out a long, slow exhale.

'That sigh is way too deep for someone so short,' he remarked before diving into the cornflakes.

'I'm hardly short, as you pointed out last night. I'm five eight. You're over proportioned.'

He couldn't help another smirk. 'So I've been told.'

Laughter burst out of her. 'I set that up nicely for you,

didn't I?' But then her expression turned serious again as she stared back at her phone. 'My sister still hasn't replied to my messages.'

He vaguely remembered a conversation about siblings. How she had one to his none. 'This is Amy, right?'

'Yep. Twenty-two and still causing me sleepless nights.'

He wondered why the sister was Sally's issue rather than that of her parents, but decided it wasn't his business and focused instead on filling his stomach.

'Oh my flaming God.' He looked up with alarm to see her staring wide-eyed at her phone. 'You will not believe how many likes we've got for our video. And the comments, jeepers creepers it's gone mad. People are actually following me now. Like tens of thousands of them.'

He didn't know much about social media. Couldn't be arsed with it. 'Is that good?'

'I don't know. I mean, it's not bad.' Head down, she scrolled through her phone. 'The comments are saying they want more.'

'More what?' He'd enjoyed touching her way too much to be comfortable about a repeat.

'More re-enactments of iconic romcom scenes.'

There were more of them? He dreaded to think what they would look like. 'Seems you've got your work cut out then.'

'Me?' She stared back at him as if he'd said something stupid. 'I can't do a romcom scene by myself.'

He clattered the spoon into his bowl. 'You can't mean what I think you mean.'

'Why not? It'll be fun.'

'We must have very different definitions of the word.' Not quite believing what he was hearing, he started to laugh. 'Can I be honest without fear of you kicking me out?'

'As long as you're not going to tell me I really do have sleep goo in my eyes, go for it.'

No way was he going to risk another look in those big blue orbs. He had enough problems in his life without adding *awkward attraction to woman whose spare room I'm renting* to the list. 'I think romcoms are dumb. I've got no interest in watching them or acting them out.'

She pursed her lips. 'You're quite blunt, aren't you?'

It wasn't the first time he'd been accused of it. 'I prefer honest.'

'So if you're being honest, what have you got against them?'

'They're unrealistic. Films are fiction, sure, but if you're going to show a fantasy, make it obvious, like give the guys wings or something. Otherwise people are suckered into thinking life can really be like that. That happy endings exist, usually against a soundtrack of violins.' Sometimes he thought it might be nice to believe in the fairy tale, but false hope just set you up for crashing disappointment further down the line.

Her eyes searched his and her expression turned sympathetic. 'You've been hurt.'

He let out a short laugh. 'Sorry to burst your theory, but there's no tragic heartbreak behind my reasoning. Sure, if my life was going swimmingly I wouldn't be renting your room, but fact is, I'm a practical guy. I prefer reality over make-believe.'

Damn, her and her big mouth. He might not have been hurt, but it was now more than obvious to Sally that her lodger was going through a tough time. 'Sorry, ignore me. I get all protective when it comes to romcoms.'

'I noticed.'

He gave her the dryly amused smile that looked so good on him. Especially when he was resting against her worktop, sweatpants low on his hips, biceps bunching beneath the sleeve of his T-shirt as he ate his cereal. Hastily, she turned away and began to fill up the water in the coffee machine. 'So, any plans today?'

'Not much. Seeing my parents.'

'That's nice.'

She heard a small huffing sound. 'Not the word I'd use.'

'Oh?' She knew some people didn't get on with their parents, but she always thought that was such a terrible waste. She'd give anything to see hers again. To feel her dad's arms around her. To talk to her mum about daft things, big things. To get their advice on how she could get through to Amy.

'Yeah, they're driving me nuts at the moment.'

The nosey part of her wanted to push, but the landlady in her realised she needed to respect his boundaries. He wasn't a talker. Two months and she still barely knew anything about him. Clearly that was how he wanted things, but it was really hard for her because she enjoyed a good chat. It was why she loved her job so much. Talking to customers was fun, fulfilling. Sometimes she could help, which was extra rewarding, but other times it was just a smile, a laugh. A bit of nonsense to brighten the day.

As the coffeemaker whirled into action, she watched him walk to the sink to fill up the kettle, her eyes straying to his roped forearms.

'You know you can use the coffee machine.' She nodded at

the jar of instant coffee in his hand. 'It kind of offends me to see you with that.'

He flashed her a rare grin. 'You get used to instant on the job. Doesn't bother me. I'll drink anything.'

He reached up to the cupboard and instinctively her gaze was drawn to the tanned strip of muscled stomach his stretch had revealed.

She needed to break this spell. To get out of the kitchen and into a cold shower. 'If you want to know what decent coffee tastes like, come down to the cafe. I'll make you our signature Love Bean Cappuccino.' Oh boy, did that sound like a come on? 'Love Bean is the name of the place,' she added quickly. 'I wasn't, you know...' She trailed off. She was acting like a teenager with a crush, and she should know. She'd had a tonne of crushes growing up.

'You weren't hitting on me?'

The clear amusement in his voice helped ease some of her tension. 'I was offering a free coffee. If I was hitting on you, you'd know it.'

Laughter spluttered out of him. 'I would, huh?'

'Absolutely. So that was definitely not me hitting on you.'

'Okay, message received.' She watched, fascinated, as he added two large teaspoons of sugar to his mug. 'Last night you said your friends were opening up the cafe today. Do you own it together?'

She slipped onto the bar stool and sipped her drink, grateful for the return to a safer topic. 'I own the place but Vince helps manage it with me. We take it in turns doing the Saturday morning shift to give us each a chance to let our hair down Friday night.' Not that she'd done much of that recently. It had been ages since she'd last had a date. That was the trouble with being such a romcom fan. Real life had a habit of proving disappointing. 'Kitty is an artist but she helps cover when we're stuck.'

He nodded. 'About Vince. I was wondering...' He trailed off, giving her a slightly sheepish-looking smile which might be cute, if she wasn't about to get really pissed off on her friend's behalf. 'Is he the drummer in the band that play in The Cat and Fiddle on Thursdays?'

Immediately her shoulders deflated, muscles relaxing. 'The Brighton Boys? Yes, he is.'

'Thought so. I've heard them a few times. They're good.'

'They are.' A little ashamed of how her thoughts had run, a lot relieved she'd been wrong, she started to laugh. 'Sorry. I thought you were going to ask me if he was gay, which he is, and he's quite open about it, but—'

'It wouldn't have been any of my business.'

'Exactly.'

He bent to stack the mug and his empty breakfast bowl into the dishwasher. Then straightened and gave her a teasing look. 'About as protective of your friends as you are of your romcoms.'

She couldn't help but smile back. 'I guess I am. Both are really important to me. So beware crossing me on either front.'

'Duly noted. I might see you later then. For the free coffee.'

'Sure. And if you change your mind about the TikTok thing—'

'I won't.'

'But if you do, let me know.' Interested, she picked up her phone and went onto the app. 'Yikes, the likes are going crazy still. And I've got thirty thousand followers now. How on earth did that happen?'

He shrugged. 'Beats me. I wouldn't even want to watch the real thing.'

But millions of people did, she thought as she watched his tall, broad-shouldered frame walk away. And if their little video was anything to go by, thousands of people also wanted to watch people trying to recreate famous moments from the films they loved.

Make that hundreds of thousands, she amended a few hours later when she snuck another peek at TikTok in a lull between customers.

Vince caught her looking. 'Still adding up your followers?'

'They're increasing by the minute.'

'Let's see what all the fuss is about. Give it here.' In a state of shock, she handed the phone over and Vince started to laugh as he watched. 'Okay, maybe I get it. Cute woman, sexy guy, having a laugh.' He waggled his eyebrows. 'And wow, if I'm not mistaken, there's chemistry, sweetie.'

'No, absolutely not. He's my lodger. Zero attraction there.'

Vince stared at her blandly. 'Me thinks she doth protest too much. Remember, I know what you're like with your little crushes.'

'Sure, when I was a teenager. I've grown out of all that now.' She didn't seem to have grown out of the nasty habit of blushing though, as she felt heat creep over her cheeks.

Of course Vince saw it and started to laugh. 'Sure you have, darling. You're absolutely not crushing on that man hunk you have living with you. A shame, really. I was on team Adam.'

'Look, Harry isn't my type, okay?'

'Umm, on that we can agree.'

All she had to do was keep reminding herself of the fact.

Chapter Four

As his mother continued to list all the things she found annoying about his dad, Harry found his attention starting to wander. He looked out of the window to the sea, more brown than blue but, hey, this was Brighton, not Barbados. Where was Sally's cafe? He knew it was somewhere on the seafront, under the arches. What had she said it was called again? Oh yes, The Love Bean. The woman was besotted with the concept.

Maybe he should introduce her to his mum. He'd like to bet five minutes of listening to her gripes and Sally would go off the idea of love, marriage or happy ever afters.

'Are you listening to me at all?'

Oops. He snapped his attention back to the woman in front of him. 'Sorry. I zoned out.'

'I wish you wouldn't. This isn't easy for me, you know. I hoped I could rely on my only son to support me.'

'You can.' Shame it wasn't a two-way thing.

'Well I would feel much more supported if you listened.' As the waiter finally placed the bill in front of them, she dabbed her mouth with her napkin. That was his mum all over. Clean. Neat. Precise. 'And it would help if you came to your senses and went back to Isabelle so your dad could come and live with you.'

He stared back at her, trying to work out if she was serious or not. 'You really think either of those things is going to happen?'

'Why not? You and Isabelle have just had a tiff, that's all.'

He decided to treat that statement with the disdain it deserved – and ignore it. 'Dad won't want to live with me.' And he was bloody certain he didn't want it, either.

'Why not? The pair of you get on okay, don't you? I mean, you argue less than me and your father.'

Because he bit his tongue. 'You know he can't drive now with his glaucoma, so how is he supposed to play golf if he lives with me?' Golf was about the only thing that got the man out of the house nowadays.

'It's just a thought.' She nodded down to the bill. 'Do you want me to get that?'

It would be nice. She was the one who'd wanted to meet for lunch in a place he'd never have gone to. He was the one with the mortgage and extra rent to pay. But, dutifully, he went to pick it up. 'I'll get it.'

'Thank you.'

Once he'd walked with her to her car and waved her goodbye, he trudged off to the seafront. A blast of sea air might cheer him up. God knows he needed something after the last two hours of misery talk. He really needed to bash his parents' heads together. They'd never been the sort of couple to star in one of Sally's romcoms, but he had a strong suspicion they'd be more miserable apart than together.

And that reminded him, he had a free coffee waiting.

When the gloom from his lunch had been sufficiently blown away by the sea air, he headed to the arches. He knew he'd found her place even before he read the name above the door proclaiming The Love Bean Cafe in a sign adorned with red hearts. Strings of heart-shaped lights surrounded windows whose frames were painted in a bright red to match the door. The board outside displayed a mug of cappuccino dusted with cocoa powder in the shape of a giant heart.

Somehow going into the lion's den felt safer.

He was about to push the door open when he noticed the dozens of note cards in the window. Each had a red heart at the centre, with two names written inside: *Sonia and Gary August 2016, Charlotte and Warren May 2017, Priti and Nadeem October 2021, Tara and Murray June 2022.* Intrigued, he pushed the door open and let his eyes roam over the space. Cosy, comfy and, yeah, okay, inviting. He'd not bargained on that. Red sofas, fresh red roses on the tables, all set against the natural brick of the arches.

He peered up at the art on the wall and almost laughed. *Sleepless in Seattle, Pretty Woman, Notting Hill...* Each painting depicted romcom movies even he'd heard of.

'Admiring the decor?'

He turned to find Sally smiling knowingly at him. 'Something like that.'

'Kitty's responsible for the artwork.'

He peered more closely and found he was impressed. 'I can appreciate the skill.'

'But not the content?'

He smirked. 'Something like that.'

'Vince,' Sally called over to her friend. 'Can you make me an americano when you've got a sec?' She turned back to

Harry. 'Unless you wanted something else? Latte, cappuccino, mocha?'

He winced. 'Black coffee is fine.'

'Please, an americano isn't just a black coffee, as you'll find out.' She waved to the red velvet sofa that looked like … a heart? God forbid, a pair of lips? 'Sit yourself down, we'll bring it over.'

As she walked away, he was bloody positive she was fighting not to laugh.

Gingerly he sat down, wondering what he looked like, big hulking builder on … this.

Pretty soon he didn't have to wonder, as Vince strolled up with his coffee and burst out laughing. 'Oh my, don't you look a pretty sight.'

'Thanks.' He accepted the coffee, which looked like the stuff he made from a jar. 'I thought the pink sofa in her living room was bad enough. Suspect she put me here on purpose.'

'She did.' Sally came up behind Vince, her smile shooting past wicked and hovering towards evil .

'Ooh the hot lips as the naughty chair, I like it.' Vince clapped his hands together, his expression gleeful. 'What did he do? Is this because he didn't want to watch *Dirty Dancing* with us? Or because he'd never heard of the lift scene?'

'Neither.' Sally grabbed a chair from a nearby table – red velvet seat pad, red heart cushion on the back rest – and sat down opposite him. 'I thought being surrounded by romantic crushed red velvet was the perfect place for him to sit while I talked him into making another TikTok video with me.'

'Gotcha.' Vince nodded sagely, as if this was a perfectly respectable answer. 'It really is a bit mean of you, Hazza, disappointing all Sally's lovely new followers.'

'Hazza?' It felt the safest thing to focus on.

'You don't like that? Harry Styles is okay with it, I believe.'

It was surreal. He was sitting in a love-themed cafe, on a pair of lips, being called Hazza and told off for not wanting to be filmed doing bizarre tributes to romance films. 'You can call me what you like. I don't want to do any films.' He looked over at Sally and then back at Vince. 'Why don't you two do them?'

Vince spluttered with laughter. 'Aside from the fact that, lovely as she is, she's the wrong sex, the followers are hoping for more of you and Sally. Don't get me wrong, I know I'm gorgeous, but I feel these new followers will be a tad disappointed if I turn up as a replacement.'

God, the man was a hoot. 'They won't be disappointed if you turn up with your band. You're good.'

'Why thank you.' Vince pretended to fan himself. 'Who'd have thought, looking at you, that you'd be such a charmer.' Before Harry could work out if that was an insult or not, Vince had headed back to the counter to serve.

'So.' Sally cleared her throat. 'Would you be willing to do some more videos if I told you we might be able to make money out of them?'

She watched as surprise flickered across Harry's usually phlegmatic face.

'How?'

Yep, now he was interested. Though not half as interested as she'd been this lunchtime when Vince had told her during a lull that there was money to be made on TikTok. 'Vince said the band regularly upload stuff on TikTok. They've got so many followers now, they're paid by a company to endorse craft beer.'

'Okay. I can see that.' Harry eased back against the red velvet and Sally tried not to giggle. His butch frame looked frankly ridiculous perched on the lush, romantic sofa. 'Music, band, alcohol. There's a link.' His dark brows drew together. 'But who the hell would want to associate themselves with bad romcom moments?'

Okay, that wiped the smile off her face. 'There is nothing bad about romcoms—'

'Put your claws in. I meant our interpretation of them would be bad.' His lips curved, just a little. 'Though I've not seen the films, so I'll reserve judgement on whether they're bad or not.'

'They're epic, which you'll find out for yourself when you go through them with me to find the most suitable moments to copy.' She smiled sweetly and he let out a low rumble of laughter.

'You're relentless.'

'I'm keen on earning some money.' Aware of how that sounded, she sighed. 'And now I feel like I'm using emotional blackmail to twist your arm. Obviously if you don't want to do this I totally understand. I just thought I'd give it another try, now you know there could be something in it for you.'

'Besides the joy of acting out' – he mimed quotation marks – '"iconic romcom moments".'

It was hard to be annoyed at his sarcasm when his grey eyes twinkled back at her.

'Besides the joy of doing that with me, yes.' Oh God, why had she added the *with me* bit? It was like her subconscious was determined to wave a big flag at him saying *she fancies you*.

'With you,' he repeated.

His eyes held hers and she felt her heart start to race. Bollocks. 'Well obviously with me, because I'm the one pestering you to do it.' She needed to throw away the damn spade because this hole she'd dug was making her feel claustrophobic. 'But you're right, we'd have to find companies keen to be associated with romcoms. Hotel chains, maybe. Perfume. Jewellery. Holidays. I'm sure there are plenty who'd be interested in pairing with us.'

'Us?' His eyebrows shot up.

Apparently she hadn't thrown the spade far enough away. 'Well, you'd want half of any money we might get, wouldn't you?' That was better. A business transaction.

He took a sip of his coffee, eyes still on her. She wondered what he was thinking. Crazy coffee lady? Nutty hopeless romantic? *Weird landlady who fancies me?* It came to something when she was hoping for the first two.

'What would I need to do for my half?' His lips curved in that little smirk he was fond of. 'Apart from perform.'

It was no wonder she was flustered. When a good-looking guy teased and smiled at you like he was doing, it was really hard to think with your brain and not your hormones. *So stop looking at him.* She forced her gaze from his and over his left shoulder. 'We'd need to agree which moments to re-enact.'

His smile slipped. 'Can't you decide? I'll go along with whatever you think.'

'So your plan is just to turn up, perform – as you so artfully put it – and bugger off?'

'Pretty much.'

She absolutely wasn't thinking about sex, they weren't talking about it. So why was it when she dared to look at him, those grey eyes were laughing? 'Fine. But you don't get to complain if I put you in … positions you aren't comfortable with.'

And now the laughter wasn't confined to his eyes. It burst out of his chest in a rumble that vibrated through her.

Leaning forward, he drew a hand down his face. 'Christ, what am I letting myself in for?'

She wondered the same, but it was too late to back out now. 'I'll put together a list of my favourite romcom moments and you can take a look. Decide which ones bring out your creative urges.'

'Oh my, that sounds promising.' Vince appeared, giving her a wide-eyed look. 'Can I look forward to more Harry and Sally TikTok moments?' He patted his heart. 'Even your names work well together.'

Sally gave her friend what she hoped he'd interpret as a giant shut up sign. 'Did you need anything?'

'Moi?' He smiled innocently. 'Adam's just called and said The Cat and Fiddle want us to play an hour earlier tonight. I came to tell you I'm going to have to head out now. Are you okay to close up or shall I see if Kitty can come over?'

'I'm fine. We're not exactly rushed off our feet.' Aside from Harry, there were two regulars and a couple who looked like they were about finished. Pretty typical for four o'clock on a Saturday. It was why they closed early, because most people were eyeing up a beer/prosecco/cocktail by now. Not a coffee.

Harry cleared his throat. 'I can stay.'

Sally wasn't sure who looked more shocked out of the three of them. 'You're volunteering to hang around and help?'

'If you want.'

'Well, that would be great, thanks.' And suddenly she had an idea. 'You know what would be even greater? We could do our next video.'

'Yeah?'

She glanced at Vince and knew, just knew – thanks to fifteen years of friendship – that he was thinking the same as she was. 'Of course, it's not a deli like it was for the other Harry and Sally.' Vince cast his eyes round the cafe. 'But it does have tables, and Hilda and Mildred would love to hear it.' His eyes twinkled. 'I'm sure it'll be something they never forget.'

'Would love to hear what?' Harry, always so calm, so sure of himself, was starting to look a little twitchy.

'The sound of me … orgasming.'

Chapter Five

Harry wondered if he'd heard Sally right. With all the innuendo leading up to this, maybe he'd heard orgasm when she'd meant ... origami. That was it. *The sound of me origami-ing...*

But he only needed to look at her face, at the way she was bursting not to laugh, to know even if the origami thing was a verb, it wasn't the one she'd used.

'I do believe our builder friend is looking a little pasty.' Vince peered at him curiously. 'And I thought you guys sat about all day wolf whistling at women and talking about sex.'

'We don't wolf whistle.' He couldn't understand why he was finding it so hard to talk. 'That's a stereotype we strongly deny.'

'So you talk about sex then?' Vince beamed. 'Maybe I should retrain because that is just about my favourite subject.'

The three of them – him, Mike and Jack – talked about what they'd watched on TV, about what was in their sandwiches. Whether Brighton & Hove Albion were ever going to win a trophy. And yes, sometimes they talked about sex, so it wasn't the word orgasm that was stressing him out. Hell, he'd talked about the film moment only last night with Sally, even cockily told her if she was doing it with him, she wouldn't be faking it. It was the thought of watching Sally orgasm – shit, *pretend* to orgasm – that was making him flush hot and cold.

Mainly hot, he thought with alarm, his trousers feeling embarrassingly tight.

'I thought you had to go?' Sally asked Vince, thankfully taking the focus away from him, and from sex.

'Damn, I do. What a bummer.' Vince sighed. 'Have fun, chickabiddies, and make sure you send me that video.'

'You'll have to watch it on TikTok like everyone else.' When Vince frowned at her, Sally grinned. 'Got to get the number of likes up somehow.'

'Who said I'd like it?'

Sally laughed. 'Come on, watching someone pretend to have an orgasm. That's right up your street.'

Harry watched Vince leave and wondered, frantically, if it would prove to be up his street, too. God, he hoped not. He really didn't want to be attracted to the woman whose spare room he was occupying.

'You said yesterday that you've seen the clip from *When Harry Met Sally*?'

Sally gave him a dimpled smile and he shook himself. This was just like the lift. Him and his, admittedly cute, landlady, having a laugh. Thankfully he didn't do cute, so there was nothing to fret about. 'I got the jist of it, yes. She's out to prove a point.'

Sally's eyes flickered over to where a man was trying to get her attention. 'If you've got your phone on you, take another look at it while I get the bill for this couple.'

Feeling like a bit of a perv, which was only enhanced by the monstrous love seat he was sat on, he typed 'Harry met Sally orgasm' into his browser and clicked on the first YouTube link.

A few seconds later, he was smiling. Yeah, this was funny. He probably wouldn't mind watching the whole film if the banter from the clip was anything to go by. He could just skip the mushy ending where, no doubt, they pledged undying love to each other.

'You're enjoying it.' Sally was back, and giving him a knowing look.

'Sure. It's funny. But they never made the sequel, where the pair of them spent so much time sniping at each other they couldn't bear to be in the same room. And then Sally went off and had an affair with her boss.'

Fuck. Judging from the way Sally's eyes were about to pop out of their sockets, that last sentence had sounded far too bitter.

There was a moment of uncomfortable silence when Harry tried, and failed, to find a way to fill it.

'Sally wouldn't do that,' she said after a while. 'She's in love with Harry, not in lust, or in like, or even crazy about, but really, truly in love. So she'd never cheat on him. She wouldn't even be interested in looking at another guy, because he's it for her.'

The way she said it, her usually bubbly voice now quietly serious, told him she believed every word she said. 'Looks like we're going with the Disney version then.' Before she could butt in with her earnest points about him being cynical, he got to the matter at hand. 'So what do we need to do for this video? Have a chat about orgasms?' Amazing how a reminder about the real-life consequences of tangling with a member of the opposite sex could cure him of his weirdness around her.

'Basically, yes. Sally is telling Harry she's glad she never got involved with him because he treats women badly. He disputes this, claiming the women he sleeps with have a good time. And that's when she asks him how he knows this. Wait.' Standing up, she reached into her back pocket and pulled out her phone. 'Let me set the video up.' He watched as she propped the phone up on a nearby table before taking a quick look around the cafe at the two customers left. 'Okay, Hilda and Mildred won't bother us. Let's do this.'

'Err, hate to put a damper on things, but I'm not sure how to segue orgasms into a conversation.'

'Just go for it.' Her big blue eyes stared back at him, unblinking. 'You don't have to try and slip it in.'

'Pretty sure it helps with the orgasm thing if I do.'

She groaned. 'Not always, and that's the whole point. Women fake orgasms.'

He couldn't resist. 'Obviously I'll have to take your word for that.'

'Because you've not seen one?'

'Not seen a *fake* one,' he countered, emphasising just to be absolutely clear.

Immediately her face lit up, and she gave him a smile that was a little sly, a lot wicked … and totally made his blood run hot. Then she started to emit a low, husky noise. 'Oh, that's good.' Another moan. 'Like really good.'

His eyes bugged out of his head. He'd been so into the conversation, he'd totally forgotten that's where this was supposed to lead.

Her moans grew louder, and his pulse start to race. He wanted to believe it was from embarrassment but the sound, the way she lowered her lids and looked totally into the moment. It was turning him on.

Sally was really getting into it. When she'd set up her phone ready to record, she'd had a burst of performance anxiety. Would she actually be able to do this? I mean, she was no Meg Ryan, that was for sure, and the thought of doing it in front of Harry was embarrassing. Yet once she'd closed her eyes to block out his stare she'd found it easier, her mind slipping into an imaginary world. She groaned again at the thought of a pair of big calloused hands cupping her breasts.

'Are you okay, dear?' Startled by the tap on the shoulder, Sally blinked her eyes open to find Hilda peering down at her.

How to go from arousal to mortification in two seconds flat. 'Umm, yes, thanks.'

She risked a glance at Harry only to find his eyes dancing.

'It's just, me and Mildred, we heard you moaning,' Hilda persisted, oblivious. 'We wondered if you had belly ache.'

Oh my flaming God. Sally slunk further down in her seat.

The comment was clearly enough for Harry and he let out a loud bark of laughter. 'Sorry.' He laughed some more, clutching at his stomach. Clearly not sorry at all.

Maybe if she hadn't been so embarrassed she'd have been able to see the funny side.

Hilda, bless her, was now looking concerned. 'Is this man bothering you, dear?'

Harry attempted to straighten his expression, but his eyes… God, those eyes sparkled like a pair of brilliantly cut diamonds. And set in such a ruggedly handsome face, on top of that broad, muscular, rugby player physique… He was stunning, she realised with alarm. She was living with a stunning-looking man she was awfully afraid she'd just imagined touching her breasts.

'Err, Hilda, meet Harry. He's my lodger.'

Harry held out his hand, which swamped Hilda's as they shook. 'Hi. I was just listening to Sally…' Oh boy, he wasn't, was he? 'Orgasm.'

'Pretend to orgasm.' Shit, she was turning bright red. 'Sorry, Hilda, we were fooling around, trying to copy that scene out of *When Harry Met Sally*. You know, the one in the restaurant?'

'Oh my, I know that one. Makes me blush to think about it.' Hilda cast her gaze over Harry again. She clearly liked what she saw because she let out a satisfied smile and patted Sally on her arm. 'Well you two go ahead and enjoy yourselves, dear. Don't mind us. Mildred's deaf as a post, and it's been so long since I had a good orgasm I can't remember what it sounds like.'

As she walked away, Sally caught Harry's eye. 'Orgasm interruptus?' He huffed out another laugh at her joke and somewhere deep in her chest she felt a flutter. Damn her hormones. 'Where was I?'

The side of his mouth curved in a crooked grin. 'I believe you were mid-groan?'

Ouch. That didn't sound as sexy as she'd thought she'd been. Pushing the thought away, she tried again, but somewhere between the belly ache comment and Harry's amusement, she'd lost her momentum. It didn't help that he was so obviously biting the inside of his cheek in an effort not to laugh. With a final push, she groaned her way to a crescendo. 'Yes. Yes. Yes.' Far too aware of Hilda and Mildred listening to her bang the table, she knew it sounded a bit, okay a lot … lame.

'Well, that was…' Harry screwed up his face and looked away, his shoulders shaking.

'You could tell it was fake?'

He hiccupped out a laugh. 'Err, yes?'

Heat scalded her cheeks. 'Maybe this was a stupid idea,' she muttered as she went to turn the video off. She'd got carried away with the thought of acting out her favourite film scene, forgetting she wasn't sexy enough to pull it off.

'What was stupid?'

'Me, trying to pretend to be Meg Ryan.' After that performance she was more … Myrtle Ramsbottom. 'Anyway, we've got some footage and I guess it keeps with the theme of epic romcom re-enactment failures because it was definitely a failure.'

'You're going to upload it then?'

'As long as Hilda's okay starring in it, I don't see why not.'

There was a beat of silence and she watched as he twisted the mug in his hands. 'It was funny,' he said finally.

When he glanced up and gave her a small smile she found it hard to stay in a funk. 'You mean the part where Hilda said my groans of pleasure sounded like I had belly ache?'

He nodded, mouth twitching.

'I hope to God I don't sound like that for real.' Embarrassed again, she looked away. This wasn't the right sort of conversation to have with her lodger. 'Anyway, enough bad acting. I'd best start clearing up.'

She was about to stand when she felt his hand on her arm. 'For the record, before Hilda interrupted, you were totally nailing it.'

Her heart gave a little jump. 'I was?'

He gave her a slow smile. 'Got me all hot and bothered.'

Wow, oh wow. She didn't know what to say. Was he flirting with her? Did she want him to be?

He rose to his feet, towering over her like only a few guys she knew could. 'What do you want me to do?'

Keep smiling at me like you just did. No, that was a bad idea. She did not want any entanglement with a love cynic whose life was not going, how had he put it, *swimmingly.* 'Could you clear and wipe down the tables for me?'

'Yes, boss.'

As he strode away she caught herself admiring his rear view. Snapping her gaze away, she headed over to speak to Hilda, who was delighted to feature in the video and insisted on watching Sally upload it. After a few attempts, she added the captions:

Epic romcom re-enactment failure take 2: When Harry kept laughing at Sally.

Half an hour later the cafe was empty of customers, surfaces and floors had been wiped and everything was in place ready for Monday.

As she walked out with Harry, she noticed his gaze drop to the cards in the window. 'They're my success stories.'

He raised an eyebrow. 'You matchmake?'

'Hell no. That would be like meddling. But locals have started to use the cafe as a place to meet on first dates. I guess it's the romance theme which we've added to over the years.' She glanced up at him. 'You should come and try our heart-shaped cakes. Or our eggs cooked in heart-shaped poachers, served with heart-shaped toast.'

He gave her a pained look. 'I think I'll give it a miss.'

'Your loss.' And probably a good thing. 'Anyway, these couples all had their early dates in the cafe and went on to get married. It's now become a thing that they fill out a card and we put it in the window. I'm proud to have played a small part,' she added defiantly.

'But how many of them will still be together this time next year, or the year after that?'

His attitude frustrated her, but it saddened her even more. 'It must be awful to live life without belief. Without hope.'

He clearly wasn't expecting that answer, because he frowned. 'Surely it's more awful to believe in a fairy tale, only to find it's all a big con?'

'But it's not.' She glanced back at the cards in the window. 'You just have to find the right person. Not only someone you fancy, you like, or you get on with. But someone you can't imagine living your life without.'

He peered curiously at her. 'And have you found this person?'

'Not yet, but he's out there. And I believe she's out there for you, too.' After setting the alarm, she caught his sceptical look and smiled. 'And when you find her, she's really going to knock you on your arse.'

'Doubtful. She'd have to charge at me like a rhino.'

For a split second their gazes collided. As she lost herself in the stormy grey of his, a bolt of something hot and sparky skated down her spine.

As if aware of what he'd said, he averted his eyes and thrust his hands in his pockets. It was too late for her heart though. Vince was right. She had started to develop a teeny, very unfortunate crush on her lodger.

Chapter Six

Harry looked round the shell of the new orangery they were building. It was getting there.

'Hey, Romeo.' Mike, the other half of WW Construction and a supposed friend, grinned over at him. 'Stop day-dreaming and help me lay this underfloor heating.'

'Ha bloody ha.' Trixie had heard from Kitty about the TikTok videos, so of course now Mike and Jack had seen them.

His life was going to be hell.

'How was it for you then, mate?' Jack's ginger eyebrows bobbed up and down comically. 'From the sound of things, the earth didn't really move for her, did it? More of a tremor than an earthquake.'

That set Mike off, and the pair of them sniggered like a couple of schoolboys.

Harry gritted his teeth. If he hadn't committed murder by the end of the week, he deserved to be nominated for sainthood. 'If you'd watched the video properly, you'd see no part of my body was in contact with hers. If it had been, you'd have seen your bloody earthquake.'

Not, of course, that any of his body parts were ever going to tangle with hers.

The orgasm scene had been a crack – at one point, when Hilda had talked about belly ache, he'd actually thought he was going to be a cliché and his sides *would* split with laughter. But he could also remember, a little too vividly, the way Sally had sounded before the interruption. And how in a rash moment, because he'd thought he'd upset her with his laughter, he'd admitted she'd turned him on. Which had led to an odd connection outside the cafe, unbalancing him enough to ensure he'd kept well away from her this last week.

'You know what, Jack?' Mike's voice bumped him out of his head. 'I reckon our Harry has got the hots for his landlady.'

'You know what, Mike?' Jack glanced at him and smirked. 'I reckon you're right.'

He wasn't going to make it to the end of the week. He was going to murder them both before the end of the day. 'Are you two going to carry on with the inane jokes or are you actually going to do some work?'

The pair of them looked at each other. Then burst out laughing. 'For a guy who claims to have no interest in her, he's pretty touchy, don't you think?' Jack, probably the worst of the two, though it was a small margin, bent to grab a cable cutter from his toolbox.

'Can I remind you pair of gossips that the last woman I dated is still firmly entrenched in my house and won't shift? I'd have to be seriously deranged or monstrously stupid to think about starting up with someone else.' Which worked, if he conveniently forgot that testosterone still pumped from his cells and possibly, just possibly, might screw with his brain when it came to a pretty woman with blonde curly hair, a wide smile and a penchant for pink.

Mike grunted. 'You need to be stricter with Isabelle. She's taking the piss.'

Tell him something he didn't know. 'What do you suggest? I go round when she's out and change the locks?'

'You could.' Mike gave him a sly smile. 'If you weren't too much of a soft touch.'

He wanted to disagree, but being a soft touch was how he'd ended up living with Isabelle in the first place. Not that he'd hadn't enjoyed having her round. Until he'd found out he wasn't the only man she'd whispered husky come-ons to.

'So when can we look forward to the next video?' Jack clearly wasn't giving up on his 'Annoy the Hell out of Harry' campaign.

'I'm hoping there won't be one.' Sally hadn't given him the list she'd promised, which made him wonder if she'd gone off the idea.

'But I thought there was money to be had?'

'Only if she gets enough followers.' Big if, considering the subject matter.

'You should do that scene from *Pretty Woman*.' When Harry gave Mike a blank look, the man raised his eyes to the ceiling. 'Come on, you know the one. It's right at the end where he turns up in the white limo holding a bunch of roses. Then climbs up the fire escape with the damn flowers in his teeth. Makes Trixie cry every time she watches it.'

'Thanks, but no thanks.' He didn't mind the two they'd done so far, but a limo and roses between his teeth? Yeah, no amount of money was going to get him doing that. He nodded over to the plasterboard. 'Enough of this shit. We've got an orangery to build.' And he desperately needed to do something … manly.

Several hours later, the boards all in place, the three of them sat on the boxes of floor tiles and dug into their lunch. His was a cheese sandwich, again, but he was hungry enough not to care. After taking a few mouthfuls, he checked his phone for messages and saw he had one from Sally.

Hi. A few options for our next videos. If you're still game [grinning widely emoji]. 1) *Ghost*: potter's wheel [ghost emoji, pile of poo emoji] 2) *Pretty Woman*: limo with roses or shopping scene [car emoji, dress emoji, shoes emoji, shopping bags emoji] 3) *She's All That*: makeover scene [lipstick emoji, lady with scissors in her hair emoji, nail varnish on fingernails emoji, wizard emoji]

Looked like there would be another video then. But a limo with roses – no bloody way. He glanced at the message and typed back.

What's with the dump?

The reply was instantaneous.

Closest I could get to clay for potter's wheel [laughing with tears emoji]

Jesus, she cracked him up. 'You guys ever watched some film called *Ghost*?'

Mike and Jack both stopped mid chew and stared at him.

'What?'

Mike gave him a shit eating grin. 'Are we going to start talking chick films in our lunchbreaks from now on?'

He ignored the question. 'Sally's come back with that as an option for the next video. Something about a potter's wheel. Sounds okay.' It beat shopping and makeovers.

His heart sank as the pair of them started to whoop.

'Shit man, that scene is steaming hot, you totally need to do it.' Jack looked way too enthusiastic for Harry's liking. 'You with your shirt off, sitting behind Sally while she grapples with a long, phallic-looking clay pot—'

'How about the *Pretty Woman* film?' he interrupted. He had enough weird thoughts about his landlady without *that* image in his head. 'She's mentioned a shopping scene.' It came to something when that sounded like the lesser of two evils.

'Well, yeah, that's funny.' Mike unscrewed the top off his flask. Harry knew it was filled with homemade soup because Trixie was still doing for Mike what Isabelle used to do for him. 'It's not hot though. It's just a woman trying on loads of clothes and a guy flashing his credit card around…'

As Mike carried on talking, Harry tuned him out and replied to Sally.

Let's go with shopping scene.

Then, in case there was any doubt, he tagged on:

As long as it's not my card.

A beat later he got a reply.

Damn. And I was planning Harrods [winking emoji]

'What's got you smiling?'

He glanced up to find Mike watching him curiously. 'Just a joke a mate sent through.'

'This mate. Wouldn't happen to be living with her, would you?'

He'd known Mike too long. 'Time we got back to work.' Ignoring Mike's knowing look, Harry shoved the lid on his lunch box, dumped it in his rucksack and picked up the drill.

Grey's Anatomy was on the TV, yet Sally wasn't fully concentrating. She kept looking at her phone. Or more precisely, at her TikTok app. She was at one hundred and fifty thousand followers now, which was absolutely bonkers. The last video had two hundred thousand views. And now she had another one in the planning.

Behind her was a clatter, followed by a loud curse. She turned to find Harry on his haunches, picking up pieces of cold pasta and dumping them back in a bowl.

'Are you going to eat that?'

He glanced up at her, his hair wet from the shower he must have dived into as soon as he'd come home. 'As opposed to decorating the floor with it?'

Still sarcastic, she noted. 'I just meant I can't remember when I last cleaned the floor.'

He grunted. 'A bit of dirt never hurt anyone.' He pushed the bowl and its contents into the microwave.

'So, I went to see my favourite shop in the Lanes about our shopping session.'

A grimace settled over his features. 'Kind of gives me the jitters when you phrase it like that.'

'My credit card, remember?'

'Yeah, still not helping.'

She watched the muscles in his back shift beneath his T-shirt as he lifted the bowl out of the microwave and sighed. Was this now officially a crush? 'Okay, maybe this will help. The owner was very happy for us to film in her shop. She's also willing to pay us commission on any sales that come from someone seeing the clip. In addition, in exchange for a mention, I've got a beauty salon to give us a quick makeover while we're shopping. So we can nail two epic romcom scenes in one awesome, money-earning video.'

He let out a low whistle, which for some reason sent a shiver down her spine. She'd never been able to do that. When she tried, all that came out was air. 'Looks like we're going shopping then.' He paused. 'Wait, you said *us* a quick makeover. That was a slip of the tongue, right?'

'I didn't want you to feel left out. We could both try on clothes, get our hair done.' She had a sudden, hot image of all that raw masculinity encased in an expensive suit.

'Err, thanks but…' He screwed up his face. 'These iconic moments were all about the woman, yes?'

'True, but these are our takes on the scenes.' Her brain threw up images of a partly clothed Harry popping in and out of the changing room.

'Nope, we shouldn't stray too far from the original.' He gave her a winning smile. 'Don't want to upset your traditionalist fans.'

Considering her mental images, it was probably just as well. 'Fine. Are you up for doing it this Saturday? I can get Vince and Kitty to cover the cafe after lunch.'

He leaned against the worktop and shovelled a forkful of pasta into his mouth. 'Yep, works for me.'

She studied him, wondering why she reacted to him like she did. Yes, he was tall and undeniably sexy in a rugged, built kind of way, but he wasn't charming. He was also far too alpha male for her tastes. She liked a man who wasn't afraid to show his soft side. A guy who'd not just cook for her but lay the table, light the candles. Then snuggle up on the sofa and watch a romcom. In a way it was reassuring to know that while she might find Harry physically attractive, might crush on him a little, he wasn't destined for her. Wasn't The One. 'Have you ever watched *Pretty Woman* or *She's All That*?'

'Do I need to?'

'I suppose you could just watch the shopping and makeover scenes on YouTube. But you're missing a treat.'

He gave her a wry smile. 'I'll take your word for it.'

She was spared any further argument by the sound of the intercom. 'Expecting anyone?'

He shook his head so she went to answer it, surprised when she heard the voice on the other end. 'Hey, come on up.'

A few seconds later she opened the door with a wide smile on her face. It slipped off the moment she saw Amy's expression.

'What the fuck, Sally?'

'Sorry?'

Her sister stomped, actually stomped, into the hallway. 'You put another video on TikTok. You know Chris follows you. He saw you pretending to orgasm and started wetting himself, then forwarded it to all his mates.' Her face flushed an angry shade of red. 'I bet you did it deliberately just to embarrass me. I hate you.'

Amy's voice was very loud and Sally hoped her lodger had disappeared back to his room with the door shut. And his earphones in.

'Is there a problem?'

Damn it. Harry stood in the hallway, hands on hips, looking like he was ready to strongarm someone.

As Sally slowly shrivelled with embarrassment, Amy twirled round to see who was talking. 'Jeez, Sis, you can stand the pit bull down.'

And the embarrassment just kept coming. 'Amy, meet Harry. He's lodging with me at the moment. Harry, this is my sister.'

Harry's bulk relaxed a fraction and he nodded over at Amy. 'Hi.'

Amy glanced between them both before she turned back to her. 'Are you shagging him?'

Good God. Now she was annoyed. 'What's wrong with you? Why are you being like this?'

'Like what? You're the one posting embarrassing videos.' Again, she looked over at Harry who hadn't moved. 'How did you persuade him to take part?'

Before she could drag Amy somewhere they could have this argument in private, Harry cleared his throat. 'She paid me in sex.' Amy's mouth gaped open, and Harry nodded as if he was confirming a drink order. 'Nice to meet you, Sally's sister.' He'd taken a couple of steps towards his room when he added over his shoulder. 'In case you're interested. It was totally worth it.'

The door to his room clicked shut. Despite her embarrassment, Sally found she wanted laugh. And when she saw the thunderstruck expression on her sister's face, the need became almost overwhelming. 'He's joking.'

'Then he has a weird sense of humour.'

'He does.' She sighed. 'Look, I'm sorry if I embarrassed you. I posted it thinking I'd be the only one embarrassed by it.'

Amy huffed. 'So why do it?'

'Because if I get enough followers there might be some money in it.'

'Right. So you're that broke you need to post dirty videos?'

'Dirty?' Ouch, that hurt. 'They're fun, not dirty. And anyway, since when did you turn into a prude?'

'Since all my mates watched my sister trying to orgasm.'

'Pretending to,' Sally clarified, willing herself to keep calm. 'And you know why the money is important.'

Amy jutted out her chin. 'I'm helping pay it back.'

Sally felt the desire to laugh again, only this time it was with frustration. Did Amy really have no idea how much debt she'd run up as a student? And she wasn't talking the usual student debt. She was talking thousands of pounds frittered away on two credit cards and a non-approved overdraft. 'I know you pay what you can.' Yet what she contributed barely paid the interest on the debt. 'Do you want to come in?' It felt ridiculous, talking in the hallway. 'I can get you a drink? Something to eat?'

'No. I only came to tell you to stop embarrassing me.'

Despite the six-year age gap, they'd once been close, though anyone witnessing them now – and she could include Harry in that – would never believe it. 'Come on, stay and have a drink. Tell me what's going on in your life. Are you and Chris happy?'

'I guess.'

'You only guess?'

'Leave it. I'm fine.'

Sally's heart ached. Amy was definitely not fine. 'I miss you, you know.' Since her sister had moved in with Chris, she'd almost been a stranger.

'Looking at who's just gone into my old bedroom, I doubt that.'

Was Amy angry that she'd rented out her room? Yet she'd told Sally quite categorically that she was living with Chris now. 'Harry is a temporary lodger, that's all. You're my sister. Of course I'd rather you were here with me. The room will always be yours. He only needs a week's notice.'

'Yeah well, don't stress. You don't need to chuck him out. I'm not coming back.'

The words sounded so final, and as Sally watched her stomp out the same way she'd stomped in, her heart felt like a lead weight in her chest. How had their relationship disintegrated so badly?

Down the hall, Harry's door creaked open. 'You okay?'

No. Suddenly she wanted to feel someone's arms around her. Wanted to be reassured that Amy was just going through a phase. She'd come back to her. But Harry wasn't Vince. She couldn't cry in his arms. 'Yes, thanks. Just, siblings, you know?'

'I don't know.' He took a few steps towards her, and she felt the weight of scrutiny. 'I take it she's not a fan of the videos.'

'She'll get over it.' Sally forced a smile. 'Not sure she'll get over being told I was using you for sex quite so fast, mind.'

'Yeah, sorry. Her attitude pissed me off.'

Tears pricked at the back of Sally's eyes and she wasn't sure if it was because he'd been sticking up for her, or because she'd needed someone to stick up for her against her own sister. 'Me too.'

Again, his gaze skimmed her face and she wished she'd learned the art of hiding her emotions. 'We can watch those films now,' he said finally. 'If you want.'

Her heart stuttered. 'You'll watch *Pretty Woman* and *She's All That* with me?'

He gave a shrug of those big shoulders. 'Sure.'

Feeling as if she'd been handed something precious, she walked with him into the sitting room and they took up a position on either side of the sofa. As she selected *Pretty Woman* from her list of recordings – yep, she had all her favourites lined up, ready – he put his arms behind his head and crossed his legs at the ankle.

'Of course I can't guarantee I'll stay awake.'

He slid her a small smile and the heavy feeling that had settled over her suddenly felt less intense.

Smiling back at him, she curled up against the cushions and pressed Play.

Chapter Seven

Hands in his pockets, Harry loitered outside Sally's cafe. He supposed he could go in, let her know he was here, but did that seem a bit, well, like he was picking her up for a date?

He scowled, cursing Mike and Jack for making him so touchy about her. Then again, Amy hadn't helped the other night with her accusation that they were shagging. Surely it was possible for a guy and a girl to live in the same flat and not have everyone assume they wanted to fuck each other senseless?

The door opened and Sally came out, those big blue eyes settling on him. 'I thought I saw you out here.'

'We said two o'clock?'

'We did. I'll just get my bag.' She opened the door wider. 'You are allowed to come in, you know.' Her eyes took on a mischievous glint. 'Unless you're scared you'll catch some sort of love bug.'

'Yeah, I'm immune to that, so no worries.' And to prove it, he followed her inside.

Kitty caught sight of him and walked over. Her hair was shaved at the sides today, longer on top. And streaked with purple.

'Well, well, if it isn't Brighton's answer to Richard Gere.'

'A good builder, is he?'

She looked like she wasn't sure if he was joking or not. He wanted to ask what her issue was with him, but he didn't get a chance because Sally was back, a pink fluffy handbag dangling from her shoulders. 'Okay, let's do this.'

Kitty put a hand on Sally's arm. 'You might want to show him the clips from the films before you head into the shop. I don't think he has a clue what he's supposed to be mimicking.'

Sally glanced questioningly at him, but he gave her a mild look. 'Umm, he should do,' she told her friend. 'He watched them with me the other night.'

Kitty's jaw gaped and Harry smirked. 'Big mistake. Huge.' He wasn't sure what had got into him after Amy's visit. Only that when he'd seen tears in Sally's eyes, he'd had to do *something*. It seemed wrongfooting Kitty was his second reward for staying awake during the three-hour romcom marathon. The first had been seeing the smile back on Sally's face.

'What was that with Kitty?' Sally asked a few minutes later as they walked along the seafront towards the pier.

'What was what?' he countered, playing dumb.

Sally glanced sideways at him. 'It was payback for the worm comment, wasn't it?'

He liked to think he had a thicker skin than that. Still, there was no arguing that he didn't like the way Kitty had seemed to pigeon-hole him as *insensitive prick out to hurt my soft-hearted friend*. 'Nope. Just winding her up a bit. Anyway, about this shop scene,' he added, keen to change the subject. 'How are we playing it?'

'You mean you haven't spent the morning working out your lines?'

A pair of vivid blue eyes stared back at him from a face that was alive with humour, the curls framing it, bobbing about in the wind. Because he had a bizarre desire to take hold of one and see how it felt, he shoved his hands into his pockets. 'Thought I'd go with the same approach as before.'

Sally burst out laughing. 'Winging it?'

'It's worked so far.'

They headed up from the seafront and threaded their way through the twisty alleyways of the Lanes until she came to a halt. 'That's the shop, just ahead of us. Before we go in, I should warn you the lady who owns it is a major *Pretty Woman* fan so she's likely to be really into this. Can you believe she's even called Mary? I mean, it's not Mary Kate, or Mary Francis like in the film, but wow. Talk about fate. Oh and Lauren from the beauty salon messaged to say she's set up at the back by the changing rooms so we should be good to start.' Sally dug into the candyfloss creation draped over her shoulder and pulled out her phone, clicking onto video mode before holding it out in front of them. 'So, here we are with another epic romcom re-enactment, this time it's *Pretty Woman* meets *She's All That*.'

'Only I'm not as daft as that Edward character in *Pretty Woman*,' he butted in. 'Sally's using her own credit card.'

She rolled her eyes before angling the video so it panned over the shop name. As they headed inside he felt the first twinge of anxiety. He might have got one over on Kitty by saying he'd watched the films, but she'd not been wrong. He had no clue what he was supposed to do, and while that didn't really matter in the scheme of things, he realised it mattered to Sally. And therefore it mattered to him.

The shop assistant gave them a wide smile. 'Hi there. I'm Mary. Can I help?'

She looked straight at him and as Sally shifted the phone camera in his direction, he felt a bolt of sheer *awkward*. What the hell was he doing? He was a builder, not an actor and he was one hundred per cent certain none of the women he'd dated would ever accuse him of being charming like Gere's character. 'Apparently we're here to spend money.'

'How much money?' Mary beamed.

He played along, mimicking the lines from the film. 'An obscene amount.'

The assistant's grin turned even wider. 'Are we talking profane, or really offensive?'

He couldn't help it, he laughed. This was so dumb. 'I guess really offensive. It is her money.'

Sally dug him in the ribs. 'Spoilsport.'

Ignoring her, he focused back on Mary. Forty-something, dressed in a smart blouse and skirt, she wasn't dissimilar to the shop assistants in the film. 'Have you got anything here to suit a curly-haired blonde with a cute nose, big blue eyes and a terrifying addiction to romcoms?'

'That's not following the film … wait.' Sally bit into her lip and the hand that clutched the phone dropped a little, as if she'd suddenly forgotten she was supposed to be holding it. 'Cute nose?'

'Yeah.' He held her gaze and felt a strange pull in his chest. Like his heart had decided to forget the bruising it had received a few months ago and perk up a bit. 'I reckon cute describes it.'

He'd always gone for beautiful over cute, like Isabelle. In

his experience beautiful women tended do the hurting, rather than get hurt. A risk he was prepared to take. Cute women were soft-hearted. They rushed headlong into relationships, falling in love and getting their heart broken. Which was why he avoided them at all costs.

'I'm sure we can find something to suit.' Mary's voice broke him out of his internal ramblings. 'If you'd like to take a seat?'

He blinked. 'A seat?'

'Of course. This lovely lady needs to try some clothes on for you.'

His gaze flew to Sally, who looked ready to fall about laughing. 'She does?'

'How else will you both get the full major sucking up experience?'

Christ, Mary was hamming it up for all she was worth. She deserved an Oscar for this.

Beside him, Sally finally exploded into giggles. 'If you could see the look on your face.'

Before he could open his mouth to protest, he found himself pushed into a huge velvet armchair. And okay, spending time in a women's clothes shop was definitely not his idea of fun, but seeing Sally so happy? He was surprised how much he enjoyed that. Besides, he had sod all else to do for the next couple of hours until he met up with Mike and Jack to watch Albion attempt not to lose against Arsenal. So he slouched back in the chair and prepared to be entertained.

Funny thing that. If there was one thing he knew about Sally, it was that he wouldn't be bored.

Sally stared back at her image in the mirror. Thanks to Lauren, her hair was now straight, her make-up subtle yet somehow managing to make her eyes pop and her lips look more … pouty. And unlike the previous outfits she'd tried on for a laugh for Harry's benefit, this one Mary had chosen. It was not only sophisticated to match the new look. It clung everywhere.

'Well, Vivien, are you ready to show our resident Edward Lewis…' Mary trailed off as Sally opened the curtain. 'Wow, you look amazing.'

'Really?' Not convinced, Sally glanced once more in the mirror. Her bum was clearly outlined, her breasts surely too big for this tight dress. As for her belly, she could now see the rounded curve that no amount of Pilates seemed to flatten. She wanted to feel sexy, but was afraid the dress and make-up all screamed *trying too hard*.

'I guarantee your boyfriend won't laugh off this one,' Mary remarked. 'He might even stop looking at his phone.'

Sally caught her eye in the mirror. 'He's not my boyfriend. He's renting a room from me.'

'Sorry, I guess I just assumed…' She smiled. 'It does explain the earlier comments. If it had been my boyfriend, I rather fear I'd have kicked him into touch.'

Harry had, in successive outfits, called her a penguin (shiny black trousers and white fluffy jumper), a canary (a bold yellow shirt dress) and a flamingo. He'd laughed particularly hard at that pink jumpsuit, even asking her to stand on one leg.

'I wonder which bird he'll call me with this one.' The dress was a slinky turquoise blue. 'Probably a parrot.' She touched her ultra-smooth hair. 'At least my feathers aren't ruffled.'

Lauren, listening from the other side of the curtain and ready to film using Sally's phone, laughed. 'Come on then, let's show him the new, not improved but different, Sally Thornton!'

As Mary ushered her out, Sally squared her shoulders and walked towards Harry who, as Mary had predicted, was looking down at his phone. 'Who's a pretty bird, then?'

She saw his lips twitch, even as he continued to type. 'Let me guess, you're wearing red and blue. Or maybe blue with an orange shirt.' He glanced up. 'Shit.'

'You were right with blue.' He didn't reply, just continued to stare at her, and Sally began to feel acutely self-conscious. 'I guess this parrot isn't as, er, trim as she could be. Too much sitting in a cage. Not enough flying.'

'Yeah … I mean no.' He shook his head. 'I don't think you're a parrot.'

She probably wasn't a bird of any description. A lumpy blue toad maybe, if there was such a thing. Mary was going to be very disappointed. No obscene amount of money would be spent today. Maybe she could find a scarf. At least a token gesture.

Feeling deflated, she set back to the changing room, anxious to get out of the dress.

'Hey, Sally.'

She stopped, drew in a deep breath and reminded herself it didn't matter what he thought. He was probably only trying to be funny and she had to not take it personally.

Slowly she turned to face him.

'The smooth hair looks good on you.' His gaze ran over her face. 'But I prefer your curls.'

'Thanks.' She supposed it was a compliment of sorts.

'You should buy the dress.'

'Why?'

His eyes skimmed up and down her body before resting on

her face, the intensity of his stare causing a tingle in the base of her spine. 'The only bird that comes to mind is hot chick. If chicks were blue and not yellow.'

She was not expecting that. It had to be the surprise that sent her heart thumping against her ribcage. 'That's a terrible pun. And hot chick is an even worse chat-up line. Not that you were trying to chat me up,' she added hastily, flushing to the roots of her very straight hair.

His eyes, usually a cool grey, or an amused silver, turned darker. Smoky. 'No?'

Her stomach swooped and it took all her effort not to read too much into his statement. He'd seen his earlier jokes had upset her and was trying to make amends. Except ... that look on his face? It was appreciation. The sort of look a guy gives a girl he fancies.

He broke the gaze and stared back down at his phone. 'Mike and Jack are meeting up for a drink before the match. Are we done here?'

'Sure.' To hide the fact he'd flustered her, she tried a joke. 'I think you managed longer than Richard Gere's character did.'

'He didn't have a smartphone to keep him entertained.'

Harry gave her a final lingering look before nodding at Mary and leaving the shop. Once he was out of sight, Lauren winked and handed her the phone back.

'He might not be your boyfriend,' Mary said, eyes still on the door Harry had left through, 'but you two definitely have a vibe.' She fanned herself. 'And I take it all back. If my boyfriend looked like that, and called me a hot chick, I definitely wouldn't kick him into touch. In fact, I might be tempted to tie him to the bedpost.'

Sally let out a burst of laughter at the unexpected risqué comment. 'I suspect the hot chick comment was just to keep the bird joke going.' She'd liked being admired by him though, even if it had been tongue in cheek.

After thanking Lauren for the makeover, she changed back into her clothes and slotted the dress back onto its hanger. 'I'm afraid we lied about the obscene amount of spending.'

Mary waved her comment away. 'Don't you worry. I enjoyed myself.' She nodded over to the dress, now sitting bright and bold on the rack. 'I'll give you that at cost, if you want it.'

She shouldn't. With bills still to pay, she couldn't afford to buy something frivolous. Unbidden, an image of Harry's face popped into her brain when he'd finally looked up from his phone. Before she knew it, she was getting out her purse. 'I do want it. Thank you.'

Later that evening, she spent a long time editing down the footage into something she could upload onto her account. She tagged it with the comments:

Epic romcom failure take 3: Pretty Woman has to use her own credit card.

She also spent far too long watching the way Harry had looked at her in that final outfit.

Yep, this was how she got when she had a crush. She went all weird for a while. She needed a distraction.

Chapter Eight

arry was sat at his favourite table in The Cat and Fiddle – the one nearest the bar – trying to focus on what Jack was saying. And definitely not on the sight of Sally in her tight jeans as she stood talking to Vince and a few of the band members as they got ready to play.

The thing people don't tell you about ending a long-term relationship? How much you miss sex. He'd gone from regular sex, to nothing. Zip, zero, de nada. And okay, for the first two months he hadn't cared because his heart had hurt and his ego had been so crushed he couldn't contemplate ever getting that close to a woman again. Why risk rejection? Worse, risk being told he was shit in bed, because at that point his sorry brain couldn't work out any other reason why Isabelle had needed to look elsewhere.

Over the last few weeks though, his libido had started to come out of hibernation. And since he'd seen Sally in that clingy number last week, it had gone to full-on Awake – and yes, that was with a capital A.

It seemed his landlady wasn't just cute. She was sexy as hell.

So it was just as well she seemed to have an admirer, he thought, as he watched her talking animatedly with one of the guys – from the instrument he was holding, he'd hazard a guess at the bass guitarist.

'…you walk up and down the prom naked with WW Construction written on your chest in red lipstick.'

'What?' He blinked and looked back at Jack, who started cackling like some sort of demonic witch.

'Thought you might appreciate a bit of advice on how to get noticed.' He inclined his head towards where Sally was now laughing with the guy. 'Might help you with the blonde you can't take your eyes off. Is that the one in the videos? The landlady?'

'Sally is over there, yes.' He'd kind of assumed she was single because he'd not seen any guys except Vince come to the flat, and for a woman who was happy to chat about anything, she'd not mentioned dating anyone. In fact, hadn't she said she'd not found *the one* yet? At that moment she glanced over and caught his eye. She smiled and, like a twit, he smiled back.

'Holy shit, you smiled at her.' Jack cackled again. 'You've got it bad, my friend.'

'I'm living in her house, dumb arse. Would be rude not to acknowledge her.' To his relief, he saw Mike and Trixie walk in. 'Mike's here. Suggest you tell him our orders while he's at the bar. We'll never get him back there.' It was a bit unfair, Mike didn't shirk his round. He just wasn't the first to get out his wallet. Or the second.

While Jack ambled off, Harry slid further into his chair. Weird how he kept looking back at her curly blonde head and wondering what she and the bass guitarist had so much to talk about. Maybe she was asking him to help with her next romcom video. It would let him off the hook and stop the incessant ribbing he was getting. News of the videos had even reached his cousin in the States who'd sent him a few messages featuring heart-filled memes.

Yes, better he got out of this while he still had a little dignity left.

'Wakey-wakey.' Mike thrust a beer into his hand and he dragged his attention back to the friends he was supposed to be with.

'Hey, Harry.' Trixie gave him a sweet smile that always made him think she was way too nice for his friend. Then again, he'd never seen Mike happier, so maybe the pair of them had something. He only hoped it lasted longer than him and Isabelle.

'Hey, Trixie.' He glanced meaningfully at Mike. 'Still not come to your senses yet, I see.'

She giggled and put her arm around Mike's waist. 'He's kind of sweet.'

His mate gave him a smug grin and Harry experienced a brief moment of jealousy at how happy they both looked. Then reminded himself it wouldn't last.

'Seems we can't escape each other.'

He snapped his head round to find Sally had joined them. Maybe the guitar player wasn't as interesting as all that after all.

'Come to support Vince?' There was a reason behind his question that he didn't want to acknowledge.

'Yep. It was pointed out I hadn't heard The Brighton Boys play for a while. Apparently only twice since Adam joined two months ago, which is shocking.'

Okay, so if she and Adam weren't a thing already, seemed they might become one. 'This Adam, is he the bass guitarist?'

'Umm, that's right. Sam's on keyboard and Eds is lead guitar and vocals.'

He definitely recognised the strapping black guy who didn't just have an amazing voice, he had the charisma to go with it. 'Bit of a hit with women, Eds,' he murmured.

Sally laughed. 'He sure is. They'll be disappointed to hear he's married. Vince and Adam are the only singles.'

He refused to ask anything more on account of the fact he definitely wasn't interested. Instead he shuffled out of his seat so he could let Trixie and Sally sit down. He couldn't charm, but he could be a gentleman.

'What have you guys got planned for the next video?' Trixie asked as they settled in. From his new standing position he was afforded a totally unplanned glimpse of Sally's cleavage. It took a heroic effort to drag his gaze away.

'I thought we could do the scene from *Ghost* where she's throwing a pot on the wheel.' Sally glanced up at him. 'If Harry's okay with that.'

'Sure.' He remembered the guys taking the piss out of the scene, but he couldn't say he was averse to the idea of seeing her grapple a lump of clay.

'Oooh yes, that's a good choice. So sexy.'

He stilled. 'Sexy?'

Trixie grinned up at him. 'Definitely. He has his shirt off for a start, which always helps when the guy has a ripped body. Then he puts his arms around her while she has her hands on the clay. There's just something about the clay, the mess, the way she leans against his naked chest.'

She shivered and Harry felt a ripple of very real concern. The direction his thoughts were currently taking, wrapping his arms around Sally while he was half naked seemed like a really, really bad idea.

Sally watched Harry's face freeze as he took in Trixie's words. It was exactly why she hadn't yet broached the idea of doing the scene with him. The trouble was, though the shopping video had received a lot of likes and comments, it hadn't really taken off like the others. She knew why, but the solution wasn't what either of them had signed up for.

'We have other options,' she said in a bid to reassure her startled lodger.

Thankfully there was no further discussion on the topic because the pub landlord announced the band were ready to play.

As The Brighton Boys stepped up to the mics, she gave Adam a careful study. Good-looking, easy-going, great smile, creative. There was a lot to like about him. It's just ... her heart didn't race, her stomach didn't dip when she looked at him. As if he was aware of her eyes on him, Adam looked over and gave her a sweetly shy smile.

Beside her, Harry cleared his throat. 'Looks like you've got an admirer.'

The low rumble of his voice awakened the butterflies that had slept quietly while she'd been talking to Adam. 'He's just being friendly.'

Harry laughed softly. 'Blokes don't smile at women across a crowded room just to be friendly.'

'*You* don't. Adam's a smiley person.'

She was aware of the movement of Harry's hands as they slid into the pockets of his jeans. 'What am I then?'

'Kitty calls you Grumpy Pants.' She risked a look at him and found a mixture of bemusement and horror cross his face. 'Bet you regret asking now.'

His eyes caught hers, holding them for a beat longer than was considered polite. 'Maybe I'm interested in the conversations you've been having about my pants.'

Damn it. Heat raced across her cheeks and her brain wouldn't come up with a suitably witty reply. Instead she ended up muttering, 'You should be so lucky.'

Again he held her gaze, but this time when he opened his mouth to speak, he closed it and shook his head. A moment later he shifted to stand closer to Mike.

———

The next couple of hours flew by and Sally didn't see Harry again until she'd said her goodbyes to everyone and was walking out of the pub. He was stood by himself, leaning against a lamp post, legs crossed at the angles, hands pushed into his pockets. Eyes scanning the pub door.

As soon as he saw her, he straightened and walked over. Again the butterflies flapped. God, they had bad timing. Why Harry and not Adam? Even if she thought sleeping with her lodger was a good idea – for the record, she absolutely didn't – the man clearly wasn't a candidate for anything more than a casual fling. She didn't mind casual, she just wasn't very good at it, and at twenty-eight, she didn't want to waste too much emotional energy on an inconvenient crush. Not when The One could make himself known at any moment.

'Heading back?'

'Yes.'

He nodded at her reply and began to fall in step next to her.

'Were you waiting for me?'

He slid her a glance. 'Either that or I enjoy propping up lamp posts.'

She wasn't sure whether to be touched or embarrassed. 'You didn't have to, you know. I can find my way back even after two glasses of wine.'

'I don't doubt it.' He exhaled a deep breath. 'Look, we don't have to walk together if you don't want to. I just figured as we were going in the same direction…'

He shrugged and from the set of his shoulders she had a nasty feeling she'd upset him. 'Sorry. I didn't mean to sound ungrateful. I didn't want you to feel as if you had to wait for me, that's all. You know, *better escort the drunk landlady home.*' Oh boy, that made her sound like some eccentric old woman.

For a few seconds he didn't say anything and the silence made her even more aware of his presence. Of the sheer size of him, the smell of the shower gel he used, which somehow turned into some sort of aphrodisiac on his skin. The soft creak of his leather jacket.

'I don't do stuff because I feel I have to.'

She could believe that. He was the type her mum used to call *what you see is what you get.* Trouble is, she was starting to really like what she saw. 'Then thank you for walking me home.'

'No problem.'

They were quiet for a while as they crossed the road, then swerved to avoid a group of loud, drunk teenage boys. She didn't miss the sweetly protective way he put himself between her and them.

'This next video then.' He scratched at the back of his neck. 'You think we should do the potter's wheel?'

'If you're comfortable with it, yes. The thing is…' She

sucked in a breath, told herself to stop pussyfooting around and come out with it. 'I think if we want to really get the number of views boosted, we need to do something more…' She tripped over the word sexy. 'Romantic.'

He came to a stop and his big shoulders rose, then fell. 'You do realise who you're talking to?'

'Yep, I know.' When he didn't say anything, just shuffled his feet in an oddly awkward gesture, she felt the need to fill in the gap. 'The comments are filled with people saying they don't think we're just flatmates. They think we're … you know.'

'No?'

She groaned. 'Come on, you can't be this dense. Our followers think there's chemistry between us.'

Another beat of silence. 'So?'

'Soooo, they're romcom fans. They want to see some of that chemistry in action. More emphasis on the rom part of the romcom,' she added, just to be extra clear.

This time the silence stretched out so long she began to feel really uncomfortable. Thankfully it was dark, and the early October evening chilly enough to cool her flushed cheeks. Still, this was a mega uncomfortable conversation to be having with her lodger.

'We don't have to—'

'This potter's wheel thing—'

They stared at each other and she nodded. 'You go first.'

'You really reckon playing around with some clay will increase the views?'

She swallowed down the disappointment, annoyed with herself. Of course that was all this was about. 'It's worth a try.'

'Okay then.'

They walked the rest of the way to the flat in silence.

Though it wasn't strained, it was full of a crackling awareness. At least from her side. Maybe he was just wishing he'd not waited for her.

It wasn't until he opened the door and stepped back to let her in that he spoke again. 'I know the real reason you want to do this scene.'

Surprised, she stared at him. 'You do?'

He flicked her a grin. 'Yeah. You want to see me with my shirt off.' With that, he turned and walked back to his room, leaving her with a view of his broad shoulders, his tight backside. And an uncomfortable feeling that he wasn't wrong.

Chapter Nine

Another day, another round of ribbing from his workmates. It had been nearly a week since they'd met Sally at The Cat and Fiddle and they still hadn't let it go.

'That landlady of yours ready to be snogged on a potter's wheel yet?'

Those were the words he'd been greeted with. Not 'Hi, Harry, how are you doing?'

Now he was eating his sandwich – nothing wrong with cheese and pickle every day. It was … filling. Yep, that's all a guy needed his lunch to be. Filling, and not filled with a million and one questions on his sex life.

Or lack of.

'Come on, H, you can't tell us you're not the tiniest bit interested in banging her?'

Jack had that sneaky look on his face. The one that said he was deliberately trying to wind Harry up. Hence the use of the term banging, deployed with the aim of getting Harry riled because who wanted someone being so crude about a woman they fancied? 'Same answer as before. Fuck off.'

'But if you weren't interested in banging her, you'd just say no, right?'

'If I wasn't interested, I'd say fuck off.'

Jack glanced over at Mike, then back at Harry. 'Well if you're not interested, I might have a go. I mean, she's a cracker to look at. Maybe she'll go for a ginger—'

Before he knew it, Harry had leaped to his feet, sending his sandwich box flying, and fisted Jack's T-shirt. It was only when he looked into Jack's face and saw the evil grin that he realised his mistake. Exhaling sharply, he gave the bastard a slight shove and took a step back. 'Bugger off.'

Jack started laughing. 'Not interested, my arse. You so want to bang her.'

And this time he couldn't ignore the crude taunt. 'Unless you want my fist in your face, shut the fuck up.'

Jack must have realised he'd gone too far because the grin slid off his face and he gave him a curt nod. For the next few minutes they ate in silence. The cheese sandwich now tasted like sawdust, and Harry didn't think it had anything to do with the dust it had fallen into. He darted a look at Mike, who'd quietly taken a pew on the box of kitchen units they were still to install.

His business partner quirked a brow.

Harry sucked in a breath. 'Fine. I like her, okay.'

'We kind of got that message.' Jack took a swig from his water bottle. 'At the risk of seeing your fist in my face, are you going to do something about it? Not that I'd try my luck if you weren't,' he added hastily. 'Gorgeous as she is, this face is too pretty to be pulverised.'

'Like she'd go for you anyway,' Harry muttered, feeling his balance, and his sense of humour, slowly return.

'Maybe, maybe not.' Jack paused. 'That guitarist in the band though. She might go for him.'

Harry felt his insides clench, but this time he had a better handle on himself so he ignored the taunt and kept on eating. He couldn't ignore the way he felt though. Like it or not, the comments on the videos weren't wrong. He and Sally *did* have chemistry. He thought she felt it, too, though he didn't think she was interested enough to act on it. But was he? On one level it was a no-brainer – she was a gorgeous blonde, he was single, why not? Yet the list of reasons why not was too frigging huge to ignore. And it wasn't just that she was his landlady, a woman who had her head in the romcom clouds, believed in love and happy endings and was likely to immediately hear wedding bells if they started dating. It wasn't even that he'd end up disappointing her because he knew she wanted *romantic* and his version – booking an occasional restaurant – and her version – likely to involve ... hell, he didn't even know. Picnics with candles and rose petals? – were never going to align. No, all that aside, there was something even more terrifying stopping him. What if he hurt her? What if, after dating him, she lost some of her wide-eyed spark, that sweet, joyful naivety? What if he became responsible for her becoming as cynical about love as he was?

He didn't think he could live with himself.

His downward spiralling thoughts were interrupted when his phone started to ring, but when he looked at the caller ID, his heart sank. With a nod to Jack and Mike, he rose to his feet and strode outside.

'Hi, Mum.'

'I need to talk to you.'

'Fine, but I'm working.' He knew how long his mum's 'talks' went on for. 'I'll pop round on my way home.' Funny how he'd started to call his room in Sally's flat his home, and his actual home *the house*. No doubt because Isabelle was still firmly entrenched in it.

'No, I'll come to you. I don't want your father listening in.'

The thought of Sally seeing that part of his private life made him feel uneasy. Then again, he'd been witness to a taste of her own family drama, so she was hardly likely to judge. 'Fine.'

A day of handling jibes from his so-called friends. An evening of handling his mum under the roof of the woman he was trying like hell to ignore his attraction to. What a treat.

Sally was already home when Harry let himself in. He'd found it really weird in the beginning coming back from work and finding someone else at home who wasn't Isabelle. All that odd dancing around each other, trying to avoid going to the kitchen when she was there. Eating his meals in his room. But then he'd realised how easy, how uncomplicated Sally was to be with. She was unfazed by his bluntness, so he didn't have to walk on eggshells around her. Plus she made him laugh. Lately he'd even found himself heading to the kitchen straight away, hoping to find her there.

His heart gave a strange bump when he saw her stood at the stove, all those curls attempting to be tamed by a pink scrunchie. She'd changed out of her work clothes and into black leggings and a baggy pink sweatshirt. He really tried not to notice how pert her bum looked in the Lycra.

'Hey.'

She turned and gave him a wide smile. A greeting he was starting to get used to. 'How's the kitchen going in?'

The other thing about Sally? She seemed genuinely interested in what he was doing. He couldn't remember the last time anyone had bothered to ask about his day. Not Isabelle, and definitely not his mum. 'Should be done by the end of the week. How's the coffee business?'

'It's good, actually. Been busier these last few weeks, ever since that orgasm scene. I think people round here recognised it.'

'That's great.' And he genuinely meant it. She'd put a lot of effort into these videos, it was good to see her getting some reward. 'Any more cards in your window?'

A slow smile spread across her face. 'Actually, yes. Jayne and David met in The Love Bean a year ago and got married last weekend. She came in today to ask if she could put a card in the window. Isn't that amazing? One more couple who've found love in the cafe.'

Her face lit up with delight and he had to turn away, aware anything he said would likely put a pin in her heart-shaped bubble. Making a non-committal noise, he opened the fridge and surveyed the contents of his two shelves.

'I don't think staring at it helps.' He gave her a quizzical look and she waved at the fridge. 'You have to actually go to the shops to get food. Wishing you had some doesn't work. I've tried it.'

He heaved out a sigh, glanced at his watch and swore. Looked like he'd have to tackle his mother on an empty stomach.

'Everything okay?'

He wanted to say no. He was tired, hungry and didn't have the energy to play dutiful son. 'Yeah. Just had enough of today.'

Harry wasn't what Sally would call a ray of sunshine. He didn't greet her with a big smile, didn't bother with phrases like *good morning* or *how are you*? Yet there was usually a flicker of amusement in his eyes, a dry quip to counter her cheeriness. Tonight though, he looked downcast. Like life was giving him a beating.

But before she could quiz him, the intercom buzzed.

'I'll get that. If it helps improve your day, you're welcome to some leftover quiche from the cafe. As long as you don't buy into that rot about real men not eating quiche, that is.' She started to move but he shook his head.

'It's my mother.'

'Oh, right.'

From the tight expression on his face it wasn't a visit he was looking forward to. As she'd always judged guys on how they got on with their mothers, hopefully the fact Harry clearly had a strained relationship with his would stop the annoying fixation she had on him.

He inhaled a deep breath, squared his shoulders and set off towards the door.

Once he'd pressed to let the visitor into the building, he glanced back at her. 'I'm man enough to eat quiche, by the way. Thanks.'

'No problem.'

The corner of his mouth lifted, ever so slightly. 'Was my manliness actually in doubt?'

She allowed her gaze to roam over him and felt a flutter deep in her belly. *Don't flirt. He knows he's a big, broad hunk of a man. No need to massage his ego.* 'According to local gossip, you were seen in a ladies' clothes shop the other day. And apparently you star in romcom re-creations and spent an evening last week watching *Pretty Woman* and *She's All That*.'

He raised his eyes to the ceiling, his smile growing wider. 'What the hell are you doing to me?'

The way her heart somersaulted at the sight of his smile, she wanted to ask herself the same question.

When the knock on the door came, Sally knew she should head off to her room, give him and his mum some space, but she was too damn nosey. Instead she started to fill up the kettle, telling herself this was her flat. She could make herself a drink if she wanted to.

Her first thought as Harry bent to kiss his mum on the cheek was, wow, they were nothing alike. His mum might have the same dark hair but she was slender, elegant.

'Well, this place isn't easy to find.'

Harry didn't reply. Instead he stepped behind her and carefully took off her jacket, going to hang it on the coat rack.

As he turned to go back to his mum, his eyes caught hers and Sally flushed, aware she'd been caught staring. Hastily, she busied herself with fetching a mug out of the cupboard.

'Who's that woman?' she heard his mother ask.

'Sally. It's her flat.'

Sally glanced over at them just in time to see his mum give Harry a pinched look. 'You didn't tell me you were living with another woman. What on earth is Isabelle going to think?'

The lines round Harry's mouth tightened. 'Do you really think I give a toss?'

His mother glared back at him. 'It's precisely that attitude that caused her to look elsewhere.'

Sally watched as Harry briefly shut his eyes. He looked like a man on the edge of his control. 'Do you want a drink?' His voice was clipped, as if his tightly clenched jaw could barely open enough to mouth the words.

'I'll have a tea. You have Earl Grey here?'

Sally felt a really terrible need to laugh. Did his mum really expect her builder son to drink Earl Grey? Yet Harry simply nodded. 'Fine.' He indicated down the hallway. 'My room is at the end.'

Awkwardly, Sally stepped out of the kitchen and smiled at Harry's mum. 'Hi, I'm Sally, lovely to meet you. Why don't you both use the living room? I'll grab my drink and make myself scarce,' she added for Harry's benefit as it was beyond obvious she'd already heard more than he'd wanted her to. The odd dynamic between mother and son, the mention of Isabelle and her looking elsewhere... So many questions buzzed round her brain, so many tiny jigsaw pieces she wanted to fit together so she had a clearer picture of who Harry was.

Why do you need to know? He's just the lodger. Swallowing hard, she dived back in the kitchen to fetch her mug.

Of course Harry followed her in.

Tension vibrated off him and he looked frustrated, yet worryingly he also wouldn't meet her eyes. She had a mad desire to wrap her arms around him, smooth the lines of tension from his face.

'If it helps, I had my ear phones in so I didn't hear anything.'

Finally he looked at her, and for a brief moment hope flared in his eyes. 'Really?'

'Sorry, no. But I can pretend I did.'

He let out a weary-sounding laugh. 'Thanks, but we both know you're burning with questions.'

She bit into her lip to stop from smiling. 'So many questions.'

He gave a shake of his head, then reached to rub at what had to be a knot of tension at the back of his neck. It made his bicep bunch sexily and of course her eyes went there. Thankfully he was too distracted to notice.

'Do you really have Earl Grey tea?' she asked as she watched him hunt around in the cupboard she'd designated for him.

He drew out a box. 'Yep.'

Surprised, she watched him pop a bag into a mug. 'You keep them for your mum?'

'No. I drink it after my spa day.'

Seeing him in a spa was almost more believable than imagining him drinking Earl Grey. So he kept tea bags for his mum yet he didn't seem to like her much? And why was she so interested? 'I'll go and watch TV in my room, let you have some privacy.'

'Thanks.'

He didn't look back at her, just focused on dropping the tea bag into the bin. Then he shocked her further by taking a lemon from the fruit bowl, slicing an end off and squeezing it into the cup. As if aware of her staring, he glanced up. 'I'll replace your lemon.'

'I'm not... That's not...' She huffed out a breath. 'I don't care about the lemon. I'm just surprised to see Mr I'll Drink Anything making Earl Grey tea with lemon.'

He shrugged. 'It's the only way she drinks it.'

Fair enough, yet it didn't fit with the profile she had of him. He was blunt, no-nonsense. Easier to imagine him making his mum a builder's tea, dumping it in front of her and telling her to take it or leave it.

She watched as he carried the drink into the living room, then picked up her own mug and headed towards her bedroom, but not before taking a furtive peek at them through the door. His mum was sat on one end of the corner sofa, Harry about as far away as he could get on the other. He was hunched forward, arms on his thighs, expression tense. Whatever they were about to discuss, it was clearly serious.

But not her business.

Yet as she shut the door to her room, her brain wouldn't stop trying to figure out which Harry was the right one. Straightforward, practical, hard-headed builder. Or the guy she'd seen glimpses of tonight, who'd possibly been cheated on by his girlfriend. And who kept Earl Grey tea for his mum despite the fact they didn't seem to be very close.

Chapter Ten

Harry successfully managed to dodge Sally for the rest of the week. He knew what was going through her head. *Is Isabelle the ex? Did she have an affair? Why did you leave the house, not her?* And perhaps also the most uncomfortable question of all: *Why is your mum on her side and not yours?*

To avoid answering questions he wasn't ready for, he'd taken to eating at the pub after work the last few days, arriving back late. Then leaving at the crack of dawn. Mike and Jack had been curious as to why he was on site so early, but when he pointed out the build would be finished a day ahead of schedule, giving them the day off, they kept their sark to a minimum.

But today was Saturday, and Sally was still home because he'd not heard the front door go.

Choices. Stay in his room, eventually die of starvation. Or, man up, go to the kitchen, eat breakfast and pretend everything is normal.

He pushed back the duvet, shrugged on sweats and a clean T-shirt and strode towards the kitchen, whistling.

She was sat at the island, drink in front of her, scrolling through her phone. When she heard him she looked up, a bemused expression on her face. 'Hello, whistling stranger.'

Everything is normal. 'Morning.' Expression carefully neutral, he filled the kettle. 'Not working today?'

'Vince is on the morning shift. I'm going in later.'

Normal, he reminded himself. 'Have you had a busy week? At the cafe, I mean. Evenings are your business.' Shite, apparently he was crap at normal. His failings were confirmed when he heard a burst of smothered laughter and turned to find her with a hand over her mouth, blue eyes bursting with humour.

'Are you really going to do polite conversation?'

'Thought I'd give it a go,' he muttered, irked. He wasn't *that* bad at it, was he?

'Why? You've not bothered before now.'

He carefully avoided her gaze. 'Fine. We can be quiet.'

Another noise, this one like a snigger that she'd turned into a cough. 'Or we can find out a bit more about each other. You know. Ask real questions rather than polite ones.'

When he finally turned to look at her, she had an innocent smile on her face. 'What sort of questions?'

She smirked, and maybe it was that, or the spark in her eyes, or the low cut of her vest top beneath the pink dressing gown. Something sent a bolt of arousal arrowing through him. He couldn't figure what was worse. Facing her questions, or facing this undeniable attraction to her.

'We could start easy, or—'

'Isabelle was having an affair,' he interrupted. 'She refused to leave the house, so I left.'

The amusement vanished from her face. 'That's awful. I'm sorry.'

'Yeah, don't be. I'm more angry at her continuing to live in my house than I am at her having sex with her boss.' Sally looked like she didn't believe him. 'I told you, I don't believe in the fantasy.'

'But you must have felt something for Isabelle,' she pressed. 'Why else were you living with her?'

'I fancied her, the sex was good, we had a laugh together.' He met Sally's searching gaze. 'Plus her landlord decided to sell the house she'd been renting and she needed a place to stay.'

Sally nodded, as if she knew the answer to a question he didn't think he'd asked. 'So you weren't together for the right reasons.'

'What other reasons are there?'

'You didn't love each other.'

He fought not to laugh. 'We've already established I don't believe in that. Isabelle and I had fun, until it stopped. I'm just pissed she didn't have the guts to tell me to my face she'd had enough.'

'She wasn't the one. That's why it ended like it did.'

This, her sweet naivety, her trust in the whole love, soulmate concept, was exactly why he had to ignore his attraction. 'It ended because that's what relationships do. They fizz for a while, then they fizzle out.'

'Some do, of course. But some deepen into something so special, it lasts for ever.'

'Maybe. Or maybe those people stay together for the sake of show, or habit. Or because it's too difficult to leave.' He didn't like the way she was looking at him. The sadness, the pity in her expression.

'What about living with someone you can't conceive *not* being with?' she asked softly. 'Who makes you smile every time you think of them. Someone to share the good times with, and help you through the bad? Who will always be there for you, fighting your corner?'

A small part of him wondered what it must be like to have her optimism. 'I think that sounds like a nice ideal. And that this is one hell of a heavy conversation for a Saturday morning.'

Her expression turned apologetic. 'Sorry. Guess we should have stuck with the polite conversation.'

'That would have been even more painful.' She smiled but it looked forced, and he felt like the school bully who'd deliberately stomped on her party balloon. 'Just because I don't believe there's someone waiting out there for me, doesn't mean it won't happen for you. And hey, maybe you're right and I'll fall flat on my arse.'

'After being charged at by a female rhino.'

Her grin was back and when her eyes met his there was a sense of déjà vu as a weird static hummed through his blood, just as it had the last time they'd had this conversation. He might not believe in love, but he definitely believed in like. And lust. And, right now, his sweatpants felt way too loose to contain what was happening inside them. 'What about Adam, then?' he asked, changing the subject. 'Is he the one?'

Her eyes widened. 'I told you, we're not involved.'

'Why not? He seems besotted.' He told himself he was asking to keep the spotlight on her.

Her cheeks reddened and she glanced away. 'So far I've not got the fuzzies.'

'Fuzzies?'

Her gaze darted back to his. 'You know, when you tingle all over, your skin gets too tight, you feel hot and achy—'

'Right.' He knew *exactly* what she meant. There was a

chance what he felt now was simply hunger though, so he dragged a bowl from the dishwasher and reached up to grab his cornflakes from the top shelf of the cupboard. All the while aware of her eyes on him.

She cleared her throat. 'Fuzzies are only stage one. You can get the fuzzies and never move on to the bells.'

He stared at her blankly. 'And the bells are important?'

'Definitely. That's when you know it's more than a crush. I've not heard them yet, but I hope to.'

'Why?'

'Because then I'll know he's The One. That it's love. For some people the bells can come straight away, but for most it starts with fuzzies.'

He fought not to laugh. 'Good to hear you've got it all planned out.'

'Of course, just because I don't feel the fuzzies with Adam now, doesn't mean they won't come in time,' she added, ignoring his sarcasm. 'They did for Harry and Sally.' He froze, and alarm shot across her face. 'I didn't mean... You know I was talking about the fictional Harry and Sally, right? From the orgasm scene.'

'I know.' Yet his eyes wouldn't leave hers. There was something else beneath her obvious panic. Something that made the air between them thicken, and those bloody fuzzies hum inside him.

'You know what, watching you eat cereal reminds me I've not had any for ages.' With a jerky movement she jumped off the bar stool and opened the cupboard door next to his. Standing on tiptoes, she reached for the top shelf.

She was tall enough, he didn't have that excuse. Yet somehow he found himself walking up behind her, his hands flying to her waist to lift her up.

Bad idea. Now her firm buttocks were pressed against his groin, which was way too thrilled to be there. And fuck, she smelled good up close. Something floral, maybe, but soft, sleepy, if that had a smell.

'Umm, Harry.'

Shit. He was standing there like a weirdo, smelling her hair. Hastily, he lowered her, but somehow his hands wouldn't leave her waist. 'Those fuzzies.'

She turned slowly and now they were face to face, and way too close. *Or not close enough.*

'Yes?' The word sounded soft and husky on her lips.

'I know what you mean.' If he hadn't just had a starry-eyed conversation with her about love, he might have forgotten all the reasons why it was a bad idea, and kissed her.

But she was a no-go zone, so he forced his hands down, and his body to step away.

Feeling flushed, her skin tight, her insides fluttery, Sally sat back down on her bar stool and focused on pouring the chocolate hoops into her bowl, alarmed to find her hand trembling. The fuzzies that currently swarmed through her system – and if she'd read his words correctly, also through his – weren't wanted. Harry Wilson wasn't the right person to be sharing fuzzies with. Surreptitiously, she glanced over at him, relieved to find he wasn't watching. Instead he was loading his bowl into the dishwasher.

God, he was sexy though. The broad back, narrow hips, tightly muscled bum. That glimpse she'd had again of his abs, of the V leading into his sweats…

Her stomach swooped and she drew in a deep breath. It was a crush. It would fade.

'So now you know why I'm living with you rather than in my own house. And why I'm prepared to sell my soul on TikTok for the promise of a bit of extra cash.' He turned and leaned back against the worktop, arms folded across his chest. There was nothing subtle about his good looks, like there was nothing subtle about him. He was bluntly handsome – all power and muscle and earthy sex appeal. 'Why are you strapped for cash?'

Avoiding his eyes, she poured milk on the hoops. 'Who said I am?'

He pointed to himself. 'I might be amazing to live with, but even I think you'd rather have the place to yourself.'

'I'm trying to pay off a debt.'

There was a beat of silence. 'That's all I get?'

And okay, she was usually happy to talk about herself, but this involved her sister. 'There's not much else to say.' She focused back on the cereal because it seemed less dangerous than looking at him.

Another beat of silence, followed by a low chuckle. 'Isn't that kids' cereal?'

'Do I look like a kid?' It was the wrong thing to say. His hot gaze travelled over her and she became acutely conscious of the fact she wasn't wearing a bra.

He paused, swallowed. 'Definitely a grown woman.'

Her nipples hardened, feeling super sensitive against the cotton of her vest top. She needed to get this conversation back on track, though what she needed to talk about wasn't likely to be any less … distracting. 'How are you fixed for tomorrow?' His eyebrows flew up. 'For the potter's wheel video,' she added hastily. 'Kitty's friend Emma is a ceramic artist and she's happy for us to use her studio tomorrow afternoon.'

'Okay. That works.'

His acceptance seemed too easy, considering what they were going to act out. 'Do you know the scene I'm talking about?'

His lips twitched. 'I know *of* it.'

'So you know what you're expected to do?' It had seemed like a good idea when she'd first suggested it. Ticked the iconic box, was likely to be fun, didn't require much effort to reproduce and was sexier than the other videos they'd done. Now she wasn't so sure.

'According to Trixie, I have to take my shirt off and put my arms round you.'

And that's *why* she wasn't convinced of her choice. Of course there was a chance he'd look awful shirtless. That all the muscles hinted at beneath his T-shirt would be too much and he'd look like a steroid-addled weight lifter. There was also a chance she wouldn't enjoy having his arms around her.

Heat bloomed across her skin. *Fat chance.*

'You don't have to take your shirt off. We can play this any way you want.'

His eyes narrowed. 'Thought you said the comments were asking for content with more oomph.'

'Well, yes.'

He shrugged the big shoulders she was starting to obsess about. 'So that's what we need to give them.'

'And you reckon a naked Harry from the waist up will do the trick?'

His gaze did that thing again, when his eyes turned from quiet grey to smouldering charcoal, in the blink of an eye. 'You think I can't do oomph?'

Her pulse began a wild beat. 'I'm sure you can.' Before she got herself in a tangle about how she was sure, she added, 'But the scene is about more than flexing your muscles.'

'I know.' He had a glint in his eye.

'It's Demi Moore, AKA Molly, reconnecting with her dead husband in a sexy, poignant yet intensely emotional encounter.'

He smirked. 'And it's making phallic shapes in clay.'

She groaned. 'That's what you took from watching the clip?'

'I've not actually seen it. Jack told me what happened.'

She swallowed her disappointment. 'Maybe you should make the effort to watch it before tomorrow.'

'Yes, ma'am.'

The buzz of the intercom saved her from having to find a cutting reply. When she went to answer it though, part of her wished she was still sparring with Harry.

'It's me.'

There had been a time when she'd been happy to get a visit from her sister. Now Amy's visits only happened when she wanted something. 'Come on up.' She turned to find Harry standing in the kitchen doorway. 'It's Amy.'

He nodded. 'What time tomorrow?'

'Let's head over at one. Gives you plenty of time to watch the whole film.'

A small smile. 'I think you need to lower your expectations.'

'How about if I tell you the hero is killed in the opening scene and comes back as a ghost? It's more fantasy/thriller than romcom. You never know, you might even enjoy it.'

Why did he have to look so damn sexy when he stared at

her like that? Mouth slightly curved, eyes alive with amusement. As if they were having a private joke.

The moment was broken by the knock on the door. Harry inclined his head and disappeared off down the hall to his room.

'Hey, Sis.' Sally smiled as Amy stepped inside. 'This is a nice surprise.'

'Hi.'

No eye contact, no smile. Not a promising start. 'Everything okay?'

'Of course.' Amy twisted her hands.

'Are you sure?' She peered more closely at her sister. She looked pale and ... twitchy. Nervous. 'You know you can tell me anything, right?'

'What if I need money?' Her expression must have given her away, because Amy let out a bitter laugh. 'Exactly. I can't tell you anything, can I?'

'Hey, that's not true. Money is tight, you know that. We're still trying to pay off your credit card bill.'

'Yeah, well, if I was allowed to get my share of Mum and Dad's money like you, there wouldn't be a problem.'

Silence, punctured by the sound of a door being shut down the hallway. Harry must have heard all that. She guessed it made them even.

'He's still here then?' Amy nodded towards her old room.

'Yes.'

'So why can't you give me the rent he pays? It is my room he's using.'

'It goes to the credit card company.' There was also the small matter of the flat actually belonging to her, not Amy. But tensions were already high and pointing that out would only heighten them. Taking a breath, she softened her voice. 'Why do you need more money?'

'Forget it. You clearly don't want to help.'

Amy made to turn, but Sally reached to touch her arm. 'Please don't go. Stay and have a coffee with me. Let's talk about this.'

'I can't. Chris is expecting me back.'

Amy had been dating Chris for the last two years but Sally had only met him a few times. On each occasion, she'd liked him less. She couldn't help but think Amy's increased spending and unsettled behaviour since graduating was due to his influence. 'So? Message him and tell him you're with me.'

'Duh, he knows that. He was the one who told me to come.'

A bad feeling settled like lead in her stomach. 'He told you to get money from me?'

Amy stiffened. 'It wasn't like that. He's going to ask his parents as well.'

But they weren't a soft touch like she was. 'Is he paying his way at all?'

Amy's face hardened. 'You've never liked him.'

'I didn't say that. I just don't like the fact you're both drifting instead of doing something with your lives.'

'I haven't decided what I want to do yet, okay? And anyway, it's not as if I'm really broke. I'll get Mum and Dad's money in a couple of years.'

Amy's share of the inheritance had been put into a trust, available to her when she turned twenty-four. Sally could only hope by then she'd grown up, ditched Chris and had a clearer view on what she wanted to do with her life. 'Two years is a long time, Amy.'

'Yeah. It's not fair you got the money at eighteen and I have to wait.'

She could point out she'd applied to get the money earlier because she'd had to buy them both a place to live. That instead of going to university like she'd planned, she'd used what was left over to buy a cafe so she could earn money yet still be there for Amy when she came out of school. But none of that would help repair the sibling bond. 'Message me with how much money you need. I'll see what I can do.'

'Thanks.' It was said grudgingly, but at least Sally knew when Amy shut the door behind her, it wouldn't be the last time she saw her.

Chapter Eleven

Harry let the hot water of the shower flow over him, washing away the sweat from his six-mile run along the seafront. He wasn't going to lie, he was looking forward to the next part of today. Fooling around with clay, and with Sally – yes, he had watched the scene on YouTube last night. Not the whole film. He hadn't been *that* engrossed.

After towelling off, he squirted a healthy spray of deodorant under his arms. He was going to be very close to her today. And shirtless. He gave himself a critical look in the mirror and flexed his pecs. Not bad. Manual labour was better than a daily gym session.

Bang on midday, he wandered down the hallway and into the kitchen where he found Sally already waiting for him. They'd not crossed paths since Amy's rather enlightening visit yesterday.

'Ready?'

The wide smile on her face, the big blue eyes. The white short-sleeved blouse, buttoned just low enough he might be able to see a hint of cleavage when he sat behind her. Yep, he was definitely ready.

He snagged his keys from the bowl on the sideboard and followed her out, noting the delicious curve of her bum in her cut-off jeans. A real bum, the sort he could wrap his hands round if he were to lift her up and pin her to the wall…

'Did you watch the film?'

He dragged his mind out of the gutter. 'I watched the scene.'

'Okay, good.' She glanced his way as they stepped out onto the pavement. 'Should we talk about how we're going to do it, or just be spontaneous?'

'Spontaneous seems to be working. I can't act for shit.'

'Fine.' She paused. 'I don't know how long the clip was you watched, but we're just doing the part at the potter's wheel. Not, you know, what happened afterwards.' Maybe it was the fresh air, but he thought her cheeks looked flushed.

'You don't want me to lift you into my arms, fondle your bum, kiss the living daylights out of you and then lower you onto a sofa?'

She briefly covered her face with her hands. 'God, this is so embarrassing.' With a shake of her head, she took in a deep breath. 'Anyway, now we've clarified that, onto less mortifying subjects. Have you ever worked with clay?'

'No.' He grinned. 'But I don't figure making a pot is what the scene is all about.'

'True.'

He thought they could both do with a change of topic. 'How are things with your sister?'

'I wondered how long it would be before you asked.' She let out a deep sigh. 'I take it you now have the answer to why I need the money.'

'I gathered it isn't your debt.' He searched her face, wondering if he should broach the subject, but too interested not to. 'Feel free to tell me to mind my own business, but what did she mean about her share of your mum and dad's money?'

'They died when we were kids. I was sixteen and Amy ten.'

'I'm sorry, that's a shit break.'

'Yeah. Mum went first, skin cancer. She left it too late to get a mole looked at. Dad, well, I don't think he could cope with watching the woman he loved, fade away. He died three weeks later. They say it was a heart attack, but I think it was a broken heart.'

'Christ, Sally.' He didn't know what to say. How could a woman who'd suffered such loss be so uncynical, so bloody hopeful about life? 'Wait, you can't have looked after Amy since you were sixteen?'

'Oh no. We went to live with Mum's sister for a couple of years. She meant well, but she lived in Somerset and we missed our friends, missed the sea. Plus my aunt was older than Mum, and her kids, my cousins, had both left home. She and my uncle were ready to retire and go travelling. The last thing they wanted was two more kids getting in their way.'

'So when did you move back to Brighton?'

'I finished school, then my aunt helped convince the trustees that I should get my share of Mum and Dad's money early. I bought the flat and the cafe and … we managed.' A sad smile crossed her face. 'Actually, we did more than that. We had some good times. Amy went back to her old school and afterwards she'd walk to the cafe and do her homework while I finished up. We were close then.'

'And now?'

'Now she's living with a guy I don't think is good for her, and pulling pints in The King and Queen a few evenings a week to pay the rent. She's got a degree, along with a lot of debt, but doesn't seem in any rush to find a full-time job.'

'And you're subbing her?'

'In a way, yes, and I don't mind. I mean, she's my sister. Of course I'm going to help.' She bit into her lip. 'I'm just not sure this is all Amy. I think I'm subbing Chris, too, and that really pisses me off.'

He suddenly had a thought. 'Am I in the way? Maybe she thinks she can't leave this boyfriend because I'm in her room.'

'I had all this out with her before I put out the ad. She was adamant she didn't want to live with me anymore.'

'But that's why you put a week's notice on our agreement.'

'Yes.' She darted him a look, and he was pleased to see the light back in her eyes. 'And I wanted to be able to chuck you out fast if you turned out to be a dud.'

He laughed. 'So the fact I'm still with you three months later means I'm not a dud?'

'Maybe.' Her lips quirked in what he thought she meant to be a smirk, but looked way too cute for that. 'Or maybe I'm desperate.'

She drew to a halt and he realised they'd arrived at the studio. Funny how he'd not even noticed the walk. Way too fascinated by his landlady's unexpected past. She might have her head in a romantic bubble but, wow, she had a backbone of frigging steel. He made a mental note to never underestimate a romance lover ever again. Just because they liked happy endings didn't mean they couldn't cope when life got tough.

'So, anyway, here we are.' She dug into the fluffy pink object dangling from her shoulder.

'Better not go to a fair with that,' he remarked idly.

'What?'

'It might get eaten by mistake.'

'Sorry?' Finally, she found what she was looking for and held out a pair of keys. 'What might get eaten?'

'The candyfloss.'

She frowned, then a second later rolled her eyes. 'Very funny. Let's hope you're still laughing when I've covered you in clay. Ready to get dirty?'

It was the wrong question to ask of a guy who'd not long ago been imagining his hands on her bum. 'Very ready to get dirty. With you.'

———

The keys dropped out of her hands. As Sally fumbled on the floor for them, her heart thumped against her ribs. The man might not do romantic, but he could sure as hell do sexy.

Harry crouched down next to her, his big, muscular thighs brushing against hers as he plucked up the errant keys.

'Butterfingers.'

'That's me.' She rose slowly, avoiding his gaze. Better he thought her clumsy than unable to cope with a bit of harmless innuendo.

He opened the door with quick, non-fumbling efficiency and stepped aside to let her through first. Manners, along with the sexy. No wonder she felt unbalanced by him.

'Do you know how to work this thing?' he asked, eyeing up the potter's wheel in the back of the studio.

'Sort of. Emma, that's who owns this place, gave me a quick demo.' Though now she wished she'd listened more attentively. 'You put a lump of clay in the middle, add some water and turn the wheel. How hard can it be?'

He burst out laughing. 'Guess we'll find out.'

She didn't think throwing the pot was going to be the most difficult part. 'So, I'll set things up and we'll just wing it, yes?'

'Sure.'

Positioning a chair behind the stool at the wheel, she filled a small tray with water and then opened the bag of clay Emma had left out. After putting it on the wheel, she went to line up the phone, resting it against a pot before shuffling it around to make sure the wheel was in the centre of the lens. 'That should do it.'

'Shouldn't you take your jeans off?'

Her eyes flew to his, pulse hammering. 'Sorry?'

He gave her a crooked smile. 'I don't know what that Molly character was wearing beneath her shirt, but in the clip I saw, there were definitely legs.'

Sally stared down at her jeans. He was right, but she didn't have Demi Moore's legs, or her elfin grace. And the shirt she was wearing wasn't long enough to hide her thighs. 'I'll stick to the jeans. Like I said, we can play this any way we want.'

'But I thought what we wanted was oomph?'

He reached for the hem of his T-shirt and in one quick, confident movement, peeled it off over his head.

She'd prepared for this moment, but she hadn't prepared for *that*. Startled, she accidentally knocked the phone over.

'Damn.' She picked it up with trembling fingers and tried to line it up again, willing her pulse to calm. Not easy because he was standing behind the wheel, that wall of well-defined muscle now in her full vision. It was immediately clear he'd spent a good deal of the summer with his shirt off. Also abundantly clear that admirers of the male anatomy weren't going to be disappointed with this clip. Holy moley, the ripple of muscles, the contained power, the sexy V where his abs met his obliques and disappeared into the top of his jeans, their path arrowed by a trail of dark hair...

'Where do you want me?'

The question, asked in a low, husky voice, sent heat rushing between her legs. She glanced up in time to catch his smirk and then an odd thing happened. She began to relax. They were flirting, and that was okay because flirting was fun. Plus it was pretty essential if they were going to do this scene justice.

After setting her phone to play 'Unchained Melody', she pressed record and walked towards him. 'If we stick true to the original, I'll start off at the wheel and then you and all those muscles' – she flapped her hand at him – 'come up behind me.'

He let out a low laugh. 'Come up behind you. Got it.'

She felt the air crackle as she reached the wheel and sat down on the stool, the haunting music echoing through the studio. Taking hold of the clay, she set it onto the centre of the wheel and started it turning. Then, after sprinkling water over it, she placed her hands on either side of the clay and tried to make the cone Emma had described.

All the while, she was acutely aware of the fact he was somewhere at the back of the studio. Shirtless.

She smelled him first, the whiff of soap and outdoors, before she felt his body settle into the chair behind her. Shivers set off down her spine as he leaned forward, breath a warm flutter against her neck. 'Keep rubbing like that and it will grow.'

It took a moment to process what he meant. Then she burst out laughing. 'You can't say that.'

'Hey, I'm not the one making phallic shapes out of clay.'

'It's a cone. I have to make that to stretch and centre the clay, then I need to squish it down.' She put the side of her hand against the top of the clay cone, the other resting round the side as Emma had showed her.

'Ouch.' She felt his big body shudder. 'Don't press too hard on the tip.'

She started to giggle. 'Stop it. This is meant to be sexy, not lewd.'

His hands settled round her waist and she felt their imprint, the warmth radiating through her light cotton shirt. His mouth brushed her ear. 'How's this?'

She swallowed. 'Better.'

That's when he shifted closer. Suddenly she felt the heat from his naked chest all along her back. 'And this?'

'I don't know.' Damn it, her heart was racing. 'Do you look as good as Swayze?'

His chuckle didn't just vibrate against her ear, it resonated from his chest and through the whole of her upper body. 'We'll have to let the followers decide.' His fingers pressed into her waist. 'Is this the part where I tickle you?'

She yelped. 'Okay, I think we covered that.'

'What about the part when Swayze asks to help, and places his hands over hers?' Harry's voice lowered an octave.

He did exactly as he said, and butterflies didn't just flap in her stomach, they started buzzing as their hands began a slow, flirty dance. This was Fuzzies with a capital F.

'And then he kisses her, right?' he asked softly.

She felt the press of lips against her neck and the low sound of him... Was that a hum? Or wait. 'Are you laughing?'

'Absolutely not.'

But she felt the shake of his shoulders. 'You are.'

'Okay, maybe just a bit. Thing is, your hair, it tickles.'

Some of the heat, the joy of the moment seeped out. 'We can't all have Demi Moore's glossy straight hair.'

'Hey, I'm not complaining.' She felt that soft press against her neck again. 'I just need to navigate it.'

And wow, he was doing a mighty fine job, she thought a moment later as his lips found the sensitive spot behind her ear.

The final echoes of the song played around the room ... *I need your love, God speed your love* ... and she lost herself in the moment. The press of lips against skin as he nuzzled her neck, the heat from his body radiating down her spine, the sensuous feel of his hands over hers as they slipped against the long-forgotten clay.

'Fuck, you smell good,' he groaned, shifting to trail hot kisses down the side of her neck and across her collar bone.

Her body melted further against the wall of his chest as her pulse hammered, her breath now short and choppy. This was more than acting out a scene, she thought, feeling dizzy. This was foreplay.

But then the music stopped.

Suddenly there was silence, just the sound of breathing. Of a moan filled with pleasure. She lurched upright. Shit, was that her? Embarrassed, she rubbed a hand over her face.

Then realised what she'd done when he started to laugh.

'Clay's good for the complexion,' she retorted, leaping off the stool. 'They use clay masks all the time. It ... detoxifies.'

'If you say so.' Amused grey eyes roamed her face and she hated to think how stupid she looked. As if he could read her mind, his expression turned soft. 'You look kind of cute.'

'Thanks.'

Now she wasn't embarrassed, she was flustered. Refusing to look at him, she walked over to the sink to wash the clay off her hands and face. Then quickly turned the video off.

'Anyway, I think we got enough footage so, well, thanks for doing that.'

'You think we gave it enough oomph?'

If the way her knees shook was anything to go by… 'I think we oomphed it up just fine.'

He nodded and went to wash his hands while she quickly discarded the clay and cleaned up. By the time she'd finished he was stood by the door, shirt back on, watching her carefully.

'What is it?' She touched her face. 'Do I still have clay on me?'

He bent his head, gaze settling on her mouth. 'Maybe just a bit. Here.'

He ran a finger over her mouth and though his hands were large and calloused, his touch was gentle enough to make her lips tingle. 'Would you…' She had to swallow to get her mouth working. 'Would you wipe it off?'

He shook his head, but the grey eyes glinted. 'I'll do better than that.' Before she knew what was happening, his mouth was brushing hers, and those tingles were skating down her spine again.

All too soon, he pulled away.

'What was that for?' Her voice sounded breathless.

'I wanted to see if your lips tasted as good as your neck.'

Her heart banged against her ribs. Should she be encouraging this? But the question was out before she could stop it. 'And?'

'They didn't.' Just as her stomach started to plummet, he smiled. 'They tasted even better.'

For a moment they stood, staring at each other. She couldn't explain why her heart raced, or how every cell in her body seemed to be on full alert, aware of him in a way she'd not been a few weeks ago. The way his eyes weren't just grey but had hints of blue. How they were framed with dark lashes that women would give their eye teeth for. How his nose wasn't strictly straight. It had a slight kink, like it must have taken a knock at some point.

'Hey, there you are.' Sally broke out of her trance to find Kitty standing in the now-open doorway, glancing between the pair of them. 'Emma asked me to check if you needed anything.'

'We're good, thanks.' Her voice sounded embarrassingly husky. 'In fact, we're done. We were just leaving.' Awkward was not a strong enough word for how she felt right now. It didn't help that Kitty was looking at her a little too closely.

'Okay.' Kitty looped her hand through her arm. 'Then you're free to come and have a drink with me.'

'Sure.'

She glanced to Harry but Kitty was already dragging her out of the studio. 'I'm sure Harry has something far more interesting to do than listen to us gossip.'

Harry gave Kitty a bland look before settling his gaze back on her, a small smile hovering on his lips. 'It was great getting dirty with you. See you later.'

As he strode off, hands in pockets, Sally sighed. 'We should have asked him to join us.'

Kitty shrugged. 'I doubt he'd have wanted to.' They started to walk and Kitty clutched onto her arm. 'Besides, if he had, I wouldn't have been able to find out what just happened here, because when I opened the door it looked like I'd burst in on something. Had I?'

'Honestly?' Sally shook her head, still able to feel the press of his mouth against hers. 'I've no idea.'

But whatever it had been, she wanted to do it again.

Chapter Twelve

Okay, so he'd flirted with his landlady, then enjoyed it so much he'd kissed her. Then enjoyed that so much, he'd spent the rest of the afternoon walking aimlessly along the seafront, trying to order his thoughts.

On one hand dangled the enticing possibility of some frigging awesome sex.

Yet the other hand was weighed down by all the reasons he'd already come up with of why he *shouldn't* act on this undeniable attraction; he'd hurt her, and in doing so, dim some of her spark. Lessen her. Plus of course there was the cringeworthy possibility he'd have to live with a woman he'd come on to, and been rebuffed by.

Yet while Sally saw life through heart-shaped eyes, she wasn't some delicate flower that might break at the first sign of poor handling. She'd coped with losing her parents at sixteen, with bringing up her sister, with running a business. Plus, with her insistence on ringing bells, she was very clear on what she wanted from a guy and that sure as hell wasn't him. So if anything *did* happen, it would be short and sweet. In fact he'd be the one to lose out because she'd not only dump his arse, she'd kick him out when she found the guy who made the bells ring for her.

The thought of her with someone else settled heavily over him, but Harry realised with a start that he was prepared to be dumped. Prepared to have his ego battered again, because the potential reward – a hot fling with a warm, funny blonde he both liked and respected – was worth it.

So maybe sex *was* on.

Buoyed by his conclusion, he headed back to the flat. He was nearly there when his phone buzzed with a message.

Sally: Need you back here pronto. Isabelle turned up [screaming face emoji]. She's not happy [monkey with hands over eyes].

Damn it. All thoughts of sex ebbed away, replaced with a simmering frustration. Isabelle had cheated on him, made a fool of him, taken his house hostage. What the hell did she want now?

He bounded up the stairs two at a time, not at all comfortable with the woman he'd been sleeping with, talking to the woman he wanted to sleep with. Flinging the door open, he yanked off his trainers and headed for the living room where he found Isabelle sitting on the pink monstrosity, wiping her eyes. Sally was sat on the opposite end of the sofa, mug in hand, looking like she wanted to be anywhere else.

'Wow, that was quick.' Sally immediately stood and gave him a wide-eyed look before nodding towards the kitchen. 'I'll, er, leave you to it.'

'Yeah.' Was she trying to tell him something? 'I'm going to get myself a drink. Do you want anything, Isabelle?'

'No thank you. Your… Sally made me a coffee.'

The moment they were in the kitchen, Sally whispered under her breath. 'She's seen the video I posted.'

'What video?'

'The one we did this afternoon. You know, potter's wheel, clay.' She glanced furtively towards the sitting room. 'You shirtless, kissing my neck.'

'I remember,' he said dryly. 'So?'

'So, she's crying.'

There was a tension to Sally's expression that he didn't like. 'Has she said anything to upset you?'

'No.' Her eyes avoided his.

'What *did* she say?' he pressed.

'She wanted to know where you were. Then she gave me a once-over and said, *"You're the one in the video"*.' Sally huffed out a breath. 'Of course I couldn't deny it, and then she point blank asked if we were sleeping together.'

Anger shot through him. 'And you told her it was none of her blasted business.'

Sally's eyebrows drew together. 'No, I told her the truth. That we weren't together and the videos were just a way to earn a bit of money.'

For some reason he couldn't put his finger on, the statement pissed him off. 'And that was all today was to you? When I was kissing your neck, you were only thinking of the money?'

Her eyes widened and she took a step back. 'That is why we're doing these scenes, isn't it?'

He exhaled sharply, aware she was right. And yet … when he'd tasted her skin, when he'd felt her lean against him, her body as pliant as the clay, his only thought had been how frigging fantastic it was to be touching her.

He turned to get some juice out of the fridge, not because

he needed the drink but because he needed to settle his thoughts.

'What's going on in here?'

Isabelle appeared in the doorway. Maybe she had been crying, but it was hard to tell because she looked immaculate as always, make-up still in place, even the eye-liner. She was beautiful, no question. But by God she was self-centred, too. 'I'm getting myself a drink.'

Her gaze skipped between him and Sally, clearly trying to work out the dynamic. 'I came here to talk to you. Not to sit on my own in another room while you flirt with another woman.'

Laughter shot out of him. 'Number one, I didn't invite you. Number two, you've clearly got a low opinion of my charm if you think this is me flirting. Number three, I can flirt wherever I like, with whomever I want to, because we're finished.' He shoved the carton back in the fridge then frowned over at her. 'How did you get this address?'

'Your mum gave it to me.' Isabelle smoothed down her already perfect hair. He couldn't help but make the comparison with Sally and all the haphazard curls that had tickled his nose. 'She's been very supportive these last few months.'

Fucking brilliant. He was supporting his mum, and she was supporting the woman who'd screwed him over. Was *still* screwing him over.

He could feel Sally's eyes on him so he forced his expression into one of indifference, hoping it hid the choking frustration, the pitiful hurt that ripped through him.

'Umm, I think I should go.' Sally pulled a face, a cross between a wince and a grimace, with a heavy dose of awkward. 'It was, er, nice to meet you, Isabelle.'

'You, too.' Sally had reached the kitchen door when Isabelle decided to speak again. 'Oh and, Sally, should you decide to do any more of those videos, please bear in mind that I'm still in love with Harry, so I'd appreciate a little … discretion.'

Sally halted and turned. 'Is that the same discretion you used when you shagged your boss behind Harry's back?'

Oh boy, the look on Isabelle's face – the utter shock that this cute, smiley woman with bouncy blonde hair had dared to confront her. Or maybe that was just *his* shock because he had a sudden urge to laugh. To high-five Sally. To thank her for being on his side. Yet he couldn't do any of that, not in front of the woman who'd just claimed to still love him.

He couldn't resist trying to catch Sally's eye though, yet when he did, he saw only apology and not the humour he'd reckoned on. With a quick jerk of her head, she walked away.

Isabelle stared at him, stony-faced. 'I can't believe you discussed our business with your landlady.'

'As it happened to me, I consider it my business.' With a sigh he dragged out a stool. 'Why don't you tell me what you came here to say?'

'I already have. Seeing you and her in that video together…' She nibbled her bottom lip in a way he'd once found distractingly attractive. 'It really upset me, Harry.'

He searched her face, trying to work out what was going on in her head. 'You don't really love me.' His mind flashed back to the conversation with Sally. 'I have it on good authority that if you did, we wouldn't have got to the stage where you were cheating on me.'

'Well I do love you, and I only fooled around with Patrick because I felt ignored by you.' She flicked her hair back over her shoulder. 'I mean, I know your mum is having a tough time, but you spent so much time helping her I felt side-lined.'

Again, he found his mind circling back to the conversation

with Sally. The one where she'd talked about being with someone who helps you through the bad, who fights your corner. Funny how she'd just fought his, yet Isabelle had not only always taken his mum's side, she'd bailed on him the moment life had got tough.

His resolve hardened. 'It doesn't matter how many times we thrash this out, the end result will always be the same. We're done and I want my house back. Meanwhile, you can start paying me rent.'

———

The moment Sally had opened the door to the drop-dead gorgeous woman she now knew to be Isabelle, it had been obvious she couldn't stay in the flat.

God, only hours earlier she'd been... What exactly *had* she and Harry been doing? Sure, making a video, yet she'd only had to look at her face when she'd played it back to know it had been way more than that. And maybe for him too, she thought as she recalled his hurt expression when she'd talked about today being about making money.

Yet she had no right to feel anything for him. Not when he and Isabelle clearly had unfinished business.

So she'd scarpered, and was now sat in the pub with Vince, Kitty, Adam and Emma. Hoping alcohol would drown her guilt, and her unruly attraction.

'Come on, let's see some of the comments on that super-hot video you posted.' Vince held out his hand and she passed her phone over to him.

'Hot and dirty, love it. No way is he just your lodger,' he read out. 'Oh, I like this one. Lodger with benefits.' Vince grinned.

'We want more like this.' Kitty took over reading out the comments from her own phone. 'More Harry without his shirt.'

She pulled a face and Vince frowned at her. 'Come on, Kit, I know you don't like him, but even you have to admit he's fit.'

'He's not to my taste, but I guess some women might find him attractive.' She gave Sally a sly look.

Immediately everyone's eyes were on her, including Adam's. 'He is attractive but he's also, you know, still Harry. So definitely not my type,' Sally finished emphatically.

Vince narrowed his eyes in that way she hated, because it meant he'd rumbled her. Yet what she'd said was true, Harry *wasn't* her type. He might give her fuzzies, but it didn't mean she wanted to date him or anything. Just, maybe, kiss him? And if that went well, was having sex with him really such a bad idea, as long as she knew it wasn't the start of some great love story?

'I'd give up my turn for the romcom pick to know what you're thinking right now.' Vince raised his eyebrows at her. 'You look flushed, sweetie, and you're way too young to blame it on the menopause.'

'It's hot in here.' To prove it, she shrugged off her jacket and told her brain to stop thinking about sex.

'Out of interest, what is your type?' Adam asked, a sheepish smile on his face.

It was a good question. A few months ago, she'd have said Adam fitted the bill perfectly, yet so far the fuzzies hadn't, well, fuzzed. Then again, she'd not really had a chance to get to know him. Hadn't she lived with Harry for a few weeks before the fuzzies had woken up? 'I'm still trying to work it out.'

Adam nodded, eyes holding hers, as if he liked her answer.

'You never said why you had the sudden urge to go to the pub this evening.' Vince was like a dog with a meaty pork chop.

'Harry's ex came round so I thought I'd give them some privacy.'

Vince eyed her thoughtfully. 'Were you worried they'd make up and you'd be forced to listen to the sound of noisy sex?'

Kitty started to snigger. 'I bet he makes terrible sex sounds. All growly like a bear.'

Unbidden, Sally pictured Harry, naked from the waist up, lowering himself over her. A growl coming deep from his chest.

'Has the ex seen that video you uploaded?' Emma's question broke through the erotic fantasy. 'I tell you, my studio has never seen such action.'

'There wasn't any action. We were just fooling around to try and get more likes and followers.' If she said it often enough, maybe she'd believe it. 'But yes, Isabelle saw it and was pretty cut up.'

'Maybe Vince is right then, and she won't be an ex for much longer.' Kitty started to giggle. 'Maybe he's already growling at her.'

'Maybe.' She hated the way her stomach twisted at the thought.

Luckily, or maybe because he saw something in her expression, Vince changed the subject.

As they walked out of the pub a few hours later, Vince whispered in her ear. 'Warning, I believe Adam is going to ask you out.'

Panic fluttered through her and Sally halted just inside the door, staring ahead to where Adam was chatting with Kitty and Emma outside. 'What should I do?'

'Do you like him?'

'Of course. He's easy on the eye and easy to talk to.'

'Plus he's not sarcastic or cynical and I have it on good authority he enjoys watching all genre of film,' Vince added with a wink.

'Even better.' Could she imagine snuggling up to Adam on the sofa, watching *When Harry Met Sally*? And why was that the film that came to mind?

'But you still have your crush on the big manly builder,' Vince supplied with a pained look.

'That is true.' She hesitated. 'What if I miss the opportunity of something real though, for the sake of a crush that I know is temporary?'

'Exactly,' Vince agreed triumphantly. 'So to come back to your question, you should say yes to Adam, if you think he'd be good company.'

'I kissed Harry,' she blurted. 'Or really he kissed me, but I didn't push him away.' She licked her lips, as if she could still taste his. 'And I enjoyed it.'

'Of course you did.' Vince let out a slow exhale, his expression now sombre. 'Who wouldn't enjoy kissing a man who looks like that?'

'Kitty?'

'She does have weird taste.' With a deep sigh, he draped an arm around Sally's shoulders and pushed open the door. 'But beyond the fact Hazza is eminently kissable, do you *like* him?'

'Yes.' The answer came shockingly easy. 'I know he's blunt

and cynical, but I don't know, he's *interesting*. There are layers to him that I want to peel off so I can sneak a peek at what's beneath.' Her mind flashed back to the hurt he'd tried to hide when Isabelle had made the comment about how his mum had been supportive to her.

Vince waggled his eyebrows. 'What layers are those, exactly?'

'I'm not talking his clothes. Well, not just his clothes,' she amended with a laugh when Vince gave her a knowing look.

'Okay, so you like the guy and find him attractive. Do you think he feels the same?'

'I don't know. The videos… It's just acting, I think. And maybe flirting a little. But he has an ex who says she still loves him, so…' There was no way she should be thinking about getting involved with him, even for a fling.

'So,' Vince filled in for her, 'there's no reason not to go out with Adam. You never know, you might like him too, when you get to know him more. And hey, he might even make those bells ring.'

'That's sound advice.'

He sniggered. 'And that's an appalling joke, but as it's late I'll forgive you.'

When they caught up with the others, Sally didn't miss how Vince deliberately put his arm around Emma and Kitty, steering them away so Adam could fall in step with her.

'That was a bit obvious, wasn't it?' Adam screwed up his face. 'I don't think Vince knows how to be subtle.'

'Definitely not.' She smiled at him, liking the warmth in his brown eyes. Wishing it sent prickles racing across her skin like the glint from a pair of smoky-grey ones.

'I suppose he also told you I'd like to ask you out.'

'He might have.'

Adam sighed. 'This feels like being at school again.'

God, he was so nice. 'Can I be honest with you?'

'Of course.'

'I think you're attractive, not to mention really cool, and I know if we went out I'd enjoy it, but—'

'You don't feel the spark.'

She looked at him in surprise. 'Well, I call it the fuzzies, but yes.'

He nodded. 'Can I be equally honest?'

'Sure.'

'I don't feel it either. But I think you're gorgeous and funny and I figured maybe if we went out on a few dates it might be fun, and maybe the spark would … spark. You know, a slow burn, like in *Love, Rosie*, or *My Best Friend's Wedding*. Or *When Harry Met Sally*.'

Flipping finally, a guy who spoke her language.

Smiling, Sally threaded a hand through his arm. 'I definitely think we should give it a try.'

Chapter Thirteen

Harry surveyed the remains of the garage they'd just knocked down. Rubble. This was one of the best parts of the job. Removing the old crap to make way for the new. The tingle of anticipation for what was to come. What he was about to help create. Sure, as his mum liked to remind him, it was only bricks and mortar; but he'd long learned to ignore her digs. There was a satisfaction in building, one neither of his parents would ever understand because they hadn't bothered to talk to him about it. Building gave him an anchor, a focus. Something he could depend on when everything else in his life seemed so unbalanced.

His parents were still doing his head in – or rather his mother was. His father, as usual, was keeping his head down and not getting involved, as he'd done throughout Harry's childhood. The silent figure at the dinner table, uninterested in anything but work, letting everything else flow around him.

Only now the man didn't have work. Now he spent his days getting in the way of his wife's well-oiled routine of lunches, book clubs and keeping an orderly house.

Then there was Isabelle, who was acting like she was the wronged party. *He's kicking me out of our house.* Yep, those were the words she'd used in a message to his mother after her visit to him. How did he know? Because his mum had forwarded it to him with the comment, *Is this really how I brought you up?*

'What have you and the landlady got planned for your next hot video clip then?' Mike asked, handing him a mug of tea from the flask Trixie had supplied. 'You gonna fool around in a hot tub with her like in *To All The Boys I've Loved Before*? Or wait, you could do the hot tub scene in *After We Fell*. That's even more steamy.' He waggled his eyebrows, grinning at his own joke.

And yep, thanks to Mike's artless probing, he was now forced to confront the other reason he felt out of sorts. He couldn't work out what his next steps should be with the woman who'd crowded his brain way too much this last week. Ever since that damn potter's wheel scene. No way was he going to admit it to Mike though, or he'd have them going on double dates and watching romcoms together. 'Have you really seen all these films?'

'Sure. Trixie loves 'em and if my woman is happy, I'm happy.' Mike grinned like he had life all sorted out. And maybe he had, Harry realised with a twinge of jealousy, because he'd never seen his mate more content. 'Besides, I get to make out with her while we're watching them.'

'I can see why she's fallen for you,' Harry commented dryly.

'Yeah, well, you haven't seen my secret weapon.' He smirked suggestively and Harry groaned.

'Don't. You're turning my stomach.'

'Trixie never complains.' Mike chuckled to himself. 'But

we're getting off the point. What entertainment have the pair of you got lined up for us next?'

'I don't know.' He shook his head. 'I can't believe people want to watch this stuff.'

'I can't believe people want to watch you with your shirt off.' Mike chuckled again. 'You've really not talked about the next one?'

'We've not seen each other all week, not to talk to, anyway.' They'd crossed paths a few times in the kitchen, but they'd both been in a hurry. Or maybe she was avoiding him. He knew she'd gone out with Adam two nights ago because he'd heard the guy's voice in the hallway.

'Maybe she's gone off the idea,' Mike suggested.

Harry thought it was more likely she'd decided to do them with Adam instead now, and fuck, that shouldn't bother him as much as it did. 'Be good if she has. Doing them is weird.'

Mike glanced over at him. 'Weird because you don't want to admit you enjoy getting up close and personal with your landlady?'

'Weird because I'm not into romcoms. Or social media. Or acting.' *But you're into Sally.* Before Mike could say anything more, he put down his mug and picked up his shovel. 'Let's get all this cleared away before it gets too dark.'

It was another late one by the time he got back to the flat. Instinctively, Harry listened out for sounds of Sally when he opened the door. Kettle boiling, TV on, humming – he found she did that a lot and he was sort of getting used to the sound now.

He ignored the pang of disappointment when only silence echoed back at him.

He'd just shoved a pie in the oven when he heard the front door open. With a nonchalance he didn't feel – his ruddy heart was thumping – he rested against the worktop and folded his arms. 'Hello, stranger.'

'Hey.' He watched as she shrugged off her big red coat – all through September it had been a pale-pink one. Clearly October warranted something warmer and brighter.

'Not seen you much this week.'

'No. I was out with Adam on Tuesday, and Kitty had a show of her paintings last night.'

'Thought you might have been avoiding me.' Damn, he'd not meant to say that quite so aggressively.

She did a double-take. 'Why would I do that?'

Yeah, Wilson, why would she do that? She obviously wasn't as unbalanced by their little kiss in the studio as he was. Probably because she was kissing Adam. 'Just thought you might be embarrassed about the kiss.' He tried to pull off a shrug. 'You know, now you're dating Adam.'

Her eyes rounded. 'Oh no, I'm not dating Adam. We just went to the cinema together.'

'You went out but it wasn't a date?'

'Yep.' She gave him a playful look. 'Apparently, boys and girls can do that. It's called being friends.'

'Smart arse,' he muttered, feeling flustered. He shouldn't be this interested. 'How did the last video do?' he asked, desperate to move the conversation on. 'Did we get enough likes or whatever you needed?'

She beamed. 'We got two hundred and fifty thousand views. That's mega, trust me.'

He whistled, impressed. 'A quarter of a million people watched us try and make a clay pot?'

She giggled. 'I know! Mad, isn't it? We should really keep the momentum going, ride all the interest while we can. I've applied to the TikTok creator fund so we might get some money through that now, but I've also reached out to a few companies to ask if they'd be interested in sponsoring some content, you know, like we did with Mary and Lauren in the shopping scene. From what I've read it's harder to get that with TikTok than Instagram, but it's worth a try.' He watched as she placed her handbag onto the island. When he looked up at her, he found her frowning. 'What?'

'Just wondering where the candyfloss went.' He nodded down to the new red, heart-shaped bag.

'The candyfloss… Oh, very funny. I needed a red bag to go with my coat.' The colour looked good on her, though he'd come to like the pink. When it was on her. 'Talking of new things, that reminds me. Mary emailed to ask how we want to be paid for our cut of the sales.'

He blinked. 'She's really going to pay us?'

'Yep. I put the link to the shop on the video and she's had a big uplift in sales apparently, though don't get too excited, we're not talking an obscene amount of money, or even a lot of money.' She grinned. 'But it all helps, right?'

He stared at her, for the first time seeing past the pretty blonde with the curly hair, the fun sense of humour and the oddball obsession with romcoms. She'd owned her own business from the age of eighteen so of course he knew she was smart, yet it was only now he realised quite *how* smart. How astute her business sense was.

'What? You're staring.'

He shook himself. 'Sorry. Just amazed at how much you

know about this stuff.' *And finding myself really bloody attracted to you.*

'Hey, don't be amazed just yet. Let's wait till we actually see the money. So anyway, you're up for doing another video, yes?'

'Sure.' He felt a ripple of what could only be described as smug satisfaction. She wanted to do another video with him, not Adam. 'Are we upping the oomph again?' There had to be more of her so-called iconic scenes where he got to put his hands on her.

'Actually, how do you feel about kissing me at a football match?'

Sally watched a range of expressions cross Harry's face. Shock, confusion and … was that interest? Or was the interest because she'd mentioned football, and the shock because he was meant to kiss her?

'It doesn't have to be a proper kiss,' she added quickly, feeling less sure about this now. 'Just, you know, a peck. In front of a few thousand people.'

'A peck?'

It's like she was speaking a different language to him. 'Yes, you know, just for show. And when I say a match, it won't be the first team. Albion weren't that accommodating.'

'Albion.'

'Why are you repeating everything I say? Albion, as in Brighton and Hove Albion. You know, the football team you support?' She looked down at the two plates he'd put out. 'Is one of those for me?'

'Yeah. There's a pie in the oven if you want some.' He

started to laugh. 'This conversation is bonkers. Can you start from the beginning? What football match, and why?'

'Why kiss?'

His mouth curved. 'I don't need a reason to do that.'

She caught his eye and the wicked gleam, the memory of that brief press of his mouth outside the pottery studio, sent heat coiling between her legs. *Get back to the conversation.* 'I thought we could build on the *will they/won't they* – or in our case the *are they an item or aren't they* – tension our followers noticed in the last clip. You know, tease them a bit about our relationship.' Too afraid to look at his face, she went to the cutlery drawer and fished out some knives and forks. 'There's this great scene in *Never Been Kissed* where she's waiting on the pitcher's mound, hoping Sam – that's the teacher she's fallen for – will turn up and kiss her.'

'Pitcher's mound? Teacher?' Harry looked bemused.

'Yes, she's a reporter and she goes undercover at this school to research teenage culture.' She waved a hand at him. 'Forget it, none of that's important to the scene. The main thing is, she comes clean and writes a story of her experience and in it she admits she's never been kissed. So she says she'll stand in the middle of the baseball field and if Sam loves her, he'll turn up and kiss her. The clock counts down from five minutes and the crowd, who are in on it, are willing Sam to turn up, but then the clock hits zero and he's still not there. She thinks that's it. He was too hurt by her lies. He doesn't love her.'

'Let me guess. Our hero parachutes in from a chopper?'

A laugh burst out of her. 'You think I'd ask you to do that?'

'I'm more interested in what you've asked the club.'

'Just if we can film this scene before one of their matches. I wanted to do it on a Saturday but they were a bit snotty about it.'

His face paled. 'You asked if we could film a kissing scene from a romcom before a Premier League match.' He swallowed. 'In front of thirty thousand football fans?'

He looked kind of adorable, all unbalanced, knocked out of his macho comfort zone. 'Why not? It would be good publicity for them. Apparently they aren't that far-sighted though, but they did say we could go along tomorrow and film it before the U23 match.'

'Okay.' He drew a hand down his face, then stared back at her. 'Let me get this straight. We turn up at the stadium tomorrow before the U23 game. You stand on … the halfway line?'

'I guess. Depends how far you want to run.'

'I'm running?'

She had to work hard to suppress a giggle at his look of dismay. 'Well, in the film Sam kind of skipped down the stairs and then, yeah, he ran, well more jogged I guess, onto the field. Or pitch in this case.'

'So I jog up to you and then, what? Just kiss you?'

'That's about it.' *Liar*. If it felt anything like that kiss outside the studio, it would feel way more than just a kiss to her. 'Or, you know, a peck would be fine.'

His gaze trapped hers before dropping to her mouth. 'I thought we were done with the bird analogies.'

'I didn't want you to think you *had* to kiss me.'

His eyes raked hers for a humming moment and then he smiled. 'What if I offered to kiss you?'

Her pulse scrambled. 'Then I'd gracefully accept.' Because she was in danger of making it into too big a deal – it was meant to be a silly TikTok video – she added, 'I'm sure it will make our followers happy.'

It was like she'd pulled out a plug. Instantly the mood flattened.

'That's the aim.' His gaze shuttered and he turned to the oven. 'Pie's ready in five minutes. Carrots and peas alright?'

'Great.' She wanted to thank him for reheating a pie big enough for both of them, but her brain couldn't find a way to do it without it sounding like she was reading something into his action that wasn't there.

Or was it there, and she'd just taken a hammer to it with her clumsy mention of followers?

She flapped around for something to say. 'Have you ever been to an U23 match at the Amex Stadium?'

'Sure, once or twice.' He emptied some frozen peas into a pan, added some pre-sliced carrots.

'How many fans do they usually attract?'

Slowly, he turned to look at her. 'Getting cold feet?'

'Not exactly.' Though she tried to picture herself stood in the middle of a football pitch. All eyes on her.

'A few thousand, maybe.' The edge of his mouth curled upwards. 'I'm sure they'll appreciate the entertainment.'

Her stomach pitched. Shit, what had she let herself in for? Good job they hadn't let her do it in front of a full stadium.

'You're looking scared.' He raised a dark brow. 'Is it the thought of the kiss, or people watching it?'

Both. 'People watching.'

He nodded, then surprised her by walking towards her, stopping just a foot away. As she breathed him in, her heart let out a slow flip. And that was before he bent and whispered into her ear. 'Relax. I'll take care of you.'

Chapter Fourteen

Harry stood on the back row of the Amex and scanned the stadium. Hairs pricked at the back of his neck. He was about to kiss his landlady. In front of a few thousand football supporters.

His words to Sally from last night kept playing through his head. *I'll take care of you.* He would, of course, do his best to make sure he didn't embarrass her today, but had that been all he'd meant? Had he been making a promise to be careful with her? They had a connection, one that was beyond physical attraction. He knew it. He thought she did, too. The reasons to ignore it hadn't gone away, but it was becoming harder and harder to remember them.

His heart jumped as the PA system screeched. And his gaze followed the female figure as she walked out through the tunnel and onto the pitch. From this distance she looked so small. A lone blonde woman carrying a microphone, dressed not in a pink dress like in the film clip he'd seen, but in a blue-and-white-striped replica Albion shirt and slim-fitting jeans.

It seemed to take forever for her to reach the centre circle.

'Hi.' She looked around her. A glance at the big screen and he saw her face up close. No make-up, wild curls.

He thought she'd never looked better.

'So, I'm not sure if you've ever watched *Never Been Kissed*.'

People in the small crowd started to look at each other as she spoke and he knew exactly what some were thinking, because he'd have been thinking the same.

'It's my favourite film!' a voice yelled from the crowd.

Nope, that wasn't it.

'We're here to watch football,' a male voice shouted. 'So if you're not here to kick a ball, sling your hook.'

Yeah, that might have been his thought, too, but listening to a bloke shout it at Sally? Harry began to walk down the stairs.

'I'll be happy to sling my hook.' A glance at the big screen and he saw her smile, but he also heard the tremor of nerves in her voice. 'But before I do that, I'm going to wait here for five minutes in the hope that this man I have a crush on will come and give me a kiss.'

Crush on? He nearly tripped up. Did she mean it, or had she said that for the video?

'Can I have five minutes on the clock, please.'

At Sally's quietly stated words, a murmur went round the crowd and a countdown began on the big screen.

'I'll kiss you, love.'

Sally's head shot round towards the direction of the voice in the crowd and Harry had seen enough. Sod the suspense, waiting for the clock to reach zero like in the film.

He charged down the steps, leaped over the advertising boards and ran onto the pitch. To his surprise, he started to hear laughter.

'Bit keen, aren't you?' a man shouted.

'Ignore them,' a female voice countered. 'Go, claim your kiss.'

As he neared Sally, he started to slow.

'You didn't wait.' But she was beaming from ear to ear.

'Didn't want anyone else taking my place.' He came to a halt in front of her and carefully cupped her face. 'Ready?'

She nodded and he bent his head, taking a moment to take in how the blue from the shirt made her eyes seem prettier. How her breath hitched. How the noise from the crowd, the cheers and claps, faded as his mouth hovered over hers.

A moment to realise how much he wanted this kiss.

Gently, he lowered his mouth to hers. Not because that's how it was in film, but because doing this slowly felt right. His lips caressed hers, exploring, enjoying their soft press, the tentative way she kissed back. It was like a first dance. A little shy, a little hesitant, but a tremor of longing shot through him. More. He needed more of her touch, of her taste. More time to continue teasing, coaxing her to open for him.

You promised you'd take care of her.

Reluctantly, he drew back, noting with satisfaction that her breathing matched his. Choppy. 'You think we did the scene justice?'

She smiled, teeth sinking into her bottom lip, which made him want to kiss her again. 'Yes.'

Applause echoed round the stadium as they walked back towards the tunnel and he couldn't lie. Being clapped off this sacred pitch, even if it was only for acting out a romcom scene, was kind of nice. And kissing her on this sacred pitch? Kind of spectacular.

It was only when they were sat in his truck that a thought occurred to him. 'Someone was filming it, weren't they?'

'I got one of the ground staff to do it.' She giggled. 'Are you worried all that will have been for nothing?'

'Hardly nothing.' He glanced her way. 'I got to kiss you.'

She didn't say anything, but her dimples came out of hiding and her cheeks flushed.

When they were back in the flat she sat on a kitchen stool, took out her phone and began to edit the clip. 'What shall we call this one?'

Harry considered the question as he opened the fridge door. *'Never Been Kissed at the Amex?'* Reaching in, he moved the carton of milk, and juice. Then smiled as he hit jackpot. 'Want one?' He waved a beer at her.

'Thanks.' She seemed to mull over his suggestion. 'I like that. But I'll change it to *Never Been Kissed at a football stadium*, so we can appeal to those rare beasts who don't follow Brighton and Hove Albion.'

'Makes sense.' He opened the beer, slid a bottle over to her, watching as her fingers raced across her phone.

'That's it uploaded.' She sat back against the stool with a contented sigh. 'Wonder how many views we'll get for this one? Hope it's enough that Albion don't regret sponsoring it.'

'I can't believe you got them to agree to letting us do that. And even made them pay for the privilege.' He shook his head, admiring her audacity.

'Hey, we're getting over a quarter of a million people watching these clips,' she replied, reaching for the beer. 'That's great publicity for these companies.'

'I guess.' He still couldn't believe so many people were interested in watching him and Sally having a laugh. *Kissing each other*. He took a swig of his beer. 'So have you got another scene in mind yet?'

A grin chased across her face. 'Asks the guy I had to practically strongarm into doing these not that long ago.'

Maybe he had sounded a bit eager. 'Didn't think I'd get to walk onto the hallowed Amex turf.' He swallowed another mouthful, then looked her straight in the eye. 'Or kiss you.'

Those dimples flashed again and he felt a tug somewhere in his chest. 'Then you might like my next idea. It would be good to keep the sexual tension up, so I thought we could kiss again.'

'Okay,' he said slowly, happy with the proposal but annoyed to realise he was disappointed with the reasoning, which was nuts because of course this was only about the views, the potential earnings.

'This time,' she continued, holding his gaze, a gleam in her eyes, 'I think we should kiss when we're wet.'

Wet… Jesus. His niggle was forgotten as his mind sank straight into the porn gutter. 'Wet works. I can do wet.'

'There are so many incredibly romantic moments that take place in the rain,' she said on a sigh, the dreamy expression indicating her mind was in a far cleaner place. 'Like *The Notebook*. I mean wow. Noah takes her out on the lake in a boat and it starts to rain and at first she tries to cover herself because that's the person she's become, all buttoned up. But then she starts laughing, because that's the real her and she can be that person with him. He joins in and they keep laughing until he looks at her, all hot and sexy even though he's drenched. They make it to the pontoon and it's still pouring with rain, Ryan Gosling's wet shirt is clinging to him and she asks the question – why did he give up on them? Because it wasn't over for her.' The words rolled over each other as her face became more and more animated. 'He tells her he wrote to her every day for a year. That it wasn't over for him. It still isn't over.' She drew in a deep breath, her expression so earnest, so completely into the moment.

He realised with a pang of sadness that what she'd just described was what she was looking for. Not the hot sex going on in his head, but the meeting of souls the films promised but he couldn't see life ever being able to deliver. 'You realise in real life she'd be complaining about getting her hair wet, he'd be pissed off his grand gesture had been ruined, and they'd both end up with pneumonia?'

God, this man. Sally would like to bet Adam had seen *The Notebook*. Also that he'd have totally understood why it rated as one of the most romantic films of all time. Yet for some reason, her body had decided it didn't want Adam.

Her mind flashed back to earlier, the way Harry had held her face between his hands just before he'd given her the most toe-curling kiss. Ever. Maybe her body wasn't so stupid, after all.

'Actually, if Ryan Gosling was stood in front of me in real life, wet shirt clinging to his body, I wouldn't give a rat's arse about the rain ruining my hairdo.'

Harry huffed. 'Swayze with his shirt off, Gosling with his wet shirt. You talk about romance, but it sounds like it's more about sex.'

The guy had a point, she supposed. But. 'The two aren't mutually exclusive, you know. Hot sex can still be romantic. I mean, Richard Gere when he kisses Julia Roberts on the piano.' She mimed waving a fan. 'That's both.'

A small smile played around his lips. 'Yeah, I remember watching that with you.'

'You'd see loads more like that if you stop being so blinkered about romance films. Sure, some of them are fairy-tale sweet, but loads are down to earth and really sexy because, guess what, falling in love also means lots of great sex.'

His eyes turned smoky grey. 'You don't need to be in love to have great sex.'

'Of course.' She'd had great-ish sex. And she had no doubt if she had sex with him, it would be beyond great. Not that she'd thought about it. Much. 'But maybe you'd have even better sex if you were in love. You'll never know though, because you don't believe in it.' She pointed to her chest. 'Me, I'm going to have the best sex ever one day, because I'm going to have it with the man I love.'

Briefly, something flashed across his face, an emotion she couldn't decipher but which made his jaw clench. 'Great sex is chemistry, pure and simple,' he countered finally, his eyes sliding down to her mouth before meeting hers.

The heat in his gaze caused a sizzle in the pit of her stomach. Time to move the conversation onto firmer ground. 'To get back to our next scene, we don't have to do *The Notebook*. There's also the closing scene in the rain from *Breakfast in Tiffany's* and the classic rain scene from *Four Weddings and a Funeral*.'

'You know I haven't watched any of them, right?'

'But you could.' She shot him a grin. 'I've got them all.'

'Of course you have.'

'You enjoyed *Pretty Woman*,' she prompted. 'Well you didn't fall asleep, so you must have been invested in finding out what happened.'

'It's a romcom,' he said mildly. 'The guy was going to get the girl.'

'But you didn't know *how* that was going to happen,' she argued. 'It annoys me when people say romcoms are predictable. In murder mysteries you know someone is going to get murdered, and someone is going to work out who did it. In action films the hero always achieves his mission.'

He put his hands up in mock surrender. 'Okay, retract your claws, I concede you have a point. But I've watched my quota of romcoms for this year, so just show me the clips.'

She sighed, more for dramatic effect than out of disappointment because she'd known he wouldn't watch the films. 'Let me get my iPad.'

She tried not to stare as he leaned over the kitchen island and watched the clips, but it was hard to tell her eyes the sight wasn't interesting when it seemed that everything about him now fascinated her. The size of his hands as they rested either side of the iPad. Hands, with their rough callouses, that she wanted to feel slide over her skin. The wide set of his shoulders, the way his well-worn jeans hugged his firm buttocks. How soft his dark hair looked, making her fingers twitch with the need to slide through it.

Suddenly he straightened, and she hastily averted her gaze.

'If we do *Breakfast in Tiffany's* I just have to stand in the rain and watch you pick up a cat.' He glanced over at her. 'Then we kiss. With *The Notebook* we need to say some words in the rain. Then we kiss. *Four Weddings and a Funeral,* I open a door and come out to you in the rain before I talk quite a lot. Then we kiss.' He quirked a dark brow at her. 'I'm sensing a pattern.'

Did he not *want* to kiss her again? 'We don't have to do any of them,' she said quickly, pushing her disappointment way, way down where she couldn't analyse it. 'We could do a rain scene that doesn't involve kissing. I mean, there's *Singin' in the Rain*, though it's not really a romcom. I know, how about the *Spider-Man* scene where he's hanging upside down and she talks to him, then she peels off his mask...'

'But just enough to kiss him.' His lips twitched. '*Spider-Man*, the epic romance film. I've watched that one.'

Okay, she could do this. Find a romcom rain scene with no kissing. 'I know, *Pride and Prejudice*. There's a brilliant scene where Darcy proposes while they're sheltering from the rain, but she takes what he says the wrong way and they argue, which ends in her telling him he's the last man in the world she wants to marry.'

'Do they kiss?'

'No.' She ran the scene through her head again. 'There's a moment when he looks at her like he wants to, though. And there's a lot of words to remember.'

He winced. 'Not going to happen.' Again his gaze dropped to her mouth, and her lips started to tingle, as if anticipating the press of his. 'FYI, I'm not against kissing you again. In fact, I'm all for it.' His eyes found hers, and she felt their pull, the heat of their promise. 'But on one condition.'

Unconsciously, she licked at her bottom lip. 'What's that?'

His eyes followed the trail of her tongue. 'We practise first.'

The air fizzed between them, charged molecules bouncing off the walls. 'But we kissed only a few hours ago.' And she wanted to feel his mouth on hers again so badly, she could taste him.

He smiled and took a step towards her. Her heart let out a loud thump. She wasn't small, but wedged between the island and the worktop, his towering presence within touching distance, she suddenly felt tiny. 'That was a sweet kiss. We should practise a real kiss.'

'A real kiss.' She swallowed. The last one had felt real enough to her.

His hands settled on her waist. 'Nervous?'

'Nope.' At least she didn't think it was nerves. More anticipation, excitement. Terror that she was going to enjoy this way more than she wanted to.

'I am.'

She studied his face, the glint in his eyes. 'You're not, but maybe you should be. Gosling nailed the kiss in *The Notebook*.'

He laughed softly, his face so close to hers she felt the flutter of his breath. 'You don't think I can nail a real kiss?'

Judging by the way her knees trembled, he'd nailed it before he'd started. 'I'm waiting to find out.'

A moment later, the wait was over. Unlike the previous kisses, there was nothing soft, nothing light about this one. His mouth captured hers, hungry, hot, his tongue leaving a trail of heat, of want, wherever it touched. Within seconds she was on fire, her body craving his touch, her hands fisting into his hair … finally, finally. And oh boy, it *did* feel soft, yet everything else about him felt so gloriously hard: the muscles of his shoulders, the wall of chest crushed against her breasts, the delicious press of his groin against her aching core.

He groaned – or maybe she did. She no longer knew what was him, what was her. It felt like *them*.

When he finally drew back, she immediately wanted to sink back into it again. 'Consider that nailed.' Her voice sounded hoarse.

He laughed, a deep rumble that sent tremors of want through her. 'How soon till we can do it again?'

Now, she wanted to scream. *Kiss me again.* But it was the hormones talking, and really she needed to escape, to think about what she was letting herself in for before she made any hasty decisions. 'I thought we could film the scene after I finish tomorrow.'

'I have to wait a whole twenty-four hours, huh?' With a soft exhale he planted another, much briefer, kiss on her lips. 'I guess I can manage that. Which one are we doing?'

After that kiss, there was no contest. '*The Notebook*.'

'And if it's not raining?'

She took a step back, needing to un-attach herself from him so she could think. 'I thought we'd do it in the shower. It will be easier to set the phone up to film. Plus there's the added advantage of no passers-by staring at us or kids wanting to get in the video.'

'You and me, in a shower. Kissing.' He shook his head as if he couldn't quite believe what he was saying. 'Consider it a date.'

Chapter Fifteen

It had been thirteen weeks and five days since he'd last had sex. Not that he was starting to obsess about it. It's just that when he looked at Sally, when he thought about Sally, it was almost impossible to think about anything else.

Not since *that* kiss last night. He'd not nailed it, because that implied he'd had any control over it. The moment his mouth had touched hers, a flame had been lit and he'd reacted on pure animal instinct. With no fans in a stadium watching, nobody filming, the only control he'd managed had been not lifting her onto the kitchen counter and burying himself deep insider her. No romance, no candles. Just pure unbridled lust.

'Your mother tells me you're still living in a bedsit.'

He jammed his hands in his pockets and forced his attention back to his dad. 'I'm renting a room off someone, yes.'

'Bloody daft, when you've a perfectly good house. You must be going soft in the head.'

Yep, there was that fatherly love again. 'I understand you

only get use of the living room on Mondays and Sundays now. Seems bloody daft when you live in a perfectly good house.'

His dad glared at him. 'Think you're clever, don't you? Well a clever man wouldn't be knocking down walls for a living.'

And right on cue, the fatherly pride. But he'd discovered that a sharp remark, delivered often enough, became blunt, lessening its ability to hurt. He was proud of the company he'd built with Mike and of the house he'd done up. Even proud that he wasn't hard-headed enough to force Isabelle out of it. 'A clever man would also be able to find a way of talking to his wife without having to go through his son,' he countered. 'So tell me why you got me over here and I'll be out of your hair.' He had a date with a hot blonde in a shower.

As if she'd heard his thoughts, his phone buzzed with a notification from Sally. He took a quick peek.

OMG, over three hundred thousand likes for last video [grinning emoji, shocked emoji, football emoji, kissing lips emoji].

He typed out a hasty reply.

300,001 – I liked it too.

'Are you listening to me?'

Feeling like he'd been caught texting in assembly, Harry snapped his attention back to the man behind the desk. They were in his dad's study, a room his mother was apparently happy not to share. 'Sorry. A work thing,' he lied. 'You were saying?'

'I don't want a blasted divorce. We had a perfectly good marriage before all this.'

'Define good.'

'Your mother took care of things at home while I went to the office. It worked for thirty years.'

He wondered how that would fit in Sally's rose-tinted view

of love, life and relationships. Then wondered why he was thinking of her. 'Now you don't go to work, and you get in each other's way.'

He hmphed. 'So she says.'

'That's because while you were at work, she had a life. She runs a book club, spends three days a week at the health club, sits on the board of two charities. Has a circle of friends she's cultivated over the last thirty years that she lunches with, goes on holidays with.' He thought back to his childhood. Had his parents ever done *anything* together? 'You need to find yourself a life, too. Play more golf. Organise golfing weekends. Find another club to join.' He stared at his dad. 'Get busy so you don't get in her way. You might find the good comes back to your marriage.'

His father steepled his hands and peered at him over the top of them. 'Not sure I should be taking relationship advice from you. What's the longest you've held onto a woman for?'

The man made it sound like landing a fish. 'We don't all want to get married.'

His dad raised his eyebrows. 'How old are you now?'

Of course he didn't know, just as he wouldn't have a clue what day he was born, either. 'Thirty.'

'Thirty years old and living in a bedsit. Good God, call yourself a man?' Harry's jaw clenched as he fought not to react. 'By your age I'd made something of myself. I'd got married, been made partner in the firm, and bought this house.'

He could tell him he did have his own house, and he was a partner in a business too, but history said there was no point arguing. 'Is that what you called me over for, to tell Mum you don't want a divorce?'

He shook his head. 'I can manage that myself. I want you to take a look at the downstairs toilet. It's not flushing properly.'

Anger fizzed through him, but again Harry clamped down on it before he blurted out stuff he shouldn't say, starting with *if you're so clever, fix your own damn toilet.* And ending with *you and Mum deserve each other.* Instead he walked outside and hauled his toolbox out of the truck.

Sally was already back from the cafe when he arrived at the flat. She took one look at his face as he walked through the door and winced. 'Someone's had a crap day.'

'Went to see my dad.' The moment he said the words he knew she wouldn't understand, because she'd loved her dad, missed him. Probably thought Harry was some sort of git for not liking his. 'Forget it.' He dragged off his boots. 'I'll just grab a drink and then we can do this thing.'

The afternoon had left a sour taste in his mouth that he needed to get rid of before he could focus on the part of the day he'd been looking forward to.

Sally scrunched up her face. 'We can re-schedule.' He watched as she twisted her hands. 'Or we can just forget it…'

'No.' Damn it. He'd been so immersed in his own issues he'd not realised how his mood might come across. But there was the woman he'd spent most of the day thinking about, now looking crestfallen. As if he'd taken something precious from her and crushed it under his clumsy workman boots. Feeling like an utter git, he dragged a hand through his hair and tried to rebalance himself. 'Sorry, I want to do this thing with you. I just need to decompress with a beer first.'

This was what happened when she started to crush too hard on a guy who wasn't the *right* guy. Disappointment crashed through Sally as she watched Harry walk down the hallway to his room, beer in hand.

So much for the sexy *Notebook*-style kiss. Before *her* kiss, Allie was rowed around the lake by Ryan Gosling's Noah. And when they finally came together on the pontoon, Noah had gazed at Allie like he didn't want to be anywhere else but in the pouring rain, with her.

He hadn't thought of the kiss as a *thing* to be crossed off. Then gone to have a beer alone in his room before he could face doing it.

She knew she'd invested too much into this moment when she felt tears prick the back of her eyes. Why hadn't she treated this as just another video clip? Why had she thought, even for a moment, that it might lead somewhere?

Her eyes fell to the boots he'd lined up neatly by the door. They looked huge.

'You know what they say about the size of a guy's feet.'

She jumped at the sound of his voice and turned to find him leaning against the wall, beer bottle still in hand, watching her with an unreadable expression. 'I thought you'd gone to your room.'

'Just went to change.' He indicated the white shirt he was wearing. 'Thought this was more like the dude in *The Notebook*?'

'Yes.' The saliva vanished from her throat. And that was just from imagining what the shirt might look like wet, clinging to his chest. She didn't dare think about the comment about the size of his very large boots. 'I guess I should find a blue dress.'

'Up to you.' His mouth curved into a crooked smile. 'I'm happy to kiss you whatever you're wearing. Or not wearing.'

Okay, she'd gone from simmering anticipation, to angsty disappointment, to her heart hammering so fast it felt like it would bounce out of her chest. 'I'll change while you finish your beer.'

'Are we doing this in my shower or yours?'

Why was it that everything he said right now woke the butterflies in her stomach? 'Mine is better. It's bigger. There's no awkward bath in the way. Just a big walk-in shower with plenty of room for … manoeuvring.' Oh crap, had she really just said that?

He chuckled. 'Sounds good.' He raised the bottle to his lips, his throat doing a sexy jig as he swallowed. 'Shout when you're ready for me.'

Her breath caught in her throat and a sliver of panic ran through her. *Was* she ready for him? She'd just experienced a glimpse of what life would be like if she let this crush go too far. Of the disappointment, the hurt she'd be letting herself in for.

Was she really prepared for that?

The bells won't ring. The panic ebbed a little as she remembered her mum's promise. She had to believe that the bells would only ring when she found the right man. Not only a man who made her blood heat, her hormones sing and tied her belly up in knots, but her equal, her partner. Her person. The one she was meant to be with for the rest of her life.

Until that time, until she fell in love, there was no harm in having some fun in a shower.

It took a while to sort out the logistics of setting up the phone to film the scene, which thankfully quietened the butterflies. The cabinet was shifted next to the shower, which worked for filming, but also meant the phone was likely to get splashed.

'We can use mine.' Harry eyed her pink iPhone warily. 'It's tougher than that thing you have.'

'Says who?'

He sighed and pulled out his admittedly rugged-looking phone from his pocket. 'There's a reason builders don't have pink phones. And it's not the colour.'

'Fine. Set it up, Builder Man. I'll stand in the shower.'

He smirked at her wording before placing his phone on the cabinet and resting it against the toothbrush holder. After a few seconds of moving it around, he stood back, clearly satisfied. 'Okay, we're good to roll.'

He stepped into the shower with her and suddenly her boast that there'd be plenty of room for manoeuvring seemed hollow. The man was built like a giant. 'You're way too big.'

'I have it on good authority women like it big.' He stared down at her, amusement making his eyes glint. 'So how do we start this?'

'We're on the pontoon. And it's pouring with rain.'

He stuck out his arm to turn on the shower and suddenly they were drenched. As she yelped and spluttered at the cold, he laughed. 'You were the one who thought it would be romantic to be wet.'

As the water warmed up, her brain began to unfreeze and she channelled her inner Allie. 'Why didn't you write to me? I waited for you for seven years. It wasn't over for me.'

'Hey, I messaged, you didn't reply. One strike and you're

out.' Sarcastic sod. She shoved at him, causing him to put up his hands. 'Okay, okay. I wrote loads of letters apparently, though seriously, who does that?'

'Men in love in a time when there were no smartphones. Or actually, men in love, because they know a handwritten letter is way more romantic than a WhatsApp message.' But discussing this was not romantic, nor was standing in a shower with her clothes on. She took hold of his arms – not technically in the script but she wanted his attention on her, on them, and not on trying to poke fun at the film. 'You wrote to me?'

As if her touch was all he needed, he stilled. 'Yes.'

His bicep tensed beneath her hands, reawakening the butterflies in her belly. They began to flap wildly as her eyes rested on his chest and the way the wet shirt clung to his pecs.

'It wasn't over.' In a flash, his hands flew to either side of her face and he stared at her, water cascading down his face, eyes a slate grey. 'It still isn't over.'

His mouth slammed down on hers. Whether he was being true to the film, or just doing what he wanted, she didn't know. Didn't care. The hard press of his lips, the way he didn't just meet her halfway, he captured her, possessed her mouth with a greedy intensity, made her feel desired, wanted in a way she'd never experienced. As he took his fill, his clever tongue tangling with hers, his hot mouth making her ache, she forgot the reason they were in the shower, the reason he was kissing her.

'Fuck.' He drew away, breath heavy, chest heaving as he searched her face. Whatever he saw there must have satisfied him because he dived back into the kiss, only this time his hands grasped her bum and lifted her so she was pinned against the shower wall, her legs automatically wrapping round his hips.

'We're going off script,' she managed as his mouth left hers to trail kisses across her neck and down, down, towards her cleavage.

'Sod the script,' he muttered. 'If Gosling had been in a shower, he'd be doing the same.'

She didn't need the screen image of Ryan Gosling, she realised, because the man currently grinding his hips against hers was just as sexy, but he was also gloriously real.

One of Harry's hands found its way behind her back, expertly pulling down the zip of her dress and shoving it aside before peeling off her bra so he could stare at her breasts. With a groan, he bent to lick her nipple. 'Your tits are bloody gorgeous.'

This was actually happening. If she didn't say something soon, she was going to have sex with her cynical, totally unsuitable lodger, in the shower. 'We should take this somewhere drier.' *That's* the part she was baulking on? Had she lost her mind?

He stopped kissing her breasts for long enough to grin up at her. 'I like your thinking.'

But he carried on playing with her, teasing her nipples with his tongue, his mouth, a nibble here, a lick there. *Tormenting* her. 'Harry.'

'Umm. In a minute.'

Even when he was worshipping her, which was how this felt, he drove her nuts. And holy cow, if he carried on doing that, she was going to come, no question. Just from his tongue on her breasts and the gloriously hard ridge of him grinding against the part of her that ached to be filled with him.

The pleasure continued to climb and suddenly she was there, spiralling out of control. 'Holy shit on a candlestick.'

As she came down she saw him staring at her, something like awe on his face. 'You came?'

'Apparently.' Maybe it was uncool to come so quick, so easily, but the look on his face said he'd enjoyed watching. That he wanted to watch her again. 'Bed,' she panted. 'Yours, mine, I don't care. I want more.'

Chapter Sixteen

He was in a fog of lust. Curves. He knew Sally had them, but he'd not been prepared for the luscious breasts that had fallen into his hands when he'd taken off her bra.

And the way she'd moaned, writhed against him, so passionate. Really frigging *eager*. If he wasn't careful he was going to blow his load before he got her to bed.

Bed.

She was right. He was totally game for sex in the shower but it was too quick for their first time – and yeah, he was absolutely planning for this to happen again. And again. He wanted to savour her, get to know her body, find out what made her moan, made her gasp. Get her naked and horizontal. With his hands under her pert rear he carried her out of the shower, setting her down by the door where he made quick work of peeling off the rest of her sodden clothes.

'Jesus.' He took a moment to just look. To admire the lush contours of her naked body. 'If I forget to tell you later, you're fucking gorgeous.'

She gave him a slow, wide smile. 'Thank you.' Then she

laughed, wrapping her arms around her. 'I'm also dripping wet.'

He snagged a big white towel and wrapped her in it. 'Hang on a minute.' He started to undress, undoing the buttons on the shirt but his fingers were too impatient so he gave up and lifted the thing over his head before popping the top button of his jeans.

'Whoa, stop there.'

'What?'

Her big blue eyes held his for a moment before dipping down over his naked upper half. 'That's quite some image.'

'Yeah?' He almost puffed out his chest. He definitely made his pecs jump around a bit. But then she reached out to touch him, her fingers searing his skin, and he stopped the posturing and hastily dragged off his wet jeans, followed by his boxers. Again aware of eyes on him.

'It's true then.' She bit into her lip, eyes dancing. 'Big boots, big … feet.'

Laughing, he lifted her up again and carried her through to lay her on the bed. There he set about continuing the feast he'd started in the shower, lavishing her breasts with attention before going lower, to the heat between her legs, driving himself crazy with want, with need. Her too, if the sounds she made were anything to go by.

'Oh my God,' she gasped, and the noise she made when she came just about blew his mind.

He needed to be inside her. Now. With the few remaining brain cells he had left, he realised there was one practical step needed before that could happen.

'Don't move. Please.' And yes, that was exactly as it sounded – a plea from a desperate man. He tore down the hallway like a greyhound on speed, snatching at the unopened box of condoms.

When he came back he found her in exactly the same position, thank you God, and a sexy little smile crossed her face when she took in what he was carrying. 'New box?'

He'd not needed condoms for a while, not since Isabelle had moved in with him. Then again, considering how she'd been having sex elsewhere, maybe he should have. Pushing the buzz-killing thought away, he quickly covered himself.

Ignoring her question, he climbed onto the bed, took her face in his hands and kissed her. So many positions he wanted her in, he thought as he deepened the kiss, the soft bump of her breasts feeling like an exquisite sort of torture as they pressed against his skin. But for now he'd settle for the old-fashioned way, him staring into a pair of midnight-blue eyes as he eased his way into the lush heat of her. A groan escaped as pleasure arrowed through him. 'Christ.' He had to pause, to try and calm the beast inside that wanted to take, to plunder. Hammer himself home.

Her hips moved restlessly against his.

'Yeah I know.' He bent, kissed the pink lips he was quickly finding he couldn't get enough of. 'Give me a minute.' But she moaned, writhing against him, and it was enough to snap his control. 'Damn it.'

Lust won and the beast took over. He surged into her, taking greedily, pleasure spiralling. Forget finesse, this was pure, uninhibited animal sex. The more he stared down at her, the more he thrust into her, the more he lost his mind. Dimly through the haze of passion he heard her cry out, felt her convulse against him as she came again. As if that was the trigger he needed, his groin tightened, tightened, tightened … and then with a guttural cry, he let go.

It could have been seconds, minutes, hours later when he finally rolled off her – he had no clue. His brain was scrambled, his body a limp wreck.

'Well.' She slid him a look as they both lay on their backs.

He huffed out a laugh. 'Well indeed.' He studied her face, feeling a niggle of concern. 'Not too rough?'

'Nope. Just right.'

Relieved, he crooked a smile. 'Fancy doing it again?'

Her eyes opened wider. 'Now?'

'Give or take a few minutes.' He drew in a deep, satisfied breath, eyes settling on the surroundings he'd not taken a blind bit of notice about earlier. The sophisticated pastels and classic oak furniture weren't quite as he'd imagined. 'Thought there'd be more … pink. Some frills, lace maybe.'

She snorted. 'You really have me down as some romantic stereotype. Just because I enjoy the genre doesn't mean I'm a lightweight, frilly person. I like pink, sure, but it's more that I believe in love, in finding your person…'

He missed the rest of what she was saying because his eyes had landed on the photo by the side of her bed. 'Are they your parents?'

She blinked, clearly surprised to be interrupted mid-lecture. But her expression softened as she shifted to pick up the frame. 'Yes.' Settling back against the headboard, she stared down at the photo, her fingers tracing the images. 'They were so similar, like peas in a pod. True soulmates. Can you see how they're looking at each other? That's what I'm talking about, what I want. A guy to look at me like Dad's looking at Mum. With complete adoration.'

The sex-fuelled euphoric bubble he'd been inhabiting, burst. Rushing to take its place, like a bossy, unwanted guest, was a heavy dose of guilt.

Sitting up sharply, he rubbed a hand across his face.

'What's wrong?'

'We shouldn't have done this.'

She recoiled as if he'd slapped her, which ratcheted the guilt up a notch. 'Well, that's exactly what a girl wants to hear after sex.'

This was going from bad to worse and the inept way he was handling it was exactly why he shouldn't have let it happen. 'This is why I hate romcoms. Real life isn't cute and sweet. It's messy as hell.' Turning, he made sure to catch her eye. 'You want the fantasy, and we both know I'm nothing like your fantasy. I don't even believe in the fantasy.'

She gaped at him as if he'd said something ridiculous. 'You're worried that just because we had sex that didn't suck, I'll fall for you.'

Ouch. Probably he deserved that, but... 'It was fucking phenomenal sex, and you know it.'

She sat up now too, and he noticed how she carefully tucked the duvet around her so he was deprived of the sight of her breasts. 'Maybe I do, but it takes more than *fucking phenomenal sex* to fall in love.'

'Okay, okay.' He exhaled sharply, frustrated with himself for not being able to communicate better. 'What I'm trying to say, and clearly doing a piss poor job of it, is I really like you.' Something tightened in his chest as he gazed into her guileless blue eyes. 'I don't want to hurt you.'

He watched the lids come down over those blue orbs before she turned away and carefully set the frame back on her bedside table.

'I might think you're hot,' she said quietly, 'but I also know you're not right for me. We are definitely not peas in a pod, not soulmates.' She smiled. 'You're Daniel Cleaver, and I'm going to fall for Mark Darcy.'

'Sorry?'

She rolled her eyes. 'And that's exactly why you don't have to worry about hurting me. My body likes you, but my brain knows we'd never work because we talk a different language. If you want to understand what I mean, watch *Bridget Jones*.'

She was right, he didn't understand her language. Nor did he understand why the thought of her with this Mark Darcy character made his gut clench and his hands want to curl into fists.

Sally watched a pained look come over Harry's face. She expected him to say something like *do I have to?* Instead, he surprised her by nodding.

'Okay.' He swallowed, stared back at her. 'Is Adam your Mark Darcy?'

'I don't think so, but who knows?' Adam ticked the right boxes, except the most important. He didn't make her insides flip, which the man next to her managed to do just by looking at her.

Silence descended between them. They'd just had – he was right – phenomenal sex. Yet that rosy afterglow was now strained by the knowledge there was no obvious path ahead. They could try and forget the sex, but that seemed impossible. She'd seen him naked, had her hands on him, been spoilt by him. Harry the Lodger was now, officially, Harry the Sex God. They could carry on having sex, but she wasn't a hundred per cent sure of the accuracy of her boast about not getting hurt. Not when this crush came with a very strong like. Yet the usual option for people who had amazing chemistry that translated into stellar sex – turning that into a relationship – was doomed before it started.

'My parents don't have that.'

His quiet words broke the silence and she turned to find him looking again at the photograph. 'You think they don't love each other?'

'Right now they don't even like each other.'

He'd given her hints that all wasn't well with his relationship with them, and she'd met his mother, felt the strange vibe between them. But this was the first time he'd spoken openly about them. 'That doesn't mean anything. Couples row, they have differences. Love and hate are said to be opposite sides of the same coin.' Feeling he was trying to connect, to narrow the gulf that had sprung between them, she gave him a gentle nudge. 'There's even a romcom called *Ten Things I Hate About You.*'

His mouth curved. 'Another one to add to my watch list, huh?'

'Absolutely. It's a classic.' She hesitated. 'Is that why you said your parents were driving you mad? Why you needed to decompress earlier?'

'Yeah. They've decided they want a divorce, which I guess is no surprise but apparently they can't be civil to each other anymore.'

'They're using you as the go-between?'

'Something like that. I've never had so much attention from them.' He drew up his knees and rested his arms on them, gaze fixed on the opposite wall. 'So, what happens now?'

She was bursting with questions of her own, but his hung like a dark cloud between them. 'I don't know.'

He twisted to face her, his eyes like liquid silver as they

stared at her lips for a beat before zeroing in on hers. 'In case there's any doubt, I want to do this again. In fact I can't imagine living here and not wanting to touch you. Kiss you.'

'I can't either.' It was like the saying about the genie being out of the bottle. You couldn't put it back, just as she couldn't tuck away her feelings now she'd had a taste of what being with him was like. *No, not feelings.* 'But it's just sex.'

His hand cupped the back of her neck and pulled her towards him for a sweetly soft kiss. 'Sex on top of like.'

Her belly dipped at the warmth in his gaze. 'You mean *Friends With Benefits* meets *No Strings Attached*.' Except... She tried to keep the smile on her face. To ignore the tug of disappointment. 'Without the Happy Ever After.'

He frowned, eyes crinkling in concern. 'Hey, just because our story doesn't end in a happy ever after doesn't mean it won't happen for you.'

'I know. The bells will ring.' It was just, for a moment there, she wanted to think they might ring with him.

'Meanwhile.' He reached down to the floor and when he leaned back up again, he was clutching at the condom box. 'Want to use these up this afternoon?'

'Ah yes, the new box.'

'Bought it after we did the *Ghost* scene.' He gave her a slightly sheepish-looking grin. 'I'm an optimist.'

She couldn't help but laugh at the boyish expression. 'You are if you think we're going to use up' – she eyed the box – 'twelve?'

'One down, eleven to go.'

A predatory expression replaced the boyish one and her pulse began to race. 'Wait. Before you start looking at me like that...'

His gaze dipped to her breasts, and she felt them tingle. 'Like what?'

'You know what.' Oh God, the heat in his eyes, the way they turned from grey to charcoal. 'Like you want to gobble me up.'

He grinned wolfishly. 'Sounds about right.'

'Before that, we need to sort out the video. It's on your phone.'

He cupped her left breast, his rough palm sending a delicious shiver across her skin. 'After.'

A moment later his mouth was on hers, hot and hungry, and editing a video was the last thing on her mind.

It was several hours – and two condoms later – before she was able to work on the clip. Harry had gone to the pub. He'd asked if she wanted to come along but she'd declined, figuring distance was needed. Despite her bold assertion she wouldn't fall for him, she was well aware that *might* not turn out to be true. Sex outside a relationship was new territory for her. As was living with a guy she wasn't in a relationship with, but wanted to have sex with every time she saw him.

So really, it was irrelevant what her head thought, because while he continued to live under her roof, it was hard to see herself not ending up in bed with him again.

Or in the shower…

Oh my God.

Her blood ran hot and cold as she watched the video back. She looked wanton. Like some porn actress overplaying her role, only this woman with her head thrown back in ecstasy, her eyes shut, her mouth open, was apparently what happened when Harry kissed her. And maybe that shouldn't be such a shock because, holy cow, his back view was hot. Big broad shoulders, muscles sliding over muscles beneath the sodden, practically translucent white shirt.

Shitting, shit, shit. They hadn't stopped the video after the kiss. Okay, you couldn't see her boobs, couldn't hear what they were saying outside the sound of the shower. *Your tits are bloody gorgeous*. She could hear his voice in her head though, the way she'd melted for him as he'd lavished attention on them. And fuckity fuck fuck, she'd not just melted.

They'd filmed her having an *actual* orgasm.

All fingers and thumbs, she messaged Harry.

Then she set about giving the footage a very thorough edit before uploading it onto TikTok.

Chapter Seventeen

It was a usual Saturday night. He was in the pub, chatting shit with Mike and Jack amongst others, and yet ... nothing about this evening felt normal. For a start, his body was shattered, but his brain felt like it had been plugged into a socket, it was buzzing so much.

Had he really just had a week's worth of sex in one afternoon – with his landlady? And if he had, and his body sure felt like it had been through one hell of a workout, what did it mean? Were they going to carry on sleeping with each other? Could he continue to live there if they did? Could he continue to live with her, see her every day, and not sleep with her?

Finally, there was the most difficult question of all to answer. Why had wrapping his arms around her, kissing her, moving inside her, felt better than anything he'd ever experienced?

The sharp end of Mike's elbow dug into his kidneys and he grunted. 'What the hell?'

'Checking you're still alive. You haven't spoken for ten

minutes. Not that I've missed your sparkling conversation,' Mike continued, clearly finding himself funny because he started to chuckle. 'But Trixie asked you a question.'

Guiltily, Harry glanced at Mike's girlfriend, here tonight with her sister, who was visiting from Dorchester and currently keeping Jack entertained. He idly wondered where Kitty was, if she was with Sally, drinking somewhere different because Sally wanted to avoid him…

'Oi.' Mike's voice again cut through his internal ramblings. 'What's got into you tonight?'

It's not what's got into me, but who I've got into… He gave himself a mental slap and focused back on his present company. 'Just family crap,' he lied, turning to Trixie. 'Sorry, what did you say?'

'I was wondering when we can expect the next video.'

'Third time she's asked,' Mike muttered unhelpfully.

'Oh wow, no worries, I can see Sally's just uploaded one.' Trixie grinned as she looked down at her phone. 'She's given it the tag *The Notebook Kiss – with a (spiral-bound) twist*.'

It definitely had a twist. The memory sent a bolt of arousal through him – frigging hell he was like a horny teenager.

'Let me see.' Mike nodded to Trixie to put her phone on the table so he could look at it.

Wanting to see it for himself, Harry got out his own mobile and clicked on the TikTok app. He was only following one person, so it wasn't hard to find.

He was vaguely aware of Mike scoffing at his comment about being big, of Trixie laughing as he said it was one strike and you're out. But then he heard nothing. He was too absorbed in how bloody sexy they looked together as they kissed, the look on Sally's face as he briefly pulled away before kissing her again. The clip ended all too soon, but the show reel in his head didn't. In there he re-lived every glorious moment.

Quickly he saved the clip to his phone. And tried not to think why he wanted to keep it.

'That's actually kind of hot.' Trixie pretended to fan herself.

'What's hot?' Typical Jack, ears pricking up the moment anything related to sex was mentioned.

'This video of Harry and Sally.' She pushed the phone over to Jack so he could watch it.

Jack, the womaniser who'd already admitted he fancied Sally. 'No.'

Harry snatched the phone off Jack, who glowered at him. 'What the hell?'

I don't want you seeing Sally like that, all wet and sexy as hell. He couldn't admit it to Jack, found it hard enough to admit to himself, because he knew how it sounded. Like he was jealous.

'I don't want you taking the piss,' he mumbled instead, handing the phone back to Trixie.

'That's what I do.' Jack stared at him, hard. 'It's what you used to do about these daft clips, too.'

'Maybe I'm not in the mood tonight.' He needed to change the subject, fast. In three long gulps, he drained his glass. 'Maybe I think you should focus your energy on getting in another round, instead.' It did the trick, and Jack reluctantly got to his feet. To further divert the attention from himself, Harry snapped a couple of photos. When Jack looked at him quizzically, he grinned. 'Wanted a record of the momentous occasion.'

Jack gave him a sly smile, then bent to whisper in his ear as he passed. 'Don't mistake me for being all looks and no brain. No way you haven't shagged her.'

Harry's hands itched to shove at Jack. His foot itched to trip the man up and watch him fall in an inelegant lump to the floor. Any reaction like that would only confirm Jack's suspicions though, so he settled for a sharp, 'None of your business.'

When he glanced over at Mike, the expression on his face said he'd been rumbled. Ignoring him, Harry focused on his beer while inside, he twisted himself into knots wondering why he was having such a strong reaction to comments that a few weeks ago, he would have laughed off.

Several pints later, Harry felt pleasantly drunk. Trixie and her sister had left, and now it was just him, Mike and Jack.

'Okay, now you can spill.'

Harry raised his eyebrows at Jack. 'You want my beer down your shirt?'

'Very funny. I want you to look me in the eye and tell me you and the cute blonde haven't had sex.'

As he knew he couldn't, he turned the heat onto Jack. 'Why are you so interested in my sex life?'

'Because he's not getting any,' Mike filled in for him.

Jack gave a good-natured shrug. 'He's not wrong. So give me the details, Casanova, so I can live vi… Whatever it is.'

'Vicariously,' Harry supplied, at the same time wondering if he could go to the john and then leg it without Mike or Jack realising.

'If that means I can get pleasure from listening about your sex life, yeah, that'll do it.' Jack's ginger brows crashed together like a couple of hairy caterpillars. 'Wait, that sounds dodgy.'

'Never stopped you before,' Harry grumbled, taking a swig

of his beer. How many was that now? And why was he drinking so much? Because he didn't want to go back to the flat yet? Didn't want to face the woman he'd spent the best afternoon of his life with?

When he looked up, he found Mike and Jack watching him like he was a lab specimen. 'Okay, okay.' He reached for the beer again, took another long drink. 'We might have hooked up after we kissed in the shower.'

Jack banged his fist on the table. 'I bloody knew it. That kiss had sex written all over it.'

'Well, well.' Mike leaned back on his chair and eyed him thoughtfully. 'I'd ask if you're going to see her again, but I guess that's kind of a done deal.' An evil smile played around his mouth. 'You know what, this is going to be fun to watch.'

Harry squirmed on his chair. 'What do you mean?'

'The love cynic and the romantic, forced together because they live together.'

Jack nodded at Mike. 'And now with the added complication of fairly decent sex.'

'Fucking phenomenal sex.' Mike and Jack looked at each other, then cackled like two naughty kids at the back of class. Figuring he'd had enough of his beer, and their company, Harry jumped to his feet. 'I'm off. See you both Monday.'

'Yeah. If you can make it out of Sally's bed.' Mike smirked.

'And your hips aren't too weak from all that thrusting,' Jack added, which of course set the pair of juveniles off again.

When he hit the fresh air, Harry turned the collar of his jacket up against the wind and set off along the prom, realising belatedly that he wasn't quite steady on his feet. Deciding he needed a moment to let his head stop spinning, he leaned against the railings and took out his phone. *You want to watch the shower video again*, a voice niggled.

He ignored it. He didn't. That would be weird.

You want to work out what was so special about it, about her.

With a huff of frustration he opened the phone, but before he could find the video, he saw he had two messages; one from the woman he'd just slept with, one from the previous woman he'd slept with.

Isabelle: Just seen latest video of you and the blonde. If you're trying to get even, it worked. Congratulations. Now I know how much it hurts when the person you love sleeps with someone else.

So many things wrong with that message, he didn't know where to start. So he pressed delete.

Sally: Plz make sure u delete video from your phone. Had to do serious editing [monkey hiding eyes emoji, face palm emoji, fire emoji, shocked face emoji].

He frowned, his alcohol-addled brain taking a few moments to work out what she was going on about. Then it sunk in.

Fuck, he'd recorded the whole kiss. And by that he meant the *whole* kiss. Desire flooded through him and in a flash he was scrolling through his photos to the thumbnail image of him and Sally stepping into the shower. Shit, there were two of them. How drunk was he? *You downloaded the edited version, idiot.* Of course. So he needed to delete, what, the first? Yep, that was it, the second was the edited version. His thumb hovered over the first video, the desire to watch it again, watch her come, so strong it felt like some inner force was going to make him press play.

She asked you to delete.

Reluctantly he sent it to the trash.

Sunday afternoon and Sally felt Adam's hand curl around hers as they crossed the road together. It was probably instinctive – he was a gentleman, she was fast discovering. And great to look at. Blond hair waving in the breeze, blue eyes popping against the sky as they walked along the seafront.

Damn it, why weren't tingles running up her arm from the feel of his fingers around hers? Why did she now prefer dark hair and grey eyes when blue-eyed blonds had always been her crushes in the past?

As if suddenly aware what he was doing, Adam let go of her hand and gave her a sheepish smile. 'Sorry.'

'No need to apologise. You were being a gentleman.'

He started to laugh. 'Yeah, not really. I was using it as a good excuse to hold your hand.'

'Oh.' She glanced over at him, torn. Did she carry on pretending she hadn't had sex with Harry yesterday?

'That's not a promising sound.'

'There's something I need to tell you.' Feeling awkward, she stuffed her hands in her pockets. 'I… Me and Harry…' God, this was embarrassing. 'We kissed yesterday.'

Adam grinned. 'I know. I saw the video. Along with hundreds of thousands of other people, from the look of the number of views you've been getting.'

'Yes, well that was the edited version.'

Silence hung in the air for a moment and Sally willed Adam to work it out without her having to actually say the words out loud.

'Ah.' He winced. 'I'm not sure what to say.'

'Me neither.'

'Was it a heat of the moment thing, or…' He trailed off, clearly finding this as excruciating as she was.

'I think it was a bit of both.' She dug her hands further in her pockets, searching for how to explain to Adam what she couldn't really explain to herself. 'I feel the fuzzies with him. But he's really not my type. I mean, he doesn't even like romcoms for a start.' *Or even believe in love.*

Adam smiled. 'I can see that from the videos. He's funny though.'

'Sometimes.'

'Are you going to date him?'

God, this was awkward with a capital A. She wasn't sure *we've just agreed to finish off a box of condoms* was an answer she could give Adam. 'I don't think so.'

'So we could carry on seeing each other then?'

She came to a stop outside the restaurant they'd agreed to have lunch in. 'Do you want to?'

He shrugged. 'Why not?'

Suddenly she had an image of Harry as he'd looked at her yesterday, with lust in his eyes. *I can't imagine living here and not wanting to touch you. Kiss you.* 'I think you've just answered that question.' She smiled sadly at Adam. 'If we can't even get excited about seeing each other as friends, this is never going to work.'

Disappointment flickered across his face and he sighed. 'I should have said yes, of course I want to see you.'

'You should have said exactly what you felt, which you did.' She gave him a gentle nudge to show there were no hard feelings. 'I still think you're cool.'

'And I still think you're gorgeous. And funny.'

Silence descended for a moment and she looked over at the restaurant. 'I'm also still hungry.'

He grinned. 'Me too.'

When Sally let herself into the flat a couple of hours later, all the nerve endings that had been happily dormant while having lunch with Adam, went into full alert. Automatically her gaze flew to the space next to the wall where Harry stored his shoes. Next to his steel-capped work boots sat a pair of rugged brown ones, and his trainers.

He was back.

As if he'd been listening out for her, the door of Harry's room opened and he appeared in the hallway. 'Hi.'

'Hi, yourself.'

They stood staring at each other, the air between them crackling with an awkward, humming, sexual energy.

He pushed his hands into the low slung jeans he wore, causing them to ride even lower. Enough that she saw a glimpse of flat stomach and of dark hair arrowing below his waist band. The hum turned up a notch.

'I see the video is doing well.'

'It is.' Talking was hard when her throat felt tight and devoid of saliva. 'Our fans are loving it. Plus we've over half a million views.'

'That's ... mind boggling.'

'It is, isn't it? Our highest views yet. I guess people must like what we're doing. It's going to make getting sponsors much easier.'

'Great.' A beat of taut, pulsing, silence. Why didn't he sound more excited? Why didn't she? Wasn't it the whole point of what they were doing? 'Been anywhere nice?'

'Out for lunch.' She paused. 'With Adam.'

Harry's big body stilled. 'You're still seeing him?'

It's none of his business. 'Why?'

'I thought...' He frowned, raked a hand through his hair. 'I thought we were seeing each other.'

Her heart gave a little bump. 'You said it was sex only.'

He shifted on his feet. 'I said sex on top of like.'

'And that differs, how?' She took off her coat and hung it up, trying to regain her balance. 'You'll have to spell it out for me because I've not done this before.'

He started to walk towards her and it was only when he stood in front of her that she saw the confusion on his face. 'You've not been out with a guy before?'

'I've dated guys, of course I have.'

'So what's the problem?'

Okay, now she was getting irritated. 'The problem is this isn't dating, is it? Per your definition, this is friends who have sex now and again.'

'I was thinking more frequently than that.' He gave her a crooked smile. 'Like twice a day more frequently.'

Exasperated, she pushed at his chest. 'This isn't funny for me, okay? I don't have sex lightly, I'm not wired like that. Up to now, it's always been part of a relationship.'

'I'm sorry.' Placing his hands on her shoulders, he squeezed gently. 'I guess I'm struggling with the issue here. You said yourself we're just a temporary thing. You're going to fall for Mark Darcy, remember?'

She nodded. She had said that, and at the time she'd really believed it, too. So why was she feeling all weirded out now?

'But until he comes along, or until you get bored of me, is there any reason we shouldn't have a bit of fun together?'

She could see the logic – it was the same logic she'd applied to their situation yesterday. But now he was talking sex and dating? Yet it didn't fit with her idea of how dating should be. With previous relationships there had always been that beautiful *what if*. *What if he's the one*.

'I've never watched *Love Story*. Or *The Fault in Our Stars*. Or *Brokeback Mountain*.'

He blinked. 'Sorry?'

'They're all films with sad endings.' She couldn't look at him. 'Asking me to date you when I know we're never going to work?' She worried at her bottom lip. 'That feels like asking me to watch a film that's going to end with me feeling sad.'

A frown appeared between his eyes. 'But what about the journey they took? Isn't that just as important? Isn't that what life is about? Not how it ends, but the experiences enjoyed on the way?'

This felt too deep a conversation to be having with a guy she'd had sex with once. 'So what are you saying? That I'll enjoy the experience of dating you so much I won't care about the ending?'

A laugh rumbled through him. 'Something like that. I'm never going to be that guy in the film you made me watch, the one about the millionaire and the hooker.'

'*Pretty Woman*?'

'That's the one, totally unrealistic storyline but anyway, just to set your expectations, I'm not going to turn up with a rose between my teeth or a red jewellery box, but we'll have a laugh.'

'Along with the sex.'

'Along with lots of sex,' he amended. 'And as for the ending, there's no reason why it should be sad. You'll get bored/frustrated/pissed off with me and be happy to dump my arse.'

'Or I'll meet The One.'

A flicker of something she couldn't decipher crossed his face. 'That's another way this could end.'

She felt better now. He was right, this wasn't like the films she'd mentioned because he wasn't her soulmate. There was a happy ending still out there for her and it wasn't with him. 'Okay then. Let's do this. But on one condition.'

He screwed up his face. 'I'm not sure I want to hear this, but okay.'

'You agree to watch one romcom a week with me.' He groaned, but before he spoke again, she added, 'And if you say anything along the lines of you're not sure the sex will be worth it—'

'Jesus, Sally.' The hands that had been resting on her shoulders slid up to cup her face. 'I'll watch a frigging romcom every night if it means I get to cuddle up to you.' He nibbled at her lips. 'Kiss you.' He deepened the kiss, one hand leaving her face to rest on her bum, pulling her closer to him. 'Sleep with you.'

This, she thought dizzily, this was what he'd meant. How short-sighted to focus only on the ending when the journey, as he'd called it, promised so much.

Chapter Eighteen

It was day five of this weird world where everything was the same – he chatted to Sally over breakfast, went to work, came back to the flat, chatted to Sally as they made dinner – except for one humongous, spectacular difference.

Every night so far, he'd ended up in her bed.

And that was both frigging fantastic, and scary as hell. It was like dating on fast forward. Dating a girl and moving in with her all at the same time. It should feel intense, too much. He was a guy who liked his own space. At his happiest when he'd dated a woman who liked her own space, too. He'd fallen into living with Isabelle and though there had been good times, he'd always been aware she was in his space.

He was now in Sally's space, yet she never made him feel that way. It was… He didn't think he'd ever say this, but it was easy. Living with a woman he liked and respected, who also made him laugh. And with the added bonus of mind-blowing sex.

In fact, there was only one downside.

From her seat on the other side of the kitchen island, Sally glanced over at him. 'Look at my face. It's sad.'

Her blue eyes danced; those soft lips he bloody loved kissing, twitched. Sod sad, she looked gorgeous. And mischievous. He swallowed a mouthful of the quiche they were sharing. Then followed it up with another because he was starving. 'Doesn't look sad to me. Looks like the face of a woman trying to con me into watching another romcom.'

And that, folks, was the one downside.

'You said you'd watch one every night,' she wheedled, giving him a smile cute enough to make his toes curl.

'You caught me at a weak moment.'

'You admitted you enjoyed *An Officer and a Gentleman* yesterday.'

To his shock, he had. 'That's because it wasn't too cheesy.'

'Not even the ending, when Richard Gere's officer character puts on that insanely hot, white navy uniform, marches into the factory where Debra Winger, aka Paula, works, lifts her into his arms and carries her out?'

Secretly, he'd thought that was pretty cool. Striding in, claiming his woman... There was something primal about it. 'I've seen worse endings to a film.' He glanced down at his finished plate. Watching another romcom with her seemed a small price to pay for having his dinner made for him. 'What do you want to torture me with then?'

She rolled her eyes. 'I thought we'd watch *Bridget Jones* because it's such a classic.'

The name rang a bell. 'Wait, is this the one where I'm supposed to be this Cleaver guy?'

'That's it.'

He didn't like the way his stomach pitched. 'And Adam's Mark Darcy still?'

She avoided his eyes. 'I don't think so.'

'But there's a chance he *might* be?' He had to work to keep his voice steady.

Finally, her gaze latched onto his. 'I'm not seeing Adam anymore, if that's what you mean. But when you and I are over, I don't know what will happen. It's up to fate to decide.'

It was a perfectly reasonable answer, so why didn't he like the idea? Why did the thought of her sharing a quiche with Adam, giving the man the same toe-curling smile she'd just given him, make his stomach turn over? Maybe he didn't think Adam was good enough for her. Yep, it had to be that. Sliding off the bar stool, he reached for the plates. 'Okay, I'll clear while you find this Bridget person. I hope she's hot.' He'd discovered watching romcoms was less painful when the lead actress was attractive.

Sally pushed her glass over to him. 'She's played by Renee Zellweger.'

He'd heard of her. 'She's cute.'

'She had to put on thirty pounds for this role.'

He looked over at Sally, at the figure that wasn't quite hidden in the leggings and T-shirt she'd changed into. 'I'm partial to a woman with curves.'

Her face lit up. 'You are?'

Could she really doubt it, after the last few days? To make sure she didn't, he strode over to her, slid his hands under her perfect bum and lifted her so he could plant a kiss on that delectable mouth. Of course, once he'd started kissing her, he couldn't stop, so he eased her onto the bar stool to properly take his fill. He wasn't sure what spell she'd put on him, but she was becoming more addictive as the days went on, not less.

When he finally drew back, his gaze took in her flushed

face, her swollen lips. 'Do you believe me now? Or do you need me to spend the next few hours convincing you?'

She let out a husky laugh. 'You're trying to get out of watching *Bridget Jones*.'

He smirked. 'What I'm trying to do is get into your pants.' For some reason that made her laugh harder. 'What?'

She shook her head, her smile all secretive. 'Watch the film and you'll realise.'

'I get to see Renee's pants?'

Sally started to giggle. Proper, girlie giggles. 'You might do.'

The sight of her laughing did strange things to his chest. Made it flipflop. And made him want to keep making her laugh. 'Is it that I'm calling them pants? Do you prefer knickers? Briefs? Drawers? Panties? Bloomers?'

'Oh God, stop.' She waved her hand at him. 'You'll find out soon enough.'

'You're just trying to make this film sound more exciting,' he murmured as he stacked the dishwasher, but she'd already gone.

A few minutes later he sat on the sofa next to her – yep, that was another thing that had changed. Now he got to cuddle her. It had surprised him at first, the way she'd nestled against him, all soft and warm. Hugging wasn't something he was used to. Not from Isabelle, who'd not been one for touching outside sex. Certainly not from his mother. Yet the moment he'd carelessly thrown his arm around Sally, it was like his heart had sighed with contentment. And yes, he was aware how corny that sounded so no, he wasn't going to admit his newfound love of cuddling to anyone.

'We need to decide on another clip,' she said, snuggling

into him. 'Keep the momentum up. So think on that while we're watching.'

'I've already decided.'

A pair of big blue eyes looked up at him. And then she groaned. 'You want to do the scene with the pants.'

'You, a pair of lacy pants. Maybe a thong.' His fevered mind could already picture it. Except … he realised he didn't want a load of blokes ogling her. Only him. Unconsciously, he drew her tighter to him.

'I suggest you watch the film and then decide.' The smile playing around her mouth had him raising his eyebrow in a silent question but she ignored it and picked up the remote.

———

She loved this film, thought perhaps it was her favourite romcom. Maybe. Certainly one of her favourites because Bridget was so utterly lovable. Even so, there was something extra special about watching it next to a strapping male body, his arm wrapped around her.

Who'd have thought Harry would turn out to be so *cuddly*? It got her wondering for the umpteenth time about what had happened to make him so against the idea of ever finding love. He'd said Isabelle hadn't broken his heart, but had he been lying? Certainly Isabelle thought there was unfinished business between them.

'Bloody hell.'

His sudden exclamation made her jump and she was horrified to realise she'd not been watching the film. First time ever, her mind had wandered during a romcom. This was not good.

'That's what you meant by the pants. She definitely needs to choose the first pair if she's going to snag Cleaver.'

Shaking herself, she focused back on the huge knickers Bridget Jones was contemplating wearing over the skimpy black thong. 'But the second pair hold her stomach in.'

Harry's hands slipped beneath her T-shirt, smoothing over her rounded belly. 'Why are girls so obsessed about a flat stomach? Guys like a soft landing.' He grinned down at her. 'Think about it, would you rather fall onto a bed of pillows, or a hard floor?' She didn't get a chance to reply because it seemed the man she'd once thought of as not very talkative had now found his voice. 'Damn, she's gone for the bloomers.'

That word coming out of his gruff builder's mouth made her laugh. 'She calls them her granny pants.' She snuck a look at him. 'Changing your mind about which scene you want us to do?'

His eyes remained on the screen. 'Nope. I'm sure you can pull off granny pants.'

She wondered why that sounded like the best compliment she'd ever had. 'Admit it, you're hooked on watching romcoms now.'

'I'm hooked on finding out if Cleaver gets to see the big pants.'

Of course he didn't have long to find out. And he laughed. Honest to God, laughed his head off as he watched Cleaver's fascination with Bridget Jones's underwear. But his mood turned strangely quiet as the film reached its final scene.

'So, what do you think?'

'She chose the wrong guy.'

Interesting. Beneath her ribs, her heart gave a little flutter. 'Why?'

'The Cleaver character was way funnier.'

'But he also wasn't the settling down sort.'

He looked nonplussed. 'Why did she want to settle down?'

The flutter stopped. He might not be a playboy, but Harry was about as likely to want anything serious as Daniel Cleaver. Her future lay with her very own Mark Darcy. 'So you think the next scene we do should be—'

'Me putting my hand up your skirt and finding a pair of … what does he say?' He smiled boyishly, a surprisingly endearing look for such a rugged face. '*Enormous* pants.'

She liked the scene, knew he'd be good at it, but after that blisteringly hot kiss in the shower, it felt like going backwards. Taking their little TikTok tease of a romance in the wrong direction. *You mean your little thing with Harry.*

And that was it, she realised sadly. Everything in her was geared towards the idea of a romance building. Of two people falling in love. Yet that wasn't what was going on here.

'You don't want to do that scene?' He placed his hand on her thigh, his thumb making a sensuous glide only inches from where she wanted to feel him.

'It's not that. I just… Reading the comments on the last few videos, a lot of our followers are as hooked on the promise of what might be happening between us as they are on the actual videos. The pants scene feels more com than rom, but that's fine.' It would have to be fine, because the real romance those followers were hoping for? It wasn't going to happen and both she and they needed to understand that.

The sex though… As his hand crept closer to her core, her pulse quickened. While the sex was this hot, how was she expected to do anything but hold on and enjoy the ride?

Just as she began to imagine how Harry would look naked, sprawled across her pink sofa, her phone started to buzz on the coffee table. When she picked it up, she sighed. 'I'll have to take this. It's Amy.'

'No problem.' He gave her a brief, tantalising kiss. 'I'll remember where we left off.'

He unfurled his long body and ambled out of the sitting room.

'Hey, Amy, how's it going?'

There was a long pause on the other end. When Amy finally replied, her voice was sharp. 'You didn't send enough money.'

'Sorry?'

'I asked for two thousand but you only sent one and a half.'

'I sent what I could.' Sally shut her eyes, tried to count to ten before she said something she'd regret. 'I think you need to come here and have this conversation.' She wanted her sister to look her in the eye when she asked for more money. Only then would she know if the girl she'd once known was still in there.

'Fine. We'll be there in ten minutes.'

'We?'

'Of course Chris is coming. This affects both of us.'

With a heavy sigh, Sally ended the call and walked down the corridor to Harry's room. His door was ajar and when she popped her head round, she found he was sat on his bed, eyes on his phone.

'Hey.'

He looked up and gave her a slow, sexy smile. 'Ready to pick up where we left off… Ah.' His eyes scanned her face and he grimaced. 'Bad call?'

'She's coming round with Chris.'

Those clear grey eyes held hers. 'Want me to hang around or disappear?'

If he was her boyfriend, she'd ask him to stay because Chris was an unknown quantity and it was late enough that who knew what he'd drunk, what he might have taken? But Harry was a temporary lover, and she had no right to ask. 'Whatever you want to do.'

He nodded. 'I'll be here if you need me.'

Gratitude flooded her. 'Thanks.'

She turned to go, but his voice called her back. 'Is everything okay?'

'Honestly, I'm not sure.' She didn't want to look weak, she definitely didn't want to give in to the damn tears that threatened to embarrass her. Guys having flings wanted fun. Not the object of their fling blubbering all over them.

'Is it money again?'

It was, and yet it was also so much more. It was Amy's life. How did she get her sister out of this bleak place and into one that had light, and joy? A place where Amy could see she had a future and it was exciting. It wasn't living off her sister in a pokey, damp flat with a guy who, instead of supporting her, dragged her down to his level? But Harry didn't want to hear any of that. He just wanted the fun part of her. So she pushed out a smile. 'Yep, she's come to raid the bank of Big Sister.'

'Ouch.' He patted the bed next to him. 'Come here.'

She shook her head. 'She'll be here in five minutes. We don't have time to … you know, start anything.'

His expression tightened. 'First, I can achieve a lot in five minutes. Second, if you think I'm that much of a tosser that all I can think of is sex even though I can see you're clearly upset, why the hell are you sleeping with me?'

'I don't think you're a tosser.' She'd angered him, but how was she to know what fell into the boundaries of this thing they were doing, and what didn't? She knew the rules when it came to dating, when it came to relationships, but with this? She didn't know what was expected of her.

There was no time to try and explain though because the intercom buzzed. It said something of how confused she was that talking to Amy seemed the easier option. At least there she knew exactly what was wanted of her, even if it was only money.

Chapter Nineteen

Harry couldn't pretend he didn't feel insulted by Sally's assumption he'd asked her to sit next to him on the bed so he could, what? Take her fast and rough in the few minutes before she saw her sister for what was clearly an upsetting conversation?

He'd wanted to *hold* her. Try and ease some of the worry he could see etched on her face.

Clearly, she saw him as some sort of sex maniac though and maybe that was on him. In his determination to set clear boundaries around their relationship, he'd confused her. If he was honest, those boundaries were starting to confuse him, too. *Sex on top of like* he'd said, and it had seemed easy, but in his experience that didn't involve the seesawing emotions he'd been experiencing recently. He'd gone from ecstatic highs – sex, without a doubt. But also that time after sex, when he held her. Felt his whole body loosen and settle. Taking the middle ground was a kind of happy contentment, he guessed he could call it. Usually experienced when cuddling up with her on the sofa, eating with her, coming home to her ... okay, just generally being in the same space as her. He wanted to blame it on familiarity, but that was trivialising something that felt way deeper and more intimate than slotting into his favourite booth at the pub. Finally, the bottom end of the spectrum was how he felt now. Easily bruised, tender, hurt. A feeling he remembered from childhood, but thought he'd hardened himself against.

Were they both just having difficulty adjusting to this change from lodger/landlady to lover?

In which case … should he start looking for another place to live? The thought weighed heavily on him. He liked living here. No, that was a lie. He'd prefer to be back at his own place – a garden to drink a beer in, space to move, his walk-in shower with seven different jets. Fact was, he liked – make that really, really liked – living with Sally.

Shit, had he monumentally cocked things up by sleeping with her?

Because he didn't want to think too hard on that, he pinged Isabelle a message.

Found a place to live yet?

Then, because he was in a sour mood, he sent another.

And I'm still waiting for the rent money.

She wouldn't be happy with the curt tone, but Mike was right. He'd been too bloody soft with her.

The voices had gone from the hallway; presumably they'd moved to the living room. The thought of Sally being outnumbered didn't sit well with him. He'd go and make himself a drink, see if everything was calm.

'It is her fucking money.'

At the sound of the angry male voice, Harry halted by the open door and eyed up the lanky male sprawled on the sofa next to Amy. Long hair that looked like it hadn't been washed in weeks, a pasty-looking face in need of sun and a diet involving the ingestion of more vegetables. And very possibly the ingestion of pharmaceuticals geared towards the health end of the spectrum rather than the *I want to get high* end.

'Not until she's twenty-four, it isn't,' Sally countered, her usually smiley face looking strained.

'Yeah, well that's not going to work, see, 'cos we need £500 now.'

There was an underlying threat to the boyfriend's voice that Harry didn't like, but as he'd promised himself he wouldn't interfere in Sally's business, he walked past the open door and into the kitchen. There he could still keep an eye out for her, but it *looked* like he wasn't.

'Why do you need another £500?' Sally addressed her question to Amy. 'I gave you what I could and I know that was enough for two months' rent.'

'We want to go on holiday.'

In the process of filling the kettle, Harry stilled, wondering if he'd heard Amy right. She wanted Sally to fund their frigging holiday?

Sally obviously couldn't believe it either, because she let out a bark of incredulous laughter. 'Seriously? I've not had a holiday for... I can't even remember when it was. Mum and Dad were both alive, that's for sure. And yet you think I should find money I don't have, so you and your boyfriend can both take a well-deserved rest from the stress of your occasional, part-time jobs?'

He couldn't help it, he chuckled.

Wrong thing to do.

Amy jumped to her feet and glowered through the open doors. 'Shut up. This is none of your business.'

'Amy.' Sally's voice held a sharp edge he'd not heard before.

Slowly, Harry settled the kettle back on the worktop. 'Yeah, you're right.' *Leave it there. You're the lodger with a side benefit of sleeping with the landlady.* Except, damn it, he couldn't. 'Thing is, it feels like my business when I see a couple trying to extort money from a friend.'

'Extort?' Amy glared at him and as for Chris … he looked like he wanted to ask Siri what the word meant.

'That's what you're doing, isn't it? Trying to get money off your sister using unfair means? Because fair would mean she owes you £500, which she doesn't.' He wasn't usually one for getting involved in other people's arguments, but he was on a frigging roll now. 'You know what normal people do when they want to go on holiday? They work overtime. Take on another job.'

Amy flushed and Chris snapped his head round. 'Keep out of this, dude.'

Harry glanced at Sally, who shook her head. Looked like he'd overstepped whatever line she'd set for him. 'I'm just saying my piece while I make myself a drink.'

'It's not that easy to get a job.' This from Amy, the girl with the degree.

'I'll give you one.' The words were out before he'd had a chance to engage his brain. Definitely before he'd reflected on why he felt the need to interfere so much he'd basically agreed to pay for their blasted holiday himself because, God knows, the business couldn't afford any more wages. Nor could it afford anything slowing them down. Mike was going to rip him to shreds.

'But you're, like, a builder.' Amy looked to her sister for confirmation.

'Newsflash, women can be builders, too.' He was safe, he realised. No way was Amy going to commit to hard labour.

Amy glanced at Chris, and Harry's stomach fell. Crap, he'd forgotten about the boyfriend.

'What sort of work are we talking?'

The guy looked like he would snap in two if asked to carry a hod of bricks. 'Depends what we've got on. It'll be hard graft. Getting your hands dirty sort of work. I'll only pay minimum wage but if you put in the hours, it won't take long to earn the £500.'

Chris snorted. 'Yeah, you just want some cheap labour. Not happening, dude.'

Harry swallowed the response that immediately came to mind, *well thank fuck for that*. 'Fine by me.' Then, because he couldn't resist, he added, 'Dude.'

As he turned, he caught Sally's eye. He wasn't an expert on deciphering her looks yet. Was she amused, or did she want to slam the doors to the kitchen shut so he'd butt out of her business?

Deciding he'd make it easier on her, he dumped the teabag in the bin, splashed in the milk and headed back to his room.

'Where does he get off talking to us like that?' Amy demanded as soon as Harry disappeared down the corridor. 'Unless, wait, are you guys sleeping together now?'

Her sex life was not a discussion Sally wanted to get into in front of Chris. 'What difference does it make either way?'

Amy slumped back onto the sofa. 'He probably thinks as he's your boyfriend he can get right up in your business.'

'He's not my boyfriend.' Sally had no clue what Harry was, but she was pretty certain he wasn't that.

'Try telling him that. He seems to think he can be rude to me.'

She hated this. More than anything, Sally wanted to put her arms around her sister. Tell her if the holiday was that important to her, she'd find the extra £500. They'd had some success with the TikTok videos. Plus ... maybe *she* could work for Harry after the cafe closed. But she wouldn't just be funding Amy, and she was damned if she was going to bust a gut or go into the red for Chris. 'Harry has a point though, doesn't he? You could work more hours to earn the money.' She held Amy's gaze. 'You could find a job that isn't just a stopgap until you decide what you want to do. A job that helps put you on a path towards a career you'd enjoy.'

'God, not this again.' Amy jumped to her feet. 'It's like you're trying to take Mum's place, except Mum wouldn't have gone on and on like you do. She'd have sympathised, understood that I don't know what the fuck I want to do. With you it's like I get all the shit parts of having a mum, the nagging, the thinly veiled disappointment, *Oh, Amy you could do so much better*, with none of the benefits.'

Wow, just when she'd thought Amy couldn't hurt her anymore. She felt like she'd been kicked in the stomach. 'I think it's time you left.'

'Yeah, don't worry, it's not like we want to be here anyway.'

We only came to get money from you. That was surely the message Amy was trying to give.

The moment Sally closed the door on them, the tears that had been burning the back of her eyes began to escape. And damn, this was another example of why this thing with Harry was so flaming awkward. She wanted to be with a guy she could cry with, because that's what people did in real relationships, they supported each other, consoled each other.

Weren't afraid to appear vulnerable in front of each other. But her relationship with Harry wasn't that.

Rubbing her face, she walked to her bedroom and shut the door – just in case the monster blubber that was welling could be heard down the hall. Then she dived onto the bed and let go.

After five minutes of crying, she heard a tap on the door.

'Can I come in?'

Oh no, no, no, no. She grabbed a tissue, wiped her eyes, then gave her nose a hefty blow. She did not want him to see her like this. 'I'm tired. I'm just going to go to sleep.'

A beat of silence. 'Right. And we're not going to talk about what just happened?'

She couldn't help it, she let out a sharp laugh. 'This from the guy who doesn't like to talk much?'

'I don't like talking through a fucking door, that's for certain.'

His voice held an edge of frustration, and yes, maybe this was daft, but she had to protect herself. If she let him in, they'd talk, maybe he'd hug her because he was bloody good at that … and then what? She'd feel better, no question, but she'd also feel worse, because he'd have wriggled into her heart that little bit more.

'Fine. If we have to do it this way, so be it.' She heard the sound of shuffling, imagined he was probably sat on the floor now. 'I'm sorry for what Amy's doing, using you as some sort of free bank. It stinks. But if you're expecting an apology for interfering you're not going to get it. You're too soft on her, which I guess is because she's your sister, but it pisses me off to see her treat you like that after everything you've done for her. I'm sorry for not being sorry, if that helps, but that's it.'

She wasn't sure what she was supposed to make of all that. 'Okay.'

'And if she can find that decent, hard-working bit of her that must still be in there as she's related to you, if she can find that and wants to earn the holiday money, give her my number.'

'I... Thank you.' God, her eyes were filling with tears again.

'Right, I've said my piece.' She heard the sound of him getting to his feet. Then a sigh so loud she heard it through the door. 'Goodnight then.'

He sounded disappointed, and that mirrored exactly how she felt. Why was she doing this – putting a wall, or more precisely a door, between them?

Because if you don't keep him at arm's length, don't keep part of yourself back from him, you'll do something stupid like fall in love with him.

'Goodnight.'

She thought he'd gone, but a few seconds later his voice sounded through the door again. 'Oh, and this isn't some sexathon, or whatever it is you think is going on between us. At least not on my side. I fucking love having sex with you, but that's not all I enjoy doing with you.'

She listened to the heavy sound of his size enormous feet as he walked away. And knew it was going to be a long time before she'd be able to sleep.

Chapter Twenty

The following night – Friday – Harry was in his usual haunt, The Cat and Fiddle, with his usual company, Mike and Jack. The last time he'd been here, he'd just had the most incredible afternoon of sex. Tonight, the woman he'd enjoyed that sex with was sitting on the other side of the room.

How had he ballsed up so badly, so quickly?

'You two had a fight, then?'

Funny how Mike, usually about as observant as a bat, was now all over him and Sally. 'Not that I know of.' And that was surely the crux of it. He still didn't know what he'd done. Or if he'd done anything. She'd smiled at him this morning, but not hung around long enough for any conversation. By the time he'd come back from work, she'd already gone out, apparently to the same pub as him.

Yet when he'd gone over to where she was sitting with Vince and Kitty, he'd not been invited to join them. Maybe Kitty had stopped her. Or maybe she'd decided they should stick to flatmates without benefits from now on.

'You're bound to have done something.' Jack grinned. 'You're a bloke, after all. We're always cocking things up.'

And that was probably true. Maybe she was still angry he'd interfered and not apologised for it.

'Or maybe you've not satisfied her.' Jack smirked as he sipped his pint. 'Maybe you're just shite at sex.'

It was a measure of how confused he was, how unbalanced he felt, that he couldn't actually dismiss that possibility as vehemently as he wanted to. 'Maybe we can talk about something else other than my on-off sex life.' He glowered at Jack. 'Like your off-off sex life.'

'We could talk about the next video.' Mike glanced over at Sally. 'Or is that all over now, on account of the fact you're not talking to each other?'

Jesus, were these two always this annoying, or was he just in a bad mood?

'From what I saw of the last one, they don't need to talk. Just, you know, tangle tonsils.' Jack made a leering face that would have given Harry the creeps if he'd not known the guy. 'You're the expert on the girlie films, Mike. What can Casanova here do next that gives him another excuse to get it on with his landlady?'

Annoyance didn't just prick, it bludgeoned him over the head. 'Will you shut up about the damn videos.'

Mike frowned, then drank down the rest of his pint and shoved the empty glass towards Jack. 'Your round, mate.'

Jack grumbled, but shuffled off to the bar. The moment he was out of hearing range, Mike asked the question Harry knew he'd wanted to ask the moment he'd come in and found Harry at the opposite side of the pub to the woman he was supposed to be starting a relationship with.

'Yesterday morning you were like the cat with the cream.

Today it's more like the cat with the sour cream. Or wait, not even cream at all. The cat with the... What do cats find disgusting?'

'How the hell do I know? I'm not a frigging cat.'

But that didn't seem to deter Mike, who clicked his fingers. 'I've got it. The cat with the bowl of broccoli.'

Harry gaped at him. 'What?'

'Everyone knows cats aren't vegetarian.' For a brief moment he entertained the hope that Mike would veer off into a conversation about feline dietary habits, but looked like tonight the man was laser focused. 'What happened between you two?'

Harry sighed and reached for his pint. He was a doer, not a talker, and as for talking about women... He just didn't go there, other than to state the basics. *Isabelle moved in with me. What time is the match on Saturday? Isabelle and I have split up. Did we order enough concrete?* Yet this thing with Sally, he'd never felt so out of his depth before. So in need of guidance, even if it was from a guy whose own track record with women was pretty shaky.

'Her sister came round.' He set the glass back down on the table. 'I think I mucked up, opened my gob when I should have kept quiet.' Yet it had gone wrong before that, he realised, when she'd assumed his asking her to sit next to him on the bed automatically meant he'd wanted sex in the five-minute window before her sister had arrived.

He decided to keep quiet about his rash offer to employ Amy, figuring neither sister would be up for that now.

'Relationships are tricky,' Mike said sagely, nodding like he was some kind of expert on the subject. Though, compared to him, Harry had to concede Mike *was* the expert. He also wasn't afraid to talk about his feelings, which might explain why he was almost disgustingly happy with Trixie. 'Navigating boundaries, agreeing how you want to move forward. It takes effort from both parties, compromise,' Mike continued. 'That's why most fizzle out.'

Harry gave Mike an ironic smile. 'They figure the sex isn't worth it.'

Mike's expression bordered on pity. 'If you and Sally were just about sex, you wouldn't be sat here, staring morosely into your pint and trying to work out how you've cocked up.'

'I know.' But sex was easy. It didn't involve emotions, tangled feelings. It didn't mean getting hurt, which he could take, or hurting Sally, which he absolutely couldn't bear to think about.

Mike stared back at him. 'You and Sally, that's going to be a real bumpy ride, I reckon.'

He decided to be deliberately obtuse. 'Why? She's laidback, even-tempered.'

'Yeah, but she's also a romantic, at least according to Trixie, and you're…' Mike snorted. 'Let's just say when they doled out romance, you weren't at the back of the queue. You didn't even know the queue existed.'

'So? She knows that. We're just having fun.' Except tonight, sitting apart from her, not knowing what was going through her head? That didn't feel fun.

Mike raised an eyebrow. 'Why interfere when it came to her sister, then? Why not just keep out of it?'

'I like her. Of course I'm not going to sit back and watch her get hurt.'

'If you'd kept quiet, you might have got laid last night,' Mike added slyly. 'And not be so cranky today.'

He wanted to laugh that off, probably had done with similar comments in the past. Yet the thought of his mood being down to the fact he'd not had sex, felt … demeaning. Insulting.

It was unnerving to realise he was in unchartered territory, his feelings for Sally unlike any he'd had before. Especially unnerving as he couldn't say what that meant, exactly. He only knew he enjoyed being around her. She was … a puzzle, full of contradictions. Just when he thought he had her sussed, he'd find out something that forced him to re-think. Like the fact he'd initially had her down as a sweet, sappy romantic, yet that was only a small part of her. The way she'd brought up her sister showed true grit. And while she was naïve and sentimental about love, she was also whip smart about other things, like owning her own business and earning money from daft videos. Threading through it all were those blonde curls that made her look cute, but that dynamite body that shrieked sexy as sin.

Furtively he glanced over to her. His pulse gave a little jump as their gazes collided. What was she thinking? Was she confused, like he was? Did she want to end their arrangement, chuck him out of her flat as well as out of her bed?

'You see those girls over by the bar?' Jack interrupted his introspection, sliding three pints in front of them, slopping beer onto the table. 'The tall redhead started to chat me up and asked for my number.' He smirked. 'Reckon she must like the idea of a bit of red on red, if you get my drift.'

Happy to be dragged from his thoughts, Harry picked up his glass. 'You sure she wasn't asking because of your T-shirt?' It stated: *If I wasn't a good electrician I'd be dead by now.*

Jack glanced down and frowned. 'You reckon she only wants me for my electrical skills?' He grinned like a big kid. 'Nah, she felt the spark.' Then he fell about laughing.

No matter how many times she told herself to stop staring at Harry, her eyes wouldn't get the message.

They greedily devoured the sight of him as he laughed with Jack and Mike.

'I thought you were angry with him.'

Guiltily, she dragged her eyes away and onto Kitty. 'Where did you get that idea from?'

'He pushes his way into your private conversation with Amy, insults her then refuses to apologise? I'd be livid.'

'That's because you've decided to always see the worst in him.' Sally glanced back at Harry, half hoping she'd catch him looking at her again. 'If you liked him, you wouldn't think of it as insulting Amy, you'd see it as sticking up for me.'

Vince narrowed his eyes. 'And is that all you feel for him, you like him?'

'Yes.' But she found she couldn't hold her friend's intense gaze.

'So why didn't you ask him to join us when he came over to say hi?' Vince asked mildly.

She could give a hundred excuses; she knew he was meeting Mike and Jack, she saw enough of him at the flat, she wanted to talk to her friends alone. But she'd never lied to Vince and Kitty. 'I'm trying to work out whether I can carry on seeing him.'

'Ooookay.' Vince frowned. 'And just to be clear, by seeing him, you mean sleeping with him, or living with him? Or both?'

'Oh no, I can't kick him out.' The thought of doing that … of not seeing his boots next to the door, his mugs in the dishwasher. Not verbally sparring with him.

Vince started to laugh. 'The look on your face. It's like I suggested you put a puppy in a cardboard box and dump it on the seafront in a force ten gale.'

'Maybe that's what you should do with Harry,' Kitty muttered. 'What?' she exclaimed when Sally frowned at her. 'You know this fling with him is going to end badly, and it won't be him left with the broken heart.'

Sally couldn't even disagree. 'You're right, of course you are. If I carry on sleeping with him, I'm going to fall. Like really hard.' She sipped her pink gin and tonic, her stomach fluttering as seemed to be the habit now whenever she thought of him. 'He's ... nicer than I reckoned he'd be. I knew he was hot but ... did I tell you he cuddles when we watch TV together? And that he keeps these tea bags just for his mum, even though she's pretty horrid to him from what I can see? Or that his ex is really taking the piss, still living in his house, but he takes it in his stride? He's angry, sure, but there's no real heat. And he's sarcastic, yes, but he's also really funny. Has me in stitches sometimes.' When she looked up, she found both her friends staring at her. 'What?'

'I think it's too late.' Vince's face was full of sympathy.

'Too late for what?'

Kitty sighed. 'Too late to worry about falling for him. You've gone and done it.'

'No, I haven't.' She snuck another look at Harry. Heard her heart thump loudly in her chest. 'It's only been five days.'

'You've lived with him for over three months,' Vince pointed out. He must have seen the fear cross her face because he reached across the table and squeezed her hand. 'Hey, come on, this doesn't have to be the tragedy you and Kitty seem to think. There's a whole range of stuff that could happen instead; you realise he's actually as bad as Kitty thinks he is so you dump his rather fine arse. You get bored of his sarcasm so you dump his arse. You fall for him a bit but then The One comes along so, guess what, you dump Hazza's arse. And, hey, maybe none of that happens and you both fall for each other. What rule says there can't be a happy ending?'

'Er, did you miss the part where I told you he doesn't believe in love, thinks happy endings are some fantasy manufactured by Disney and Hallmark? Or if that's not enough for you, how about the part that he's only looking for fun, sex and a roof over his head until he gets Isabelle to leave. Or hey, maybe until he decides he wants to get back with her.'

Vince screwed up his face. 'Okay, I admit there are a few potential hurdles there.'

Kitty snorted. 'A few?'

'Then again,' Vince countered. 'If he'd wanted to go back to his ex, he'd have done it by now. And as for not believing in love, guys have been known to change their minds, you know. The other Harry did, the one in *When Harry Met Sally*, and there must be a tonne of other examples.'

There were. Again, Sally looked over to her Harry. The one who was cynical and unromantic, his own words, yet had sat on the floor outside her room last night and empathised with her over Amy. No, more than that, he'd *hurt* for her over Amy. Then gone on to say he wanted to do more with her than have sex. Even though he apparently really enjoyed that.

'You shouldn't encourage her.' At the sound of Kitty's voice, Sally turned to see her friend giving Vince a death stare.

'Hey, I am here, you know.' She smiled at Kitty to take the edge off her words. 'I appreciate you're only looking out for me, but maybe Vince is right. I am sort of rushing to the ending even though I've only just started the film.' Maybe she should watch *Brokeback Mountain*. Maybe Harry was right and the middle was more important than the ending.

'Speaking of films.' Vince glanced over her shoulder. 'Looks like the would-be hero of yours is on his way over.'

Her heart did a little jig as she watched Harry stride over to their table, looking casual but hot in black jeans and a red Henley shirt.

'Hey.' The word came out scratchy, her throat suddenly too dry. Turns out having an adult crush was just as tortuous as a teenage one.

He smiled, eyes crinkling sexily at the corners. 'Let me know when you're ready to leave. I'll walk back with you.'

Before she had a chance to reply, Kitty snorted. 'That kind of assumes she wants to leave with you. She might not.'

Harry gave her friend a mild look. 'Point taken.' Then he turned back to Sally and bent in a dramatic bow. 'Would you allow me to escort you to your flat?'

Sally bit down on a smile. 'Yes, I will. Thank you, kind sir.'

With a final nod to her, he turned and strode back to his table.

'Well,' Vince said into the silence. 'Seems the lodger is a gentleman after all.'

Kitty's eyes narrowed as she watched Harry. 'Maybe.'

As Kitty and Vince argued in the background, Sally stared at Harry's retreating figure. Gait loose-limbed, his shoulders straight and broad, he wasn't cocky, not like Kitty thought. In fact, for a man who looked as good as he did, with and without his clothes, he had surprisingly little swagger. His whole demeanour was understated, not flashy. Just an ordinary, gorgeous-looking bloke with a really attractive, down-to-earth confidence. *This is me, like it or lump it.*

And, for better or worse, she really, really liked it.

Chapter Twenty-One

A s he waited outside the pub for Sally, Harry watched her say goodbye to her friends and wondered, for the umpteenth time, what Kitty had against him. He knew he wasn't everyone's cup of tea – sarcastic, blunt, stubborn, hard-headed were just some of the adjectives hurled at him by people who didn't appreciate his way of thinking. Still, he'd never had anyone dislike him so much, at least not someone he'd not slept with.

He could see why Vince and Sally were such good friends. Both had a warm, easy-going nature that made people want to talk to them. If he was going to go with animal analogies, Sally and Vince were Labradors, Kitty a cross between a chihuahua and a pit bull.

'Ready?'

He shook himself out of his canine musings to find Sally giving him a hesitant smile.

Normally, he'd reach to hold the hand of his date, but after yesterday he wasn't sure where he stood so he kept his hands in his pockets as they started walking.

'Did you have a good evening?'

He halted, shook his head. 'Are we really doing polite chit-chat?'

He had a second to see hurt flash in her eyes before she glanced away. 'We don't have to talk.'

'You've got me wrong. I *want* to talk, but about important stuff. Like, are you angry with me?'

Her eyes widened. 'No, of course not.'

'Okay.' He didn't realise how much it had mattered, until now. 'So why didn't you open the door to me last night?'

Again, her eyes wouldn't meet his. 'I didn't want you to see me like that.'

'You didn't want me to see you crying? Why the hell not?' When she didn't reply, just bit into her bottom lip, he pushed. 'Your other boyfriends didn't see you cry?'

'Of course they did, but that's not what we're doing here, is it?'

He exhaled sharply, suddenly aware that he *was* the problem, just not in the way he'd thought. She wasn't upset with him for interfering. She was upset by the boundaries he'd set.

'Harry?'

'I don't know.'

She blinked up at him. 'What do you mean?'

Frustrated with himself, he jammed a hand through his hair. How could he articulate what he didn't understand? 'I mean I don't know what we're doing.' He drew in a breath, tried to get some handle on emotions that were spiralling out of control. 'I only know I don't like it when you shut me out. If I see you're upset, I'll want to help. I'll want to console you.'

She nodded but didn't reply. Instead she looked down at the pavement and he found he was holding his breath, waiting to see whether he'd said enough to persuade her not to give up on him just yet. Finally, she caught his eye, a small smile on her face. 'You want to see me with red eyes and a puffy face?'

He barked out a laugh as relief flowed through him. 'If that's what happens when you cry, then yes.'

'Okay then.'

A shiver ran through her and it was only then he realised they were standing on the prom on a cold November evening. And her jacket was made for fashion, not a gusty Brighton seafront. Shrugging off his own heavy-duty parka, he draped it round her shoulders. 'Before you say anything, this isn't some big gentlemanly gesture.' She nodded, but he could see she was fighting not to smile. 'I don't want to see you cold, that's all. I should have had this talk back at the flat.'

'But then you'd have lost the opportunity to be my romantic hero.'

Mischief lit up her eyes and he gave up trying to warn her he wasn't romantic hero material. She had to know that by now. Instead he threw his arm around her as they walked back, feeling the tension between them ease. The moon glinted off the sea and as they talked about their days, about little things that had made them laugh, his balance returned.

As they were about to cross the road, she whispered, 'Wait a second.'

He watched as she hurried over to a scruffy-looking guy sat on the seawall. His bearded, craggy features brightened when he saw her and they shared a few words before she dug into her purse and slipped him a note.

Damn if his heart didn't do some sort of acrobatic leap in his chest. This woman was way, way too good for him. Of course she'd realised it already. Hence her belief she wasn't going to fall in love with him. And though that was what he wanted, the knowledge left him feeling strangely flat as he opened the door to her place.

'Are we okay?' he asked as she handed him back his coat. He had the sense she was still holding back on something. 'What did Vince and Kitty have to say? I assume you were talking about us, the way Kitty kept scowling over at me.'

He received the first real smile he'd had all evening. 'She thinks I should put you in a box and dump you on the seafront.'

And yeah, that was probably true. 'She's not my biggest fan.' He gave her a wary look. 'Are you considering that?' It was sobering, realising how precarious this all was. He could lose not just her, and her friendship, but also the roof over his head. And sure, he wouldn't be entirely homeless, not like the poor guy she'd just given money too, but his house was currently occupied by his ex.

Then again, was he lying to himself that Isabelle was the reason he didn't want to go back?

'You think I can find a box big enough for you?' Sally asked, oblivious to his internal meltdown.

'That's the only thing stopping you? The size of the box?'

'Well, there is the fact that even if I found a box, I couldn't carry you.'

'Both good reasons not to kick me out.' He swallowed, unexpected nerves squirming in his stomach as she gave him a long, contemplative study.

'Last night, you said sex wasn't the only thing you enjoyed doing with me.'

'I meant it.' He felt helpless in the face of these muddled thoughts. Before, he'd always known what he was doing in a relationship. First, set the boundaries. Then enjoy, until the enjoyment stopped. But this felt different, and it wasn't just that Sally was different to anyone he'd dated before. He felt different. 'I'm not saying—'

'I know. You're not about to go and fall in love with me.'

The blunt statement settled over him like a dark, angry cloud. He wanted to be the man who could fall in love with her, the man she wanted him to be. 'I'm sorry.'

'No need to be. You've been clear from the start.'

Damn it, why was this so hard? She knew he wasn't right for her, he knew he wasn't right for her. 'If it helps, if I was to fall for anyone, I think I'd fall for you.'

She bit into her lip, eyes welling. 'Thank you. And if I was daft enough to fall for a cynical, unromantic type, I think I'd fall for you.'

He forced a smile, still feeling off kilter. 'So where does this leave us?' He glanced around. 'Assuming you don't have a large cardboard box hidden away.'

She glanced over his shoulder for a beat. Then seemed to come to a decision, her gorgeous blue eyes locking onto his. 'I think it leaves us enjoying the time we have together.' His heart decided to thump loudly as she held out her hand. 'Take me to bed, you big stud, or lose me for ever.'

What? But then the penny dropped. 'Hey, that's from *Top Gun*.'

She smiled. 'See, we do have some film tastes in common.'

He liked that thought, yet as he walked with her towards her bedroom, it was the previous words that weighed heavily on his mind. *It leaves us enjoying the time we have.* Because that time was finite.

Sally had taken some solace from the conflict she'd seen in Harry's eyes as he'd told her if – big, sad *if* – he was to fall for anyone, he thought it could be her. Still, she couldn't find the strength to step away from this now.

Instead she'd put her faith in love, and the belief that she would find her person. Perhaps, as Vince said, the end wasn't already written and there was a chance it would be Harry. And if it wasn't, if she'd not yet met the man she was destined for, then what was the harm in enjoying a fling with a good man she had a laugh with and who she really liked?

It was why she'd taken his hand last night. And why, when she'd woken up next to him this morning, his arms around her, she'd decided to be grateful, not fearful.

And that gratitude ratcheted up a notch as she took in the sight of him walking out of her en suite with only a towel around his waist.

Dragging her eyes from his chest, she remembered what she'd meant to tell him last night. 'Don't get too excited, it's not mega money, but we've gained another sponsor for a video.'

He paused, raised his eyebrows. 'Who?'

'You know I can read what you're not saying, just from looking at your expression.' She met the challenge in his eyes and lowered her voice to mimic his. 'Why on earth would any sane company want to sponsor a dumb romcom remake?'

He let out a soft chuckle. 'Busted, but don't let my surprise take away from the fact I'm also seriously in awe of your ability to wheedle money out of them. Now answer the question.'

She named a coffee brand. 'We use that brand at the cafe so I figured why not ask them if they want us to do a product placement in a future video? It'll be good business for the cafe as well. To be honest, I'm bummed I didn't ask them when we did that scene from *When Harry Met Sally*.'

'You mean when you fake orgasmed.'

'I do.' She shook her head at him. 'Look at you, you're like a schoolboy saying a rude word.'

His grin turned to a smirk. 'I'm not grinning at the word, I'm grinning at the memory.'

She felt a blush creep across her face and briefly buried her head in her hands. 'The belly ache, according to Hilda. God, I was so bad.'

Suddenly he was in front of her, the taut muscles of his still damp chest, glistening. She'd kissed all that sexy flesh only ten minutes ago, yet still her belly flipped.

With a smile that settled deep into his eyes, he kissed her gently on the lips. 'Fake you was funny yet a surprising turn-on. Real you is the sexiest sound I've ever heard.'

Her insides turned to goo. His compliments might not be traditional, but they packed a punch. 'Thanks, but I'm not sure the TikTok world is ready for real me.'

His eyes narrowed, turning from shimmering silver to warship grey. 'Only I get to hear real you.'

'Yes.' There was something intensely gratifying about his tone. 'While we're together.' As the words echoed ominously back to her, a lump formed in her throat. 'That sounds...' Awful. Unbearably sad.

His expression tightened, his exhale heavy. 'I know.'

'So anyway, back to the coffee.' She forced a smile. 'We'll have to re-think the next video as I'm not sure we can do the *Bridget Jones* pants thing in the cafe. We'll give Hilary and Mildred a heart attack.'

His eyes scanned her face and he seemed to come to a decision. 'I definitely want to see you in – and more importantly then out of – big pants, but leave the cafe thing with me. I've got an idea.'

She stared back at him, taking her own inventory. The square jaw, the cheekbones women would die for. Ditto the dark lashes that framed what she considered his best feature. Those striking grey eyes. His wasn't a poker face, his eyes were a mirror to how he was feeling. And right now they were… 'You've got squirrelly eyes.'

His eyebrows flew upwards. 'Sorry? Squirrels have beady brown eyes. Mine are grey and non-beady.'

'I mean you've got a squirrelly look, as if you're hiding something.'

He glanced down at his towel. 'Like my nuts?'

She had to fight not to laugh. 'Yes, like your squirrel nuts.'

'Hey.' Now he looked affronted. 'I've not looked closely, but I suspect squirrels have tiny brown nuts. Mine are—' He groaned as she cupped him. 'Oh yeah, I'm not hiding my nuts from you. Feel free to play with them anytime.'

He thrust into her hand, his expression playful yet with an edge of arousal that sent her own blood heating. But she had work to get to, so she gave him a final squeeze before regretfully stepping away. 'Much as I'd love to play, my Saturday morning regulars aren't going to be happy if I open up late.'

He sighed, but then pressed a kiss to the tip of her nose. 'Don't worry. Me and my nuts will be here when you get home.'

Home. It sounded so domesticated, yet though this was her home, he'd soon be moving back to his… *Stop it*. She smiled brightly. 'That's good to know. So what are you up to today?'

His face took on a pained expression. 'Going to see my parents.'

'You're not expecting it to be fun.'

He gave a small shake of his head. 'Fun is not a word I'd ever use to describe either of them.'

It was so different to her own experience, she found it hard to comprehend. 'They must have been when you were growing up?'

He just smiled, a small, sad curve of his lips that didn't reach his eyes. He looked for all the world a big, strapping, confident male, yet here was another hint to the life he might have had as a boy. It tugged at her heart.

'What's the quietest time for you today?' he asked, clearly wanting to move the subject on.

'Thinking of coming to see me?'

His smile was back to playful. 'Maybe.'

'From around four onwards. You should remember,' she teased. 'That's when we gave Hilda and Mildred a treat.'

'Oh, I remember.' He winked at her. 'Maybe today we'll give them another one.'

As she watched him walk out, the towel pulled tight across a mesmerising pair of round, firm buttocks, her heart gave a long, slow flip. Suddenly she couldn't wait to open up the cafe.

Chapter Twenty-Two

Harry felt his left leg bounce up and down, something that hadn't happened since he'd been an eighteen-year-old. It wasn't nerves, it was mounting frustration, bordering on anger, that couldn't have an outlet. As an adult, he'd learned not to keep a lid on his feelings. If he was annoyed, he let it show. As a kid, growing up in this house, he'd had to bottle things up because nobody was interested in hearing how he felt.

But he wasn't that kid anymore. Nor that eighteen-year-old who'd finally got up the guts to tell his parents he didn't want to go to university. He wanted to become a builder.

'Will the pair of you shut up.'

His mum's eyes widened with horror.

'Don't speak to us like that.' His dad's voice was tight with anger.

'I'll be polite if you are, which means talking to each other, not over each other.' The leg quieter now he'd had his outburst, he glanced between them. Sat on either side of the kitchen table, they were like a pair of marble statues: cold, detached, selfish. Fleetingly, he wondered what Sally would make of them. She'd already met his mum and he knew she hadn't been impressed. Their personalities couldn't be more different. One radiated warmth, empathy, joy. Had selflessly gone to work at eighteen so she could bring up her sister and now lived in a bubble filled with friends, love and happy ever afters. The other viewed life through a clinical eye, unable to love, to form any sort of relationship except with a man as detached and selfish as she was. Unease wormed through him. Had he just described *himself*?

'I'm done being the mediator here.' He thrust a business card onto the table. 'This woman runs a mediation service. They're professionals, trained to sit down with couples who are splitting up and work a way through it.'

His dad let out a dismissive sound. 'And I bet they charge a ruddy fortune for it.'

'They're cheaper than lawyers. I've spoken to them and they can meet up with you next week. The only other alternative is you sort it out yourselves, which clearly isn't working.'

'So that's it?' His mum looked astonished, as if she really couldn't understand why he didn't want to be dragged into their constant battles. 'Our son palms us off to some strangers after all we've done for him?'

The damn leg started bouncing again and he jumped to his feet. 'I'm going before I say something I regret.' He nodded down at the card. 'Give them a call.' *And leave me the hell alone.* Words he'd never say, because at the end of the day they were his parents. They'd ticked all the boxes when it came to how to bring up your child: a stable home, tick, healthy food, tick. The best schools, tick. He couldn't complain, he knew plenty of people who'd had it far worse. Again, he thought of Sally. Or people who'd had it far better, yet then had it cruelly snatched away from them.

She was on his mind as he climbed into his truck and set off to his next duty call. His own home.

His heart lifted a little as he pulled up outside the Victorian terrace in the North Laine. Yeah, she was a beauty alright. A dump when he'd bought her, sadly neglected for sixty years, he'd transformed the three-bed house into something he was truly proud of. He'd kept the period features; the fireplaces, the bow window, but now she boasted two modern bathrooms and a snazzy kitchen leading out to a small patio garden that was still work in progress.

He wanted to live in her again, no question. But … when he pictured himself there, he wasn't alone. Sally was curled up next to him on the sofa. Or sitting on a lounger in the garden, sunglasses hiding those big blue eyes as they soaked up the evening sun. She was there, too, in the huge oak bed he'd temporarily moved into her flat, wearing her cute pink pyjamas that shouldn't be sexy, but somehow were. Reading a passage to him from her latest romance book because it had touched her so much she just had to share it. Even though she knew he'd just roll his eyes.

A nervous ripple ran through him. He'd never had a vision of a future with someone before. When he'd been working on the house, he'd only ever seen it as *his* home. Sometimes he'd imagined a dog by his side – a black lab. Never a woman.

What, if anything, did it mean?

Brushing the thoughts aside for another day, he jumped down from the truck and rang the bell. Yep, he was the sad git ringing the bell on his own house.

Isabelle answered, hair glossy and straight, her slim frame

dressed in skinny jeans and a soft blue cashmere jumper. No baggy jumper and leggings for Isabelle on her day off.

'Come on in.' He raised an ironic eyebrow and she had the grace to look awkward. 'Sorry, force of habit. Do you want a drink?'

'I'm not stopping. Just wanted to find out your timeline for moving out.'

She stared up at him. 'You didn't reply to my message.'

He cast his mind back, remembered something about the last video and him sleeping with Sally. 'Didn't think it deserved one.'

'That's it? You're just going to sleep with other women now?'

'What I do is not your concern, hasn't been for several months.' He fought to keep his voice even. 'You need to get it into your head that I want you out of this house. Right now you're squatting, and if you don't start paying me rent, I'm going to begin legal proceedings.'

Her mouth tightened, and a flicker of worry crossed her face. 'Wow, you've turned really cold.'

He stilled, dragged in a breath. Had he? Was this who he'd become? He'd lived with this woman, shared a year of his life with her and now he was threatening her with lawyers?

An image of his parents flashed through his head. Damn it, maybe he *was* a chip off the old block. Feeling suddenly nauseous, he stepped away from the doorway. 'Please, just find somewhere else to live so I can have my house back.' *My life back. The one where I knew who I was.* But that life didn't have Sally in it.

Isabelle searched his face and whatever she saw there made her draw in a breath. 'This is it, isn't it? We're really over?'

'We are.'

Sadness settled in her eyes and he felt a dart of the affection he'd once had for her.

Feeling melancholy, he climbed back into the truck and pulled out his phone. One final thing on his list of crap things he had to do today. Dialling the number he'd got from Sally, he waited for Kitty to answer.

'Hi, it's Harry.'

There was a long pause. 'Well, well. If it isn't the toolbox-wielding TikTok hero.'

The woman made porcupines look cuddly. 'What is your problem with me?'

Another pause, even longer this time. 'I don't have an issue with you, per se. I just think you'll hurt my friend. Sally's got a soft heart, she falls too easily. She needs protecting from people who don't know how to cherish her. People like you.'

His stomach clenched, anger vying with guilt that maybe she was right. 'For someone who's supposed to love her, you don't understand her very well. She's strong, tough. Not some hothouse flower who needs your protection.'

'Says the man who thinks he knows her because he's having sex with her.'

He shut his eyes, swallowed the sharp retort on his tongue. No good would come of trading insults. 'I'm phoning to ask a favour. And before you cut me off, this is for Sally, for the next TikTok video.'

His thoughts were muddled as he finally let himself back into the flat. Five months ago his life had felt stable, the ground solid beneath his feet. Isabelle and he had rubbed along fine. Living with her had been comfortable, their relationship founded on good sex, mutual like and an understanding that what they had wasn't permanent. Then he'd caught her with her boss and things had become messy for a few months but his ego had recovered, his anger dimmed and he'd started to enjoy living with a different woman, under a different roof. Solid ground again.

But then he'd had sex with Sally, and now the ground kept shifting; one minute a bit of fun until he had his house back, the next he was imagining her in his house. One minute a casual relationship based mainly on sex, the next he was bulldozing into her relationship with her sister like an over-protective boyfriend, unhinged by yo-yoing feelings he didn't understand. And wishing he was someone else. Not cynical, like his parents, but open to possibilities, trusting. Someone more like her.

Now he was about to put a suit on for her, he thought wryly as he dragged the thing out of his wardrobe. He could tell himself that what he had planned was purely for the sake of their TikTok venture, but was it really? Hadn't he decided to do this because on one level, he *wanted* to?

The door to the cafe opened, and Sally whipped her head round to see who'd come in.

Beside her, Vince laughed softly.

'Shut up.'

He mimed zipping his mouth, but his eyes were highly amused.

'I just want to know what he has planned, that's all.'

'Of course.' Vince inclined his head with exaggerated solemnity. 'You're not excited about the prospect of you and Hazza having your very own romantic moment in the slightest.'

She scoffed. 'We both know him well enough to know he's not romantic.'

'Oh, I would hardly put my knowledge of him on the same footing as yours.'

She elbowed him, causing Vince to yelp, but before she could give him a more eloquent repost, the door opened again.

'Umm, something tells me Kitty isn't quite the visitor you were hoping for,' Vince murmured as he went to refill Hilda and Mildred's mugs.

Kitty gave her a little wave, but weirdly she didn't come up to see her. Just stepped inside and took out her phone.

A few beats later, the door opened again. The sight that greeted her made the bottom fall out of her stomach. And the spoons she was carrying drop from her hand onto the floor.

'Holy crap.'

The tall, dark-haired stranger in the immaculate charcoal suit quirked his lips in a familiar manner, then began to stride purposefully towards her, those beautiful grey eyes fixed on hers.

'Oh boy.'

Vince's jaw dropped as, like her, he watched Harry's long legs propel him past the tables and up to where she stood, heart pounding, behind the counter.

'Er, hi.' Butterflies swarmed like crazy in her stomach. 'Nice suit.'

He grinned, and maybe it was the freshly shaved face, the crisp white shirt or jazzy turquoise tie, but the sight sent the butterflies swooping. 'Figured it was more appropriate than my work uniform of jeans and tool belt.'

'More appropriate for what?'

'This.' He bent his head and kissed her. In her cafe, with people watching, he kissed her, drew back, smiled. Then kissed her again, his lips warm and soft against hers, teasing with light nips, yet with a sensual undertone that turned her insides to liquid.

A giddy moment later, his arms wrapped around her and he lifted her up, her feet dangling as he turned them round and round, adding to the dizziness she was already feeling.

Then his right arm curled under her thighs and suddenly she was hoisted into his arms. Automatically she threw her own arms around his neck, breathing him in, her fingers curling into the soft hair at the nape of his neck.

'Your cafe's too small,' he murmured, feathering her another kiss. 'Gere's character had way more room to make his entrance.'

She laughed against the hollow of his neck, feeling totally undone. An untethered balloon floating freely, bouncing joyfully in the breeze. 'Are you seriously doing the final scene of *An Officer and a Gentleman*?'

'If you have to ask, I'm doing a shite job of it.'

He turned and it was only then she realised Kitty was videoing them. And Hilda and Mildred were gawping like a pair of love-struck teenagers.

'Are you going to carry her out, dear?' Hilda asked.

He winked. This blunt, no-frills builder actually bloody winked at the seventy-five-year old. 'That's the plan.'

'Way to go, Sally.' Vince, who could recite every detail of the scene if asked, started to clap, a broad grin on his face.

The other customers joined in – Mildred and Hilda, a family in the window table. Two ladies, hearts in their eyes, who couldn't take their eyes off Harry.

'Oh my, that strapping young man is going to whisk you off your feet.'

At Mildred's words, Sally drew in a shaky breath.

It was quite probable that he would.

There were no bells, she reassured herself, yet she had to question that hypothesis now. Love surely wasn't about what she heard, or saw, but what she felt. And right now that strange sensation in her chest? It felt like a gloved hand had taken hold of her heart and was gently squeezing, making it harder and harder to breathe.

'This is crazy,' she whispered as he carried her towards the exit to the sound of applause.

'Damn it,' he mumbled. 'I forgot the hat.'

She kissed his neck, the skin warm with a zesty tang. 'You're forgiven.'

'Gere didn't have a door to negotiate either.'

Somehow he managed to open it without dropping her.

'You can let me down wherever you want.' But her arms tightened around his neck, impossibly touched by what he'd just done. By *him*.

He laughed, looking out at the sea. 'If it was summer, I might be tempted.'

She followed the direction of his gaze and screwed up her face. 'You'd drop me into the sea?'

'Maybe?' His expression softened, a mix of humour and fondness that sent a flood of warmth into her chest. 'Thing is, I'm not an officer or a gentleman.'

She didn't like the hint of regret in his voice. Clasping a hand to his face, she drank in his gorgeous features. 'Who cares? You can really rock a suit.'

He huffed out a laugh and for a few humming seconds they stared into each other's eyes. It had to be the romance of what they'd just done – please God it was – but that hand seemed to tighten around her heart.

'I've stopped the video. You can let her down now.'

Kitty's voice crashed into the moment and Harry let out a deep sigh, his chest shifting up and down. Then he slid her slowly to the ground.

Maybe she should be grateful to her friend for the timely reminder that this was an act, but she wished Kitty had waited a little longer before butting in.

'I've sent it to you.' Kitty was clearly determined to break whatever mood she thought she'd interrupted. 'Harry told me this was being sponsored, so in one part I focused in on the logo of the coffee company.'

Was that a deliberate reminder that this was all about money? 'Thanks.'

Harry looked annoyed, but she didn't know if that was for the same reason she was, or if it was just his usual default when Kitty was around.

Tension swirled between them, Kitty clearly waiting for Harry to leave, Harry standing his ground.

'Thanks for doing this.' Wanting to feel that connection again, Sally reached for his hand. 'I loved it.'

'Let's hope your followers do.' Kitty was obviously not going to give up on her quest to bring Sally back down to earth.

Harry stared at Kitty, and it seemed to Sally that he was trying to compel her friend back inside using the power of his mind, or at the very least make her feel awkward enough that she'd leave them alone. But Kitty was stubborn as heck and she stared back at him. In the end Harry shook his head, a wry smile on his face. 'Fine, I don't mind an audience.'

Turning to Sally, he gently tilted her head up to his. Then he kissed her, at first teasing, his tongue darting, his lips a soft, sensual press against hers. But then he deepened the kiss, tongue tasting her, hands sliding down her shoulders and round to her back, drawing her closer. Soon Sally forgot Kitty was watching, forgot the customers who might be gawping through the window. She felt her body go boneless against his, her own hands disappearing under his jacket, feeling the heat of him, the strength beneath the thin layer of cotton shirt.

When he finally drew back, he rested his forehead against hers. 'See you back at the flat.'

The husk in his voice, the heat in his eyes. It wasn't a question, it was a promise.

'He's going to break your fucking heart,' Kitty stated, her expression sombre as her gaze followed Harry's retreating figure.

'Maybe.' But in that moment it didn't seem important. Not nearly as important as closing up and getting back to that promise as fast as humanly possible.

***

Later that night – much, much later – she gave the video a quick edit and uploaded it onto TikTok with the caption:

Not an Officer, maybe a Gentleman? Can definitely rock a suit.

Chapter Twenty-Three

The groundwork to the new extension had been completed and the buildings inspector had approved the foundations. Next up was sorting the wiring and laying the bricks up to the damp course.

For big jobs they got a brickie in, but Mike and Harry figured they could manage on this one. He liked laying bricks. Sure, it was monotonous, but there was something therapeutic about the process of layering brick on top of brick, seeing the wall grow.

Mike shouted over at him. 'Your turn.'

Lugging the bricks from the front drive to where they needed them wasn't a part of the process he enjoyed. Still, it gave him a workout. Kept the muscles toned that Sally seemed to like running her hands over.

'Oi, dreamboat, get your head out of the clouds.'

Harry lurched guiltily to his feet and tossed Mike a dirty look. He supposed he'd been called far worse. Much as he enjoyed filming the TikTok videos, swanning into the cafe, lifting Sally off her feet, kissing her before carrying her out like some sort of screen hero? He couldn't deny he'd got a buzz from *that* particular scene. He also didn't mind reading all the speculation about his and Sally's relationship, even though everyone and his dog seemed to have a view on whether they were an item or not. Let them wonder. What made him cringe though, was the stuff about him being a hunk, dreamboat, hottie, stud. Embarrassing enough to read. Annoying as fuck to have his mates call him that. Which of course was why they insisted on doing it.

'Hey, beefcake, hurry it along.' Jack started to chuckle.

Before Harry could think of a suitably crushing response, his phone started to ring. When he saw who it was, all the irritation seeped out of him. Marching out of earshot, he pressed answer.

'Hello, hot cafe owner.'

Sally laughed. 'Thanks, but we both know that was one of the kinder comments.'

'Jealousy, pure and simple. Besides, you're a hot cafe owner in my eyes.' It had upset him to see a few spiteful remarks on Sally's weight, and how hard it must have been for him to lift her. He'd been ready to fire off a cutting reply, but she'd stopped him, saying it was all part of putting the videos out there.

'Thank you.' He heard the smile in her voice as she added, 'Especially nice to hear coming from, what was the most popular comment? Ah yes, "every girl's fantasy".'

'It was the suit.' Bought to impress would-be clients, he'd spent a small fortune on it at the time, but it had repaid him many times over. Apparently a builder in a suit said 'professional'. Odd, because to him it said 'slick bastard who charges too much'.

'It wasn't the suit people were talking about in the

comments,' she countered dryly. 'In fact, you've been really good for business. So many customers have come in the last few days wanting to meet the man who swept me off my feet.'

He was genuinely thrilled all this nonsense was helping the cafe. 'Maybe I should drop in and try it again.'

'Maybe you should.' She gave a little cough, like she was clearing her throat. 'The sponsor was impressed with all the views the video had.'

'That's good to know, but I'm more interested in impressing the hot cafe owner.'

There was a pause, and he hated that he couldn't see her face. 'You definitely impressed her.'

'Good.' When had what she thought become so important? He didn't know, only that it now governed so much of what he did. Would Sally enjoy this? Would it make Sally laugh? If he did x, y or z, would Sally be pleased / disappointed?

'Speaking of impressed, that leads me smoothly onto what I'm phoning about. You must have made an impression on Amy because she wants to talk to you.'

'Is that a *keep away from my sister* conversation. Or a *stop putting your oar into my business* one?' His stomach knotted as he realised there was a third *give me my fucking room back* option.

'I think she wants to know more about what she'd have to do if she worked for you.' While he registered the shock of that, Sally quickly added, 'Don't feel you have to give her a job. I know you only said it to make her realise she can't just expect handouts, she needs to work. If anyone is giving her a job it should be me.'

He thought he knew the answer, but asked it anyway. 'Has she worked for you before?'

'No.' A sigh, and again he wanted to see her face. To kiss

away the small frown he knew had formed between her eyes. 'I've offered, of course, but she never wanted to. Always said serving people coffee all day was lame.'

'And serving alcohol isn't?' He thought both jobs were tough and involved far more interpersonal skills than he possessed, but it was hard to see how Amy could argue against the first while doing the second.

'Her sister works in a cafe, not a bar,' Sally replied, her voice quieter.

The more he heard about Amy, the more he wanted to shake her. 'I'm happy to talk to her but be warned, my diplomacy skills are non-existent.'

Sally let out a soft laugh. 'I'm well aware. Then again, mine haven't worked so I don't think you can do any further damage.'

'Let's hope not.' He glanced over to where Mike and Jack were making no attempt to hide the fact they were trying to listen in. 'Tweedledum and Tweedledee are watching so I'll hang up now. See you at home.'

After he ended the call Jack clutched dramatically at his chest. 'Aw, Mikey, how cute is that? Loverboy is calling it home now.'

Mike roared with laughter. 'Do you think they have matching slippers by the bed? His and hers dressing gowns hanging up in the bathroom?'

Ignoring them, because a) it pissed them off if he didn't take the bait, and b) the fact that he'd called it home again was not something he wanted to dwell on, he punched the number Sally had given him into his phone.

'Amy, it's Harry. Hear you want to talk about earning some money.'

'Maybe.'

He didn't have time for games. 'If you want to discuss it further, meet me here in half an hour.' He rattled off the address they were working at, then ended the call before looking uneasily at Mike and Jack. Mike was going to question his sanity, especially as he'd have to deduct Amy's wages from his own earnings because no way was he putting that on his partner. He'd definitely have to get Isabelle to pay him rent now. As for Jack, he was going to drive him to insanity when he realised what Harry was prepared to do to help Sally out.

Half an hour later, and surprisingly on time, Amy appeared on the front drive as Harry was heaving another load of bricks into the wheelbarrow.

He eyed her white Converse trainers, designer ripped jeans and soft pink hoodie. 'You realise this is a building site?'

'You said come to discuss, not to work.' She shoved her hands into the front pocket of her hoodie.

'Fair enough, but you get dirt on your clothes, it's on you, not me.'

'Fine. Say what you've got to say and I'll go.' She shuffled her feet. 'It's not like I want to be here.'

'I *want* to be watching football and drinking beer but work is what happens when you grow up.'

He received a full-on glare from eyes as big and blue as her sister's though they lacked Sally's sparkle. 'I don't like you.'

Standing to his full height, he crossed his arms and looked down on her. 'Funny, I think I could probably like you. You're Sally's sister, and I like her a lot. You must have some of her genes. But I don't like the way you treat her. You're acting like a spoilt brat to a woman who's given up one hell of a lot to take care of you.' As red spots formed on Amy's cheeks, he zeroed in on her gaze. 'You lost your parents way too young, and that's a shit deal. It's made you angry with the world and I get it. But you weren't the only one who lost them. Sally did, too, only she didn't get the luxury of wallowing in grief and self-pity. She was four years younger than you are now when she opened the çafe so you could move back here where your friends were.'

'Her friends were here too.'

'That's all you took from my big speech?' He wasn't sure whether to be angry at her for being so clueless, or at himself for failing to get her to understand. 'If you want to earn your holiday money you need to turn up on time, do what we say and pull your weight. I can't afford to pay you for more than three weeks. That work for you?'

'Depends.' She stared back at him. 'What if I don't like it?'

'Then you leave and find some other sucker willing to give you a job. Or don't go on holiday.'

She sighed, kicked at the ground. 'Fine.'

'Come on then, I'll show you around.'

She looked down at her trainers. 'Can't you talk about it here?'

What the hell had he got himself into? 'You need to see where you'd be working, what you'd be doing.' With a deep sigh, he put a hand on her arms. 'I'll lift you, okay?'

She yelped as he lifted her into the air so her feet dangled a few feet above the ground, but as he marched her round the back, she did something he really didn't expect.

She giggled.

And it sounded so much like Sally, he felt a surprising tightening in his chest.

Sally watched her sister carefully as she chatted away to Vince, who'd just served Amy with a large mocha latte. Normally she wouldn't think twice about seeing them together because Vince had always had this amazing ability to get on with everyone he met, which included getting Amy to talk even when she was at her most belligerent.

Today she looked different though. There was colour in her cheeks, for a start.

As if aware she was being studied, Amy looked over at her.

'Hi.' Sally smiled as she went over to them. 'Did you manage to speak to Harry?'

'Yep.' Amy stared down at her drink.

She could talk to Vince, but not to her sister? Sadness rolled round her gut like a lead ball.

Vince cleared his throat. 'Amy was telling me she's been with Hazza all afternoon.'

'Oh?'

'I worked there for a few hours.' Amy ran her finger round the rim of the mug. 'He said so I could get an idea of what I'd be letting myself in for.'

Tread carefully. 'What did you think?'

Amy shrugged. 'It's okay.'

She caught Vince's eye and he gave her a sympathetic look and mouthed *keep going.* 'Will you be going back?'

'Kind of have to if I want to go on holiday, don't I?'

Ouch. Sally turned away so Amy wouldn't be able to see how much that had hurt.

'He made me put bags over my shoes.'

Amy's voice pulled her attention back and this time her sister met her eyes. 'I looked kind of stupid but I guess my trainers didn't get dirty. He said he'd buy me some proper steel-capped boots for tomorrow.'

A handful of words, yet Sally wanted to sit down so she could process them all. There was the fact Amy was actually talking to her all, which felt like an olive branch. That she was going to work for Harry again tomorrow. And he was buying boots for her.

Her heart flipflopped and as she went to serve the customer waiting at the counter, she had to tell herself to slow down, not read too much into it all. Amy was being nice because Vince was there. Harry was a decent guy, of course he'd make sure she had the right gear when working for him.

Still, as she closed up with Vince an hour later, she couldn't help break into a dippy smile.

'Okay, so that look on your face. You're … let me guess, thinking of Hazza naked?' Vince smirked. 'How bad would it be if I said me too?'

'Very bad. Best friends don't imagine their friends' partners naked.'

He nodded, eyes dancing with mirth. 'So he's your *partner* now, huh?'

She batted him away. 'I couldn't say boyfriend, it would have been too many "friends" in the sentence. You know this.'

'Umm. I also know Amy was way more excited about working for your Harry than she let on to you.'

Your Harry. She should contradict him, point out that wasn't where they were headed, but the two words sounded far too right to her at that moment. 'Really?'

'Oh yes. She couldn't stop talking about it. Apparently they've knocked down a ropey old garage and are building a two-storey extension in its place. She got to lay some bricks and watch Jack – that's Jack who cracks her up, by the way – do something clever with the electrics.'

'Wow.' Sally let the words settle over her. 'She said all that?'

'Indeed.' Vince grinned. 'I'm looking forward to the day Kitty has to admit I'm right, and that our Hazza is a force for good and not the evil she's determined to believe.'

She couldn't help but laugh. 'And now he's ours, huh?'

'What can I say? I was all for team Adam, but clearly that turned out to be a non-starter, so I'm happy to jump ship. Especially if it means proving Kitty wrong.'

'She doesn't believe Harry's actually bad,' Sally protested. 'Just that he's bad for me.'

'And what do you think?'

She smiled sadly. 'I think he could be perfect, except for one tiny problem. He'll never fall in love with me.'

Vince shook his head as he set the alarm and shooed her out of the door. 'Never say never, that's defeatist talk and you, my dear, are the most positive person I know.'

When she let herself into the flat a little later, there were no boots by the door and the place was quiet. Deciding that when he got back Harry deserved a thank-you meal at the very least, she busied herself making mac and cheese. Not gourmet, but she happened to know he was a fan of both pasta and cheese. By the time she heard his key in the lock, she had the meal bubbling in the oven.

Thump went the boots, clatter went the keys. Even the noises he made were typical Harry – straightforward, unpretentious. Male.

Her stomach dipped when he appeared in the doorway. 'Hey.'

She wondered if her heart was in her eyes. Certainly it had made its way to her throat. 'Hey, yourself.'

His gaze scanned the kitchen, taking in the dirty pans. 'What would you say if I told you I was starving?'

'I'd say it was lucky I made a mac and cheese large enough to feed a hungry builder.'

Grey eyes glittered as he smiled. 'I could get used to this.' Her face must have given her away because his smile froze and he looked away. 'I just meant—'

'I know.' Tension pinged round the room, unwanted, uninvited. This was so hard, so unlike how she imagined she'd feel when she finally fell in love. And yes, maybe it wasn't quite love. The bells were silent. There were no big fluffy clouds to walk on. No visions of red hearts, white dresses or sitting on the beach watching the sunset forty years from now. It was entirely possible that Harry was just a sexy, funny, beautiful diversion on the way towards it. And that this ache in her chest, this pull on her heart every time she saw him, was only a taste of what would happen when love finally hit her head on.

'Shit, Sally.' Three strides and he was in front of her, one of his big, rough hands cupping her face. 'I don't want to hurt you.' He looked so earnest, his gaze turbulent.

'I know.'

'It's just … the life you want, it isn't something I ever imagined for myself.' His eyes fluttered closed for a moment as he seemed to struggle with his thoughts. 'I've never seen myself having kids, growing old with someone.'

Each statement was like a slice through her heart. A steel-capped boot trampling over any shoots of hope. 'That sounds so sad.'

'Does it? Because to me the alternative sounds far more miserable. Staying with someone you don't like for the sake of your kids, then finding yourself too old, your lives too tangled, to easily part ways.'

He was describing his parents' marriage and her heart ached for him, and the future he seemed to have promised himself. 'We'll have to agree to disagree.' Reaching up, she pressed a hand to his cheek in a mirror image of how he held hers. 'Don't ever worry about hurting me. I went into this relationship with my eyes wide open.' She tried a smile. 'My Mark Darcy is still out there, remember?'

Beneath her palm she felt his jaw tighten. 'I remember.'

'Be warned though, when it is time to say goodbye, I'll definitely embarrass myself and cry. But I'll also feel blessed for what we shared.'

'I don't know if I can ever say goodbye.' His voice sounded thick with emotion. 'I think that will have to come from you.'

But what if I never want this to stop? She swallowed the words, choosing instead to rise up on her tiptoes and kiss the lips that hovered so enticingly over hers. The present was all she could control, and she wanted Harry in it.

Chapter Twenty-Four

Harry watched Amy chat to Mike as they prepared the lintels for the windows in the new extension. Her whole attention was on what he was saying, a small frown between her eyes as she concentrated. So much like her sister.

He was starting to see the real Amy, he thought as he set about fitting the cavity wall insulation. The one Sally had loved so much she'd forgone three years of carefree student life to bring her up.

'You'll have to ask Harry that.'

He looked up at the mention of his name and found Mike and Amy both staring at him. 'What do you need to ask me?'

'Amy wants to know how you cost up a build.' Mike glanced back at Amy. 'I'm assuming he doesn't just put his finger in the air and think of a number.'

Amy giggled, and again Harry marvelled at how different this woman was from the one who'd first walked onto the site in her white Converse trainers only three days ago. 'It's a complex process, hence why I'm in charge and not Mike.'

Mike gave him the middle finger, but Amy laughed and

when she caught his eye, he shared a smile with the woman who, earlier in the week, had said she didn't like him.

As he began to explain his process, how he costed things out, she asked smart questions, not just about the build but the role of others involved, like the architect. It struck him that maybe the reason she'd changed so much from the start of the week wasn't down to him, or Mike and Jack and their winning personalities. It was because she was interested in the work itself.

'You know, there are a tonne of career opportunities for women in the building industry.' He gave her a considering look. 'Plumbing, electrics, labouring, architecture, quantity surveying. If you're interested, I can put you in touch with a builder friend of mine. I'm sure she'd be happy to give you her take on what it's like to be a woman in this industry.'

Amy eyed him suspiciously. 'Did Sally put you up to this?'

'Nope, just figured the fact you keep turning up must mean you don't hate it, at least.'

Her mouth curved in a small smile. 'It's okay, I guess. Beats bar work.' She glanced about her. 'I like being outside.'

'Wait till it rains.'

She scoffed. 'I'm not bothered by a bit of wet.' She scuffed the floor with the toe of her boot – the steel-capped boot he'd bought her because he didn't want to be responsible for breaking Sally's sister's toe. 'This woman builder, ex-girlfriend, is she?'

'Fishing for gossip?'

She blushed. 'Just interested to find out about this guy my sister is seeing.'

'She's the daughter of a mate.' He paused, wondering what Amy knew. 'My ex works in marketing and wouldn't be seen dead on a building site because it would mean shoving a hard hat over her carefully styled hair.'

Amy's eyes widened. 'She's nothing like my sister then.'

He laughed. 'Definitely not.' Then, because he wanted Amy to know how important Sally was to him, he added, 'Your sister isn't like anyone I've ever met before. She's special.'

A few days ago, Amy might have argued back, declared the only thing special about Sally was the fact she'd kept money from her, but this new, improved version simply nodded. It wasn't as good as *I know*, or *you're right*, but it gave him hope that the pair of them would be close again one day.

Even if he wasn't around to see it.

'I hear she's got some jewellery company sponsoring your next video.'

'Yep.' He didn't like talking about the money side of it. Sure, he'd gone into it wanting to make money, but now … if he was honest, he didn't want to plan the clips on the basis of who was sponsoring them. He wanted to make videos that were fun. And yes, though he'd never admit it out loud, that gave him a chance to be with Sally in a way he knew he couldn't be in real life. He'd watched the video of him carrying her out of the cafe on more than one occasion. 'Sally's considering some clip featuring a big arse yellow diamond—'

'*How to Lose a Guy in 10 Days*,' Amy interrupted with a grin. 'That's the film you're talking about. Kate Hudson's character gets loaned this fuck off necklace to wear at a gala that Matthew McConaughey's character helped organise with a jewellery company.'

'Right.'

'It's not very romantic though.' Her face fell a little. 'At the end of the gala she has to take it off and they have this big row. If you want to keep up the speculation about whether you guys are an item you should go for the *Pretty Woman* scene. You know, the one when Edward presents Vivian with a necklace to wear for their posh night out at the opera, and just when she's looking into the box, he snaps it shut.' Harry found himself riveted, not on what Amy was saying, but the animated way she was saying it. 'Apparently that part wasn't scripted but it was well funny and also like, wow, the way they looked at each other. Talk about chemistry.'

'You sound like your sister.'

'Yeah?' Amy looked pensive, seeming to absorb his words. 'After Mum and Dad died, me and Sally watched loads and loads of romcoms. It was like we were keeping them alive, in a way, 'cos Mum was such a huge romcom fan and the pair of them were so soppy in love, at times it felt like we were living in our own romcom, you know?'

He not only didn't know, he couldn't even imagine. Still, he felt he'd been given a precious insight into the woman who was taking up more and more space in his mind. 'So we should go for the *Pretty Woman* scene?' He thought he could remember it. At least he could remember the actress looking knockout in a red dress. His pulse kicked at the thought of Sally wearing red velvet.

'Definitely. But you need to charge way more for this extension if you're going to buy her that necklace.'

He laughed, but a little part of him regretted he didn't have the spare cash to do things like buy Sally a sparkly necklace. Then he wondered if he'd been hit on the head and not realised it. When had he ever wanted to buy a woman jewellery?

Unable to get the damn scene out of his head, he walked round to the front of the house, away from beady eyes and wagging ears, and phoned the person who kept inspiring these strange romantic desires in him.

'Everything okay?' Sally sounded breathless, like she'd had to leg it to the phone.

'Yes.' He realised belatedly she'd put two and two together and made seventeen. 'You've added Amy plus building site and imagined blue flashing lights and a hospital dash.'

'Guilty. Then again, you've never phoned me when you've been at work, so…'

'So, in between playing with live wires, using a heavy drill and carrying more than twice her weight in bricks, Amy and I had a chat about this next video.'

There was a beat of silence on the other end. 'I'm not sure if I'm more suspicious of the chat or the live wire/drill/brick scenario.'

God, he loved her sharp humour. 'Amy says we should do the *Pretty Woman* necklace scene. Less sad. More…' Okay, it didn't make him soft to say the word. 'Romantic.'

Another pause, longer this time. 'And that's what you want? Romance? Now I really am suspicious.'

Was this how he sounded? All cynical and disbelieving? 'Just passing on your sister's judgement.'

'It would mean a second clip from the same film. Then again, *Pretty Woman* is an absolute classic, so I don't suppose it matters.'

'And the bonus is I'd get to peel you out of tight-fitting red velvet,' he added hopefully.

Her laughter burst down the phone. 'The scene with the yellow diamond necklace features a slinky yellow silk dress.'

Oh boy. 'Okay, as long as I'm taking you out of a dress, I'm down for either.'

More laughter. 'You're easy to please. How about I see what I can find dress wise and we work it from there?'

'Sold. But if there's a choice, can we have a long zip down

the back that I can pull down, leaving it to pool at your feet. Then you step out of it, wearing only a tiny red or yellow matching thong…'

It was several seconds before he realised she'd cut him off and he was left talking to himself. A few minutes later he got a message.

Sally: Had to stop you. Customers with flapping ears. [monkey with hands over eyes emoji, flushed face emoji, elephant emoji].

He was smiling at that when he got the second message.

[Kissing face emoji]

His smile turned into a grin, and his heart did a somersault in his chest.

The grin was wiped off his face a short while later when he got another message from her.

Sally: Amazing news. Adam is mates with the manager of Seaview Hotel. He says we can film the necklace scene there tomorrow pm [grinning emoji, dress emoji, high shoes emoji, crown emoji]

Was she still in contact with Adam? His fingers itched to ask the question but he didn't want to come across as some jealous twat, so instead he messaged:

[Crown emoji?]

Sally: Closest I could get to a necklace [laughing with tears emoji, grinning with eyes shut emoji, girl wearing a crown emoji].

PS I have red velvet and borrowed necklace. You need to bring yourself in suit.

'What are you smiling at?'

Amy walked up to him and he nodded down at his phone. 'Your sister. We're on for *Pretty Woman*. Looks like I'm dusting the suit off again.'

'Suit?' Amy pursed her lips. 'Richard Gere wore a tux for that scene, but I guess a suit would be okay. It's not quite the fantasy though, is it?'

No, it probably wasn't. Then again, neither was he.

And it was the fantasy Sally wanted.

Chapter Twenty-Five

I t was Saturday afternoon and Sally was walking with Harry to the hotel to film the *Pretty Woman* necklace scene. Harry had their suit carriers flung over his arm.

'You could have worn your suit,' she remarked as they dodged a pair of kids on roller skates.

'Thought about it, but then remembered all those comments from the last time I wore it, you know – hot stuff, dreamboat.' He winked at her. 'Didn't want to cause too much of a stir.'

She rolled her eyes and decided not to give him the satisfaction of telling him he caused a stir anyway. Tall, built, ruggedly handsome guy walks along seafront wearing faded jeans and a brown leather jacket. Yep, he was attracting attention anyway.

'Isn't that the guy from the other night?'

Spotting the bearded figure ahead of them, she waved. 'It is.'

'What?' Harry asked when he noticed her eyeing him curiously. 'I saw you give him money.'

'Oh.' She'd tried to be discreet. 'I didn't think you'd noticed.'

He gave her a loaded look. 'I notice everything about you.'

Her heart twisted and she couldn't hold his gaze. When he said things like that it gave her hope, but hope was dangerous. 'Jim lives in the shelter. He's a good guy going through a tough time.'

'And you try to make it less tough.'

It had taken a lot of persuasion for Jim to take money from her. Even now, he would only accept it on the understanding he'd spend it in The Love Bean. 'The cafe has links with the shelter. All part of helping the community.' Feeling uncomfortable at the admiration in Harry's gaze, she changed the subject. 'Adam said he'd meet us in the hotel lobby so he can introduce us to his friend, Peter. He also agreed to hang around and film it for us, which is really handy as I'm not sure how it would have worked otherwise. I didn't really want to ask Peter as it's weird enough doing this, never mind doing it in front of someone we've not met.' Harry slowed to a stop and when she turned, she found him staring back at her with a tight expression. 'What's wrong?'

'Do you still see Adam?'

'I still keep in touch with him, yes, of course. We're friends. But that's all we are.'

He drew in a breath, seemed to shake himself. 'Okay.'

She wanted to make a tart reply about the fact he was still seeing the woman he'd lived with for a year. But then she remembered what Isabelle had done to him. 'I would never cheat on you. I hope you know that.'

His mouth curved in a wry smile. 'Actually, I do.' His shoulders raised, then lowered as he sighed. 'I was just being a jealous prick. Sorry.'

She felt that squeeze on her heart again and reached up to kiss him. 'Forgiven.'

Adam was waiting in the lobby when they arrived, talking to a dark-haired guy with glasses. Introductions were made, Harry shook hands with both men and Adam kissed her cheek, which felt a little awkward after the conversation she'd just had with Harry. She didn't miss the way Harry threaded his arm around her waist immediately afterwards.

He cares more than he lets on.

'There's a spare room on the first floor you can use to change in,' Peter said, looking down at the suit carriers Harry was holding. 'And the shop dropped the necklace off. They said to leave it here and they'll pick it up later.'

Excited, she bounced on her feet. 'Ooh, can I see?'

Harry gave her an admonishing glance. 'Did the bloke Gere was playing—'

'Edward Lewis.'

'Did Edward Lewis show—'

'Vivian.'

He grinned, like it was weird she knew their character names. 'Did Vivian get to see the necklace before she got dressed?'

'No.' She pouted, but really she was thrilled he wanted to do this properly. 'Okay, I'll go and squeeze into the dress.'

'Sounds promising.' He gave her that small, sexy smile he used to such devastating effect. 'I'll change down here so you can make the full entrance.'

After handing her phone to Adam, she took the carrier from Harry and walked towards the lift. Butterflies flapped in her stomach which was daft. They were acting.

Yet it didn't feel like acting. Not when she was doing it with the man she was falling in love with.

The red velvet dress, loaned from a friend of Kitty's who was in charge of costume at the theatre, fitted a little too well. After applying a coat of red lipstick and clipping her curls up into some sort of style, she looked in the mirror. The dress was knee length, not long like in the film, and she didn't have the waist that Julia Roberts did. Or the hair. Or the face. For Sally Thornton though, she'd scrubbed up pretty well.

The butterflies began to flap again as she stepped into the lift. *It's only Harry. Only a video clip on a mobile phone.* But the fluttery feeling wouldn't let up. She was excited to see him in his suit again. Excited and nervous for him to see her.

The lift door opened and she stepped out.

Her heart almost detonated. He was wearing a tux. The down-to-earth man, who claimed to be unromantic, had actually gone to the trouble of hiring a tux. And he looked like every woman's fantasy.

He smiled when he saw her. 'Can't remember what Gere's character says at this moment, but you look frigging gorgeous.'

'I could say the same.' She couldn't stop the tremor in her voice. 'You went all out.'

'What, this?' He looked down at the suit, then back up at her. 'Found it in the back of my wardrobe.'

It was so clearly a lie, she started to laugh, but then he stepped towards her and cast his gaze deliberately up and down. 'Something's missing.'

Okay, they were back onto the scene. 'Well I can tell you that nothing else is going to fit inside this dress.' Vivian's lines, but also wholly accurate. '*I* barely fit inside this dress.'

He reached behind him to pick up the box sitting on the sideboard. 'The something is inside here. Don't get excited, it's only on loan.' He named the company who'd sponsored the clip, then opened the box.

Just as Vivian had done, she peered into it. Okay, it wasn't a quarter of a million dollars' worth of diamonds, but the red heart necklace was beautiful. Suddenly the lid shut, and she stepped back, shocked. Then looked at Harry's laughing face and realised she'd got so carried away with seeing the necklace, she'd forgotten what came next.

Her heart beat crazily as he carefully set the necklace around her neck, the brush of his hands against her neck sending goose bumps skittling across her skin. 'You're supposed to ask how much it cost,' he whispered, his breath warm against her ear.

She had to swallow to get the words out. 'If you were going to buy this, how much would it cost?'

He laughed softly. 'Damned if I know.' She shivered as he placed a kiss against the nape of her neck. 'But far more reasonable than the quarter of a million dollars for Vivian's necklace, that's for sure.'

God, this man. Why did her heart beat so crazily for him? His good looks, the pretty eyes, the way he made her laugh? Or was it that the more she got to know him, the more she liked what she saw inside as well as out? *Keep on track with the video*.

'So where are we going?'

He did a very Richard Gere-like secret smile. 'It's a surprise.'

When she said the next words from the film, it didn't feel like acting. It felt like the truest words she'd ever spoken. 'If I forget to tell you later, thank you. I had a really amazing time tonight.'

His eyes turned dark, a mix of heat and some emotion she couldn't identify. 'Me too.'

He held out his arm and she grasped it gratefully as they walked along the lobby towards the door. It was only when they neared it that she became aware of Adam filming ahead of them. Remembering the scene, she touched the necklace.

'Even when you're fidgeting, you look bloody gorgeous.'

She caught Harry's eye and along with the amusement she saw a quiet sincerity that sent her heart jumping into her throat. 'And tall?' she supplied, mimicking Edward's line in the film.

'I guess, but as I'm way taller than Gere, you look kind of short arse next to me.'

It was typical Harry. Compliment her to make her knees weak, then bring her down to earth with a quip. Yet she was coming to enjoy that matter-of-fact side of him. He didn't dish out false charm. His compliments were like nuggets in a gold prospector's pan. Rare, but oh what a thrill when they appeared.

They came to a halt by the entrance and disappointment settled in her stomach. Fantasy time was over.

'Thanks, Adam, you can end it there.' She glanced down at her dress. 'Cinderella won't be going to a ball tonight, alas.'

He laughed and handed over the phone. 'I hope I got everything. I zoomed in on the necklace like you said, but you might want to film it in the box, just to make sure. I'm no expert at photography.'

'Good idea.'

She reached to take the necklace off, but Adam stepped forward. 'I'll do that—'

'I've got it.' Suddenly it was Harry's surprisingly deft

fingers undoing the necklace, Harry's hands sliding it from her neck as he gently removed it.

'I think he's trying to tell me something,' Adam whispered as Harry walked over to the reception desk.

'He is being a bit proprietary. Sorry.'

'No worries.' Adam looked over to where Harry was now placing the necklace in the box. 'I don't blame him. I'd do the same in his position.'

'Thank you, but...' She gestured awkwardly between the two of them. 'Please tell me you're not feeling a spark here?'

'Ah, no, I don't think so.' Adam let out a wry smile and pushed his hands into his pockets. 'I guess I'm just wishing I did, you know?' He glanced again towards Harry. 'The pair of you have so many sparks firing you light the place up. It makes a guy envious.'

Don't be, it's heading nowhere.

And yet, it didn't feel that way, not when she was with him. Not when he was looking at her like he was now. As if he was only one nudge away from stalking over to claim her.

Because she knew how she felt when Harry saw Isabelle, she thanked Adam, then walked over to the impossibly sexy man in the tux and took hold of his hand. 'Guess it's time to get out of these clothes.'

He gave a little shake of his head. 'Not yet.' His lips found hers in an all-too-brief kiss. 'Grab your stuff and meet me down here.'

Five minutes later she and Harry were stood outside the hotel. He'd taken off his bow tie, but the mix of casual open white shirt and formal black dinner suit still looked ridiculously gorgeous on him. Elegant, yet slightly rumpled.

A taxi pulled up and Harry went to open the door for her. 'It's not a private plane, and we're not heading to the opera—'

'Thank God.'

He laughed. 'My thoughts exactly.' With a hand behind her back, he eased her towards him and kissed her gently on the lips. 'But before we go home, I figured we should eat.' Once again he looked her deliberately up and down. 'Then I get to peel you out of the dress, as promised.'

It seemed the butterflies weren't getting the night off. They flapped wildly as he slid in beside her and asked the driver to take them to The Grand Hotel. And they kept flapping as they ate, the conversation easy yet with every eye contact, with every brush of his leg against hers, came the promise of what would come later.

———

The following day, she edited the video, giving it the strapline *Heading out, Pretty Woman style*. It was beyond obvious that they were dating now. Adam was right, the sparks between them lit up the screen.

As she gave it a final watch before uploading it onto TikTok, her breath hitched. The way she was looking at him … and yes, he at her. There was a warmth, a fondness that shimmered between them, so transparent she almost expected to hear the bells ring. And wasn't sure whether to be relieved or disappointed when she couldn't.

Chapter Twenty-Six

I t was the first Friday in December, and instead of enjoying a pint down the pub, Harry was sat on a pink sofa, glass of margarita in his hand, about to watch some romcom called *Love Actually* with the three musketeers, as he'd started to think of Sally, Vince and Kitty. Apparently watching this film together was some sort of tradition for them.

'You'll enjoy it, just you wait.' Sally grinned up at him, looking like a pig in shit with her big red Santa Christmas jumper on, bowl of popcorn in her lap, fluffy socks littered with red hearts on her feet. A frigging gorgeous pig in shit, he amended. His heart did a strange wriggly thing in his chest and he pulled her more tightly towards him.

'He won't enjoy it,' Kitty muttered. 'Because he's got no soul.'

'I enjoyed the last one we watched,' he protested, letting the barbed comment roll off him. He was starting to think Kitty was all bark and no bite. 'The one with Will Smith.'

'You mean *Hitch*?' Kitty glanced sideways at him. 'What part did you like the most?'

He sensed a trap, but couldn't remember enough about the film to navigate round it. 'All the parts with Will Smith in them?'

'Exactly,' she said with a triumphant expression. 'He's funny, so you liked watching him. Bet you didn't even realise there was a romance going on, did you?'

He might have glazed over at those bits, but he wasn't going to let Kitty know that. 'I watched the whole thing.'

'Any scenes you think you could do for the next video?' she asked.

'The first date,' he replied confidently, pleased he could remember it. 'The part where he accidentally kicks her in the face as he gets on one of those jet skis. Or when his face blows up because of the allergic reaction to the scallops.' Though actually, thinking about them... Yep, he'd stumbled right into the frigging trap. 'What's wrong with funny, anyway? People enjoy watching our clips *because* they're funny.'

'Not necessarily,' Sally interrupted as she pressed the remote. 'A lot of people like the love story they think they're seeing play out.'

Think they're seeing. He hated the way that sounded. Like what they had was a sham, a pretence to notch up the views so the sponsorship would keep coming in.

'Speaking of love stories.' Vince wore a slightly smug expression. 'We may have one of our own brewing.'

Sally gasped. 'You've met someone? Who, where, when?'

'Well.' Vince mimed a drum roll. 'His name is Justin and he's followed the band for a while now, turning up to most of our gigs. We all thought he was a fan of the music.' Vince grinned coyly. 'Turns out he was a fan of the drummer.'

Kitty squealed, and Sally leaped up from the sofa to throw her arms around him. As the two women grilled Vince for more details, Harry couldn't help but feel marginalised. It wasn't that he minded not being involved; he knew the three of them were tight and had a history that spanned over a decade. It's just … where had the excitement been for him and Sally?

It hit him with a force then, how Sally must have felt when he'd laid it out so baldly for her that he didn't believe in love. They were excited for Vince because, even though his relationship with Justin was in the very early stages, there were possibilities. Hope. In contrast, he'd put the brakes on his relationship with Sally before it could even get off the starting line.

Sadness crept over him and he had to look away, take a big glug of margarita. This time next year, Vince would likely be sat here with Justin, Sally next to them, cuddled up to her Mr Right, whoever he might be. Possibly Adam, he thought, his stomach rolling as he imagined the sound of the film track they were watching, drowned out by the noise of sodding bells, ringing merrily in the background.

Meanwhile he'd be in his own house, sitting alone. *Watching what you want to watch. Drinking what you want to drink.* Why couldn't he get excited about it?

'Harry looks like he's been slapped round the face with a wet fish,' Kitty remarked. 'Come on, you might be too closed off to let someone into your life, but can't you be happy for those who aren't emotionally detached?'

He flinched. He'd been wrong about her lack of bite. Stiffly, he rose to his feet, aware he needed to get away from Kitty before he said something he regretted. 'I'll be back in a bit. You can start the film without me.' Because Kitty had pissed him off, he couldn't resist adding, 'I think I'll manage to pick up the plot.'

Walking into the hallway, he shoved on his boots and coat, picked up his keys and headed out.

He was halfway towards the seafront when he heard Sally call out his name.

'Wait. Please.'

He halted, slamming his eyes shut, not ready to talk to her, to anyone. Not until he had his emotions – *see, Kitty, I'm not a fucking robot* – under some sort of control.

A hand curled round his, the fingers warm, the skin soft. 'Kitty talks first and thinks later.'

'I don't care about what Kitty says or thinks.'

'Then why are you out here?'

He turned to face Sally. Blonde hair blowing in the wind, blue eyes full of concern, for him. His chest felt way too tight to take the breath he needed. 'Because I care what *you* think.'

She swallowed, eyes glancing away from his. 'You're not emotionally detached, if that's what you mean. I think you have your reasons for not believing in love, reasons I wish I understood, but it isn't because you aren't capable of loving anyone.'

Some of the tension left his body, but his mind was still restless, unable to rid itself of the image of her watching romcoms on her daft pink sofa, cuddling up to a guy who wasn't him. 'You said you wanted what your parents had in that photo, but what if that was just a snap shot of how they felt on that day? What if the next day they were back to arguing with each other? What if they did that far more than they ever smiled into each other's eyes?'

'I don't know how that would have felt, how it would have changed my view of things. I only know what I grew up with, and that was the certainty that they not only loved me and my sister, they loved each other.'

'Yet they died far too soon.' He shook his head, unable to understand how she could be so positive. 'How can you still believe in happy ever after?'

'Because they died having spent twenty years loving each other.' She sighed, took hold of both his hands. 'I'm not stupid, I know nothing is guaranteed in life, but I know true love is out there, and I'm going to find it.'

She would, he realised, and it felt like a vice had gripped his chest. Could he really stand by and let her go? Was he so stubborn-headed that he wasn't prepared to open up to the possibility that he could be wrong? That just because he hadn't witnessed love, didn't mean it was myth? That because he'd never seen himself with kids, didn't mean one day he couldn't change his mind? He'd already imagined her in his house, and that was a future way more appealing than the one he'd imagined of him sitting alone.

Carefully, he tucked a wayward curl behind her ear, let his gaze roam over the face he loved waking up to every morning. 'You once talked to me about bells. Do you think it's possible you could hear those bells with someone like me?'

Her eyes widened, and those cute as hell dimples seemed to wink at him. 'Harry Wilson, what are you trying to say?'

'I don't know.' He really didn't, had no clue what this feeling was. 'I just know I care for you more than I've cared for anyone.' He sucked in a deep breath. 'And it scares the everloving shit out of me to think of you buggering off with some Mark Darcy.' *Or Adam.*

Her hand touched his cheek, the feel of it warm, soothing. 'I'm not going anywhere, except back inside to watch the film.' She smiled into his eyes. 'Are you coming?'

On Sunday, Sally walked with Harry to the Lanes to meet his mother for lunch. She knew he was on edge from the way he kept glancing at his watch. For a guy who came across as supremely confident in his own skin, unconcerned by what others thought, it was a really odd look on him.

'We're not going to be late,' she told him for the second time.

'By normal standards, no.'

Okay. If he was trying to make her nervous, he was succeeding. She glanced down at her leggings and what she'd considered a meeting-the-mother-appropriate cream, loose-fitting jumper sporting a giant sequined heart on the front. 'She's not going to be smart, is she? Because you said it was casual, but now I'm thinking people who are meticulous about timekeeping are probably meticulous about how they dress.'

He pointed to his jeans. 'Do you think I care?'

'But you care about being late.'

'I don't. I just hate being on the back foot with her.'

The nerves wriggled, burrowing into her stomach. 'Maybe it's best if I don't go? I mean, we're hardly in a meet-the-mother sort of relationship.'

'You've met her already.'

Ah, good point.

Suddenly he halted. Placing his hands on her waist, he pulled her towards him and planted a soft kiss on her forehead. 'I need to make two things perfectly clear. Number one, you look sexy as hell in those leggings. Number two, you're here to help make the meal less tortuous, not to get some sort of approval from her. In fact, if she likes you, I'll start to worry, so be as obnoxious as you like.' He shook his head, letting out a small laugh. 'I bet you can't even do obnoxious, can you? I should have asked Kitty.'

She wanted to object, but he was right. Kitty had been obnoxious to him the other night. 'Kitty's being over-protective right now, but that's what we do, have each other's backs. It's been that way since school.'

'Vince seems to manage it without the need to kick me in the balls.'

He was hurt, she thought. Far more than he'd let on, and probably far more than Kitty realised. With a sigh, she wound her arms around his waist. 'At school there was this group of guys who thought they were the top dogs, you know? They went about trying to look and act macho. Kitty being Kitty, she didn't flutter her eyelashes at them like they expected. She told them what she thought of them. I think they were intimidated by her, but to hide that they called her names and started a rumour she was a lesbian, because of course she couldn't possibly be heterosexual and not fancy them.'

'And you're telling me this, why? I've always been polite to her.'

'I know, but...' She needed to choose her words carefully. 'You're like those guys to her. She's comfortable with quiet, arty types, and you're blunt, big, sarcastic. You bring out the worst in her.'

He nodded and she could almost see his mind churning over what she'd said. 'Did these bullies get at you, too?'

'This all happened around the time my parents died and I was too immersed in grief to care what anybody said to me. But I do know Kitty was the one who took those guys on. She drew the attention away from me and Vince and onto herself.'

His breath came out in one long sigh. 'I get it. I take back the obnoxious comment.' He glanced back at his watch and swore. 'Now we really are going to be late.'

Sally was out of breath by the time they arrived at the restaurant, but as Harry had predicted, his mum was already there.

'Nice of you to finally turn up.' She rose to her feet and accepted the perfunctory kiss on the cheek Harry supplied before turning her cool gaze on Sally. 'We meet again. Only now I take it your involvement with my son is more than a monthly rent payment.'

Wow. Way to make it sound sordid. Rent a room, have sex with the landlady for free.

Harry's face hardened. 'Sally and I are together. If you can't be civil to her, we're leaving.'

Despite the tension at the table, her heart gave a little kick at the phrase *together*. Coming after his admission on Friday, it felt as if they'd turned a tiny corner. That hope now felt tangible. Dangerous to cling to, yet impossible not to reach for.

'I see.' His mother met Sally's gaze and she saw the resemblance to Harry's, though where the son's grey eyes held a smoky warmth, often along with a twinkle of humour, the mother's were steel grey. 'Good afternoon, Sally. You can call me Beverley.'

'Hi.' She smiled because that was the decent thing to do, but it felt frozen on her face. What must it have been like having this woman as a mother growing up?

The waitress took their order and Sally wanted to laugh at how clichéd their choices were. Harry with the no-nonsense cheeseburger, her with the trying-to-watch-my-weight-a-bit smoked chicken salad, ruining it by ordering a side of fries, because who wanted a bowl of salad by itself? Beverley ordered the steamed halibut, which Sally would have liked to bet the chef hadn't cooked for so long he'd forgotten how to do it.

'So, I'll get to the point.' Beverley took a sip of her water. 'Your father and I have spoken to the mediator and come to a financial agreement. However, when I look at the money I'll get from my half of the house, and what I can buy with it in the same area, I'll have to do some considerable downsizing.' While his mum was talking, Sally snuck a peek at Harry and found that, for once, he was poker-faced. 'One way I could retain at least a little of my current standard of living,' Beverley continued in her cool monotone, 'would be to buy an older property that requires considerable renovation.'

Sally's eyes nearly bugged out of her head. She wasn't going to ... was she?

'I can recommend a good builder.' Harry's tone was as bland as his expression.

Beverley's lips moved in what Sally supposed was a smile. 'I knew you'd see it my way. Obviously I won't be able to move into it until it's ready, so I thought I could move into your house temporarily. That way it would be easy to discuss the renovations.'

'We're booked out for work for the next year.' A muscle ticked in Harry's jaw, but other than that he showed no hint of his feelings. 'When I said I could recommend a good builder, I meant someone other than me.'

'But you renovated your own house while you worked.'

'Yeah, in the evenings and weekends. I had no social life for eighteen months.'

His mother laughed humourlessly. 'I had no social life for eighteen *years* while I was bringing you up. Do you think *that* was fun?' She took another delicate sip from her glass of water. 'Eighteen months doesn't seem very long in comparison.'

And there it was, Sally realised with a searing dose of clarity. The reason Harry didn't believe in love. At first, she'd thought it was because of what Isabelle had done to him, then because of what he'd seen in his parents' marriage and sure, both of those things had helped cement his view. But surely the reason he didn't believe in love was because he'd never actually experienced it. Not from a partner, but importantly, if this conversation was anything to go by, not from his parents.

'I'll see what I can do when the time comes.' Harry's tone was flat, his expression resigned.

As she listened to the pair of them talk, it became painfully clear that Harry would help his mum, because that's what a son should do. Just as he kept Earl Grey tea bags for her. Out of duty, not love, because that's how he'd been brought up.

Deep inside her chest, her heart began to ache at what he'd missed out on. Parents who couldn't be bothered with him and no siblings to soften the loneliness. It all pointed to a miserable childhood.

'I don't like your mother,' Sally told him as they walked back after the lunch, slipping her hand round his.

His fingers squeezed hers. 'Not sure I like her much right now, either.'

'That's not how a parent is supposed to be. What she said, about bringing you up being no fun? How could she? Parents are supposed to love you unconditionally.'

He laughed softly. 'I have no clue what that means but I did better than some.'

'You deserved more than meals and a roof over your head.' Tears welled in her eyes as she imagined five, eight, ten-year-old Harry, sitting alone in his room.

'Hey.' His eyes filled with concern as they took in her face. 'I hope those aren't for me. I was fine. And I made it into adulthood without too much damage so...' He shrugged his big shoulders.

But there *was* damage. She wasn't sure if it could be repaired, but she wanted to try. To show him the love he'd clearly never experienced so he could see how special it was, if only he opened his heart to the possibility of it.

Chapter Twenty-Seven

I n a bid to take his mind off the conversation with his mother yesterday, and because he figured Sally would like it, Harry took a detour on his way back from work to pick up a Christmas tree. As he hauled it out of the back of his truck, he wondered if he should have asked her first if she was a real tree or fake tree person. Or maybe not a tree person at all.

She loves fairy-tale films with over-the-top romantic gestures and sugar-coated endings. Yep, she was not going to hate Christmas. In fact, he'd bet good money that she filled her place with fairy lights and decorated her tree with pink – or maybe red – baubles.

A warm, happy feeling filled his chest when he realised he might be here, in the flat he'd moved into temporarily four and a half months ago, for Christmas.

'What on earth?'

Once he'd managed to squeeze the tree through the front door – maybe he should have gone for the five-footer rather than the six-footer – he found Sally gaping at him.

'Never seen a tree before?'

She rolled her big blue eyes at him. 'Not what on earth is it, but what on earth are you doing with it?'

Maybe he had got this wrong after all. 'I bought it for the flat.'

She nodded, but her expression was clearly confused. 'Where are you planning to put it?'

He glanced again at the tree, which admittedly looked huge in her hallway. 'I can take it back.' Though actually he couldn't imagine the guy letting him. Maybe he could take it to his own house. In her last message, Isabelle had finally said she'd found somewhere and might be moving out in a couple of weeks. He'd believe it when he saw it, but clearly living in his house and paying him rent was not as attractive a proposition as living there rent free.

'No way are you taking it back.' Sally moved to touch the tree, which was still trussed up in its netting. 'Can we put it in the living room?'

'Your tree, your flat. You can put it where you want.'

She stared back at him, eyes searching his. 'You bought this for me?'

'No. I bought it to put in my bedroom because I'm a huge fan of fairy lights and pine needles in the bed.' He gave her a mild look. 'What do you think?'

She bit into her lip, and her eyes glistened. 'I think I can't wait to decorate it.' Reaching up, she kissed him. 'Thank you. Nobody's bought me a tree for a long time.'

'No problem.' He felt faintly embarrassed. 'I drive past a guy who sells them, and I have a truck, so…'

'It was easy,' she filled in for him. But then took his hand, squeezed it. 'But that's not the point. You thought of me, when you drove past.'

While he absorbed what she'd said – he had thought of her,

which wasn't a surprise because he thought of her all of the time – she pushed the door to the living room open. 'Come on, let's get it up. I'll fetch the holder and the decorations.'

He was going to make a pun about having no problem getting it up, but she disappeared, returning a few minutes later with a huge box covered in Father Christmas wrapping paper. And a beaming smile.

'Come on,' she encouraged, pulling baubles and lights out of the box with the enthusiasm of a six-year-old.

It was then he realised how easy it was to please her. She might love big romantic gestures but she seemed equally as thrilled with small, thoughtful ones.

Under her excited gaze he shoved the tree into the holder and wrapped the lights round it because it was easy when you were tall. After that he plonked the star on top because, again, the tall thing.

'I'll leave you to jazz it up.'

She nodded distractedly, her focus on the baubles she'd excavated from the box. He watched as she put a few on the tree, then stood back, surveyed her handiwork. And swapped two of them round.

Smiling to himself, he went and took a shower.

———

Later, they sat down in the kitchen to eat the pasta he'd thrown together while she'd been faffing around with pink baubles – apparently they matched the sofa. If Harry thought about it, he'd be amazed how quickly, how easily, they'd settled into the routine of not just having sex together, but living together in the full sense. He no longer had shelves for his stuff. Somehow it had all merged into *their* stuff. Now they shopped together, cooked for each other, ate with each other.

'We should do another video clip this week,' she remarked as she shovelled a large forkful into her mouth. She ate like she made love. Lustily. 'We don't have a sponsor lined up, so we can do what we like.'

'Good.'

Her eyes widened. 'I thought you wanted the money?'

He squirmed on the bar stool. 'Sure, money is always useful, but Isabelle's paying me rent now, so things aren't so tight.' He looked over at her, decided he'd always spoken his mind, even if it got him into trouble. 'It's more fun when it's just you and me, having a laugh. Doing our thing.'

Her face softened. 'It is, isn't it?'

'So what do you want to do?'

'As it's the run up to Christmas, we should do something from an iconic Christmas film.' Her eyes twinkled over at him.

'*Bad Santa? Elf?*' He clicked his fingers. 'I've got it. *Die Hard*. Not sure I fancy walking over broken glass in bare feet though. Or climbing through an air-conditioning vent. Or, wait, you mean the bit where he leaps off the very tall building clinging to a fire hose?'

A few months ago, she'd have got exasperated with him. Now she simply smiled. 'You know exactly which film, because you watched it last week. And I bet you can guess the scene, too, because you have to have been living under a rock not to have seen that repeated in adverts or other sketches.'

He nodded. 'You want me to do what that Mark character did for Keira Knightly and stand outside the flat holding up bits of cardboard for you to read.'

She laughed. 'Wow, it sounds so romantic when you say it like that, but yes. Are you up for doing a bit of *Love Actually?*'

'I've lifted you over my head, shopped with you, made a pot with you, kissed you in front of football fans, showered with you, carried you out of a cafe, put on a tux for you.' He shrugged. 'I reckon I can manage to knock on your door.'

'While holding cards that tell me how you feel,' she added, then blushed and looked away. 'Not that you have to do that, obviously, because we're mimicking the scene. If it helps, we can write the cards together. I can probably remember what they said off by heart.'

If she thought he was going to copy some sappy film word for word... 'Isn't what the cards say supposed to be a surprise?'

'Well ideally, yes.'

Her eyes caught his again, and the light in them, together with the smile on her face, hinted at an anticipation he couldn't possibly live up to. 'Remember this is me though, not whichever romantic heartthrob you're thinking of right now.'

She slipped off the stool and pressed a kiss to his cheek. 'You're the only heartthrob I'm thinking of.' And damn if that didn't make his heart do a crazy dance in his chest. 'Shall we do it tomorrow? Does that give you enough time to work on what to put on the cards?'

Again, he felt a ripple of unease. What was she expecting? 'Tomorrow's fine, but I've got to swing by my house after work. Apparently the shower valve is leaking.' He glanced up at Sally who was now clearing their dishes away. 'Isabelle says she's found a place to move into.'

'Oh.' She was facing away from him, so he had no clue whether that was an *oh I'm going to really miss you*, an *oh great, finally I get my flat back*, or just an indifferent *oh well it was good while it lasted*.

He walked up to her, placed his hands on her waist and

turned her to face him. 'It doesn't have to change things, if you don't want it to.' He smiled, trying to judge her thoughts, his heart now beating a hard rhythm. 'Just means we have options for places to sleep.'

Her body relaxed against his. 'I like the sound of that.'

So did he, he thought, bending to kiss her. So did he.

———————

The following day, Sally found herself humming as she wiped down the tables in the cafe. Every now and again she'd look up at the heart cards in the window. Would her own name ever feature on a card with the other success stories? Technically she'd not been on a date with Harry here, but he had watched her fake an orgasm, and he had carried her out, *An Officer and a Gentleman* style.

'Oh dear, you've got it bad, girl.' Vince's expression was full of sympathy as he caught the direction of her stare.

She tried to play the innocent. 'What do you mean?'

He simply sighed. 'You think I don't know you, Sally Thornton? You're imagining your name next to Hazza's on a card in our window. I'm not sure what date you've got in mind for the wedding, but let's go with summer next year. Only you forgot the small part about him not ever wanting to get married.'

She tried to laugh off his comment, to put a *duh, of course I've not forgotten* look on her face, but it all went horribly wrong and she was left with this strangled-sounding noise. The accompanying expression must have looked terrible, because Vince winced. 'Let's park this conversation until after we close.' He took another glance at her face. 'And I'll call Kitty, see if she can come over.'

'I look so bad you need reinforcements?'

'You look beautiful, as always.' He squeezed her arm. 'But two brains are better than one, even though mine is clearly superior.'

'Well, Mr Modest, you can relax, I'm fine.' She scanned the pleasingly humming cafe, reassured herself they weren't needed. 'Kitty will only give me the doom and gloom, he's going to break your heart lecture again, and that's okay, maybe she's right.' She finished wiping the table and placed the heart-festooned sugar dispenser back in the middle. 'But last night Harry bought me a Christmas tree, which I know sounds like nothing but coming from him, it seemed like *something*. And then he told me Isabelle was leaving his place, and I thought he was going to say that was it, we were over, but he didn't.' She inhaled a deep breath, let it out slowly. 'He said it doesn't have to change things, that we can keep seeing each other if I wanted to, which of course I do, so…'

'So now it's hard for you not to get carried away. Not to dream,' he finished for her, his eyes as soft as his voice.

'Yes. I had lunch with him and his mother the other day, and I now know why he's so cynical about love. His mum was really cold with him. Can you believe, she wants him to renovate a house for her in his spare time and she doesn't care how much it impacts his life because, and I quote, *I had no social life for eighteen years while I was bringing you up. Do you think that was fun?*'

Vince shuddered. 'Ouch.'

'Exactly.' Every time she thought about it, she felt like crying. It had been brutal to lose her parents when she had, but at least for sixteen years she'd known nothing but unselfish, unconditional love.

The door opened and they both turned to watch as Amy

walked in. She gave Sally a hesitant smile, and Vince a wider one.

'Finished work already?' He raised a brow. 'That boss of yours must be getting soft.'

'Ha ha.' Her gaze darted to Sally. 'Harry said I could go early 'cos I wanted to talk to my sister.'

'Oh right, don't mind me, girls.' Vince made a big play of pulling out a chair. 'Sit yourselves down. I'll do my level best to cope with our unruly customers.' He nodded over to the occupied tables: several groups of young mums with their toddlers, four pensioners, a single woman typing away on her laptop and a middle-aged couple doing a crossword together.

'He's crazy,' Amy said fondly, sitting down.

'You always did have a soft spot for him.' Vince and Kitty had not just been her friends, her support when their parents died. They'd been there for Amy, too.

She shrugged. 'He's easy to like.'

'And how about Harry? Are you getting on better with him now?' She braced herself, but Amy shocked her by giving her a goofy smile.

'Yeah, he's alright.' She reached for the sugar dispenser and started to play with it. 'Actually, he put me in contact with this woman he knows who's a builder.'

'Oh?' A useful word, she'd found, when she wasn't sure what to say.

'I had a good chat with her on the phone and we're meeting up tomorrow.'

It all sounded so positive, Sally was afraid to push in case it sent Amy back into defensive mode. But then she didn't have to, because Amy carried on the conversation. 'It probably sounds dumb, but I sort of like working on the extension. I mean, Jack and Mike are a right laugh, and Harry's okay.'

The devilish light in her sister's eyes caused a lump to settle in Sally's throat. How long had it been since she'd seen that look? 'Only okay, huh?'

Amy's mouth twitched. 'Yep.' They shared a smile, something Sally had been afraid would never happen again. 'But it's not just that we have a laugh. Building, the stuff that goes into planning for it, it's way more interesting than I thought it would be.'

More interesting than bar work? It was a question she should be able to ask, but their relationship had been far too strained over the last year for Sally to risk it. And anyway, Amy coming and talking to her about it was a huge step. Enough that she was content to simply smile and say, 'I'm glad.'

'Everything okay with Amy?' Vince asked later as they closed up and set the alarm.

'Actually, yes.' She couldn't help the satisfied smile. 'It sounds like she might have found a new career direction.'

'Umm, can't say I'm surprised, not after talking to her the other day.' He grinned over at Sally. 'Like I said, your Harry seems to be a force for good.'

This time she had no desire to correct him, not on either point. He *was* her Harry, at least for now. And whatever happened, he would always hold a piece of her heart. Not only because of the joy he'd brought her these last few months, but because of how he'd helped Amy. Maybe her sister wouldn't go into the building trade, maybe they would never find the relationship they used to have, but Harry had done something she'd not been able to do. He'd got through to Amy and made her realise there was a better path than the one she'd become lost down.

Chapter Twenty-Eight

Harry whistled as he climbed out of the truck and hauled out his toolbox. Nothing was going to ruin his mood. He'd started the day with his body wrapped round the gorgeous curly-haired blonde who was the cause of all these new feelings blooming inside him – warm, happy feelings. He'd had mind-blowing sex in the shower – triggering a very different set of warm, happy feelings. The rest of the day he'd spent fitting window and door frames to a build that was now a few days ahead of schedule. He only had a leaking shower valve to fix, then it was back to Sally.

Cue another rush of those feelings.

Isabelle opened the door and for once she looked frazzled. Her hair unbrushed, her face without its usual make-up. 'I've come to fix the shower as requested.'

She stepped back to let him in. 'Thanks.'

'Everything okay?'

'Fine.' Her gaze turned cool. 'I'm having to move because I've been booted out of my home, but other than that…'

He sighed. 'I'm not here to argue. Is it the shower in the en suite?'

'Yes.'

He walked into the kitchen, peeled off his jacket and headed up the stairs.

'Do you want a drink?'

Halfway up, he halted and turned. 'No thanks, I'm good.' He didn't want to be here any longer than necessary.

'So you really are shagging the landlady, huh?'

Anger coiled in his gut. 'Knock it off.'

'What? It's pretty obvious you're with her, looking at all the videos.'

'I'm not here to discuss my love life, or yours.' He carried on up the stairs. To think, he'd once been cut up by what she'd done to him. Now he could only think what a lucky escape he'd had. Living with her had been easy, but compared to what he had with Sally? There was no comparison. He'd been sleepwalking through life until he'd met Sally.

'Your phone has buzzed with a message,' Isabelle called up to him five minutes later.

He frowned, realising he'd left it in his jacket pocket. 'Leave it, I'll look at it when I've finished.'

But a few seconds later Isabelle was there, holding the mobile out for him. 'Considering who it's from, you probably want to read it now.'

He glanced at the screen and saw a notification from Sally. But with one hand holding the valve in place, the other unscrewing it, he was tied up. 'Just leave it.'

'Sure you want to risk ignoring her? Might be important.' In the blink of an eye Isabelle took the screwdriver from him and slapped the phone in his hand. Figuring it was quicker not to argue, he tapped to open it.

Sally: Do you like anchovies? Being lazy and about to order pizza… [pizza emoji, licking lips emoji, fish emoji, kissing face emoji]

'Doesn't know you that well then, huh?'

He glanced up to find Isabelle staring down at the screen.

We don't spend a lot of time talking. He opened his mouth to say it, but slammed it shut again. He wasn't going to demean what he and Sally had, bring it down to sex when it was way beyond that now. 'She knows the important stuff.' Like why he was screwed up when it came to relationships. She'd not said as much, but he'd seen the understanding in her eyes after they'd come out of the restaurant following lunch with his mother. His childhood hadn't been terrible, but it also hadn't given him any reason to aspire to being married or having kids.

Hastily, he replied to Sally.

Like anchovies about the same as I do romcoms…x

Sally: you'll put up with them because I do [grinning widely emoji, smiley face emoji, hearts in eyes emoji]

He laughed, shaking his head.

Yep x

Before he could slip it back into his pocket, Isabelle took the phone and handed him the screwdriver. 'I'll put it back in your jacket. Safer there.'

This helpful Isabelle was slightly weird. 'Thanks.'

When he emerged fifteen minutes later, he found her in the living room, picking a photo off the mantlepiece. She smiled at him sadly. 'Do you remember when that was taken?'

He gave it a cursory glance, not interested in the trip down memory lane. 'Before you started sleeping with Patrick.'

Her face hardened. 'I had sex with him in his office twice.

That's all.' She bit into her lip. 'We ended it the day you came to meet me.'

'You ended it, or he did?'

She glared back at him. 'What difference does it make?'

'You're right, it makes absolutely no difference to how I feel.' With a sigh, he turned and headed to the door. 'Let me know when you have a move date. I'll help you shift your stuff into the new place.'

'Make sure I'm gone, huh?' Because he figured there had been too much bad feeling between them, he ignored the comment and opened the door. 'Do you love her?'

The question made him pause. It was none of Isabelle's business, but he didn't want her thinking there was any way back for them. 'You know me. I don't believe in love.' But then he stared Isabelle directly in the eye. 'But if you're asking me if things are serious between me and Sally, the answer is yes. I can't imagine myself with anyone else.'

Isabelle nodded, her expression a mix of confusion and sadness. 'If I hadn't slept with Patrick, we'd be still together though.'

He thought of what he had with Sally, and what he'd had with Isabelle. 'Don't kid yourself. We weren't right for each other.' He gave her a wry smile. 'I guess I should thank you. If I hadn't had to find somewhere to stay, I might never have met Sally.'

It was fate. The clichéd line echoed back at him as he climbed into his truck. Yet he couldn't deny that it was a quirk of fate that had found him living with Sally, and that she'd brought something to his life that he'd not known was missing.

And it wasn't romcoms, he thought with a smile. Then sobered when he realised they were meant to be doing the next scene tonight. Damn. He needed to get some cards on the way home.

Then figure out what the hell to write on them.

———————————

Harry had disappeared into his room almost the moment he'd stepped into the flat. He'd taken off his boots, hung up his jacket, come to give her a brief but knee-trembling kiss … then vanished with a slim package under his arm.

That had been twenty minutes ago.

Suddenly Sally heard his door creak open and she darted out of the kitchen to find him standing in the hallway, hands on hips. His hair was damp from the shower and he'd changed into grey sweats and a long-sleeved black Henley T-shirt. How was it fair that sloppy looked so frigging good on him?

'We don't have to bother with the carol singers, do we?'

'The carol singers … oh.' She started to laugh. 'That's what you've been up to. You're writing the cards for the *Love Actually* scene?'

He heaved out a sigh. 'Trying to. I mean I can write. It's just what to write that's proving hard.' He stared back at her. 'Are we doing this as us, or as the couple in the film?'

It was just a daft scene and yet … her pulse spiked as she thought what he might write. Pretence would be easier to handle, because what she wanted to be on the cards and what he would write were going to be very different. But while they'd copied scenes, they'd never done it as the characters in the film, they'd always been themselves. 'We're doing it as us.'

He drew a hand down his face, and it was only then she saw he looked … stressed.

'We don't have to do it all.' Feeling guilty, she walked up to him, smoothed the frown lines on his forehead. 'This is meant to be fun.'

His eyes roamed her face, like he was trying to read her. 'Are you sure? Because I'm worried you have … expectations. And whatever they are, you need to lower them. I'm shit at this stuff.'

'Shit at making me smile? Making me laugh?' She cradled his earnest-looking face and kissed him softly. 'You're epic at it.'

'You'd be okay with that?' He looked like he didn't believe her. 'Just playing it for laughs?'

She pictured the scene from *Love Actually*, remembered how emotional she felt every time she watched it. But that was fiction. Staring into Harry's concerned grey eyes, she felt a hard tug on her heart. This man in front of her was real, and yes it meant he had faults but, boy, so did she. 'I'll be okay with whatever you want to write.' Because it still felt too heavy, she grinned at him. 'And guess what, if I'm not, we can always do a re-take and *I'll* write the cards.'

His face relaxed. 'Okay, good. I'm ready then.'

'You're sure? Don't want to check them?' she teased. 'Worry a bit more about how upset I'm going to be with your corny jokes?'

He gave her a mock-offended look. 'I don't do corny.' Then he stepped inside the room and came back out with a stack of large cards under his arm.

'Looks like we're doing this then.' She eyed the cards, and, despite everything she'd said, her belly wriggled with anticipation. 'I'll set the phone up on the sideboard and let you know when I'm ready.'

He started walking towards the door but stopped in front of it and looked down at his sweatpants. 'Is this okay?'

'If you mean will your fanbase still call you a hottie when they see you in joggers instead of a tux?' She let out an exaggerated sigh. 'The answer is yes.'

A pleased smile spread across his face. 'Good to know.'

The door closed behind him and she held a hand over her heart, willing it to quiet. Dear God, she was losing it. He'd been right to be concerned; the romantic in her was way too invested in this.

Quickly, she set up the phone camera so it had a good view of the door. Then she called out she was ready, pressed Play, and waited for the knock.

When it came, she inhaled a deep breath and answered it.

Harry held up the first card.

Hi

She laughed and he held up the second one.

Good start huh?

Figuring she'd stick to the original scene for her part, she smiled but kept quiet.

But now I'm stuck

Next card.

Words have never been my thing

This is more my thing

On the card he'd stuck some photos out of a magazine.

There was a pint of beer, a few guys playing football and a hammer.

Her heart shifted. This big hunk of a man might not be romantic, but he was ridiculously, loveably, *sweet*.

Then he held up the next card, and her heart somersaulted.

But with you I want to try

Now her heart was in her mouth.

So it may not be Wordsworth or that bloke on *Love Actually* but…

She stared back at Harry and he shrugged, though the intensity of his gaze, the swirl of emotion in his eyes, belied the gesture.

That fantasy of yours?

Her breath caught as he held up the last card.

You make me want to give it to you.

Heart hammering now, she looked into his eyes. Did he mean he wanted to, but he couldn't? Or he wanted to try?

He gave her a crooked smile. 'That's all I've got.'

The vulnerability in his expression caught at her throat. Whatever his meaning for the future, it was beyond clear that he'd tried to make *this* fantasy come true.

'Just as well.' Feeling choked, she wiped her eyes. 'Any more and I'll be a blubbering mess.'

Remembering what had happened in the shower scene, she

squashed her need to smother him with kisses just long enough to turn off the video. Then she ran up to him and flung her arms around his neck.

'Whoa.' The cards clattered to the floor as he lifted her up, her legs wrapping round his waist. 'It was okay, then?'

She kissed him, then kissed him again, wanting to get as close as she could, as quickly as she could. To burrow into him. 'Did you mean it?'

He nodded, eyes fixed on her. 'Of course.'

'Then take me to bed.'

'Or lose you for ever?'

She smiled, but inside her heart was telling her he would never lose her. In fact, if he wanted, he could *have* her for ever.

It wasn't until the next day, during a lull in customers, that Sally remembered to upload the video onto TikTok. She wanted to give it the line *Love Actually?* but she knew she was getting ahead of herself and besides, that was far too private an observation. She settled with *Harry meets Sally to do Love Actually*.

Chapter Twenty-Nine

Harry studied the partly completed extension and felt a rush of pride. Forget the hard graft, the days when it rained and everything that could go wrong – *did* go wrong. Creating a space for people to enjoy was deeply satisfying.

'Oh no, cover your ears, young Amy.' Jack's voice floated over to him. 'Any minute now Harry's going to deliver his sentimental speech.'

Amy put down the tape measure she'd been using. 'What do you mean?'

'He does this every time we get the shell of a new build up.' Jack smirked, face full of mischief. 'He looks at it like some doting dad gazing at his newborn babe. Then he waxes lyrical about how rewarding this job is, how we make the world a better place, blah, blah blah.'

Okay, so maybe he had been about to say that. Didn't mean he was predictable. He was proud, that's all.

He didn't get the chance to get into a dingdong with Jack though, because his phone started to ring, number unrecognised. Settling for a middle finger at his supposed mate, he answered.

'Who's this?'

'It's your worst enemy. What the fuck do you think you're playing at?'

What the hell? 'Is that Kitty?' It was only as she confirmed it was that his brain took in the second part of what she'd said. 'What's wrong? Is Sally okay?'

'Of course she's not fucking okay.'

Now his heart was galloping. 'Is she sick?'

'Sick of you, most definitely.'

He calmed a little. A row with him, he could deal with. 'Where is she?'

'In the cafe. And, trust me, you're the last person she'll want to see.'

As if he gave two fucks what Kitty thought. 'I'm on my way.'

He silenced her objections by pressing end on the call.

'That was Kitty. I've got to go,' he told Mike. 'Something's upset Sally.' When Amy jerked her head up, he shook his head. 'It's me she's pissed at for some reason. I need to sort it.'

He didn't wait for Mike to answer. The job wasn't important, not in that moment. All that mattered was making things right with Sally.

He pushed open the door to the cafe twenty minutes later. A quick scan showed no sign of Sally or Kitty but Vince was there, serving a couple. Harry hung back, waited for the guy to finish.

'Where is she?'

Vince nodded to the back of the cafe. 'In the office.' He stared back at Harry, then shook his head. 'I don't want to think you had a hand in this.'

'Hand in what?' Frustrated, he jammed his hand through his hair. 'Kitty didn't say, just that Sally is upset with me for some reason.' They'd had epic sex this morning, he'd kissed her before he left. What the hell had happened between then and now?

'You'd better ask Sally.'

He marched through to the back and knocked on the door to the office.

'Who is it?' Kitty's voice.

'Harry.'

'Fuck off.'

More alarmed than angry, he pushed the door open and stepped inside. Ignoring Kitty's murderous look, his eyes settled on the woman sitting in the chair. The woman Kitty had her arms around.

Sally glanced up, and the sight of her tear-streaked face caused a fierce pain in his chest, like his heart was tearing in two. 'What is it, what's wrong?'

'Have you looked at TikTok this afternoon?' Sally's voice was small, her eyes, usually so full of life, were horribly flat.

'I've been on site.'

'You'd better take a look.' Kitty's voice was hard as stone. 'First, check out the comment from Isabelle on the video itself. Shouldn't be too hard to find. It's the most liked.'

His heart hammered a frantic beat and his fingers felt too fat as he opened the app on his phone to find their account. Clicking on their latest video, the one mimicking *Love Actually*, he pressed to read the comments.

Harry said he wanted to give it to her. He certainly did from the look of things #HarrydoesSally.

'What?' He was confused.

'She's referring to the cards you wrote for Sally. The last one said "you make me want to give it to you". So romantic,' Kitty added cuttingly.

'The fantasy. I wanted to give her the fantasy.' He willed Sally to look at him. Surely she'd known that was what he meant, not this sordid version that Kitty and Isabelle had made it into.

But Sally was avoiding his eyes, and Kitty was talking again.

'Search for #HarrydoesSally. Then explain to us how Isabelle got that video.'

Dread curdled in his stomach. What video were they talking about? After a few fumbling attempts, he typed the words in and found the video of him kissing Sally in the shower.

'Keep watching.'

He wanted to enjoy the sight of her melting in his arms, relive the perfect moment, but the knots in his stomach, the clawing dread … he knew what was coming next.

Shit.

He'd deleted the original video, hadn't he?

'I don't know.' His voice shook and he looked straight into Sally's bloodshot eyes. 'I don't know how Isabelle got hold of that.'

Kitty snatched the phone from him and began to scroll through his photos. 'There it is. That's the video you were supposed to have deleted.'

He had a flashback to the night Sally had messaged him about it. He'd been drunk. Had he deleted the wrong one?

'Wait.' He pressed Play, and watched with his heart in his mouth. 'It's the edited version that Sally put onto TikTok. I downloaded it.'

Kitty looked like she couldn't believe it. 'Why would you keep that?'

He glanced over at Sally. 'She knows why.' Sally's head jerked and she stared back at him. 'It was a special moment. An epic moment.'

He couldn't read her. He thought her eyes had softened a little, but there was so much sadness there still and he got it. He was about to tell her that, when Kitty swore.

'You bastard.' Kitty sent him a look that would have shrivelled a stone. 'You might have deleted the original, but it's still there, in your deleted photos file. And here's a message you sent to Isabelle, forwarding it to her.'

She shoved the messenger app under his nose and he looked at it with mounting horror. 'This is bollocks. For fuck's sake, why the hell would I do that?'

Kitty waved the phone at him, her expression clearly saying *but I have proof you did*.

Desperately, he recalled when Isabelle might have had his phone... Shit, when he'd fixed the damn valve.

Kitty laughed humourlessly. 'Now you remember, huh? A drunken moment with your ex?'

Anger fizzed down his spine but he reined it in, well aware that having a full-scale row with Kitty wouldn't help anything. Most of all, it wouldn't help Sally, who remained horribly quiet.

'Sally.' He silently pleaded with her to look at him. 'You know I didn't do this.'

She felt numb. Sally was aware of the conversation going on around her, of Kitty's harsh words and Harry's shell-shocked expression, but she couldn't connect. All she kept seeing was the video of her coming apart in Harry's arms in the shower. Of that intense, intimate, highly private moment, now being watched by thousands of people.

Harry was talking to her, his eyes begging her to believe him.

'What other explanation is there?' Kitty again, clearly determined to believe the absolute worst of Harry, and yet right now her friend was the life raft. The one person she felt she could cling to.

'How about the one where Isabelle got hold of my phone?' There was a hard edge to Harry's voice.

'And how did she do that? Did you go back to your house for lunch? Meet her in your bedroom maybe?'

Harry's face flushed and Sally reached for Kitty's hand. 'That's enough.'

'I went to my house to fix the shower valve after work yesterday,' Harry said tightly, jaw muscles jumping. 'Isabelle handed me my phone so I could reply to Sally's message. She must have gone through it when she took it downstairs to put it back in my jacket. Probably forwarded the video to herself when she found the message from Sally asking me to delete it.' He rubbed his face, and for the first time Sally noticed how shattered he looked. Like he'd been punched, repeatedly. 'I don't know why she'd do that. Or decide to upload it.'

'Because she's a bitch?'

Sally squeezed Kitty's hands again in a silent warning to back off.

Silence echoed round the small office for a few seconds. Then she heard Harry's deep exhale. 'I'm sorry if I've—'

'If?' Kitty ignored her warning and jumped to her feet. 'There is no if. You didn't delete the original video from your phone properly, leaving Sally vulnerable to this. You let your own phone get into the hands of your vengeful ex.' She stabbed a finger at Harry. 'You may not have *meant* for anything to happen, but it doesn't alter the fact that Sally has been hurt because of your actions.'

Harry ignored Kitty and crouched down on his haunches in front of her, his expression tortured. 'Please, Sally, talk to me. Say something. I'm dying here, thinking you believe I'm responsible for this.'

She wanted to tell him not to worry, she knew he hadn't done this, yet Kitty's words wouldn't budge from her brain. Sure, it hadn't been intentional, but two of the most special moments in her life – the start of her sexual relationship with Harry, and the moment he'd admitted, via the cards, that he wanted to give her the fantasy – were tarnished now, ruined.

'I don't think you're responsible.' She gazed into his turbulent grey eyes. 'But I do think this could be a sign.'

His brow furrowed. 'A sign?'

She swallowed, emotion a hard lump in her throat, her eyes burning with more tears. 'A sign we should end things.'

'You've got to be fucking kidding me.'

She gave him a sad smile. 'Maybe you were right about love. Maybe opening your heart to someone just leads to heartache and pain.'

He gave her an agonised look and tried to reach for her hand but Kitty pushed him away. 'You need to leave. You can see she's upset.'

'She's not the only one upset here.'

His voice sounded rough, gravelly, and when she saw the devastation on his face, the glitter of unshed tears in his beautiful grey eyes, her heart crumpled.

Yet much as she wanted to reach out to him, to tell him to

forget what she'd said, the words stuck in her throat. Her mind felt like a boggy field, and she was sinking in it, unable to move forward. As if she sensed her friend's turmoil, Kitty pushed Harry out of the door. Then slammed it behind him.

There was a finality to the noise that sent a tremor through her.

Kitty gave her a wry smile. 'Don't think I'm not aware he could have stuck his ground and I wouldn't have been able to budge him.'

'He didn't want to upset me any more than I already am, so he left.'

Kitty sighed and went to hug her. 'I know. Just as I know this isn't all totally his fault. I'm not quite the hard-nosed bitch he thinks I am.' Her arms tightened around her. 'But I can see you're hurting and, to quote from *Star Wars*, the protective instinct is very strong with this one.'

Sally let out a strangled laugh. 'I know.' She slumped back against the chair. 'What a mess. I was so happy today when I uploaded the video, watching it again, reliving what Harry had written…' A sob broke free and she reached for the box of paper napkins Kitty had scrounged from the stock cupboard. 'I really felt there was a chance for us, but now I feel like I've been kicked in the teeth.' She shuddered. 'I'm terrified to see how many views Isabelle's had.'

'We've complained about it. They'll take it down soon. I'm surprised it wasn't automatically removed. Probably dodged their anti-explicit content technology because mostly it's just a view of Harry's back.'

Mostly. Except if anyone looked closely. Saw her come undone. Sally dabbed her eyes, wondering if the waterproof mascara would live up to its name. 'I hope they ban her. And give her a serious bollocking. Enough to make her think twice about ever pulling a shitty stunt like this again.'

Kitty glanced towards the door she'd pushed Harry out of. 'Something tells me that will already be in hand.'

'So you believe he had nothing to do with this?'

'You mean did I really think he went to shag Isabelle in his lunch break?' Kitty sighed. 'When I realised the video had been forwarded from his phone I saw red, said stupid stuff in the heat of the moment. But he *was* stupid not to realise the video would still be in his deleted files folder. And even more stupid to let her get her hands on his phone.'

Sally recalled Harry's ravaged face and felt her eyes well again. 'Or maybe he was just naïve about technology, and too trusting.'

'I guess that could also be true.' Kitty perched on the edge of the desk. 'So what happens now?'

'First, I delete the last video, so that removes her bitchy comment.'

'You could just delete her comment. Deleting the video removes all the views,' Kitty pointed out.

'I don't care about the whole TikTok thing anymore. The moments we acted out, I got too carried away. They meant far more to me than they were supposed to. Especially that last one. I can't bear to see it again.' Another sob left her. 'I won't be recreating any more romcom scenes.'

'You could create them with someone else.' Kitty smiled. 'Adam would be up for it, I'm sure.'

Sally shook her head, her heart aching. 'If you think I can recreate with Adam what I had with Harry, you really don't understand how I feel about Harry.'

Kitty searched her face, and her eyes swum with sympathy. 'Okay. You delete the video. I'll help Vince finish up here.

Then, if you want to come and stay with me tonight, we can go back to your place and pick up some clothes.'

She didn't want that, Sally realised as Kitty quietly slipped out. She wanted to go home, to where Harry was. To be folded into his arms and for his deep, rumbling voice to tell her everything was going to be okay.

But… She bent forward, holding her head in her hands. Hadn't she always known this was going to end? The pain she felt now was exactly the big, flashing warning sign she needed to stop her from dreaming. Stop her from hoping for the impossible. Harry might have wanted to give her the fantasy, but it didn't mean he would. Or even that he could.

Weariness hung over her and she closed her eyes, but all she saw was his face, the raw hurt as she'd suggested they should end things. He might not love her like she loved him, but she wasn't the only one deeply invested in this relationship. He didn't deserve her disappearing off to Kitty's. Not without a proper conversation.

Chapter Thirty

Harry paced the flat, beside himself. Now he understood where the phrase tearing your hair out came from. He'd dragged his hands through his so much, it was a wonder he wasn't bald.

He hadn't returned to work – for the first time ever, he'd phoned Mike and told him to finish up the day without him. Mike must have heard something in his voice because he hadn't made any sarky comments. Instead he'd said no problem, then followed it up with a message.

Anything you need, call me, anytime.

Emotions all over the place, Harry had choked up when he'd read it.

Next, he'd gone round to his house to confront Isabelle. One look at the expression on his face and her haughty look had collapsed. 'You're angry about the video.'

'What the hell was going through your head?' he'd demanded, at a loss to understand how someone he'd once cared for could do something so vicious, so spiteful.

Tears had filled her eyes but he'd been far too incensed to

feel any sympathy. 'I don't know,' she'd whispered. 'I wanted to see what sort of messages you and Sally sent each other, but then I found one about a video, and when I saw it, I just ... I lost my mind for a bit. I thought if I posted it, she'd kick you out. Then you'd come back here and it would be like old times.'

He'd told her bluntly that their time had been over well before Sally had come into the picture. Then he'd watched over her as she'd deleted the video, only to find not only was her post no longer there, their *Love Actually* clip had vanished, too. His heart had shuddered to a stop as he'd considered the implications of *that*.

Finally, he'd told Isabelle he expected her to be gone when he came back tomorrow morning. No excuses.

He was done being Mr Nice Guy to a woman who'd shattered the best thing that had ever happened to him.

Now he was pacing. Sally should have been back an hour ago. Was she even going to come back? Or would Kitty waltz in here and tell him to leave, like he'd just done to Isabelle?

He came to an abrupt halt as he heard the key in the lock.

'Hey.' His heart thumped like a drum in his chest as Sally stepped inside. 'I was afraid you weren't going to come home.'

Home. The word curled around his insides, evoking images of a future he'd never imagined for himself. Until he'd met her.

She dipped her head, not quite meeting his eyes. 'I thought we should talk.'

'Yes.' He walked towards her, half afraid she'd bolt. 'But first can I please... Can I hold you?' It was a few heavy beats while he held his breath before she crossed the space between them and he wrapped her in his arms. 'I'm so fucking sorry,' he murmured, lips close to her hair, breathing in her coconut shampoo, breathing in *her*. 'Kitty's right, I should have realised the video wasn't fully deleted, and that Isabelle couldn't be trusted with my phone.'

She wriggled out of his arms. 'I don't blame you.'

'Are you sure?' *Because if you don't, why does it feel like you're punishing me?*

'Maybe part of me does a bit. I mean, I wish you'd been more careful, but it's not like you meant any of this to happen.'

She turned away and walked into the kitchen, busying herself with filling the kettle when he was damn certain a drink of tea was the last thing she wanted.

'I deleted that last video.' She glanced up at him. 'I hope that's okay. I know the money from the sponsorship was nice but—'

'I don't give a fuck about the TikTok stuff.' She startled and he inhaled slowly, trying to calm himself. 'It was always your thing, not mine.' When she nodded stiffly, he knew she'd taken that the wrong way. Christ, for a guy who prided himself on plain speaking, he had to get better about talking about his feelings. 'I meant it was your idea, your genius and hard work that got us to the place where we were making money out of it. I liked the money, but I liked having a laugh with you even more.'

She gave him a sad smile. 'They were fun, weren't they?'

'They still can be.' She didn't reply, just carried on with the mechanics of making the drinks. That included getting two mugs out, which he wondered if she'd done out of habit. 'Look, you say you don't blame me, but if that's the case why are you over there and I'm over here?' Her eyes looked huge in her face as she met his gaze. 'I know you're upset, and I get that what Isabelle did was inexcusable, but if you don't blame me, why won't you let me hold you?'

Silence, except for the hiss of the kettle. Even when he'd

only just moved in and they hadn't known each other well, there had never been this strained atmosphere, this sense that he was walking on eggshells.

'I don't know.' Her voice was painfully quiet, lacking all the usual energy, the exuberance he always associated with her. 'It just feels like everything is ruined, and I'm sorry if that sounds dumb to you, but it's how I feel.' Her eyes met his, and he saw her pain. 'I want to be able to shrug this off, not care that who knows how many people have watched me orgasm, that what I thought were really special moments have been hijacked by your ex and made into something sordid.' Her voice started to crack and she wrapped her arms around herself. 'But I'm sorry, I can't. Those videos, those moments, they meant a lot to me. At the time I thought we might be building towards something, but now this has happened and I realise I got that wrong. I wanted the fantasy so much I was seeing things that weren't there.'

He hated this. Seeing her so distraught, knowing he was responsible, it sliced him in two. 'How do you know they weren't there if you end us before we get to find out?'

Tears spilt down her cheeks. 'Because we want different things. We've always wanted different things.' She sobbed out a laugh. 'I got blindsided by our chemistry but I think when I take a step back I'll see you weren't the man I'm meant to be with.'

'Jesus, Sally.' He felt crushed, like someone had taken his heart and squeezed the life out of it. First, he wasn't enough for Isabelle. Now it seemed he wasn't enough for Sally. 'So that's it?' She nodded, and that crushed feeling intensified, bringing with it a burst of anger at what she was throwing away. 'You told me once that you know real life isn't like a romcom, but I'm starting to seriously doubt that. Seems to me you want the perfect man, the perfect moments – the guy who'll sweep you off his feet. But that perfect guy doesn't exist, and in between those moments, life's messy. People make mistakes, get hurt.' He shook his head, emotions all over the place. 'But if they care for each other, I'm pretty certain they don't bail at the first bloody road bump.' Staring at the two mugs, white with matching pink hearts, he laughed humourlessly. 'You really think we can sit down now and drink tea together? Eat together? Stay in the same flat as each other?'

Her hand trembled and she put the kettle back down. 'I don't know. I wasn't thinking.'

'It would be awkward as fuck if I carry on living here with you now.' And hurt like hell to go back to polite conversation and separate bedrooms, he added silently.

It was unravelling too fast. She'd come back to talk to Harry, but now he was leaving. A sob tore from Sally. This wasn't what she wanted.

She opened her mouth to tell him not to go, but then slammed it shut again. This was for the best. They needed distance, *she* needed distance – from him. She'd not been kidding when she'd told him he distracted her. How was she supposed to make clear, sensible decisions when he looked at her as he was now? All frustrated and pissed off, yet with such yearning in his eyes that all she wanted to do was fling herself at him and never let him go.

'I'm going to miss you.'

He leaned back against the worktop and briefly shut his eyes. When he opened them again, he looked almost angry. 'Don't say stuff like that.'

'Sorry.' She bit into her lip, scared to ask the next question but needing to know. 'Where will you go?' *Back to your house. To Isabelle.*

He was an expert at reading her expressions. 'I'm not going to move back to my house while Isabelle's still there. Give me some credit.' He pushed himself off the counter. 'I'll crash on Mike's sofa till she's gone.'

Tears pricked the back of her eyes. 'I feel like the bad guy here, but you have to know this isn't just about the video.' She held his gaze. 'Can you tell me you love me? Or even that you might love me one day?' He didn't say anything, but she could see by the way his jaw was working that she'd made him think. 'That's the real issue here. Do I stay with a man I'm falling in love with, but who can't love me back and will one day leave me?' He jerked, eyes avoiding hers. 'Or do I get out now and see if I can find someone who would, maybe, fall in love with me, too?'

A tortured look crossed his face. 'That's not fair.' His voice sounded rough, heavy with emotion. 'This isn't a film where the ending is tied up in a neat bow. I can't say what the future holds. Nobody knows that.' Grey eyes filled with pain met hers. 'I might never want to leave you.'

She smiled sadly at him. 'But that's the thing. If you loved me, there would be no might about it. You'd *know*.'

He hung his head, and her heart ached for him because she knew he was struggling to understand what he was feeling. And also because she knew he was hurting, just like she was. Unable to stop herself, she walked over to him, slid her arms around his waist and pressed her head against his brick wall of a chest.

Immediately, his arms wrapped round hers and they stood for a few minutes, united in their misery. This moment had been on the cards from the day she'd slept with him. Maybe even before that, because heaven help her, she'd crushed on him for months now. But it would be too easy to rewind, to go back to the way things were and continue to ride this amazing wave a while longer. At some point, the wave would end, and she would get dumped into the ocean, churned around and finally spat out.

So she untangled herself from his arms and stepped back. Watched silently as he walked out of the kitchen, broad shoulders not quite as straight as usual, gait not as fluid.

She'd just finished making the tea when he appeared in the doorway again, holdall in his hand. 'Let me know when I can come back for the rest of my stuff.'

Her heart felt as if it was dragging on the floor. 'Sure.' He'd be taking his bed, she thought with a wrench. The same bed they'd spent hours, sometimes whole days, rolling around on.

With a single incline of his head, he opened the door and disappeared.

A sob burst of out of her the moment it shut behind him. And the tears fell faster when she walked into the hallway to find no boots by the door. No coat hanging on his peg. And his set of keys still in the bowl on the sideboard.

———

Sally tried to distract herself by watching a film but it brought back too many memories – lying sprawled across the sofa with Harry, listening to his teasing gripes about whatever romcom they were watching. So instead she had a shower, turned on her Kindle and tried to focus on reading.

When her phone rang ten minutes later, she clutched at it,

only to feel a crushing disappointment when she saw it was Amy, not Harry.

'Hi.'

A pause, then Amy's voice. 'Is everything okay? You sound, I dunno, off.'

'You can tell that from one word?'

Another pause. Then a sigh. 'I am your sister.'

Already in emotional overload, those four words, the reminder of the bond they'd once shared, was too much for Sally. She burst into tears.

Ten minutes later, Amy rang on the bell.

'You didn't have to come,' Sally mumbled, opening the door to her. 'I told you, Harry and me have split, but I'm okay. Nothing a bit of time, distance and a margarita won't fix.'

'Yeah, well, maybe I wanted to see for myself.' Amy studied her face. 'You look like crap.'

'Thanks.' Sally gave her a weak smile. 'Could always rely on you to bolster me up.'

'That's what siblings are for.' Amy pushed her into the kitchen. 'Come on then, let's get stuck into the margaritas and you can take me through the gory details behind the split.'

It didn't take long to give Amy the rundown. Intensely private video posted by lover's deranged ex. 'Okay, I get that was mega embarrassing, but how come you kicked Harry out? It wasn't like he meant for any of that to happen.'

'I know, and I didn't kick him out. He chose to go.'

Amy scoffed. 'Right, because he wasn't really into you or anything, so of course he wanted to leave.'

'How do you know he was into me?'

Amy rolled her eyes. 'Come on, why else did he give me a job? I can tell you, it wasn't because he needed the extra pair of hands because I'm not exactly useful. More of a hindrance because he has to keep stopping to explain stuff to me.' She shook her head at Sally. 'He told me you were special, gave me this big speech about how much you'd given up to take care of me. That man is hooked. So why is he not here with you now?'

Sally reached for a tissue, blew her nose and tried to gather her thoughts. 'He told me right from the beginning that he didn't believe in love, never saw himself married or with kids.' Her throat tightened and she had to take a breath to power through it. 'It didn't matter because we were just having fun, right? But then Isabelle posted that video and it all went south. I know it's not Harry's fault, but it feels like a sign, you know, like the bells, only the opposite. A sign we're not meant to be.'

'The bells?'

'You remember Mum telling us about the bells, that we'd hear them ring when we found The One? Well, I've not heard them, so Harry isn't the man I'm meant to be with. And that's okay, I always knew it.' Deep in her chest, her heart began to ache, as if it knew what she'd said was a lie. 'It's just going to hurt for a bit while I get over him.'

'Oh my God, and I thought you were the smart one.' Amy gave her a sympathetic smile. 'Mum never said you were going to hear like *real* bells.'

'I didn't think I'd see a man walk down the street ringing them,' she retorted defensively. 'Just, I don't know, something going off in my head.'

'Well, what Mum actually said was if falling in love had a sound, it would be church bells at a wedding. Something about the sound being full of joy, of making you want to burst with happiness when you heard it. So I guess you have to work out if that's how you felt when you looked at Harry.'

She didn't need to work it out. She'd always known, on one level, that she'd fallen head over heels in love with him, but she'd tried to kid herself that no bells meant she'd be okay. She'd still be able to get out without her heart being ripped in two.

Now she knew this awful pain in her chest wasn't going to go away in a few weeks, a few months.

'So?'

Amy was waiting for an answer. 'It doesn't matter whether I love him or not. He doesn't love me, he'll never love me, so there's no point in carrying on.' She raised her chin, stared back at her sister. 'We both deserve the deep, lasting love that Mum and Dad had, and neither of us should put up with anything less.'

Understanding dawned in Amy's eyes. 'You're talking about Chris now and it's okay, I get it.' She picked at the sleeve of her hoodie and suddenly she looked like the fourteen-year-old girl Sally had once had such a strong bond with. 'I don't think we're going to last much longer. I figured he'd be happy for me, you know, that I've found something I enjoy doing. That makes me feel, I dunno, like I'm useful. But he keeps sniping about how I'm no fun anymore because I don't want to drink and party when I know I have to get up in the morning for work.' Her tear-filled eyes met Sally's. 'He doesn't get it.'

Amy started to cry then and Sally pulled her into a hug. An hour ago, it felt like her life was imploding. Now, though her heart was crushed, she knew she would survive this. She'd lost the man she loved, but, thanks to that man, she'd got her sister back.

Chapter Thirty-One

Harry slowly pulled himself up into a sitting position. Slowly because every muscle in his back was shouting at him, clearly disgusted at the cramped position it had been forced into during the night.

'Morning.' Mike stood in the doorway. 'The sofa fought back last night, did it?'

'Bloody thing is too small.'

'That's because I bought it to sit on. Not for sad six-foot-four singles to sleep on.'

Singles. Harry rubbed at his face, trying to get some blood circulating. He was single again. That was good, wasn't it? He could do what the hell he liked now. Didn't have to eat leftover quiches from the cafe. Didn't have to put up with Kitty and her barbed comments when she and Vince came over. Best of all, he didn't have to watch any more frigging romcoms.

'Remind me why you spent the night on my sofa instead of in the place you're renting. Or the place you own?'

'I told you, I got dumped.'

Mike shook his head. 'Not buying that. You said Sally

didn't blame you for the video, so why would she suddenly kick you out?'

He stretched, trying to iron out the kinks in his neck, his back, his legs. 'She ended things. I could hardly carry on living there after that, could I?'

'Yeah, but she had to have a reason.'

'Leave it.' He had no desire to rake over the dying embers of another failed relationship. For a guy who didn't want heavy or serious, it was kind of ironic that he'd lived with two women in the last six months. One had bruised his ego. The other had... He felt the punch in his chest as he recalled last night. *When I take a step back I'll see you weren't the man I'm meant to be with.* Yeah, the other had taken a knife, jammed it into his chest and yanked on it for good measure.

Yet hadn't she also said she was falling for him?

He dropped his face into his hands. Christ, his head hurt.

A few minutes later he became aware of Mike standing over him. When he looked up, the man shoved a cup of coffee into his hands. 'Fat lot of good you're going to be today.'

'I'll be fine.' Bleary-eyed, he clutched gratefully at the mug. 'You ever been in love?'

Mike's eyebrows flew up. 'Not the conversation I expected to have with you before breakfast but okay.' A slow, soft smile spread across his face. 'Matter of fact, I have. I am.'

'You and Trixie?'

'I've hardly got another woman on the go, have I?' But then that goofy smile erupted again. 'I'm going to ask her to move in with me, so be warned, this sofa will be off limits soon.'

'Assuming she says yes.'

He looked affronted. 'How could she not want to live with me? I'm frigging adorable.'

Harry tried to smile, but he couldn't help but think that

was part of his problem. He *wasn't* adorable. Isabelle had had no problem cheating on him. Sally clearly thought she could do way better than him, which okay, she could, of course she could, but shit, that hurt. *She didn't say find someone better, she said find someone who might love her.* But better was implied, because he had to be defective in some way if he couldn't love someone as amazing as her, didn't he?

'How do you know you love Trixie? I mean, how does it feel?'

Mike looked at him like he was deranged. 'You don't know?' He must have seen the desperation in Harry's face because his expression softened and he came to sit next to him. 'Okay, let me think.' He scratched at his chin. 'It's probably different for different people, but with me? I want to spend any free time I have with her. When I'm not with her I'm thinking of her.' He waved at Harry. 'Especially when I've got a lump like you sat on my sofa with a face like a slapped arse, ruining all my happy vibes.'

'Sorry.' He wanted to leave it there, slap Mike on the back and thank him, then get the hell out and back to work. A place where he knew what he was doing, what was expected of him. But he pictured Sally's face, the future he'd seen but been too scared, too dumb, to grasp. 'I think I love Sally,' he blurted. 'But I don't know. And I have to know, don't I? Have to be sure or it's not fair on her.'

'Some people know straight away. Others it takes longer. What's important is you have to be open to the possibility of it. Be willing to *try.*' Mike gave him a sideways glance. 'All these years we've been mates, and I can't remember ever having a conversation about relationships with you.'

Harry gave him an ironic smile. 'Guess we figured it would lose us some macho points or some crap like that.'

'Probably,' Mike agreed. 'Pretty daft considering that working through this stuff, analysing your feelings, your emotions, is way more important than analysing Albion's leaky defence.'

He let out a weak laugh. 'Yeah, but I know a damn sight more about football.'

'You and me both.' Mike shifted forward, resting his forearms on his thighs in a mirror image of Harry's. 'Nobody said relationships were easy, so don't beat yourself up for not having all the answers. Take the time to figure out what you really want.' He flicked Harry a look. 'If you want my take though, I've never seen you so cut up over anyone before, which should probably tell you something.' Jumping to his feet, he punched Harry on the shoulder. 'Come on, haul yourself into the shower and let's get to work.'

***

Half an hour later, they were on site. Harry was about to drag some plasterboard to the back of the house when he saw Amy standing hesitantly on the driveway.

'Morning.'

She pushed her hands into the pocket of her jacket. 'Hi.' But she didn't move.

'What's up? Not working today?'

Her eyes darted towards the house. 'I dunno. Am I?'

With a sigh, he dropped the plasterboards and walked over to her. 'Look, what's between me and Sally doesn't affect what goes on here but if you want out, no problem.'

'I don't. I just figured you might not want me here.'

'Have you talked to her?'

'I went to see her last night.'

He felt a dart of satisfaction. 'That's good. Are you two overcoming your differences?'

'You mean do I realise I've been a right cow to her? Yeah.' She looked pensive. 'I told her I'm gonna break up with Chris.' Her eyes caught his. 'Now you've gone I can move back into my old room.'

He felt a wrench in his chest when he thought of never going back to the flat. Never sitting on the sofa he liked to scoff at but was actually pretty damn comfortable. But at least with Amy going home, something good was coming out of all this. 'I'll clear my bed out and put yours back after we're done here.'

'Cool.'

He heaved up the boards again and they started to walk round to the back of the house. 'How is she?'

'She's okay. Sad but okay.' Amy glanced over at him. 'She told me we both deserve what Mum and Dad had, and we shouldn't put up with anything less.'

Emotion gripped him like a fist to the throat and he had to work hard to keep his voice from cracking up. 'She's right. I hope she finds it.'

The ache that seemed permanently lodged in his chest, deepened. Yet again he wished he was the man she wanted. The one who could go down on bended knee and promise to love her for ever. But if he said the words now, it would be because they were what she wanted to hear. Not because he believed them. Don't get him wrong, he couldn't imagine ever *not* wanting to be with her, but how could a guy who prided himself on honesty, say words he didn't understand, or make promises he had no clue if he could deliver on? He'd like to bet his parents had given each other some bullshit words about love when they'd got married and no way in hell did he want to end up like them. Miserable together, yet their lives so entwined it was messy and painful to separate them.

He glanced over at Mike, who was laughing with Jack, no doubt already anticipating seeing Trixie tonight, and felt the weight of sadness, of loneliness, settle over him. What was wrong with him? Why could Mike and Sally talk so easily about being in love, and he couldn't?

———————

Sally felt her stomach knot as she closed the door on the last customer, the message from Harry still fresh in her mind.

Spoke to Amy today. Is it okay if I swap the beds round after work?

All business. No kiss, not like she'd had in the messages before she'd told him they were over.

With a sigh that came from deep inside, she went to sort out the till.

'Everything okay?' Vince wandered over and gave her a careful study.

'You mean aside from splitting up with the guy I fell in love with but who doesn't love me back?'

He kissed the top of her head in an affectionate gesture that brought tears to her eyes. 'I'm sorry.'

'Me too.' She drew out the cash drawer, hands operating on autopilot. 'He's coming round tonight to swap the beds round. He replaced Amy's old one with his because hers was too small.' Vince looked like he was trying to suppress a smile. 'It's okay, you can laugh. I'm done with crying.'

'I was just imagining him in Amy's old bedroom. Funny, I'd not considered it before, but if I remember correctly it was a rather vivid shade of pink.'

'He painted it, changed it to some dark-blue green colour.' It had suited him, she thought with an ache as her mind threw up an image of him, chest muscles rippling as he'd eased over her the last time they'd made love there. *It was sex*, she reminded herself sternly.

'I won't ask what you're thinking about right now.' Vince gave her a knowing look. 'Do you want me to come round? Moral support.' He clicked his fingers. 'Wait, I've got a better idea. We'll get Kitty to come as well, get the margaritas out and watch a film. That way you don't have to have anything to do with him.'

Gratitude shot through her and she hugged him. 'That sounds great, thank you.'

An hour later, Sally was sat with her best friends on her gorgeous sofa, trying not to think about the fact Harry was down the corridor, dismantling his bed.

'How about *Notting Hill*?' Kitty suggested, flicking through the romance films.

Instead of joy, she felt a swell of misery. 'No.'

Kitty frowned, then nodded. 'Okay, I get it, that's too much of a weepie. How about *Think Like a Man*? That's funny.'

It was, and yet… 'I'm sorry, I don't think I can watch any film with people falling in love.'

They both gaped at her.

'This is bad. Like serious, never happened before, bad.' Kitty looked over at her in concern. 'How about we go with a Marvel film then? Superpowers sound just what you need right now.'

They settled into the film and Sally tried hard to focus on

Chris Hemsworth and how swoon-worthy he was ... and not on how Harry looked a little bit like him without his shirt on.

At the sound of a throat being cleared, they all turned round. Harry's frame filled the doorway. Automatically her heart somersaulted, not having read the memo that it needed to detach from all things Harry Wilson, pronto.

'All of my stuff is out and Amy's bed is back.' His gaze found hers and despite her determination to be unaffected, her pulse scrambled. 'I'll have to apologise to her for the change in colour scheme.'

'She's probably grown out of the pink anyway.'

He nodded and an awkward silence filled the room. She felt sure he'd turn and go, but instead his eyes flickered over to the TV which Kitty had paused. 'What are you watching?'

As if she sensed Sally was finding this hard, Kitty replied. '*The Avengers.*'

His eyebrows shot up and this time he stared directly at her. 'Not a romcom?'

Sally avoided his eyes. 'I wasn't in the mood.' The pain, the heartache, it all churned around in her stomach. 'I'm beginning to think you were right. They are a silly fantasy.'

She'd expected a smile, not a smug one because he was too sensitive to how she was feeling for that, but at least a little wry humour. Instead, his face... There was no other word for it. It crumpled. 'I don't want to be right.'

The raw emotion in his voice caught at her. 'I don't want you to be right, either.'

Everything faded around her as their gaze caught, held. She forgot Vince and Kitty were watching them. Forgot she was meant to be putting up a shield around her heart. All she wanted to do was be wrapped up in those strong arms and never let go.

He was the first to blink, to look away. 'I'll leave you to it then.'

A few beats later, the door closed quietly behind him.

Vince was the first to speak. 'I've finished with guys because I didn't think they were really into me, not as much as I was into them, and I can tell you, they looked relieved. A bit angry, maybe, because I'd beaten them to it, but mainly relieved. None of them looked like our Hazza just now. As if his world had shattered.' Vince looked sadly at Sally. 'Remind us again why you ended things with him?'

'You know why,' Sally whispered, her voice breaking. 'Kitty said he was going to hurt me and, guess what, she was right.'

Kitty screwed up her face. 'Normally those words would be music to my ears, but looking at Harry just now, it doesn't feel like I'm right. It feels like he's hurting as much as you are.'

'But he doesn't love me,' she protested, a desperate edge to her voice. She'd done the right thing, hadn't she? 'I deserve a guy who loves me, don't I?'

'Of course you do.' Vince reached to squeeze her hand. 'But just to be pedantic here, he told you he doesn't *believe* in love, and from what I remember you said you weren't surprised, not after seeing him with his mum.'

'I don't think he's experienced love first hand. Not seen how beautiful it can be. But that doesn't change anything, does it? How can he ever love me, ever love anyone, if he doesn't believe in it?' Her heart broke that little bit more, this time for Harry and what he would miss out.

Vince looked over at Kitty and whatever silent communication they shared, it led to Kitty let out a deep sigh. 'What Vince is trying to say, is just because Harry doesn't believe in it, doesn't mean he won't ever feel it. It's just that he won't be able to recognise it.' She huffed. 'That man is a blunt, straight talker. He's never going to say anything he doesn't honestly mean.'

Sally pictured the torment on his face the other night as he'd told her he might never want to leave her. But might wasn't good enough, was it? 'What am I supposed to do, stay with him and hope?' The thought of falling deeper and deeper in love with him, only to find he would never feel the same way? 'That seems like prolonging the inevitable while signing up for the mother of all heartbreaks.'

Vince gave her a sympathetic smile. 'I guess that's the thing about love. It's all a risk.' He glanced at the TV, then back at her. 'You know, in a way your love of romcoms isn't helping. The films make us want the words, because that's what steals your breath, what touches your heart when you watch them. But all the words, they're no guarantee. Plenty have said them, and it's meant nothing. Equally, just because the words aren't there, it doesn't mean love isn't there. It means you have to look for other signs.'

Unconsciously, her gaze locked in on the tree he'd bought her. Had that been a sign? Like the one he'd written on the card, saying he wanted to give her the fantasy? Was she so set on that fantasy, on the gestures, the words, she'd missed the other clues of how he felt? Or was she so desperate for him to love her like she did him, she was seeing things that weren't there? Emotions on overload, she put her head in her hands. 'I'm too all the over the place to think about this right now.' Wearily, she raised her head. 'Can we please just ogle Thor?'

Chapter Thirty-Two

The last few weeks had been Shit, and yes, that was with a capital S. Usually Harry enjoyed the run up to Christmas. People tended to be in a better mood, even those whose projects had been delayed or hit snags. Mates were more inclined to socialising, which meant more time down the pub. Always a good thing. Except when you were feeling as miserable as sin.

This Christmas, he'd avoided The Cat and Fiddle, much to Mike and Jack's disgust. 'You're going to let a woman scare you off your local watering hole?'

He'd wanted to defend himself, say he wasn't scared, just respecting her space. Truth was though, he was terrified of seeing Sally again. If he did, there was a distinct possibility that he'd drop to his knees and beg her to forget he wasn't the right man for her. Then plead with her to let him back into her life.

He'd not had a limb ripped off, but he imagined this would be how it felt. Thinking about it all the time, missing it like crazy and sometimes, especially after a few drinks, forgetting it wasn't there. Then feeling a tearing pain when he realised it was really gone.

Yeah, comparing her to a torn-off arm was exactly the poetry she'd want to hear.

Morosely, he levered himself off his sofa and went to the fridge in search of another beer. Happy frigging New Year.

His phone buzzed, dancing across the coffee table, and he checked the caller ID, unwilling to acknowledge how his heart sank when he saw it was Jack.

Get your arse through the shower and put some clean clothes on. I'm coming to pick you up in ten minutes.

Before he could protest, the line went dead.

He stared down at the ketchup stain on his jeans, the one from his McDonald's take-out three days ago, and let his head fall back against the sofa. Fuck, he was better than this.

Fifteen minutes later – Jack had never been punctual in his life – Harry's doorbell rang.

'Come on, you saddo, time to get out of hibernation. New Year's Eve is when we drink, and party. And drink.' He waggled his eyebrows. 'And did I say party?'

How to admit to the man he wasn't up to New Year jollity without sounding like the total saddo Jack thought he was? 'Good of you to come by, mate, but—'

Jack put his fingers in his ears. 'Nope, not listening to any excuses. I've strict instructions to use any means necessary to drag you out.' He did the bodybuilder pose of balling his hands into fists and making his biceps pop. 'You might think you're bigger than me, but I pack a mean punch. And I fight dirty.'

Harry's shoulders slumped. It was easier to give in, stay for a pint, then slip out when nobody was looking. 'Fine.'

He grabbed his jacket from the peg and shrugged it on. Then zipped it up as he felt an arctic blast of wind the moment he stepped outside.

'How was Christmas?' Jack gave him a sidelong glance. 'As bad as you expected?'

'Yep.' He didn't want to talk about the time he'd spent at his parents'. Not how he'd had polite conversation with his dad in the morning in one room, then walked through to share a turkey crown with his mum in a different room. Or how they'd both given him a bottle of whisky. Sure, he liked the stuff, but it had been the same gift every bloody year since he'd turned eighteen. Only this year, because they'd split up, he'd received two. Nor did he want to talk about the fact he'd asked them both if they'd ever loved the other, and been told love was fanciful. Respect was more important.

He'd pointed out that they were hardly respecting each other now.

'How was yours?' he asked, more to direct the conversation away from himself than out of a deep fascination with how Jack had spent the holiday.

'We all went to my sister's this year. Her kids overdosed on chocolate and threw up, my dad overdosed on booze and fell asleep in the chair. Rest of us lazed about, watched shite television and polished off the rest of the kids' chocolates. It was cracking.'

'Sounds it.'

At Harry's dry reply, Jack laughed and slapped him on the back. 'Maybe you had to be there.'

The warmth of his expression, the fondness in Jack's tone as he spoke of his family, all made Harry realise how lonely, how sad his life was. Sure, he had mates, but they increasingly had their own lives. Mike was now living with Trixie, next Jack would find someone. He had parents, but, unlike Jack, he only saw his out of duty. He'd never really minded before, but having lived with Sally these last few months he now realised what he was missing out on. It wasn't just a person to come home to, or a warm body in his bed – he'd had that with Isabelle. It was having someone who got you, warts and all. Who didn't care that you put your feet up on their coffee table, or took the piss out of their favourite movies. Someone who stuck up for you, who you could talk absolute bollocks to, slob around in your sweats in front of, without them judging you.

———

The pub was heaving and they had to push their way through well-inebriated revellers to find Mike and Trixie.

His heart almost fell out of his chest when he saw who else they were with. Vince was standing next to a guy Harry hadn't met but it had to be Justin, surely, from the adoring look they were giving each other. Then there was Eds and a stunning black woman Harry assumed was his wife. Next to her was Adam, and along from Adam was Kitty. In between them both, stood so close to Adam it sent Harry's pulse roaring, was Sally. And she looked fantastic. Was that the parrot-blue dress she'd tried on for him when they'd filmed the *Pretty Woman* shopping scene?

He knew the moment she saw him, because she jerked her head back, as if she'd not expected him to turn up. The thought sent disappointment rocketing through him. Stupid because of course she'd not been hoping to see him. Far more likely she'd been told he'd not been out in weeks, so figured it was safe to risk coming.

'Usual?'

Jack's question shook him out of his trance. 'Yeah.' *Pull yourself together, act normal, get out of here as fast as you can.* He slapped a smile on his face and added, 'Not sure if it can be called usual if you're offering to buy it.'

Jack peered at him and then let out a satisfied smile. 'Maybe the old Harry is still there.'

He looked over to where Sally was now talking to Kitty and felt a deep ache in his chest. He didn't think the old Harry was still lurking inside him. More, he wasn't sure that guy would ever be back.

Sally had known there was a chance she'd see Harry, but nothing had prepared her for how she'd react when she did.

'Ah.' Kitty followed her gaze. 'Things might just have got awkward.'

'I don't want it to be awkward. He lived with me for over three months. We made videos together. He brought Amy back into my life.' *We laughed, cuddled, talked about everything and nothing. And had loads of hot, incredible sex.* She swallowed down the boulder sized ball of emotion that had lodged deep in her throat. 'I want us to be friends.'

'Easier to do that with someone you haven't fallen in love with,' Kitty murmured, glancing pointedly at Adam who was chatting to Eds and his wife.

'Well, if it isn't the rare breed that is Harry Wilson.' Mike's voice boomed over the group as Harry walked up to them. 'A vanishingly uncommon sight these days outside daylight hours.'

Harry's eyes flicked over to hers and his jaw tightened enough to show her he felt as uncomfortable as she did. 'I've been busy.'

The two men exchanged a look and Mike nodded with what seemed to be an apology for raising the subject. 'Well, it's good to finally see you out and about.'

Chatter started again and somehow – she'd have said it was deliberate on Kitty's part if her friend didn't dislike Harry so much – Sally found herself stood next to the man who filled her daylight thoughts and haunted her night-time dreams.

'Nice dress.' He gave her a crooked smile. 'You still look like a hot chick.'

'Thanks.' She could barely get the word out. It was almost impossible to talk, to think, while he stared at her like that. All smouldering appreciation, nostalgia and hurt feelings.

'I'll head off soon.'

Now he couldn't bear to be in the same room as her? This was awful, just *awful*. And yet around them people were laughing, saying goodbye to the old year, anticipating the new. 'Before midnight?' she managed, throat tight, eyes burning.

His gaze found hers. 'Unless you're planning to let me kiss you?' Her heart jumped and she had to look away. 'Guess I've got my answer.'

Hearing the edge to his voice she glanced back at him and saw he was staring at Adam. 'If I was to kiss anyone at midnight, it would be you.'

His shoulders relaxed a fraction and this time the breath he let out was soft. 'If I thought there was the smallest chance you would, I'd stay.'

Tears stung her eyes and she couldn't reply because what her heart wanted and what her mind thought was best were such polar opposites.

Was it stupid to end a relationship with a man she loved just because he couldn't say the word back? Because he couldn't make a promise about forever, when his brutal honesty prevented him saying things he didn't one hundred per cent believe?

They stood silently as the sound of laughter, of cheers, of chatter and clinking glasses swirled around them. Eds, Vince and Adam downed their drinks and walked towards the small stage.

'Will you stay for a dance?' If she could just feel his arms around her, press her head against his chest. Breathe him in. One more time, so she could preserve it in her memory for the lonely nights ahead.

He stared down at her, one hand sliding to her waist, the other cradling her face, his eyes a turbulent storm of grey and silver. 'Are you asking?'

Her smile wobbled. 'I am.'

The music started and he drew her against him, moving his hand to rest on the small of her back. Instantly, a delicious warmth spread through her. Feeling choked, she wound her arms around his neck, pressed her head to his solid chest and listened to the thump of his heart. Not steady, not tonight. In fact, it felt as jittery as her own.

The more he held her, the more the background noise dimmed and it began to feel like just the two of them in their own cocoon, sheltered from the outside world, suspended in time. She was aware only of him, of the gentle press of his lips against her hair, the way he rested his head on hers.

Song after song they stayed like that, just swaying together, while around them people danced and applauded the band.

Finally, the music stopped and Harry took a step back, his

arms dropping away and falling to his side. 'I'm going to go before I do something embarrassing.'

His voice sounded ragged, his expression mirrored the pain she was feeling. 'Like?'

'Like beg you to take me back.' As her heart somersaulted, he inclined his head in a small, tight action. 'Happy New Year.'

She felt a tear escape and leave a wet trail down her cheek. 'And to you.'

He seemed to hesitate, beautiful grey eyes taking an inventory of her face before finally zeroing in on hers. 'I hope the bells ring for you.'

He turned and her chest felt hollow as she watched his tall, broad figure cut through the crowds. As if her heart had wriggled out from it and gone to join him. She wanted to tell him she'd got the bells wrong, that it wasn't a noise after all, but a feeling. And that she had that feeling every time she saw him, like she was going to burst with emotion.

'Oh, Sally.' Kitty's arm reached round her and her friend's gaze raked hers. 'What is it?'

'Harry's just said he hopes the bells ring for me, but I got it wrong. Amy told me. All this time I thought I'd hear bells when I found the one, but I misunderstood what Mum had been trying to say.' A sob erupted as the words tumbled out of her. 'What if that's not the only thing I've got wrong? What if I don't need the words, or the promises that nobody can really make. What if the most important thing is that someone wants to try?' She turned to Kitty, everything she'd once believed in now feeling so fragile. 'I want what Mum and Dad had, but I didn't see the start of their relationship. Maybe Dad never promised to love Mum for ever or vice versa. Maybe that only came in time.' Tears ran down her face unchecked. 'Maybe I've just said goodbye to the one man I'm meant to be with, but I've turned him away because he didn't adhere to some stupid stereotype I've got in my head.'

Kitty found her some tissues, hugged her, then whispered something to Vince who enveloped her in his arms and held her while she cried some more.

Chapter Thirty-Three

The wind whistled around him as Harry marched, head down, back along the front and then took a left towards the station. All he wanted to do was put distance between himself and Sally. Distance meant he was less likely to turn around and run back to her.

Distance meant he could drag his mind away from thinking about what he'd lost and onto stuff he wanted to think about, like putting together the quote for the next job, laying a new patio in his own house.

'Hey, slow down.'

He halted and turned to find Kitty trying to catch up with him. Just what he needed. 'What?'

He knew his tone was belligerent, but he'd had enough of Kitty and her sly digs. One good thing about his split with Sally: he no longer needed to bite his tongue where her friend was concerned.

'I've just left Sally in tears.'

His chest tightened painfully. 'If you think the thought of that doesn't slice me in two, you're wrong.' Agitated, he shoved his hands into his pockets. 'But I don't know what you expect me to do about it. It's not like I want to be here, walking in the other direction from her.'

Kitty stared at him so long it took all of his stubborn streak not to be the first to look away. But then a really weird thing happened. She gave him a half smile. 'You know what, I actually believe that.'

Fan-fucking-tastic. 'Am I supposed to thank you?'

He was six feet four to her five foot a bit, but he jumped, honest to God jumped like a startled rabbit, when she strolled up to him and threaded her arm through his. 'No. You're going to take me back to your place.'

'Whoa.' Now he was like a startled virgin rabbit and he attempted to extricate himself from her.

She rolled her eyes. 'Oh for crying out loud, get over yourself, you're not my type.' Her fingers wrapped round his arm. 'We're going to discuss a plan of action.'

'Action.' He still wasn't certain she wasn't planning to jump him. 'What sort of action would this be?'

'Not the sort of action you're worrying about.' He felt a shiver run through her. 'But let's have this discussion somewhere warmer. Sally said you live in North Laine, yes?'

'Yes,' he said distractedly, his mind still on the woman he'd left in the pub. 'But whatever you have to say to me, it can wait. It sounds like Sally needs you right now.'

Kitty's brown eyes warmed, ever so slightly. 'She's okay, Vince is with her. And I'll be back as soon as we've had a chat.'

They walked the rest of the way to his place in silence. He wasn't sure what to think, but figured whatever she had to say to him, it was probably better than sitting in his house alone, running through every word he and Sally had said to each other tonight, every look, every touch.

Kitty refused a drink and went to sit on his sofa – brown leather, rugged, manly. Yet he missed the pink velvet. Or at least he missed the person he'd sat on the pink velvet with.

'It's nice.' When he just stared at her, she grinned. 'Okay, I admit it, I thought your place would be a typical boke dive. Empty beer cans, sterile except for a giant TV. Seems I was wrong.'

'Not entirely wrong.' He sat on the armchair by the fire and leaned forward, resting his arms on his thighs. 'You said I'd end up hurting Sally, and somehow I did.'

'I think,' Kitty said slowly, 'you ended up hurting each other. You couldn't say what she wanted to hear, but she wanted to hear those words so badly I think she forgot that other words could be just as powerful.' Her gaze rested on him. 'Have you ever really told her how you feel?' He opened his mouth to answer, but she waved him away. 'Before you say "of course", remember what you're asking of her. To be in a relationship with you, she has to open her heart, make herself utterly vulnerable to you, because that is the only way she knows how to love. Yet at the same time you're saying you can't offer her that love back. You can't offer the one thing she's wanted all her life. To be part of a love so all-encompassing there is no question of either of you ever wanting to be with anyone else.'

Of course he didn't want to be with anyone else. Tears burned the back of his eyelids. Embarrassed, he furiously rubbed his eyes. 'I don't know what you want me to say.'

'Love isn't a word. It is a feeling. I want to know what's in here.' She touched her chest. 'Tell me how it felt when you saw her tonight. And when you left her. Tell me what you think up here' – she touched her head – 'when you go to bed at night, and when you wake up.'

'It felt like my chest was being ripped apart with a blunt hacksaw, and she's all I fucking think about, all the time, day or night.' He glared at her. 'Is that what you wanted to hear?'

A satisfied smile crossed her face. 'It's not what I want to hear, it's what Sally will want to hear that counts. You need to find a way to tell her what you've just told me, but it might help your chances if you can do it with a little more … finesse.'

'Finesse.' He rubbed his forehead, feeling the beginnings of a headache. 'That is not what I'm known for.'

'I'm sure you'll come up with something.' She rose to her feet. 'Happy New Year, Harry.'

'Yeah, and to you.' He walked her to the door, what she'd said still buzzing through him. 'You think I've got a chance? If I tell her how she makes me feel?'

'If you stop being a coward and open up to her then I think you've got a shot, yes.' She raised her hand and for a split second he wondered if she was going to slap him. Considering their past interactions, it wasn't too far out of left field. 'Relax, I was going to pat your cheek, because, shocking as this might sound to both of us, I'm rooting for you.' She was halfway out of the door when she looked back at him. 'Oh, and by the way, if you want to put a word to that hacksaw and chest ripping you described to me, it would be love.'

He stood in the doorway a long while after she'd gone. Love, seriously? If it was, he couldn't understand why the film industry depicted it with frigging violins and the romance industry used rose petals and fluffy hearts. Love fucking hurt.

Still, for the first time in weeks he felt lighter, a smidgen of hope threading through him, straightening his spine, pulling up his shoulders. For too long he'd focused on the fact that Sally had ended their relationship, and not on the most important thing she'd said before that. *Do I stay with a man I'm falling in love with?*

Sally believed in love, and she'd already opened her heart to him, but so far he'd offered nothing concrete in return. Kitty had been a pain in his backside for most of the time he'd known her, but she was also right. He was a coward. Too terrified of ending up like his parents to question why their relationship hadn't worked. No wonder Sally had wanted out.

Well, it was time to pull his big-boy, Bridget Jones-eat-your-heart-out pants on. Time to show her how much she meant to him.

It was a week into January and Sally was flicking through her mail after her Saturday shift at the cafe. A late Christmas card from her notoriously tight cousin who'd probably bought her cards in the sale, an energy bill, a company wanting to sell her clothes she didn't need and had no room for... She put the brochure on her to-read pile. Maybe buying something would help cheer her up.

Next, an envelope with a handwritten address? Curious, she ripped it open and scanned the single sheet of white paper with the bold, black handwriting.

Her heart skipped a beat when she saw who it was from.

Dear Sally

You once told me you wanted to find a love letter in your post. The last letter I wrote was to my aunt to thank her for my Christmas money. I was ten. So this isn't going to be up to much, but I'll try.

I miss you so fucking much.

Her hands started to tremble and her knees felt like they were about to give way so she stumbled into the living room and threw herself down on the sofa before continuing to read.

I tried to work out how it felt to not wake up to you, not cook with you, eat with you. Laugh with you. Cuddle up with you on the sofa, even if the sofa is pink, and the film we're watching is a love story. Best I could come up with is it feels like my right arm has been ripped off.

Yeah, not very poetic, I know. But it's honest.

I hope you're doing okay, but not so okay that you don't miss me a bit too.

A sob tore out of her and she had to take a moment to grab a tissue from the coffee table and wipe her eyes before reading the last few lines.

I saw Amy yesterday. She told me she's back with you now. Must be good to have her sleeping in her old room again. At least she'll be better than that surly lodger who kept crashing in your bed instead of keeping to his own.

I did warn you I was shite at letters. Still, I hope this was better than another bill.

Harry

x

Carefully, she folded the letter and pushed it back in the envelope where it would be safe from her tears. God, what was he doing to her? How could she possibly defend her heart against him when he did things like that?

She recalled her words to Kitty on New Year's Eve. *What if the most important thing is that someone wants to try?*

There was no doubt in her mind that Harry was trying. She had to decide whether that was enough for her.

And while she did that? She dug her phone out of her pocket and called him. He answered on the first ring.

'Hey.'

She'd forgotten how deep his voice was. How just a single word could send a shiver of longing down her spine. 'I got a letter in the post today.'

'Ah.' A beat of silence, and she imagined him running a hand through his hair. 'Was it from Wordsworth?'

A smile tugged at her mouth. 'I don't think so. Not sure Wordsworth ever used the F word.'

'No? Maybe the writer should get extra marks for using words Wordsworth hadn't thought of.'

'The writer doesn't need the extra marks.' She drew in a breath, tried to calm the jitters in her chest. 'Not when the reader loved what he wrote.'

There was a beat of silence and she wondered if he'd heard her. But then his voice came back, the rough husk telling her that he was feeling as emotional as she was. 'That reader must have lower standards than the writer had dared to hope.'

'No, her standards are high.' She scrambled to find the right words. 'But maybe she didn't make herself clear before now. She doesn't need poetic fluency. In fact, she's become a big fan of blunt honesty. As long as it comes from the heart.'

Another pause, and she wondered if he knew what she was trying to tell him.

'He'll bear that in mind.'

Silence descended again and she could hear his breaths, a faint brush of clothing when he moved. She wanted to reach through the phone and clasp his hand, tell him she was sorry for having such tunnel vision when it came to what she thought a happy ending should look like. That it didn't matter that he didn't love her like she loved him. It was enough that he missed her, that he'd bothered to put pen to paper and write to her. That he wanted to try.

But how could she take such a big leap without seeing his face? Without looking into his eyes and trying to read at least some of the signs Vince had spoken about?

On the other end of the phone, Harry cleared his throat. 'How is my old room? Amy said she's painted it pink again but I had a feeling she was kidding.'

It was only then she realised it was the second time he'd mentioned her sister. 'It's still as you left it. She prefers the blue apparently. No accounting for taste.' She nestled back against the sofa, enjoying just talking to him again. 'Is Amy still working with you, then? I thought that had stopped.'

'It has, we couldn't afford to pay her any longer, but she's dropped by a few times.' This time she heard a smile in his voice. 'Think she misses the banter.'

It was her turn to smile. 'Mike and Jack are funny.'

His soft laughter wrapped around her and she felt her heart swell. 'Now I know you're kidding. Nobody would describe Jack as funny.'

But you are. And kind, and surprisingly gentle. Tears filled her eyes again. What was it with this emotional overload?

'Did Amy tell you she's applied to do a post-grad course in building surveying?'

'She did. Guess we didn't put her off totally.'

'You did so much more than that.' Emotion clawed at her, and she knew her voice wasn't steady as she added, 'More than I can ever fully thank you for.'

He exhaled heavily. 'I don't need your thanks. Aside from the fact I like her, she's your sister.'

He didn't embellish the sentence any further, but she heard the unspoken words. And there had been a lot of them, she realised belatedly as she ended the call. If only she'd listened more carefully. Not just why he'd helped Amy, but why he'd put on a suit and tux and acted out scenes from films he didn't even like. How jealous he'd been of Adam. How he'd been so cut up about her ending things he'd had to get out and sleep on Mike's sofa.

As she lay on her bed that night, the future didn't seem as bleak as it had. She'd made a mistake, but it wasn't insurmountable. All she needed to do was work out a way to get back to him.

Just before she drifted off to sleep, her phone buzzed with a message.

Thought we should do one more romcom video for our followers. Will swing round the cafe next Saturday afternoon. H x

Chapter Thirty-Four

K itty had assured Harry that everything was in place. Wait, everything wasn't the right word, because that implied he had a clever plan, with a lot of neat ideas coming together in one big Hollywood crescendo. Instead it was him, in a suit because he thought it might give him an edge – and he needed every bit of help he could muster. Essentially though, he was going to try and win Sally over with just … himself.

He yanked his phone out of his pocket and dialled Kitty's number. 'This is a shite idea.'

He heard her long drawn-out sigh. 'Winning Sally back is a shite idea?'

'Damn it, you know that's not what I meant. I should have thought of something more dramatic. I could have done this on a Ferris wheel, you know, like in *Love, Simon*.'

'First, I'm impressed you've watched *Love, Simon*.'

'Yeah, well, nothing much on TV this time of year.'

She snorted. 'Liar. You're missing Sally so you're watching romcoms because that way you feel closer to her.'

There was a pause, and he knew Kitty was waiting for him

to agree but he kept schtum. They might not be enemies anymore, but no way was he admitting she was right.

Another sigh echoed down the line. 'Second, it's January. You don't want to drag Sally onto some Ferris wheel in the cold and wet when it's not the gesture that's important here. It's you, talking to her, telling her how you feel.'

And that was exactly why he was breaking out in a cold sweat. 'I'm crap at words. You know it, I know it. This can only end badly.' He grimaced at his image in the mirror. Smart suit, red tie with hearts on it that looked frankly ridiculous but he hoped she'd like it. Face that looked about as terrified as he felt. 'I'll be with you in ten minutes.'

As he headed out, he tried to remember what Sally had said to him after she'd read his letter. *The reader doesn't need poetic fluency. In fact, she's become a big fan of blunt honesty. As long as it comes from the heart.* Looked like he was about to find out if she meant it.

His heart was beating like a ruddy pneumatic drill as he reached the cafe. A quick glance inside and he caught Vince's eye. The man had obviously been looking out for him because he winked, gave a thumbs up and then nodded over to where Kitty was talking to Sally. When Sally saw him, she smiled tentatively, her confusion obvious. She was probably trying to work out which romcom scene he was trying to copy.

And hell, now his heart was going so fast he was afraid it might take off and leap out of his chest. Probably trip him up as he walked in.

Get a grip.

He sucked in a breath, pulled out the rose he'd stuffed into his pocket and jammed it between his teeth. Then, feeling like a twelve-year-old kid about to ask the girl he fancied out for the first time, he pushed the door open.

Sally's face, that gorgeous face that was all he saw when he closed his eyes, exploded into a grin when she saw him.

Heart still hammering, he yanked the rose from his teeth and handed it to her. 'Hi.' Not a great start, but at least he'd said something. The rose looked kind of droopy in her hand though. Maybe he should have put it in water.

Sally opened her mouth to speak, but he held up his hand. 'Sorry, I need to say the stuff I've been rehearsing in my head before it leaks out.'

'Okay.' The soft smile remained, as did the spark in her eyes, and Harry felt his heart settle, along with his nerves. She wanted what he was about to say, he realised. She didn't care if it was daft, or raw. In fact, he probably didn't need to say anything at all because just being here, with the suit and the wilted rose, was enough of a signal if she'd learned how to read him.

But she deserved more than him just turning up.

'You're probably wondering what scene I'm trying to copy here. I was told a Ferris wheel was too cold.'

Her eyes danced. '*Love, Simon.*'

He nodded. 'And the Empire State building is too far from Brighton.'

Like an excited child, her hands clasped together. '*Sleepless in Seattle.*'

He pretended to frown. 'I was thinking more *Superman* or *King Kong* but yeah, okay, I guess Tom Hanks was there too.' He tried not to get too distracted by the brightness of her smile. 'Maybe I could have at least got you on a plane, but I have it on good authority that people get in the way when you're trying to make dramatic pronouncements.'

'*Crazy Rich Asians.*'

God, he hoped she liked what he had to say as much as she

was enjoying his trip through romcoms. 'I thought about bringing a shoe, instead of a rose, but I figured a rose was easier to hide in my pocket.'

'A shoe, way too easy, that's *Cinderella*. The rose has to be the final scene in *Pretty Woman*, but without the limo, fire escape and *La Traviata*.'

'You're too good at this.' *You're too good for me*. What the hell was he doing, trying to be this romantic hero, when his role models were two people who couldn't even live in the same house as each other now? Feeling panicked, his gaze slipped to Kitty, who was holding up her phone, videoing it all. She gave a single firm incline of her head. Translation. *Stop thinking. Do what you came here to do.*

He swallowed, tried to calm the nerves in the pit of his stomach. 'So anyway, in the end I thought rather than copy a scene, I'd try and create a new one, though maybe I'd pinch some of their words. Some might call it cheating, but I reckon it's knowing my limitations.' Heart in his mouth, he took a few steps forward so he was stood right in front of her. Then he clasped one of her hands, raised it to his lips and kissed it.

Funny how a cheesy gesture could feel absolutely fitting, with the right person.

Sally felt her heart execute a perfect flip as Harry held her hand and looked straight into her eyes. From the moment he'd stepped into the cafe, looking like a larger-than-life romantic hero with his sharp suit, ruggedly handsome face and a wilting rose between his teeth, she'd known it didn't matter what he had to say. She was his, totally, utterly, whether he wanted her for a week, a year or a lifetime.

Still, a thrill ran through her as he cleared his throat.

'I can't say you had me at hello.' He gave her an embarrassed smile. 'To be honest, when I first met you, I thought you were nuts. Frigging gorgeous, yeah, but totally nuts.'

'I thought you were blunt and sarcastic.' Emotion lodged in her throat. 'But I liked your bum.'

He laughed softly. 'Good to know. So anyway.' His face took on a serious edge, his eyes turning from quicksilver to pewter grey. 'I've heard it said that when you realise you want to spend the rest of your life with somebody, you want the rest of your life to start as soon as possible.'

Oh God. Those eyes snared hers, and though she knew he'd borrowed the words, there was no doubting he meant them. *'When Harry Met Sally.'* Her voice came out as a whisper.

His mouth tugged in a soft smile. 'Seems appropriate. And accurate.' He swallowed, hand tightening around hers. 'I've missed you like fucking crazy, Sally Thornton. If I was that Jerry Maguire bloke, I'd probably say something smart like you complete me, but you told me you didn't want poetry, just words from the heart. So instead I'll tell you that it hurts like hell to be without you.' His eyes darted briefly to Kitty before resting again on hers. 'I told Kitty these last few weeks it felt like my chest had been torn open with a blunt hacksaw. She told me that was because I was in love.'

Sally felt her eyes well, and her heart swell so much it hurt. 'It sounds painful.'

'Exactly. Love's supposed to be like walking on air, right? Floating on the clouds, sliding down rainbows, cuddling puppies.' Those grey eyes pressed hers, ardent, insistent. 'Guess for all that to happen, I need to be with you, not apart from you.'

Bugger it, she was crying now. 'That can be arranged.'

His eyes flared with an emotion she couldn't read. 'Yeah?'

It was the rough voice, the slight shake to it, that clued her in. Hope. The hulking fool still didn't realise that he'd literally had her at 'hi'. 'Have you finished the speech? Because if you have, I've got some stuff I need to say to you.'

'I was going to add a few more quotes, like I'm just a boy, standing in front of a girl, asking her to take a chance on him.' He angled his head, Adam's apple moving as he swallowed. 'Would that help my chances?'

She reached to touch his face, her fingers tracing the lines of his jaw, bumping over the slight bristle of his five o'clock shadow. 'I'd say if it worked for Anna Scott in *Notting Hill*, it's a safe bet it's going to work for you.' Whatever he was about to say next, she cut off because she'd stood here too long without doing the one thing she'd wanted to do ever since he'd stepped inside the door. She threw her arms around his neck and kissed him. And kissed him again.

She was so enthusiastic that he wobbled for a second, but then his arms tightened around her and he was kissing her back, letting her feel his desperation, his need to get as close as he could to her.

Yet through it all, the sensuous slide of his tongue, the press of his body, the grip of his arms, she heard... Was that clapping?

Suddenly she remembered where they were, who was watching. He must have remembered too because he pulled away but his eyes, oh God his eyes, were alive with joy, with pleasure. And, yes, he'd claimed not to believe in it, but they blazed with such adoration she could no longer doubt that he felt what she felt.

'I was just saying to Mildred, it's never a dull moment here.' Hilda beamed over at her.

Embarrassed, Sally bent her head, laughing into Harry's chest. When she heard a deep rumble, she knew he was laughing, too.

'Maybe you two should take this to the office.' Kitty waved towards the back of the cafe. 'Stop frightening the customers.'

Aware she was probably grinning like a maniac, Sally took Harry's hand and led him into the back. The moment the door closed behind them, he groaned and took her back in his arms, kissing her as if his life depended on it for a few intense, spectacular minutes until he finally drew back, breathing heavily.

'There's stuff I want to do to you now that would give Hilda and Mildred a heart attack,' he told her roughly. But then he slid his hands up her arms and over her shoulders until they came to rest on either side of her face. 'Are we okay?' He cursed, giving his head a dismissive shake, like he was annoyed with himself. 'What I mean is, can we go back to how we were, only this time sometimes you stay over in my house, instead of just my room? And when you've had enough of going between our places, and Amy's settled, maybe you move in with me?' He paused, searched her face. 'Or maybe we can buy a place together?'

Her breath hitched. 'You said you didn't picture yourself getting married, having kids.'

'I didn't.' A slow smile tugged at his mouth. 'But then I met you. So, what do you say? Will you be with me, Sally Thornton, in whatever way you want, as long as it means I get to wake up with you every day, and go to sleep with you every night for the rest of my life?'

She bit into her lip, tears of joy now running freely down her face. 'Yes, a thousand times yes.'

A big smile lit up his face. 'Whatever film that's from, I'll take it.'

'It's actually from *Pride and Prejudice*. And it undervalues how I feel. I should say a million times yes, a billion times.' She kissed him, then kissed him again because she'd missed being able to do that so much. 'You make me happy, Harry Wilson. Even when you're awful – even when you're insulting my romcoms – I would rather be with you than with anyone else in the world.'

He narrowed his eyes. 'Damn it, I know that one.' She opened her mouth, ready to help him, but he stopped her. 'No, I've got it. Not technically a romcom, but *Me Before You*.'

She laughed delightedly. 'Now you're an expert, huh?'

He smiled, but then his expression turned serious, those eyes a swirl of emotion. 'Not an expert, not even close, not in any of this. But nobody will try harder than me to make you happy.'

A fresh slew of tears fell down her face. He might not be a typical romantic hero, but he was *her* romantic hero.

Chapter Thirty-Five

Waking slowly, Harry rested his head on his elbow and stared down at the woman lying next to him. She slept like she lived, embracing it, her face peaceful, even a small smile on her face, as if whatever she was dreaming was full of the heart-shaped mushy stuff that she loved.

Except amazingly, she also loved him.

Her eyes blinked open, drowning him in their soft blue gaze.

'Morning.' He bent to kiss her, a light touch of her lips, his libido momentarily taking a step aside to this other feeling she managed to wrench out of him. A mix of ferociously protective yet embarrassingly sentimental. One look at her and all he wanted to do was bundle her into his arms and never let her go.

'You look pensive.' She ran a finger down his cheek. 'What are you thinking?'

'That I'm in my favourite place.'

She smiled. 'My bed?'

He shook his head. 'Nope. Next to you.'

Her face took on this soft expression. 'See, you are romantic.'

He huffed out a laugh. 'Maybe all those films you made me watch are starting to rub off.'

'Umm.' Her smile turned a tiny bit sly. 'You know not all of those films you quoted yesterday were ones we'd watched together.'

Busted. A flush crept up his neck and he shifted onto his back, pulling her with him so her head rested on his chest. 'I may have resorted to watching one or two over the Christmas holidays. Choice of that or the same old Christmas films they churn out every year.'

'I get it.' She raised her head, her smile teasing. 'Wouldn't be because you missed them.'

'Nope. I missed you.' Her face gentled and it felt like the most perfect reward. How easy to express his feelings when it was obvious how much his words, however unpoetic, meant to her.

'I missed you, too. Christmas is a crap time to be heartbroken.' Her fingers trailed over his pecs and a shiver of arousal shot down his spine. 'Too many sentimental films on the TV.'

'But you and Amy spent it together, yes?'

'We did. And Kitty and Vince joined us later. Vince brought Justin. They're really cute together.'

He pulled a face. 'Please don't tell me we're cute together.'

She laughed, pressing a kiss to his chest. 'I don't think cute is the right word for us.'

'Hot.' That was certainly how he felt right now. 'That's a better word. We're hot together.'

'We'll have to upload the video Kitty took yesterday and see what our followers think.'

'I don't need anyone else to tell me the woman I love is hot.'

It wasn't until Sally's face took on this look of wonder, her lips curving in what he could only describe as smug delight, that he realised what he'd said.

'Okay, fine. Seems love does exist.' He thought of his Christmas. 'At least for some people lucky enough to find it.'

Her eyes searched his. 'Are you thinking of your parents?'

It was as effective as a cold shower. 'That was how I spent my Christmas Day, an extremely polite hour with Dad discussing politics, then a bland turkey lunch with Mum. Not because any of us wanted to actually spend time together but because that was expected.' He grimaced as he remembered the awkward as shit day. 'I was so angry at them, at myself, I even asked them if they'd been in love. You know what they told me?'

Sympathy shone from her eyes. 'What's love?'

'Close. They told me it was nonsense and that respect was more important.' He felt the same flash of anger as he had then. 'As if it was only possible to have one or the other.' He made sure to catch her eye. 'I bloody respect the hell out of you, you know that, right? I respected you way before I fell in love with you.'

She pressed another kiss to his chest. 'I know. So are they still selling the house?'

'Funny thing. Before I left, I told them both there was zero respect in the way they were treating each other now. A few days ago I got a call from Mum saying they've decided not to sell the house, after all. They're not back together, not in the sense you would associate with marriage, but they figure they can at least continue to live with each other without resorting to his-and-hers sections of the house.' He sighed, drawing a hand down his face. 'I've been invited to lunch with them next weekend. Both parents eating at the same time, in the same place. Something of a novelty.'

'I'm sorry. Not that they're staying together, but that your relationship with them is one of duty, not love. That sucks.'

She slid over him, her naked breasts crushed against his chest, and his libido woke up again. 'If that's your way of distracting me, it's working.'

'Good.'

But just as she started to kiss him, there was a knock on the door. 'Do you two want a drink or are you too busy bonking each other's brains out?'

He slammed his eyes shut. 'We're going to need to stay at mine more.'

Sally giggled. 'Probably. But I think we should take a rain check on my distraction.' She bent to give him a brief kiss. 'I've got a video to edit.'

He wanted to protest, but the sight of her naked body walking across the bedroom and into the shower stole the breath from his lungs. And besides, he could hardly complain when the final video had been his idea.

***

Sally found herself tearing up as she watched the video Kitty had filmed of Harry walking into the cafe.

'Mum and Dad would have loved it.' Amy, who'd been watching with her, smiled.

'They would.' Just as they would have loved Harry. How could they have failed to love the man who'd brought her and Amy back together?

'So what are you going to caption it?'

'I'm thinking *When Harry wooed Sally*.'

'Wooed?' Harry's voice came through from the kitchen. 'No bloody way do I woo. Seduce.' He nodded, obviously proud of his choice. 'Yeah, that's a better description. *When Harry seduced Sally*.'

'Umm, maybe, but why should we put you first? How about *When Sally said yes to Harry*.'

He angled his head, considering it. 'Yeah, not sure I like that. Sounds like you saying yes to me is a rare occasion.' His mouth curved into a smirk. 'I'm pretty sure saying yes to me will be a daily occurrence. Maybe twice a day.' He waggled his eyebrows up and down comically and Amy groaned.

'When I said I wanted to come back and live here I didn't think I'd end up in the middle of some X-rated romcom.'

'I take exception to that,' Harry mumbled. 'There's nothing cheesy about me and Sally.'

They both looked at each other and, in sisterly synchronisation, threw a cushion at him.

His eyes widened in shock. 'What did I say?'

'Don't ever diss the romcom,' she told him sternly.

'Hey, I've got a caption for you.' Amy gave her a secretive smile. 'How about *When Sally heard the bells ring*.'

Harry, who was picking up the cushions, halted mid-grumble and looked over at them. 'You heard them?' Sally nodded, biting back a smile. 'Seriously? No bullshit now, you really heard the bells ring when you looked at me?'

Amy glanced at her, and mouthed, 'Are you going to tell him?'

There was something about his expression, like he was trying hard to act casual yet beneath that veneer was a sort of desperation. It was as if he needed to think she'd heard bells, not because he wanted to believe in the myth, but because he wanted to believe he was the one. And that's when she realised Harry hadn't just once believed he couldn't fall in love. Thanks to his parents' disinterest, he hadn't believed anyone could love *him*. Right then, she promised herself she'd tell him every day that she loved him. As for now?

'Yes,' she told him clearly, walking up to him and planting a soft kiss on that sexy mouth. 'I really heard bells.' In a way it was the truth because the joy in her heart when she looked at him was almost overwhelming. Like the loudest church bells that had ever been rung. Just as her mum had promised.

He cocked his head, eyes darting over her face. 'Bells and fuzzies eh? Any violins?'

The man who hadn't believed in any of it, now wanted to believe in all of it. 'We can make our own music. We don't need violins.'

He laughed. 'Frigging good answer. I always thought I'd be more drum rolls and cymbals.' He leered suggestively. 'If you get my drift.'

'And you call romcoms cheesy. You two are gross.' Amy jumped up from the sofa. 'I'm out of here. I'll catch up with you later when you've got this out of your system.'

Harry's shoulders starting shaking. 'When do you think I should tell her I'll never get you out of my system?'

Her heart swelled and she reached to kiss him, wondering if there would ever be a time when she wouldn't melt as those big warm hands slid down her back and over her hips.

'So, about this strapline.' He smiled into her eyes. 'How about when Sally heard the violins?'

'I thought it was cymbals?'

'Good point.'

She leaned further into him, arms around his big, solid body. 'I'm not sure I want to upload the video after all.'

He tilted his head back to look at her. 'Not that I care either way, but why not?'

'It's our special moment.'

His arms tightened around her. 'And me and Isabelle already ruined two special moments.'

'Isabelle tried to ruin them,' she corrected firmly. 'Only Isabelle.'

He didn't say anything for a few moments. But then she felt the press of his lips in her hair and he drew back. 'I've got an idea. Trust me?'

'Totally.'

'Okay, give me your phone.' He smiled. 'I want to make a quick video.'

She opened it and handed it over. He raised it up so it was pointed at them both as they stood with her arms around his waist. 'Hi,' he said into the camera. 'As you guys have been following us, we thought you'd like an update.' He stared down at her, eyes filled with adoration. 'Harry's fallen in love with Sally.' Yep, she was never going to get bored of hearing him say that. 'From now on our story will be private, but thanks for taking part in the journey.'

He pressed End and threw the phone onto the kitchen island. Then he picked her up, sliding her legs around his hips, and carried her to the sofa. 'Now it's time for that private part.'

'Oh good.' She glanced down at the pink velvet. 'Are you sure the colour isn't going to put you off your stride?'

He laughed softly. 'Pretty sure I'm man enough to make love to you on a pink sofa.' His gaze settled on hers, quieter now. 'We need to put a card in your window.'

'Sorry?'

'In the cafe. We need one of those cards with our names and today's date. Because this is the start of our happy ever after.'

Dear God, this man had no idea what he did to her. It was like a dam had opened and all the love trapped inside him had suddenly found a release.

And she was the extraordinarily lucky recipient.

As she melted into his arms, she just had time to reflect that there, *right there*, was the reason romcoms were so important. Of course they didn't mirror true life – few films did. But they inspired hope.

Dreams *could* come true. You just had to believe.

Acknowledgments

It is such a thrill to see my name on the front cover and yes, I wrote the words, but many more people were involved in getting the final story into your hands. This is my chance to thank them and make sure at least some of them get their name into the book, too.

The first thing any writer needs, is an idea, and though I'd love to take the credit, the genius behind this story wasn't me. It was my agent, Hannah Todd. When she mentioned her thoughts about a potential plot, I almost peed my pants (yes, you know which romcom that comes from!) What could be more exciting for a romance writer than writing about a couple who recreate iconic moments from our favourite romcoms? Not just because the opportunity for both romance and humour was huge, but because I was forced – oh yes, absolutely forced, for the sake of accuracy you understand, to binge on romcoms. I thought I knew all the iconic moments, yet when Hannah and I started chatting about the scenes we felt just had to be included, some films Hannah mentioned I'd not seen – imagine that! I was sent away with the homework of having to watch romcoms like *Ten Things I hate About You*, and *Never Been Kissed*. Err, did I say how much I love my job?! So thank you Hannah, you didn't just provide the brilliant idea and help hugely in pulling the book into shape, you also introduced me to some cracking films I might otherwise have missed.

Next on my thank you list is the amazing team at One More Chapter. It's a joy to work for such a professional, supportive publisher. Charlotte Ledger – where would I be without you? Thank you yet again for taking my rough draft and gently, but expertly, showing me how to make it soooooooo much better. And for coming up with such a brilliant title. And for the encouragement, the support…and being a generally awesome person to write for.

A big thank you also to the rest of the One More Chapter team who work seamlessly behind the scenes to get this book from first draft into the version that is finally read. That includes designer Lucy Bennett and illustrator Amelia Flowers who have created yet another stand out cover. I will make it into a canvas and put it on the wall in my study with the rest of the covers from my romcom collection. A great source of inspiration when the words get stuck.

I'm not just lucky in my publisher. I'm lucky to have a gang of really supportive friends and family who were there from the start of my writing career, keeping my spirits up when finding a publisher seemed impossible. Ten years later, they're still there, trying not to glaze over when I ramble on, and on about my next book. The roll call includes my dear mother-in-law Anne (Mum 2), cousins Shelley, Karley, Kath, Kirsty and Hayley, my sis-in-law Jayne, nieces Maddi, Tiggi and Gracie, friends Charlotte, Laura, Sonia, Jane, Carol, Tara and Priti. And not to forget my biggest fan – yes, that's you Mum! Thank you all for your unflagging support.

Thanks too, to my hubby, Andrew, who told me all those years ago to stop talking about writing a book and get on and do it (that's the polite version). I don't think he realised quite how many I would go on to write – and that he would have to subsequently show an interest in. I must also mention my sons,

Harry and Ben, for putting up with a mum who writes romcoms. Will this be the book of mine they finally get around to reading?!

I'm not sure where any of us writers would be without the amazing book bloggers who are kind enough to read, review and shout about our books, so very grateful thanks to you all. A special hug to Rachel Gilbey and Anne Williams who were also there at the start of my journey, and are still cheering me on. You are superstars.

Finally, the most important thanks of all go to YOU. Thank you so much for reading this book. I hope you enjoy Harry and Sally's journey through the romcoms as much as I enjoyed writing (and researching!) it!

ONE MORE CHAPTER

YOUR NUMBER ONE STOP

FOR PAGETURNING BOOKS

The author and One More Chapter would like to thank everyone who contributed to the publication of this story...

Analytics
Emma Harvey
Connor Hayes
Maria Osa

Audio
Charlotte Brown

Contracts
Georgina Hoffman
Florence Shepherd

Design
Lucy Bennett
Fiona Greenway
Holly Macdonald
Liane Payne
Dean Russell

Digital Sales
Michael Davies
Georgina Ugen
Kelly Webster

Editorial
Charlotte Ledger
Nicky Lovick
Bethan Morgan
Jennie Rothwell
Kimberley Young

Harper360
Emily Gerbner
Jean Marie Kelly
Juliette Pasquini
emma sullivan
Sophia Wilhelm

HarperCollins Canada
Peter Borcsok

International Sales
Hannah Avery
Alice Gomer
Phillipa Walker

Marketing & Publicity
Emma Petfield
Sara Roberts

Operations
Melissa Okusanya
Hannah Stamp

Production
Emily Chan
Denis Manson
Francesca Tuzzeo

Rights
Lana Beckwith
Samuel Birkett
Rachel McCarron
Agnes Rigou
Zoe Shine
Aisling Smyth

The HarperCollins Distribution Team

The HarperCollins Finance & Royalties Team

The HarperCollins Legal Team

The HarperCollins Technology Team

Trade Marketing
Ben Hurd

UK Sales
Yazmeen Akhtar
Laura Carpenter
Isabel Coburn
Jay Cochrane
Sarah Munro
Fliss Porter
Gemma Rayner
Erin White
Leah Woods

And every other essential link in the chain from delivery drivers to booksellers to librarians and beyond!